A HUGE WHITE YA

W9-CBQ-922

INTO VIEW OVER THE HORIZON.

"They must be turning," Dugan remarked.

"Turning?" Veronica asked.

"Either that or they're slowing down. I'm hoping they're turning."

"Why would they be slowing down?"

"That's a question I'd rather not have to answer. Keep playing with that fishing rod. Make it look good."

It was true, boats could slow down and pull alongside just to be friendly. But they didn't do it very often.

"Try to look like we're out here to get a tan and catch a fish, okay? Don't follow me below, don't act like we might be worried."

"You are worried, aren't you?"

"Just a little bit."

She searched his face, then nodded and sat back in her chair.

Below, Dugan unlocked the drawer where he kept a Glock 9mm . . .

RAVES FOR RACHEL LEE'S PREVIOUS ROMANTIC SUSPENSE NOVELS

AFTER I DREAM

"A fabulous romantic thriller with the accent on thrills. . . . Fast-paced and filled with suspense and tension. This author deserves much acclaim for her exciting tales of romantic suspense." ***—Midwest Book Review***

more...

BEFORE I SLEEP

"A wonderfully crafted, suspenseful tale with just the right balance of romance and mystery." —***Rendezvous***

"A powerhouse novel full of excitement and romance. Ms. Lee is an accomplished writer, and her expertise in setting scenes, developing characters, and creating suspense is evident. . . . The plot never faltered . . . you will not be disappointed." —***Mystery News***

"A powerful writer. . . . *Before I Sleep* is a gripping romantic suspense book . . . and much, much more. It's a compelling emotional novel." —***Heart to Heart***

"A nail-biting, engaging story . . . a web of suspense and emotion . . . BEFORE I SLEEP is not a book you want to begin reading late at night unless you plan to go without sleep. It immediately grabs your attention and pulls you in. Very satisfying and enjoyable." —**Bookbug on the Web**

"Tight and dramatic . . . a well-written piece of romantic suspense. . . . It keeps the reader glued to the page."

—***Affaire de Coeur***

"Terrific author Rachel Lee does a masterful job turning on the tension and suspense."

—***Romantic Times***

"Moving . . . may be Ms. Lee's best novel to date. Fans of romantic intrigue will be caught by this novel that provides immense pleasure."

—**Harriet Klausner, *Painted Rock Reviews***

"Exciting and challenging . . . a gripping tale of sexual tension, intrigue, and suspense that will keep you on the edge of your seat until the last word. . . . It is definitely one for the keepers shelf."

—***Under the Covers***

ALSO BY RACHEL LEE

Before I Sleep
After I Dream

ATTENTION: SCHOOLS AND CORPORATIONS
WARNER books are available at quantity discounts with bulk purchase for educational, business, or sales promotional use. For information, please write to: SPECIAL SALES DEPARTMENT, WARNER BOOKS, 1271 AVENUE OF THE AMERICAS, NEW YORK, N.Y. 10020

WHEN I WAKE

RACHEL LEE

WARNER BOOKS

A Time Warner Company

If you purchase this book without a cover you should be aware that this book may have been stolen property and reported as "unsold and destroyed" to the publisher. In such case neither the author nor the publisher has received any payment for this "stripped book."

WARNER BOOKS EDITION

Copyright © 2000 by Sue Civil-Brown
All rights reserved. No part of this book may be reproduced in any form or by any electronic or mechanical means, including information storage and retrieval systems, without permission in writing from the publisher, except by a reviewer who may quote brief passages in a review.

Cover design by Diane Luger
Cover illustration by Franco Accornero
Hand lettering by David Gatti

Warner Books, Inc.
1271 Avenue of the Americas
New York, NY 10020

Visit our Web site at
www.twbookmark.com

A Time Warner Company

Printed in the United States of America

First Paperback Printing: November 2000

10 9 8 7 6 5 4 3 2 1

To the love of my life.

Thanks to Katie V. for inviting me into her world of deafness. I'm so grateful for the masterful way you were able to give me analogies that helped make the silence real for me.

Thanks to Margaret A. for her perspective on working with the deaf, and the mechanics of hearing loss. And thanks to many others who in their various ways taught me what silence means.

Prologue

Orin Coleridge had six months to live. He regarded the prospect with little fear, but with a whole lot of impatience. Six months wasn't long enough for what he needed to do, especially when his strength was failing, and treatments were only going to make him weaker.

The only thing he feared was that his daughter wouldn't outlive him. He watched her sit in a corner, rocking endlessly and staring out the window at the brilliant Florida days as if she couldn't even see them.

A man had done that to her. Her *husband* had done that to her. Orin looked down at his frail, trembling hands and wished they had the strength to strangle Larry Hauser.

The bright candle flame that was his daughter had nearly been extinguished, and months later it showed no signs of leaping to life again.

She was too thin. Too withdrawn. Counseling had been useless because she wouldn't speak. Her once raven black hair now had a silver streak in it, speaking of what she had endured. Of what Larry had inflicted on her.

Orin sighed heavily and went to stand beside her, looking out through the filtering leaves of an ancient live oak at the sunbaked street beyond. He didn't care what happened to him, but he needed more time, time enough to find a way to put the spark back in his daughter's eyes. A way to give her back her life before he gave up his own.

Reaching out, he touched Veronica's shoulder and felt her shrink away. His heart breaking, he withdrew his hand.

There had to be a way to reach her, he thought, as tears burned in his eyes. Some way to reach the little girl who had once grasped life with both hands, hungry for experience. Some way to reach the woman who had followed in his footsteps, becoming a professor of archaeology.

He had so many memories of her, all of them full of light and life from the time she took her first steps to the time she had come to him with sparkling eyes and showed him her first published monograph. Surely that woman couldn't be gone forever.

There had to be a key to the lock of silence and despair that imprisoned her. There had to be a way to fan the spark back to life.

Closing his eyes against a swelling surge of grief, he tried, as he always had, to focus on the problem at hand.

Then, to his amazement, for the first time in twenty-five years, he heard the sound of his late wife's voice. It seemed to waft to him on the air, carrying the mysterious lilt that had first drawn him to her.

"The mask of the Storm Mother."

A chill went through him as he recalled all the trouble that quest had brought into his life. And yet, looking at his daughter as she slowly faded away from lack of will to live, he wondered if renewing the quest could possibly be any more costly.

The answer was plain. He just hoped the mask wouldn't

bring his daughter back to life only to take her away again. Because, to this day, he was convinced his wife's death was no accident. Whenever he let himself think of it, her loss filled him with anguish and rage.

And fear.

Chapter 1

Dugan Gallagher sat in the small jumbled office where he spent his days, with his feet propped up on the desk, tilted back in his chair so he could see the harbor.

He wore his usual costume of khaki work shirt, khaki shorts, and topsiders, about as formal as he ever got since quitting his job as a stockbroker ten years ago. Of course, the nice thing about being a business owner was that he got to set the dress code. And this was Key West besides. Even the lawyers came to work dressed this way, and kept a suit hanging in their offices for the times they needed to go into court.

Watching the *Sea Maid* put out with her current cargo of tourists who wanted to dive a wreck, he felt pretty good. All his captains and dive instructors had shown up today, which meant he, Dugan Gallagher, didn't have to get wet. Which was just fine with him. He might live on an island and have an office on a harbor, and make his living from boats, but he hated to get wet. Period. The bathroom shower was his maximum preferred water exposure.

He also preferred to stay holed up in his tiny office as

far away from the tourists as possible. Oh, he was well aware of the irony in the fact that he owned a diving business that catered to tourists when he hated both the water and tourists, but life was ironic any way you looked at it. Besides, never having to wear a tie again was reward enough for putting up with the other annoyances.

The *Sea Maid*—not the most original name in the world, but what the hell, he wasn't angling for awards, just for business—eased out of the harbor and sailed away with her precious cargo of tourists and compressed-air tanks. From experience, he knew that everyone was talking and laughing with excitement, and that Jill, the instructor on board, was encouraging them with her own enthusiasm.

He almost snorted, then reminded himself not to get too cynical about what he did. It might show. The dives they took the tourists on were relatively tame, for liability reasons. But while he might be jaded about diving wrecks, his customers weren't, and he needed to keep that in mind.

Besides, this job was better than Wall Street any day. Unfortunately, it was also a little more hectic then he'd planned on when he had dropped out ten years ago with the express intention of becoming a beach bum. Instead, he'd wound up buying a dying business and turning it into a profitable concern. He figured he must have a loose screw somewhere.

On the other hand, you couldn't beat the view of the harbor, or the lazy pace around town, or the nightlife that never seemed to end. So he was a productive beach bum. It didn't exactly call for hand-wringing and *mea culpa*s.

There was a knock on his door, and Ginny, his office manager, the lady who dealt with ninety percent of the onshore crap of the business, stuck her head in. "Couple of people want to see you, boss."

He didn't even stir, but kept looking out the window at the mast of the sailboat riding at dock just outside. Maybe it was time to take the *Mandolin* out for a long, long sail in Caribbean waters. Maybe two weeks of long sail. "I'm busy," he said.

"I can see that. When you get through contemplating your navel, you might want to see these folks. They're talking about a long-term charter."

That perked his interest a bit, though he was reluctant to show it. "Yeah? What . . . two days?"

"Open-ended, probably several months."

He was about to say no way. Then he realized that he was curious. He turned his head and looked at Ginny. She was a thirtysomething redhead who'd spent too much time in the sun and had done too many drugs until the day she woke up and realized her live-in boyfriend was sucking her dry, leeching her meager income, and killing her with cocaine. She'd thrown out the boyfriend, kicked her habit, and come looking for a job. Dugan had never regretted hiring her.

"Okay," he said.

"Okay? Okay, what? Charter the boat? Send them in here? Make them wait?"

Count on Ginny to give him a hard time. While he never regretted hiring her, sometimes he thought of her as his thorn in paradise. "Send them in."

Then he went back to contemplating the navel of the world—or in this case, the mast of the sailboat. Which to him was the same thing, since he thought of sailing as the center of his personal universe. For somebody who didn't like to get wet, he sure liked to be out on the water.

He heard the door open again and turned his head just enough to see his visitors. The first to enter was an elderly man who leaned on a cane. Dugan didn't need to be a doctor to recognize the signs of cancer. The man looked like too many AIDS victims he'd seen on the streets of Key West.

But his eyes were bright blue and lively yet, though his face was gaunt and his head absolutely hairless. He wore casual khakis, too, and Dugan decided he could probably deal with this guy—unless the old man wanted to arrange to have his own ashes dumped somewhere out there. Dugan hated people who insisted on burial at sea. Mainly because when Dugan was forced to go in the water, he didn't want to be thinking about what he might be swimming through or by. Not that he was squeamish. He just figured some things were better buried.

Behind the man came a young woman, maybe thirty, with brilliant blue eyes and hair as blue-black as a raven's wing, except for one intriguing white streak. He couldn't tell how long her hair was, because she had it pinned tightly to the back of her head.

That was the first thing he didn't like about her, the tightly pinned hair. The next thing he didn't like was the very, *very* nice figure barely hidden by a tank top and shorts. He didn't like it because he couldn't ignore it. He also wondered if she had any idea how fast even that tawny skin of hers was going to burn in the subtropical sun.

"What can I do for you?" he asked the man. He knew he should have stood and shook hands, but he'd sworn off formality and didn't see any reason to break his vow for these two.

"We'd like to charter one of your boats for several months," the man said.

Dugan could have told him he never did that. He could have pointed him to a charter boat business. But he didn't.

He was curious why they'd chosen him, and why they wanted the charter. They sure as hell didn't look like drug runners. So instead of saying no, and saving himself from all the trouble—a significant error, he was to realize shortly—he said, "Why? Better yet, why me?"

The man nodded to one of the chairs, and Dugan waved him into it. Then, falling back on dusty manners, he waved the woman to the other chair. His feet were still on his desk, and he had no intention of taking them down, not even when he realized the woman was looking at him with disapproval. He resisted the urge to belch and scratch his chest—just barely.

"Well," said the man, "perhaps I'd better tell you who we are."

Dugan didn't especially want to hear this part, but it had to be better than going back to his bookkeeping, so he nodded.

"I'm Orin Coleridge. This is my daughter Veronica Coleridge. We're both archaeologists."

And now Dugan guessed exactly what was coming. If he'd had an ounce of brains, he'd have shown them the door immediately. He didn't want any part of their headache. "People have gone broke and died young hunting for treasure."

"That may be," said Coleridge, with a small nod that acknowledged Dugan's quickness. "But my daughter isn't in any danger of going broke in this lifetime, and we have good information on the location of a particular wreck."

"So have a lot of people." Dugan put his feet on the floor and faced the old man directly. "It took Mel Fisher sixteen years to find the *Atocha*—after he finally got good information. I won't even mention the twenty years that came before that. Do you have any idea how much seafloor there is out there? How far a wreck could have drifted over the years? How unlikely that there's still enough of it in one piece to identify?"

"We're archaeologists," Coleridge said.

"And then there's the permits. Have you got permits?"

"We certainly have. We've done our legwork, Mr. Gallagher."

"Maybe so. But have you talked to anyone who's actually hunted for a wreck? Are you prepared to devote the rest of your life to this search?" Which, as soon as he said it, struck him as an utterly insensitive thing to say to a man who probably didn't have much life left. Too late now.

But Coleridge didn't seem to take offense. He smiled faintly. "That should be *my* concern, not yours. We simply want to charter a boat from you for the next three months."

"Why me?"

"We need a dive boat. And we need divers. You have a good reputation."

Having a good reputation in Key West could mean a lot of things, depending on who you talked to. But there was one thing Dugan wouldn't give ground on to anyone: He had safe boats, good instructors, and the best equipment. In that respect he wanted a good reputation. The rest of it he didn't care about. "I don't rent boats for three months at a stretch. I need all my boats to handle the tourist demand. If I start turning people away, it won't be good for my business." Which wasn't strictly true, because he turned people away all the time for lack of room. He just didn't want to be cutting back his schedule by one boat.

"Well, we can rent a boat elsewhere, I suppose," Coleridge said, looking at his daughter. "It's just that you were highly recommended."

Did he really want to throw this job to a competitor?

Three months of easy work, charter fees. . . . He looked out the window again, pondering. Of course, he'd have to get wet.

Hmm.

"Three months," Coleridge said. "We'll pay in advance, whatever you'd make off the boat regularly plus twenty-five percent. We'll pay all costs, and we'll pay for your diving services and one or two other divers of your choice."

"I don't know."

The woman spoke, too loudly. "Will you look this way when you talk?"

He turned sharply, prepared to take umbrage, but Coleridge was waving a hand. "Forgive my daughter, Mr. Gallagher. She's deaf. She can't read your lips when you look away."

Dugan's anger deflated almost before it was born, and he looked at the woman with new interest. Deaf? What a goddamn shame. Not his problem, of course, but when he considered some of the shysters and hucksters around here who might try to take advantage of a deaf woman and her ailing father, he felt something akin to a moral qualm, a feeling so rare that he almost didn't recognize it.

"Yeah?" he said.

"Yeah," she said.

Okay, so she was good at the lipreading thing. He looked at Coleridge again. "Just three months?"

"At this time. After that, we'll have to reconsider and possibly get different equipment."

"You can't search a whole lot of seafloor in three months," he said, making a point to look at the woman when he spoke.

"We can search enough," she said succinctly, and still too loudly.

He decided he didn't like her at all. "It's your money," he said finally. Only then did he realize what he had just walked himself into.

Oh, Christ, the whole damn town was going to be laughing at him. Dugan Gallagher, treasure hunter. He'd rather be called an asshole.

"One stipulation," Veronica said.

"Yeah? What's that?"

"Nobody at all is to know what we're doing. Nobody."

He sighed. "Lady, you can't keep a secret in Key West. It's impossible."

"You're not to tell anyone," she repeated. "No one. No information. I don't care if they know we're looking for a wreck, but beyond that everything has to be secret."

"Well, sure, okay." Like anybody would be interested anyway. People were always looking for treasure around these parts and coming up empty. No big deal. His reputation could stand it.

Coleridge spoke. "We need you to find us some more divers. Trustworthy ones. We'll pay their rate."

"Slow down a minute." He waved a hand and propped his feet back on the desk. "Just searching, right? No dredging or anything."

"Not unless we find something."

"I'll have to look into the equipment I'll need to get."

Coleridge nodded. "We've already ordered the metal detectors and magnetometer. They'll be arriving Saturday."

"So that's all you want to do? Sweep the seafloor for metal?"

"Right now, that's it."

Chickens for the plucking. The phrase crept into Dugan's mind, and that's when he knew he absolutely had to do this. Not so he could pluck this pair of chickens, but so that he could keep someone else from doing it. The old guy was nigh unto death, and the woman was deaf. Under those circumstances he couldn't fall back on the P.T. Barnum philosophy of life. Nobody else might be able to live with him, but *he* had to.

"What happens if you find something?" he asked.

"Then we consider a salvage attempt."

Of course. That was obvious, so obvious that asking the question was stupid. "Sure. Okay. So where are we searching?"

"You don't need to know that," Veronica said.

"Not until we have a contract," Coleridge added. "Not until we're ready to go."

"Like the state doesn't already have a record."

"The state has a record of a very large piece of water," Veronica said. "That's all they have."

"And you have a more refined idea?"

"What did you say?"

"I asked if you have a better idea where this vessel is in this large piece of water."

"Much better."

He nodded slowly, wondering if this woman was as crazy as she was deaf. Enunciating with considerable care, he said to her, "Regardless, you *do* understand that you're searching for a needle in a huge haystack?"

"Of course." She said it dismissively.

"Well, it's your money. When do you want to start?"

"As soon as we sign a contract and get the metal detectors," Coleridge said. "Saturday or Sunday."

Dugan rubbed his chin, thinking about it. In spite of himself, he was intrigued. He'd been thinking about a vacation on his boat, and this would be a kind of vacation, even if he *did* have to dive. "Water depth?"

"No more than thirty feet."

"Okay. Why the hell not. Just as long as you understand that a three-month search isn't going to turn up anything except a lot of mud. Cripes, I'm practically fleecing you."

Coleridge shook his head. "You can't fleece someone who is getting exactly what they're willing to pay for."

"Right. I hope you feel the same way three months from now."

"We will."

Dugan wished he was half so sure.

Dugan had plenty of time to regret his hasty decision to help the Coleridges. All afternoon and early evening in fact. By the time he saw his last boat back in harbor and cleaned and readied for the next day's business, he'd had ample time to wonder if P.T. Barnum had been talking about *him*.

Feeling like a royal sucker, he strode home through the busy streets, sidestepping crowds of tourists who were having a hell of a good time and drinking a bit too much. Finally he reached his own home, a blessed four blocks from Duval Street, where everything was quiet and dark except for the occasional passing motor scooter.

He'd bought the house when he'd first arrived, never realizing what a good investment it would turn out to be. It was a Key West original, built sturdily by a ship's carpenter, and likely to last forever. At the time he bought it, it had been sadly neglected, but it had been exactly the therapy he'd needed to get over Jana. He had no idea how many hours he'd spent working on the place, repairing, repainting, improving, and remodeling the interior. Now he had a showpiece, a white-clapboard house with green tropical shutters, a wide shady porch, and a backyard—a small,

Key West backyard—filled with a pool and tropical foliage that made it feel like the most private place on earth. And it was worth far, far more than he had put into it.

Which was a rather odd thing for a man who'd come to Florida determined to waste his life away in bars. But then, so was the business, which he'd bought from Tam Anson. Tam and he had met up in a bar one night, neither of them really sober. Tam had been bemoaning the fact that his diving business was going belly-up. Dugan, not thinking too clearly, had offered to bail him out. Which was how he'd come to own Green Water Diving, Inc. A piece at a time, anyway. He'd started by buying in as a partner, but as time passed, Tam had wanted less and less to do with it, and had sold the rest of the business to him.

Now Tam was his tenant, renting the upstairs apartment in the house and working for him intermittently as a diver while he tried to find himself. After eight years, Dugan figured Tam was never going to find himself, and probably wouldn't pay the rent ever again either.

Which was okay by Dugan. He'd left his cutthroat ways behind in New York. And he kind of figured he owed Tam something for getting him into the diving business.

Besides, Tam was a good buddy and kept him from forgetting that he'd come here to lie back, not to rev up to Wall Street speeds. Tam was always ready to party, be it bar-crawling along Duval or taking a boat out to celebrate the sunset.

Tam was lying in the pool area, reading a copy of *Mad Magazine* and drinking a longneck. He was wearing blue swim trunks, still damp from the pool, and had a towel slung around his neck. He looked like the perfect beach bum with his sun-streaked blond hair and moustache. There'd been a time when Dugan had envied that look.

These days he was content that his dark brown hair was still thick.

"Hey, what's up, dude?" Tam asked, looking up from the magazine.

"Nothing much," Dugan replied, resisting the urge to 'fess up to his stupidity. He'd get around to that later. "You?"

"Just hanging around. Thought maybe I'd invite a couple of guys over for poker, but everybody's busy."

That surprised Dugan. Sometimes he thought most of Tam's friends did nothing except party. "What about Serena?" Serena was Tam's current interest, a girl too young to be running around Key West on her own, in Dugan's opinion, but what did he know? Twenty-one was twenty-one.

"She went home for a week. Her dad's sick."

"Sorry."

Tam shrugged. "It happens. Grab yourself a beer, man, and hop in the pool. Water's warm."

"Funny. Very funny." Tam knew damn well he'd put in the pool only to enhance the property's value, and because that particular summer he'd had an overwhelming need to dig a deep hole.

He went into the house and popped open a Heineken, carrying it back out onto the deck with him, pausing to flip on the yard lights and some reggae on the outside speakers. A golden glow and quiet, upbeat music filled his private tropical paradise.

The beer did its work rapidly, considering he hadn't eaten since breakfast. Soon he was relaxing and thinking maybe he hadn't just made the biggest mistake of his life. There could be advantages to a job that involved sailing around a quiet piece of ocean and diving. Plenty of peace and quiet for one. As long as Veronica Coleridge wasn't talking all the time. The old man at least would be easy to deal with. The woman he wasn't sure about.

Basically, it might be a little more intensive than that vacation he'd been thinking about, but probably not much. How much work could be involved in taking a few shallow dives each day and running a metal detector over the seafloor? Low stress, that's what it would be, because he didn't give a damn if the Coleridges found anything at all.

Yeah, it'd be okay. Three months of sea and sun. Except for the getting wet part, it was his favorite way to spend time.

So . . . no big deal. And feeling better about it, he didn't mind telling Tam what he'd done. He was aware that his major failing was his reluctance to admit he'd messed up, but he couldn't see any good reason for trying to change himself.

Tam chose that moment to dump the magazine and jump in the pool. A splash went up, and Dugan watched water drops darken his khaki shorts and shirt. Some people, he thought, never grew up. The fact that he was one of them didn't mean he couldn't notice it in other people.

When Tam resurfaced, he grabbed the edge of the pool and shook his wet hair back from his face. "You oughtta come in, dude. Great way to cool down."

"No thanks. I'm not hot."

Tam gave him a wry look. "Yeah, right. You were a cat in your last life, right?"

"Maybe. Or maybe I'm one this time around. I just have a good barber."

Tam laughed.

"So, you want a diving job for the next three months?"

"Taking tourists out? I don't know." Tam dropped the

beach-bum attitude and grew serious. "You know I'm not that reliable, Dugan. I'll drive you nuts."

"Way I figure it, if you're on a boat, you're reliable. This isn't for Green Water."

"No? What then?"

"Some crazy woman and her dad want to look for a wreck. They figure they can find it in three months."

Tam lifted both eyebrows, then hefted himself out of the pool by his arms and sat on the edge dripping. "Three months. You're kidding, right? Or did they come from Mars?"

"They think they have a pretty good idea where it's at."

"Yeah. Sure. They're crazy."

"I think I already said that."

"I'm agreeing with you."

"Ahh."

Tam shook his head. "So what exactly do they want us to do?"

"Use metal detectors. Two divers, one boat, just a search."

"Sounds like a vacation."

"That's what I'm thinking." And, now that he thought about it, feeling a tad guilty, too. Was it any more honest for him to take these people's money just to protect them from somebody who'd take twice that or more? Or was he just rationalizing the fact that he was a sucker?

Tam, who hadn't completely forgotten what he'd learned as a businessman, asked, "You didn't make any promises, did you?"

"Hell, no. I even tried to talk them out of it. They said they'd done their research. Well, if you ask me, if they'd done any serious research, they'd know they're probably never going to find that wreck, even if they spend the next thirty years looking."

"Did you see their permits?"

"Yep. I'm not crazy enough to get into something illegal. It's all on the up-and-up, Tam."

"Then maybe they're not as crazy as they seem. I hear only a few people get those permits every year, and hundreds try to get them. They must have something going for them."

"Maybe. But I figure it's not my problem. They want one boat and two or three divers for three months for an easy job. Nice money, nice work, no hassle, right?"

"Sounds good to me."

Tam at least wasn't asking the questions that Dugan was asking himself, such as, How could he be thinking about getting tangled up in something like this when he was already as busy as he wanted to be with the diving business?

But, he acknowledged, there was still some of the beach bum in him. Still something of the guy who'd wanted to lead a laid-back, hassle-free existence. Something of the man who'd been so singed by a bad marriage that he'd vowed never to get involved in anything serious again.

And running the diving business was beginning to seem too much like work. Seven days a week. Bookkeeping. Employee problems. The list was endless. He also had not the least doubt that with minimal supervision Ginny could run the business. No problem there. He made a mental note to give her another raise.

"So," Tam asked, "what wreck are they looking for?"

"I haven't a clue. They're keeping all the information under wraps."

Tam snorted. "Cripes. Like everyone around here hasn't talked about every wreck and every salvage operation forever. Like anyone around here would give a shit that some new group is going after a wreck. They could come put up banners and nobody would think twice about it."

"Maybe they don't want to look like fools if it doesn't pan out."

"If they're gonna look like fools, there's a whole herd of fools running around here." He shrugged and let it go. Tam wasn't one to let unanswerable questions trouble him for long. "Three months. Now I've heard everything."

Dugan nodded, but his thoughts were already drifting on to something else—namely the hunger gnawing his belly. He really needed to eat lunch. But since it was too late for that, he decided to get a pizza. And maybe it was time to call Linda. She was always a good evening of fun. Light fun. She was no more interested than Dugan in getting seriously involved, so their relationship was comfortable for both of them.

And that was the whole point, wasn't it? he asked himself. To be comfortable. That was the mistake he'd made with Jana. It had never been comfortable.

Damned if he was ever going to be uncomfortable again.

Chapter 2

"Why don't you put in your hearing aids?" Orin asked his daughter.

Veronica didn't hear him, and he didn't want to shout. So, finally, he picked up the waterproof case she'd bought to store them in for the trip and carried them to her.

Her gaze slipped from the window of the cottage they were renting down to the case he held out toward her. She shook her head and looked up in time to read his lips.

"Why not?"

"Because I hate them," she said. She could hear her own voice, barely. It was distant, unformed, and she had to trust that her lips and tongue were doing the right things from memory.

"They help," he said. "I want to talk."

Reluctantly, she reached for the case and opened it. Inside were the reminders of her disability, and she looked at them with a hatred beyond words. Then, irritably, she snatched them up and inserted them into her ears. Drawing a quick breath, she listened. They were adjusted right.

And now every sound was annoyingly loud, including

the grinding roar of the air conditioner and the hum of the refrigerator in the kitchenette.

"Thank you," Orin said.

To Veronica it sounded like "aaaaa ooooo." She had to watch his lips to identify the consonant sounds she could no longer hear at all.

"I don't understand," he said, "why you hate them so much, Veronica. They help you hear."

"They help me hear everything, Dad. *Everything*. Right now I can barely hear you over the roar of the air conditioner." Could barely distinguish his words from the invasion of other sounds.

He nodded, but she guessed he would never really understand. Would never understand that the amplified noise in her ears was every bit as bad as the silence she experienced without her hearing aids. Would never understand that for her there was no good solution, there was only bad and worse, depending on the situation.

"What did you want to talk about?"

"This search." He had learned to keep his sentences relatively short to make it easier for her to follow him.

"What about it?"

"We're probably not going to find the vessel. Not in three months."

She shrugged and wished she could turn her attention back to the window. Watching the top of a palm turn into a dark shadow against the red smudge of the sunset sky interested her more than this conversation. But she no longer had the luxury of looking at something else while she listened to someone speak.

"Gallagher," her father said, "was right. You might spend your entire life and fortune searching and never find a thing."

"I know that." But it wasn't going to stop her. She had nothing else to live for anymore, except vindicating her mother's quest. She had lost everything else that had mattered to her. *Everything.*

"Veronica . . ."

"Look, Dad, we've been all over this. If you didn't want me to do this, then why the hell did you tell me about the mask and Mother?"

She must have been speaking even more loudly than usual, to judge by the way he pulled back.

He shook his head. "I told you because I wanted you to have something to live for."

"Well, now I do. It's all I have. So let me do it."

"I don't want you to be disappointed."

As if anything could ever disappoint her the way Larry had disappointed her. She laughed bitterly and turned her back on her father, effectively ending her conversation with him. If he said anything, she would hear vowels. Just vowels. Unintelligible. If she could even hear him over the roar of the air conditioner.

She was angry with him, and had been ever since he'd told her about the mask. Her mother had died when she was five, and Veronica had grown up with a great big hole in her life. Discovering that her father had concealed her mother's obsession with the mask from her had infuriated her because it was such an important part of her mother's life. For twenty-five years he'd painted her mother in a light that was not her mother at all. She felt betrayed and cheated. Even more, she felt he had betrayed her mother, by hiding an essential part of her as if it were something of which he was ashamed.

Worse, she was angry at herself for being angry with her father. It seemed so wrong to be unable to forgive him when he was so close to death. Yet she couldn't find it in herself to do so. Not after he had steadfastly lied to her all these years.

Sometimes, merely looking at him filled her with an almost uncontainable rage . . . and the rage was always followed by self-loathing.

He touched her arm, causing her to jump, forcing her to look at him.

"Veronica, please. You need to know. Just sit down and listen to me, please."

She battled down her anger, burying it under the cold lump of lead in her heart, and sat in the chair by the window. It wasn't a very comfortable chair, but she didn't care about that. She felt tense, irritated, ready to fly or fight. Over what? The fact that her father wanted to caution her? For every bit of help he'd given her with research over the past months, he'd also given her warnings. She continuously felt as if he were urging her forward with one hand and holding her back with the other.

He took the other chair and faced her, taking her hands in his. The rumble of the air conditioner drowned out his first words, and she had to ask him to repeat himself. She hated that. God, how she hated that. She hated every single reminder of her disability.

"You need to be careful," he said more clearly. He'd said it a thousand times since she'd undertaken this quest, but he'd never told her why. She was getting sick of the warnings without explanations.

"Why?" she demanded. "You keep saying that, but you never say why."

"Because sunken treasure is valuable," he said. "Men will do anything for gold. Because . . . because . . ."

She watched him look away, unsure if he'd said any

more than that, if his words had been lost when he turned his head. Before she could ask, he faced her again.

"Honey," he said, "your mother died under suspicious circumstances."

"She fell off a boat and drowned!"

"Your mother could swim like a dolphin."

"She hit her head."

"Maybe. That's what the coroner thought. I'm not so sure." His face tightened, and his eyes darkened. "Just be careful. The artifact's value is greater than gold."

Indeed it was. Far greater. Because so few of the golden artworks of the Native American cultures had survived the Spanish plunder. So much had been melted down into gold bars for transport back to Spain, so much had been turned into coinage used to pay the armies of conquest. Very little of the beauty remained. But the mask was even more important because if it were found, it would be the *only* surviving artifact from a lost culture, a people whose passing had left almost nothing of archaeological value, a people whose culture was known only as a few footnotes in the journal of MesoAmerican conquests. A people without a name.

Veronica was not about to be deterred by vague warnings. "I'll be safe, Dad. How could I be anything but? It's kind of hard to sneak up on a boat on the open sea."

"People don't have to sneak up at sea, Veronica. They come as bold as you please, because there's going to be no one around to protect you."

She shrugged and looked away, letting him know she didn't want to discuss this anymore.

So he changed the subject, which forced her to look at him again. "What did you think of him?"

"Of whom?" she asked, having missed the first part of what he said.

"Gallagher."

"Him. Oh." What did she think of him? She let her gaze wander back to the window, but found the night had grown dark and all she could see was her own reflection in the glass. "I don't know. Drew was sure about him."

He touched her hand again, drawing her attention back to him. "Drew's a fairly good judge of character. How did he know Gallagher, anyway?"

"They went to Harvard together."

Both of Orin's bald eyebrows raised. "Harvard? Gallagher's a Harvard man?"

She nodded. She was getting tired from the effort of talking with her father, tired from the battery of noises coming through her hearing aids. "MBA, apparently."

Orin said something and shook his head, but she was through listening. Pulling out her hearing aids, she put them back in the container, letting him know that she was done conversing for the evening.

There was one advantage to being deaf, she thought bitterly, even as her own petulance bothered her. She could bail out of a conversation in an instant, and nobody could force her to listen.

But she couldn't silence her own thoughts. Her father's question, What did she think of Dugan Gallagher, followed her into the quiet.

What *did* she think of him? She hadn't been particularly impressed to find him lazing back in his chair with his feet up on the desk on a business day. On the other hand, she had colleagues who assumed exactly that pose when they were thinking, so maybe she shouldn't hold it against him.

She hadn't liked his lack of manners, though, and she found the cluttered mess of his office distasteful. Bottom line, she hadn't really been impressed with him. She was even less impressed by the thought that someone with a Harvard MBA was wasting himself on a small diving business.

But her friend Drew Hunnecutt, an oceanographer whose idea of a holiday was to dive the reefs off the Florida Keys, had recommended him highly. "His barrel may be a little bent," Drew had said, "but he's a straight shooter."

And a straight shooter was exactly what she needed. She needed someone she could count on to tell her the truth, because there was so much she didn't know about this whole treasure-hunting business that she could get into serious trouble. She needed someone she could rely on not to steal or conceal their finds. If they made any.

Drew had been a great help to her, studying the ocean currents in the area where *Nuestra Señora de Alcantara* had probably gone down, and had done some extensive computer modeling of how the wreck might have drifted over nearly three hundred years. He'd targeted a relatively small area of seafloor out toward the Marquesas as the likeliest place for a discovery.

She knew perfectly well his models could be all wrong. She knew she might never find a thing, not even some ballast. She was willing to live with that. What she wasn't willing to live with was never having tried.

As for Gallagher . . . she could control him. After all, she was paying for him, his boat, and his time. Besides, she trusted Drew, and if Drew thought she could rely on Gallagher, she probably could.

But she had no doubt that it was going to be a bumpy ride.

* * *

Night was settling over the mountains of Venezuela. Emilio Zaragosa sat on his patio, awaiting his dinner, and watched his garden turn into shadows and shades of gray. In a little while his wife would call to him, and he would join her in a repast fit for a king.

Emilio lived well. He had grown up the hard way on the streets of Caracas, in the gutters basically. Hungry, half-naked, and unwanted, he had learned life's lessons well. He had learned that if he wanted something, he had to take it. He had learned that the only thing he could rely on was his wits. He had learned a man could never be too wealthy.

And he had learned that it was a man's responsibility to provide for his family. These days, Emilio Zaragosa had family. A great deal of family. He had six daughters and two sons, four of them married, and seven grandchildren. If Emilio had anything to say about it, not a single one of them would ever go hungry as he had.

So now he was in his fifties, a proud man with the fortune of Croesus, all of it made by dealing in antiquities from all over the world. He had a good business in producing fake artifacts that tourists loved to buy all over Spanish-speaking America, but he also had a healthy and very illegal trade in the priceless relics of ancient civilizations.

Wealthy men were acquisitive, he had discovered, and had a particular taste for forbidden things. He was more than willing to pander to their tastes because they were more than willing to pay generously for their pleasures.

But he had developed a certain acquisitiveness himself over the years. Maybe because he didn't entirely trust currencies, stocks, or bonds. But the value of ancient artifacts never fell, and as they became increasingly difficult for private hands to obtain, they became increasingly priceless. So he had a collection of his own, a hedge against the ills that could befall a man who put all his eggs in one basket. A hedge against years in which he might not find some new artifact to market.

His caution did well by him. He could have retired at any time and still been sure his children and grandchildren would have been well provided for. But that was not his way. The memory of hunger dogged his heels like a ravening wolf.

So when he heard that a Tampa archaeologist was searching for the lost mask of the Storm Mother, he put his ear to the ground, so to speak. He'd heard of the mask once before in his early days, a rumble on his network of informants. A Tampa archaeologist had been looking for it then, too, and a great many acquisitive people had been bidding for it even though it was unlikely to be found.

But all the furor had interested Emilio in the mask, and he'd looked into what little he could learn about it. And what he had learned had whetted his appetite considerably. How rare indeed it would be to have the sole surviving artifact of an extinct culture. A golden artifact.

He had never been able to learn where the mask might be found, and the Tampa archaeologist had been murdered by one of Emilio's competitors, who mistakenly thought she had found the mask. But now someone else was searching, and Emilio was never one to overlook a possibility.

He always paid attention to the permits issued by the state of Florida for exploration for ancient wrecks. The contents of those wrecks, after all, were his bread and butter. He had a Florida state employee who kept him advised of all applications and grants, and Emilio made it a habit to check out all of them. Most he discarded as pipe dreams.

But this one was different. This one had given him a gut-clenching thrill when he learned of it. Not just because of the mask.

No. Because the new archaeologist was the daughter of the one who had been killed. Emilio had always suspected there was some knowledge there that wasn't shared by the world at large. Now he was sure of it.

The letter in his hand confirmed it. Dr. Veronica Coleridge had left for Key West. She believed she knew where the mask was.

And Emilio Zaragosa was going to keep a very close eye on her.

He was just deciding which of his informants to put in place when his wife called him for dinner. When the glass door opened as she stuck her head out, he could hear the laughter of his grandchildren.

The sound hardened his resolve. He would let Veronica Coleridge do the hard work, then he would step in and take what he wanted as he always had. Because those children inside his house were never going to be hungry or homeless.

Not while Emilio Zaragosa lived.

Veronica woke up from a nightmare, and momentarily felt frightened and disoriented. She didn't recognize the shadows in the room where she slept, and her deafness struck her afresh, offering her no cues to her whereabouts.

Adrenaline coursing through her, she searched frantically for a light, and finally found a small lamp on the night table. As soon as she switched it on, she knew where she was. In the cottage in Key West. The cottage she was renting from a friend of Drew Hunnecutt's. Her father, she recalled, was sleeping in the loft above.

Throwing back the covers, she climbed out of bed. The air was still and warm, and she imagined the air conditioner must have turned off. Making her way barefoot into the kitchenette, she turned on a light and poured herself a glass of milk. Then, sitting at the bar, she pulled out the papers where she had listed all the things she needed for her exploration.

But she couldn't concentrate on it, because she was aware of the crushing silence around her. At night there were no sounds to pierce the cocoon of her deafness. There was nothing to orient her in the world, and she might have been adrift in a vacuum.

And that night it was even worse, because in her dream she had been hearing. She had been on a boat on a sunny sea, listening to the waves lap against the side of the vessel. She'd been standing at the bow, watching waves roll toward her, listening to the ceaseless whisper of the water. Listening to the wind hum in the rigging behind her.

Listening to the wind hum in the rigging.

That detail surprised her. Where had her mind drawn that sound from? She had sailed on small boats, with small sails, and she knew the sound of wind in canvas. But this had sounded bigger, much bigger, and her mind had insisted that she was on a large boat sailing swiftly before a strong wind.

But they had been sailing into a dark cloud. A black cloud. As she had stood at the bow, rising and falling on the waves with the sound of wind power behind her, she had watched the black wall of cloud grow larger, darker, denser, until it filled the sky. And with its growth had come the terror that had awakened her, every instinct shrieking for flight.

The dream, she told herself, was the result of all the

warnings her father had been giving her, and nothing else. His uneasiness about her quest had begun to make *her* uneasy.

She forced herself to look at her lists and notes. Underwater metal detectors, the best brand made. A magnetometer, absolutely essential for finding the areas to dive and sweep. Buoys to mark those areas. A Global Positioning System so she could record and return to interesting positions. The list was, to her way of thinking, surprisingly short. But, upon reflection, she realized that the exploration part was relatively uncomplicated. Use the magnetometer to detect iron deposits, dive to check them out, and sweep the immediate area with metal detectors. Simple enough.

The hard part was locating the wreck. Despite what Dugan Gallagher might think, she wasn't deluded about the difficulty of the search, or about the vast areas that might need to be covered.

Information about where old wrecks had gone down was unreliable at best. Survivors rarely knew the exact position of the vessel at the time it broke up or sank. At best they knew the last *measured* position—and that might have been taken hours before the disaster occurred, and might well have been inaccurate.

In this case, there had been only two survivors, one of them an infant. The conquistador who had managed to save himself and his child had washed aground on some unnamed island. There he had made a boat to carry himself and the child island to island until he made the mainland of Florida, where he then spent more than a year hiking his way up the coast until he reached St. Augustine. He thought the ship had gone down in the Straits of Florida. But a few things in his description had led Veronica's mother and now Veronica herself to believe the boat had been seriously off course at the time the hurricane had hit.

In fact, Veronica was so sure of it that she was prepared to sink a lot of money into her own theory that the boat had gone down somewhere southeast of the Marquesas.

She had left the conquistador's original account, faded ink on parchment, safely locked up in her bank, but she had a translation copy with her, something she had typed up without identifying the source. The document itself was a family heirloom, a treasure she would never risk losing.

Juan Bernal Vasquez y Maria had been an old man at the time he wrote the account, which had passed down to Veronica. She allowed for the fact that he might have misremembered some of the details of his arduous journey with a two-year-old child through the wilds of Florida at a time when mosquitoes and Indians were both deadly threats. He might also have exaggerated greatly. Memory and time had a way of enlarging things.

But what she didn't doubt was his description of the island where he washed ashore with the child, nor of the length of the journey he took from that island to the next. And while he might indeed have washed up on any of the Keys that ran along the Straits of Florida, she was willing to give Juan Vasquez credit for being able to tell the direction of his travel by the stars.

If the ship had gone down where the *legajos* her mother had found in the archives in Spain had suggested, then Juan Vazquez couldn't have traveled as far east as he claimed without being lost in the Atlantic. Her mother, Renata, had believed the *legajos* were more accurate than Bernal's account, and had concluded that over the years the conquistador had exaggerated the length of his journey. Veronica believed otherwise. The *legajos* had no accurate information about what had happened to the ship after it departed port, whereas Bernal had been there. Playing jury, she had decided the eyewitness was probably more reliable than the official records.

Combining his description of his journey with a map, it hadn't taken all that long for Veronica to conclude that the ship had gone down somewhere between the Marquesas and Key West. Nor was it completely unlikely that the ship had gone so far astray from the Straits, not with the cloud cover that had existed for two days before they were caught in the edge of the hurricane that had caused the ship to founder.

The fact that the ship had foundered, rather than broken up on reefs, added to her conviction that the vessel hadn't been in the Straits when it went down.

The *Alcantara* had been within sight of land when it foundered, but only Vasquez and his infant daughter had made it to shore. He had strapped the child to an empty barrel, then clung to it, keeping the baby upright, while the waves carried them to land. There he had watched the wind and rain batter the ship and sweep its remains away "to the southeast," he said.

Veronica assumed he came up with that direction after the clouds had cleared and he could observe the heavens again.

So, unless he had misremembered, and unless her calculations were completely off base, she thought she had a pretty good idea where the wreckage would be found.

There wouldn't be much of it, she was sure. The area she was looking at wasn't isolated. If there was enough of that ship left to see from the surface, someone would have found the remains by now.

Instead she was going to be seeking broken remains,

probably deeply buried in silt and sand. And gold. The *Alcantara* had been heavily laden with plundered gold, an estimated ten million dollars of it, melted into bars.

But she didn't care about that. It was merely a signpost to the one treasure she really wanted: the mask of the Storm Mother.

Chapter 3

Life is what happens when you're making other plans. The sign hung on the wall facing Dugan's desk. The quote was attributed to John Lennon, but Dugan had read somewhere that it was really a quote from some female writer in the 1920s or '30s, except that he couldn't remember her name. He figured since she wasn't around to make a stink about the attribution, there was no point in him worrying about it either.

But what that quote did, whoever was responsible for it, was help him keep his cool when everything seemed to be blowing up. Which it regularly did. Which it was doing today.

He'd come to work to find out that one of his divers hadn't shown up, and one of his boats had major engine trouble. Apart from the loss of income, he'd had to face the irritated clients who'd had reservations for the boat that morning. Some were laid-back about it, of course, taking it philosophically that they might have to wait a day or two for their dives. But others were irate at having their vacation plans ruined, and they were vociferous in telling him so.

By noon he'd managed to rearrange the schedule, cut break times, increase the number of runs each of his boats was to make each day, and was left only with objections that they'd been *promised* a dive at a certain time of day. There was nothing he could do about that.

Just as he was figuring the worst of the storm had passed, the Coleridges showed up in his office. Veronica, looking a little pink from the sun, at least had her shoulders covered.

Orin took a seat without invitation, apparently deciding to practice manners the way Dugan did. Veronica stood in the corner, her arms folded beneath her breasts. It may have been a protective pose, but from Dugan's perspective all it did was heighten his awareness of one of her better assets. Maybe her only asset.

Today she had her hair tucked behind her ears, though, and for the first time he saw her hearing aids. He felt a twinge of pity for her, which evaporated the instant he met her blue eyes. They were sparking, defying him to feel sorry for her.

So he looked at her father. Here, at least, he found a human being he could relate to. "What's up?" he asked, not at all sure he wanted to know. Orin's next words confirmed that ignorance could indeed be bliss.

"We've hired a plane to do a low flyover of the water in the area where we're planning to search. I can't go, so I want you to accompany Veronica. It only makes sense, since you're going to be our captain and chief diver."

"You want me to go?" Next to getting wet, Dugan hated flying. He most definitely did *not* like having someone else in control of his survival. Life required him to get on large commercial planes sometimes, and he did it, feeling rather like a cat whose fur was being stroked in the wrong direction. But a small charter? Sweet Mother! "I don't have time."

"Certainly you do. We've hired you beginning Friday. Tomorrow. Look, Gallagher, you might as well be in on it. If we can see any signs of wreckage from the air, it'll help our search, and help you know what you're looking for."

"It's a waste of time," he said, more out of a growing sense of desperation than any real objection.

"Absolutely not," Orin said. "Many wrecks have been spotted from the air. Flying a hundred or two hundred feet above these waters can be a great help in finding wreckage. This could narrow our search area considerably."

Flying a hundred or two hundred feet above the water didn't bother him. Having someone else in the pilot's seat did. "I'm too busy. I've had a diver call in sick, I've got a boat that's disabled, and a hundred tourists really pissed at me. Find someone else."

He glanced at Veronica again and saw that her eyes were narrowed and irritated-looking. He wished she would say something because then he could tell her where to get off. Then it occurred to him she might not have completely followed his conversation with her father, and that narrowing of her eyes might indicate nothing except that she was trying to piece things together.

Oh, shit, he felt another moral qualm coming on. The woman was deaf. Her father couldn't go. Was he going to cast her to the wolves? Or more specifically, some wolf who might want the treasure himself?

He looked at Orin. "Are you sure you need me?"

"It would be a great help. We have a GPS, but someone is going to have to write down the interesting coordinates while someone else watches. And it would really help to have a set of eyes looking out *both* sides of the plane."

Well, it might shorten his three-month sentence if they found something right off.

Dugan leaned back in his chair and looked out his window at the harbor. "Okay, I'll do it. Ginny can handle the mess here, now that I've set the ball rolling to cope with it." Which made him remember that he still hadn't told her he was giving her a raise.

"I'm starving," he decided abruptly. "Let's go get some lunch."

Because all of a sudden he had to get out of that office, breathe a little fresh air and sunshine, and try to find some reason he shouldn't just bail on this project.

Not that he was going to. He was a man of his word, unfortunately, and he'd already said he'd do it. But he would feel a whole lot better if the ice queen would thaw a degree or two, since they were apparently going to be in close quarters quite a bit.

He stood up and started toward the door when he caught sight of Veronica's frustrated expression. She didn't know what was going on, he realized. He hadn't been looking at her when he spoke, and she probably hadn't caught a tenth of what he'd said.

Something inside him, something well guarded behind high protective walls, nibbled at him, telling him to take it easy on her. Something very sharp slipped past his barriers and pierced his heart with an unwelcome pang of sympathy.

He stopped, facing her, and said clearly, "Let's go to lunch. My treat."

She darted a surprised glance at her father, then nodded. "Okay."

He picked a restaurant not too far from the dock, a place that always kept its doors wide-open, as did most Key West businesses, and its air-conditioning set at forty below zero. "Great seafood," he said to the Coleridges, taking care that he was facing Veronica when he spoke.

He noticed she took the seat across from him at the table, apparently determined not to miss any more of what he said. He found himself wondering what life must be like for her, and how handicapped she really was.

And he figured, judging by the expression on her face a few minutes ago, that he would go nuts from frustration if he suddenly lost his hearing. He wondered if she'd been deaf all her life, or if it was something recent.

And he concluded that it was none of his business, so he didn't ask.

He ordered a beer, and Coleridge ordered a glass of wine. Veronica, he noted, asked for ice water. Uptight in every way. She and he were not going to get along at all.

But somebody had to break the ice, and by the time they ordered their meals, it was pretty apparent that it was going to have to be him.

"So," he said, "tell me about this wreck we're looking for."

Again that look of mild irritation flitted across Veronica's face, and he figured she hadn't understood him. Lifting his head, he repeated his question slowly, simplifying it. "What wreck are we looking for?"

She understood this time. He also noted, with interest, that her father didn't leap into the breach and answer for her. Instead, Coleridge seemed fascinated by the passersby beyond the window.

"*La Nuestra Señora de Alcantara,*" Veronica replied. Her voice, he noticed, was still too loud, but in the restaurant, which was filling up with a noisy lunch crowd, it wasn't exceptional.

"*Our Lady of Alcantara,*" he translated. "Spanish treasure ship?"

She nodded.

"What happened to it?"

"Near miss with a hurricane. The cargo was doubling as ballast, and the captain wouldn't let them throw any of it overboard when the seas got rough. They foundered."

He nodded. He almost asked where this had happened, then decided against it. Some details were better not bruited about in public. "Survivors?"

"Two. One of them recorded the events afterward."

Original source material. That was always useful. "You know, don't you, that a lot of those ships made navigational errors?"

She cocked her head. "What?"

"A lot of those ships made mistakes in calculating their positions."

She nodded. "I know. I'm going by other information."

Maybe she *had* done her homework. Although he would readily admit he didn't know a whole hell of a lot about the subject himself. That little fact probably didn't make him the best judge of whether she knew what she was talking about.

Then she surprised him by actually asking him a question. "You've done some wreck diving, haven't you?"

He nodded. "But only a little. Just for fun. No serious treasure hunting." Back in his early days in the Keys, he'd wasted some time diving the reefs and the known wrecks. "I've used submersible metal detectors, but that's about it."

Her eyes were narrowed again, as if she hadn't quite followed what he'd said. It occurred to him that conversing with her could be exhausting. Then he realized that if it was exhausting for him, it was probably even more so for her. "Metal detectors," he said.

She nodded inquiringly.

"I've used them."

She gave another nod, a bigger one this time, one that said she comprehended.

There, he told himself. That wasn't so bad. Although he had a feeling that if he had to spend the next three months repeating everything twice, it was going to be a serious nuisance.

"I'm sorry, Mr. Gallagher," Orin Coleridge said. He turned toward Dugan in a way that cut Veronica out of what he was saying. Veronica noted it instantly, Dugan saw, and she didn't like it.

"The background noise," Orin said. "It makes it more difficult for her to make out what you're saying."

Dugan didn't get that. Now that he thought about it, he didn't understand the hearing aids, either. "Maybe somebody ought to explain this to me, so I know what I'm up against here."

"My daughter still has some hearing. Her loss mostly lies in the middle ranges where most daily sounds occur. Where speech occurs. With the help of hearing aids, speech can be amplified enough that she can hear some of the sounds you make, but not the consonants. Unfortunately, as she has told me so often, the hearing aids also amplify all the other sounds. So right now I would venture to say that your voice is getting lost in all the other noise around us."

He nodded, absorbing that. "So what do I sound like to her?"

She answered, apparently having read his lips. "Ooo ow eye iiii."

It took him a minute to realize that she had said, "You sound like this." No consonants. Thinking about it, he guessed he could see it. Consonants were kind of quiet. So he sounded like that to her, did he? Then he could damn well understand why she was having trouble. "So you get the consonants from watching my lips?"

"Yes."

"Wow." He could scarcely imagine how difficult that must be. So maybe instead of feeling so irritated by her irritation, he ought to just pay more attention to looking at her, and enunciating clearly. It sounded easy enough, but he knew it was going to be a strain, because he wasn't used to doing that.

And it might be a good time to get back to the subject at hand. "So, okay, how long are we going to be out tomorrow?"

"We'll be out for a couple of hours and probably make two flights," she said. "That should cover most of the area I'm interested in."

"What if you don't find anything?"

"We'll still look. There's an eyewitness report that the ship broke up, so we might not see anything from the air."

He nodded, but was thinking that this was a fool's quest. "When did this ship go down?"

"In 1703," Orin answered.

"Three hundred years." If it had gotten buried in sand of mud, there might be quite a bit of timber left, but if it hadn't gotten buried, there wouldn't be much except cargo and cannons and some of the ship's iron fittings. And all of that could be scattered over several square miles. Three months? In your dreams, lady.

But he didn't say what he was thinking. No point in it. It was on her dime, not his, and he figured that if she was going to yield to reason, she would have done it before she showed up in his office. So he acted like this was a perfectly rational thing to be doing. "I've got another diver for you, a friend of mine."

She picked that up well enough, and nodded. "Good."

"So maybe two is enough to start?"

"Why?"

"No point in hiring anyone else until we're sure we need the extra hands."

She thought about that, but something about her eyes told him she wasn't too happy about it.

"Look," he said. "You want to keep this under wraps. That means you go at it in a small way. Now if you don't care what the world knows about this, we'll hire another boat, string a cable between them and use it as a guideline for a whole team of divers to swim in parallel."

"I don't follow," she said.

So he grabbed a napkin and drew a sketch, using it to show her what he meant as he explained again. She nodded her comprehension, then shook her head.

"I thought you'd feel that way. Look, first we do the flyover, right?"

"Yes."

"Then we go out on the boat. You said you have a magnetometer?"

"Yes."

"When we find something worth checking out, Tam and I can do it. You won't need more than the two of us right away. Later, we might, but right now, two divers will be enough to check out the possibilities."

She looked at her father. He nodded. "Mr. Gallagher is right. Two will work for a start."

"Call me Dugan," he said.

"Okay," Veronica said. "Two to start. But if I think we need more, we get them."

"Sure." If they found anything, they'd need the extra hands. But at least for now he figured two divers were going to be overkill. In fact, he was willing to bet they wouldn't see anything from the plane, and willing to bet her magnetometer wouldn't find anything either.

Cripes, he might not know much about treasure hunting, but he'd been in these parts long enough to know how difficult it was going to be to find a sunken, broken-up Spanish treasure ship. Three hundred years could do a lot of weird things to wreckage. Wood would be mostly gone, coral would have grown on the remains, hiding them. Unless they found something that looked distinctly artificial, they were apt to get nowhere fast.

Not his problem. His problem, the way he saw it, was to get these two lambs through the next three months of disappointment and heartbreak without being fleeced. And without drawing the attention of some less-savory elements who might think the Coleridges knew an easy way to get rich.

Which was quite enough of a burden for a man who had decided to avoid moral burdens like the plague after he'd been taught that other people didn't have moral qualms. The rule was every man for himself, and anybody who didn't play by those rules was bound to be a loser.

He'd been a loser, once. And he'd finally carved out a niche where he didn't have to face those conflicts anymore. So what was he doing getting involved in this mess?

The question kept rearing its head, irritating him because he'd already answered it numerous times since yesterday. He didn't want to think about it anymore. He just wanted to get through these next months.

"What time tomorrow?" he asked.

"What?"

He stifled a sigh and looked at Veronica. "The plane," he said. "What time tomorrow?"

"Eight. Wilson Air."

Oh, God! He knew Butch Wilson. Worse, he knew Wilson's reputation. The guy had started his life as an aviator in Vietnam, where he'd developed some seriously bad habits related to careful flying. Then he'd run drugs up from Jamaica, back in the days when drug running had been a primary industry around the island. He'd long since gone legit with a charter service, but his attitude hadn't improved any. He still liked treetop flying and quick thrills.

Maybe he needed to pick up some Dramamine for the flight.

On the other hand, Butch was as honest as the day was long. The Coleridges had lucked out, picking him.

"Butch is a good man," he said finally. "How'd you pick him?"

"You know Drew Hunnecutt?" Veronica asked.

"Hell, yes. We went to Harvard together, and I take him diving a lot." Not on the regular tours, either. When Drew came to town on vacation, he was looking for something special, and Dugan had long ago developed the habit of scheduling a vacation himself at the same time, and taking Drew out on the *Mandolin.*

"He recommended both you and Mr. Wilson."

"Figures." Drew liked his thrills, too. But then Drew had always been a little bit insane. Dugan liked the sea as much as the next guy, but spending your life studying coral reefs had always struck him as the next best thing to taking up basket weaving.

"Well," he said, taking care to face Veronica directly, "I hope you have a strong stomach. Butch can be a madman at the controls."

She shrugged. "Drew warned me. But he said Mr. Wilson was an honest man who could keep a secret."

"That's true." Sometimes he figured Butch kept more secrets than a graveyard.

Orin Coleridge bailed out right after lunch, insisting he needed to rest. Which left Dugan with the lady, who was looking at him as if she didn't like him any more than he liked her. He was going to have a word with Drew about sending him this crew.

He ordered another beer while Veronica had a fruit bowl for dessert. She wasn't very talkative, probably for good reason, which left him feeling awkward and irritable. He was used to people who had plenty to say, and conversations that were freewheeling.

"Is your dad going with us on the boat?"

Her head snapped up. "Did you say something?"

"Yes. Is your dad going with us on the boat?"

"I don't think so. He's not well and needs a lot of rest."

"I thought so." Great. Him, Tam, and this woman. What a happy group they were going to make. Unless he could find some way to make common ground with her, a place where they could talk more easily without ruffling each other's feathers.

"Why are you so sure you're going to find this boat in three months?"

"I'm not."

The answer surprised him. She'd seemed so definite about it yesterday. "You're not?"

She shook her head.

"Then why the deadline?"

She looked down at her fruit, then pushed it away with something like distaste. She looked at him again. "It's a long story, Mr. Gallagher."

"Call me Dugan. Please. And I've got time to listen. How about this evening? Have you seen our sunset celebration yet? You don't want to miss it. I'll pick you up around six-thirty."

She looked as if she wanted to say no, but he wasn't going to let her. The more he thought about it, the more questions he had about this little operation. And the more he wanted to know why a deaf woman and her terminally ill father were so hot on doing this search right now.

"No arguments," he said, donning his most charming smile. "Six-thirty. I'll come for you."

"You don't know where I'm staying."

"So tell me. Believe me, you don't want to miss the celebration. Lots of local atmosphere. A great show."

She hesitated, then gave him a location on Elizabeth Street. Ten minutes later, when they parted ways, he was at least sixty percent certain that when he appeared at her door tonight, she wouldn't be there. Well, it wouldn't be the first time he'd been stood up, and he wasn't particularly attracted to the idea of spending an evening with Veronica Coleridge.

But he did want to hear her story.

Veronica, who'd barely come out of the house since she'd lost her hearing, did something unusual after leaving Dugan Gallagher: she walked around Key West. In the anonymity of the crowds, she didn't need to hear or to read lips. She could simply wander around without anybody realizing she was deaf, and without exhausting herself by trying to converse.

The level of the noise bothered her, though, and finally she popped her aids out and tucked them into a pocket. She wasn't fully ready to admit it yet, but there were times when silence was a blessing. Without her aids in, every sound was distant and muffled, as if coming from a very long way away. And many sounds didn't reach her at all.

It was still unnerving at times to see people laughing and not be able to hear them. For some reason that bothered her almost more than anything else. So she didn't look at the people's faces, but contented herself with looking in the shop windows.

She just wished she hadn't let Dugan talk her into the sunset celebration. Not that he'd exactly talked her into it. He'd steamrolled her. Sort of.

Deep inside, though, at some place where the Veronica she used to be still resided, she wanted to go to the celebration. Wanted to do the ordinary things that other people did. Things she had once taken for granted.

Things she would have done without a second thought, before the accident, and before Larry had left her. Before having a simple conversation with a stranger had become one of the hardest tasks in her life.

She could lipread her father reasonably well, because they'd been practicing it for the last six months. Dugan Gallagher was a lot harder to read, although not nearly as hard as most people she encountered. But because of that limitation, she found it hard to speak with strangers at all, and that's why her father had come along on this trip. Much as he probably would have preferred to stay home where he could get all the rest he needed more easily, he had chosen to ride shotgun, to be there to deal with all the people who might as well have been babbling, as far as Veronica was concerned.

Everyone from gas station attendants to clerks in the supermarket was a problem for her. Since becoming deaf, she'd realized how little people actually looked directly at the person they were talking to. Usually they looked down or away. And then there were so many people who hardly moved their mouths at all when they talked, leaving her completely at sea about which consonants they were using.

All of which had seriously chipped away at her self-confidence. She was aware of the erosion, but she didn't seem to be able to stop it. Even a trip to the convenience store had become a task to avoid because someone might speak to her.

Because she was embarrassed and ashamed. Embarrassed to be flawed, and ashamed to have to keep asking people to repeat themselves, or to have to explain she was deaf. She kept telling herself that it was nothing to apologize for, but she kept feeling apologetic anyway, because she could no longer function like the rest of the "normal" world.

And behind her wall of silence, she told herself how little she was really missing. What did it matter if she couldn't tell that the clerk was saying, "Hi, how are you today?" A meaningless question that demanded no answer other than, "Fine." Whether she was fine or not. So she was cut off from the banalities and trivialities.

And how many people really had anything worth saying, anyway? When she really needed to understand, she could ask for repetition until she got it. The rest of the time, conversation was all just so much wasted breath anyway.

Or so she told herself.

But she didn't really believe it. When she was honest, she admitted she missed all that casual talk about nothing important, and that she missed gabbing with her friends about nothing in particular. That she missed, most of all, the long talks she and Larry used to have over their work.

That she missed Larry most of all, even if he was a splay-footed jerk who should hang his head in everlasting shame. Good God, *he* had been driving the car. He had had too much to drink and lied to her about it, claiming he'd only had one beer. *He'd* been the one who was too dazed to avoid the other drunk driver who had crossed the median and plowed into them. So how dare he have the nerve to tell *her* he couldn't deal with *her* deafness?

She realized she was getting blindingly angry, and the sensation frightened her. She didn't get angry like this. She didn't feel rage so strong that she wanted to rip nails from boards or smash something. This wasn't like her.

But that was what she was feeling. More and more since coming out of her depression she'd begun to feel angry. Anger at Larry, mostly, for dumping her after she'd lost her hearing and the baby. Anger for her loss. Anger at her father for dragging her out of her depression with the story of her mother's quest.

The last thought caught her unawares, and stopped her in her tracks. Crowds moved around her, some people glancing at her as if she were crazy, but she hardly noticed them.

Angry at her father for pulling her out of her depression?

That was insane.

But deep inside she knew it was true, knew it as sure as she knew she was angry that he was dying, and angry that he'd kept the secret for so long.

Angry. That's what she was. *All* she seemed to be anymore. Angry at everyone and everything.

God, it had been easier when she was depressed. At least then she'd been able to hide deep inside herself, where nothing but the ache of loss and despair could touch her.

This anger hurt even worse.

A hand touched her arm and she jumped. A stranger had touched her and was saying something. She couldn't hear him because she didn't have her aids in, and his mouth was giving her no clue because it was concealed behind a heavy beard.

Embarrassment flooded her. Something about his face said he was concerned about her. She managed a weak smile, then made the humiliating admission: "I'm sorry, I can't hear you. I'm deaf."

Comprehension dawned on his face. Then he pointed to the nearby bar, and held up one finger. She nodded to him, although she had no intention of waiting to see what he was going to do.

But before she had fully passed the bar, he caught up with her. Into her hand he thrust an icy cold bottle of spring water. She looked up at him, startled. He pointed to her, then wiped his forehead with the back of his hand. He was telling her she looked too hot.

From some graveyard inside her, a genuine smile emerged. It felt strange as it lifted the corners of her mouth.

The man smiled back, waved, and walked away, leaving her in the middle of crowded Duval Street with an icy bottle of water in her hand.

Suddenly all she wanted to do was cry. And she didn't know what the hell to make of the kindness of a stranger.

Chapter 4

Dugan Gallagher was as good as his word. He arrived at the cottage promptly at six-thirty. Orin let him in, looking surprised to see him.

"I'm here for Veronica," Dugan explained. "I'm taking her to the sunset celebration."

"Oh."

"Did she run out on me?"

"Uh, no. She's here. . . ." Orin looked around, as if not at all certain where his daughter had gone to. "Sorry, I was napping. I think she's in her room. Just a moment."

Dugan waited just inside the door as Orin walked down a short hallway and opened a door. You couldn't knock for the deaf, he supposed, unless you wanted to hammer really loudly.

"Dugan's here," he heard Orin say. He couldn't hear Veronica's response, although he could hear her voice. He wondered if that was what the world sounded like to her all the time.

"She'll be just a minute," Orin said, returning. "I'm surprised you got her to agree to this. She doesn't much like to go out in public anymore."

"I didn't give her much choice."

A smile creased Orin's drawn face. "Maybe that's what it takes."

"Well, we'll see how much of me she can tolerate."

Veronica appeared wearing white shorts and a bright red tank top that Dugan suspected put his blood pressure through the roof. God, what a body, he thought. Too bad she didn't have the personality to go with it.

She said good night to her father and followed Dugan out onto the street. Elizabeth Street wasn't a main thoroughfare, so it was quiet despite the crowds of tourists who had jammed every available parking place.

It didn't take him long to realize that they couldn't walk and talk at the same time because she couldn't see his face. And if he turned to look directly at her, neither of them was paying attention to where they were going.

Not good. He paused and touched her elbow. She automatically turned to face him.

"I've got us a table reserved at the dock. We can have a few drinks, maybe something to eat if you want."

"That sounds nice."

Well, he supposed that was a good start. When they reached busier streets, he automatically tucked her arm through his, and he was relieved when she didn't seem to object. He was probably being overprotective, he realized, and he wouldn't have blamed her if she'd informed him that she was perfectly capable of walking down a street without leaning on a man.

But she didn't, and he wondered if the crowds were intimidating her. It wasn't exactly shoulder-to-shoulder crowding , but it was close to it. The only reason they were moving as swiftly as they were was because pretty much everybody was heading toward Sunset Dock and Mallory Square for the nightly festivities.

But he had connections, and they had a table waiting for them at the dock. With any other person, he would have placed them both on the same side of the table, looking out toward the west, so they could both enjoy the sunset without craning. But this was not just any other person, so he put his own back to the sunset, facing her.

Veronica still wasn't sure what she was doing there with him, or why she had let herself be pressured into this. But at the moment, it didn't seem to matter. The breeze was balmy, the sun was sinking low, and the excitement on the dock was contagious as people gathered for the celebration. The murmur of many voices was becoming a steady drone in her hearing aids, but it wasn't yet annoying. And she could still hear Dugan when he spoke to her.

"Would you like something to drink?"

Well, no one was driving anywhere, so after a moment's reflection, she said, "A Tom Collins, please."

"Sure thing." At least she thought that's what he said. He spoke too rapidly, and his head had started to turn as a waiter approached.

She couldn't make out what he ordered, but she supposed she would find out when it was delivered. She pretended that it didn't bother her to be cut out of even such minor things, but the truth was it did. She just didn't want to think about it just then. It was too beautiful there to be tormenting herself with thoughts of things that made her unhappy.

But she wished she could hear the sound of the water lapping against the pier. In her mind, she could hear the gentle sound, and she strained her ears to pick it out from all the other sounds that were bombarding her. She had no luck.

A seagull flying overhead let out a sharp cry, distracting her. Her gaze leapt upward, and she felt a twinge of envy for that bird.

Dugan said something she couldn't make out, and she looked at him again, the sense of frustration welling in her. It was always like this, and God knew how she was going to learn to live with it. "I didn't hear you."

"I know," he said, speaking slowly and forming his words with care. "But I didn't want to just reach out and touch you, and talking was the only other way I could think to get your attention."

"Oh. Sorry." Sorry for what? Why did she feel so apologetic for something she couldn't help?

"No need," he said, smiling. He had the devil's own smile, she thought, incredibly charming. Just seeing it made her feel warm, and she didn't like that. Didn't want anyone to be able to affect her so easily. She had enough other problems in her life.

He spoke again. "I just wanted to know if you'd like some conch fritters for an appetizer."

"That sounds good."

He nodded and turned to the waiter who was serving their drinks and gave the order. At least that was what she assumed he was doing. She hated this, always having to make assumptions about what people were saying. She made them every time someone spoke to her, when she had to piece things together, trying to figure out the sense when some of the individual words eluded her. She was getting better at it, but she was also beginning to understand that it would always be this way for her. Always.

The breeze caught her hair, ruffling it, and she had to

push it back from her face. Her gaze strayed to the water and the two islands beyond. Boats were making their way down the channel, some of them tall with masts and sails, some motor launches, all headed out to sea.

Dugan touched her arm and she looked at him. "The boats are going out to watch the sunset."

She realized she would like to do that. And maybe she would, once they started searching for the wreckage. For the moment, though, she contented herself with watching others do it, including a large schooner. Judging by the number of people aboard, she figured they were paying for the ride.

She sipped her drink, enjoying the tart-sweet flavor of it, enjoying the coldness of it in her hand and against her lips. Dugan was sipping on a beer and looking longingly at the schooner.

She recognized that longing. It wasn't so very different from what she felt when she saw someone with a newborn baby, or a couple laughing happily together. The things she had lost in a few split seconds one rainy Friday night. The ache that was never entirely gone pierced her anew, and she closed her eyes for a moment.

But closing her eyes now cut her off more than ever before in her life, and it wasn't long before she opened them again so that she could sort out all the sounds that were battering her through her hearing aids.

"Do you want a schooner?" she asked Dugan, more to get her mind off the direction of her own thoughts than because she was really interested.

He looked at her. "Not really. But I love to sail. Sometimes I think I was born a century too late."

"Why? You can still get a sailboat."

"I *have* a sailboat. But it's the wrong century for someone who wants to captain a . . . on a voyage to. . . ."

"To where? A what?"

He spoke more clearly. "A clipper ship."

"Oh." She had seen pictures of those. "They were fast, weren't they?"

"Very. Six months to China and back." He gave her a crooked grin.

"Why did you go to Harvard if you wanted to be a sea captain?"

"Good question." He laughed, shook his head, and shrugged. "I guess I was being practical. Besides, nobody is looking for a clipper captain anymore."

"How did you wind up here?"

He cocked his head as if he didn't quite understand her question. "Wind up here? What do you mean?"

"Harvard MBAs don't usually wind up in places like this."

"Oh." He lifted one dark brow. "Snobbery?"

"No, just curiosity."

"I got here by way of Wall Street. You could say my, um, principles weren't flexible enough."

It took her a few moments to be sure she'd heard him correctly. "They wanted flexible principles?"

"Yes."

"That's reassuring."

He laughed. "It's all about power and money. Nothing else matters. At least not in business."

That was cynical, but his opinion was probably justified. She certainly had no experience with the world he spoke of that might make her think otherwise. "So how did you come to be here?"

"Oh, I decided to become a beach bum."

"A beach bum?"

He spread his arms, as if to tell her to look at him.

She couldn't resist saying wryly, "It didn't quite take, did it?"

"Apparently not." He laughed again, an engaging sound that made her smile. Whatever else she might not like about him, she *did* like his self-deprecating sense of humor.

"I'm happy," he said. "I don't have to work any harder than I want to." Which wasn't strictly true, but he refused to admit it. "And I've got everything I want." Well, mostly. "What about you?"

"Me?"

"Why did you become an archaeologist?"

"I never thought about doing anything else." And that was true. She'd grown up with an archaeologist father, and had spent her summers accompanying him on digs all over Central America. And then there had been her mother. Nearly forgotten, because women of thirty didn't have very many memories of being five, but she'd grown up knowing her mother had been an archaeologist, too.

"Why not?" Dugan asked. "Why didn't you ever think of anything else?"

The question made her uncomfortable, although she wasn't sure why. Maybe because it sounded so dull to have only wanted to be one thing in one's entire life? "I don't know," she said finally. "It's just what I always wanted to do."

"Fair enough. I was just wondering if you felt pressured to follow in your father's footsteps."

"No, never." And for some reason she didn't resent the question, although she felt she should have. But the way he offered it seemed innocent, and not at all critical. Just curious. Well, she was curious herself, about him.

The waiter appeared with the conch fritters and offered to bring them fresh drinks. Dugan shook his head, and Veronica was relieved that he didn't have another beer. It made her nervous now when people drank too much. He looked at her questioningly, and pointed to her drink. She shook her head.

Reaching out, she took a fritter, dipped it in hot sauce, and bit into it.

"It's good, isn't it?" Dugan said, watching her expression. "If I ever had to leave here, I'd have to find a way to get these things shipped to me."

She could understand why. Just then a blond man with a moustache came up to the table, pulled out an empty chair and sat. He was talking rapidly to Dugan and grinning, and Veronica couldn't catch more than a word or two of what he said.

Dugan must have seen the confusion on her face, because he spoke to the other man, then said, "Veronica, I'd like you to meet your other diver." Then he added something she didn't quite catch.

The man turned and beamed at her. "You're the boss lady?" He stuck out his hand and she shook it.

She forced herself to say, "I didn't get your name."

"Tam. Just call me Tam."

"Tam?"

"That's it."

"Veronica is . . . hard of hearing," Dugan said. "Try speaking slowly and clearly, Tam."

"Sure, okay. No problem." He looked at her ears, and Veronica felt a pained flush coming to her cheeks. Then he said something else she didn't quite catch. His moustache wasn't helping a whole lot.

"Look, Tam," Dugan said, making sure his face was

turned so Veronica could see his lips. "We'll talk later, okay? Veronica and I have some business to discuss."

"Yeah, sure." Tam smiled at her. "Nice meeting you, boss." Then he rose and walked away.

"Sorry," Dugan said, when Veronica's gaze was once more on him. "Tam's . . . exuberant. Actually, I think he's still living in the sixties."

She laughed. She had to laugh. "He's too young."

"I know. But I think he's been crushed ever since he realized he missed Woodstock. Speaking of which . . ."

"Yes?"

"What do you know about your pilot tomorrow?"

"Butch Wilson? Just that he's very good. Drew thinks highly of him. Why? Is something wrong with him?"

"No. No. I just wondered." He turned his head to look at the sky. Streams of high clouds were beginning to glow golden as the sun nearly touched the water.

The dock was crowded, the buzz of voices loud in Veronica's ears. Almost in spite of herself, she felt the growing anticipation, too. There was something almost surreal, she thought, about a place that took time every day to celebrate sunset. Something pagan.

But there was no disapproval in the thought, only a kind of admiration for the vivacity and vitality of it all.

Dugan looked at her again, catching her eye. She waited. "Why three months?" he asked. "Why that time limit?"

"My father's not well."

"I can see that. How bad is it?"

"He finished chemo a month ago and seems to be in remission. But there's no telling how long that will last. I don't have a whole lot of time to do this because *he* doesn't."

Dugan nodded understanding. "But . . . he must know as well as anyone how unlikely this search is."

Veronica shrugged. She was getting tired of people telling her this probably wouldn't work. She *knew* that. But unbeknownst to the people who kept telling her that, she had twenty years of her mother's research behind her. All she had done was interpret it somewhat differently. It wasn't as if she was coming to the search out of nowhere. "In three months he has to go back for tests. In three months we might find out he's sick again. There is no more time."

"I see." He reached out then, startling her by covering her hand with his.

The touch affected her more than she wanted to admit. She wasn't used to being touched anymore. It was as if her deafness had locked her up inside a bell jar. She could see everything around her, but she couldn't hear it . . . and she couldn't touch it. Not when it came to other people. Her father was the only one who touched her anymore.

She wondered why that was. She'd always been a touching sort of person, and was used to exchanging hugs with her friends when they met. But these days, on the rare occasions when she met her friends, they seemed reluctant to touch her at all, as if they were afraid she was too fragile. Or as if she might be contagious. She couldn't explain it. She just knew in that instant, as Dugan's hand covered hers, that she had missed this kind of human contact.

His palm was warm, dry, and surprisingly rough. He must, she thought, do something besides sit at a computer all day. His were hardworking hands.

She looked down at the hand on hers, noted the fine fair hairs that dotted the back of it, noted assorted small scars and a deep tan. The feelings his touch was giving her were scaring her, though, because they were making her want things she'd sworn never to want again. She was about to jerk her hand away when his fingers closed around it, holding it snugly.

Her startled eyes flew to his face.

"I'm sorry," he said. "About your dad."

She didn't know what to say. She was sorry, too. But her paramount need just then was to break physical contact with him, because it was disturbing her.

He glanced over his shoulder, still holding her hand, then looked at her. "Do you want to watch from here, or would you like to take a stroll?"

"Let's walk." It would be safer, she reasoned. Safer to be moving through the crowds than thinking about how barren her life had become in the last year. It was a mark of how empty she had become that a simple touch could affect her so deeply. Time to be wary, because she had just discovered an unexpected weakness in herself.

He rose and helped pull her chair back. Then, before she could think of a reasonable objection, he tucked her arm through his and began guiding her away from the Sunset Dock toward Mallory Square.

And she was instantly at war with herself. Having her arm tucked through his gave her a sense of security in the crowds, and she hated feeling that way. There had been a time when she would have walked here all by herself without a single qualm, but that confidence had been stripped away from her, and she hated the weak need to lean on someone else emotionally.

But however much she detested her own weakness, she didn't pull away. She couldn't make herself do it. It was as if having him beside her surrounded her with a protective shell. If someone spoke to her, she wouldn't be at a loss. Dugan would hear them. If she had trouble understanding, he would explain to her. He buffered her against normal, everyday things that shouldn't have frightened her. But they did.

And more than frightening her, they stressed her. The influx of sounds through her hearing aids was overwhelming and irritating. Trying to understand the speech of other people was exhausting. Casual conversation had become an obstacle course for her, and being among strangers had become a threat.

When they reached the square, he found a low stone wall where they could sit and watch the sunset. The clouds were turning darker shades of rose, and the sun's fiery ball had half sunk into the water.

Mingling with the sounds of people talking and laughing, she detected bagpipe-and-flute music.

Dugan looked at her, smiling. "Even after ten years I still love this."

"It's like a carnival."

"It sure is. So why is this search so important to you?"

It took her a few moments to get what he'd said. The subject change was abrupt, and she didn't fully hear the question, so she had to piece it together.

"I'm an archaeologist."

"And I'm not buying it."

She stiffened and inched away from him. "Why not?"

"Because you're not here on a grant."

"Who told you that?"

"Your dad, when he said you wouldn't run out of money in this lifetime."

"Oh." She looked away, reluctant to pursue this conversation. It was really none of his business.

But he tucked a finger under her chin and turned her face back to him. "That's cheating," he said, but there was a humorous glint in his eye. "If you want me to shut up, just say so. But don't shut me out by looking away."

Her cheeks grew hot, and she was sure a bright blush must be staining them. She hoped he thought it was the red glow from the sun, which was almost gone.

"So why is this so important that you're spending your own money on it?"

She couldn't bring herself to be rude enough to tell him to butt out. She didn't know why, because she was usually quite capable of telling people to get their noses out of her business.

But so much about her had changed since the accident, and she didn't know if it was her loss of confidence that kept her from being rude to him. Or maybe it was having his finger under her chin, a gesture that was almost lover-like.

Finally, she pointed to the southwest. "Out there is a small island."

"There are lots of small islands out there." He said it humorously, but he dropped his finger from her chin, and waited intently.

"There was one small island in particular. A tribe of people lived there until 1703. They're mentioned briefly in some of the records of the time, but almost nothing is known about them."

"What happened to them?"

"A hurricane wiped them out. The same one that sank the *Alcantara*."

"Okay. Why do I think they're connected somehow?"

A moment of almost forgotten impishness overtook her. "Maybe because I mentioned them when you asked about the ship?"

He laughed, that warm, wonderful sound that plucked something deep inside her. "Okay," he said. "Go on."

"Anyway, they were a Stone Age culture in terms of artisanry. They didn't build stone monuments; they lived in dwellings made of cane and thatch. The most anyone's found of theirs is some basketry, some shards of unfired pottery, and flint and stone tools. Nothing else is left but some fire pits. Because they didn't have any gold, they weren't of interest to the Spaniards, and they were pretty much left alone, So basically we don't know anything at all about them."

"Where does the ship come in?"

"About 1700, the Spaniards started to take an interest in the island, with the intention of converting the inhabitants to Catholicism. Some monks arrived, and with them a few soldiers. One of the soldiers married a holy woman of the tribe and later they had a child. After a couple of years of marriage, the soldier persuaded the priestess to come to Spain for a visit."

"And they were on the ship?"

"Yes. Along with the only major artifact ever made by this culture, a mask that the holy woman wore during religious rites. It was made of solid gold."

He nodded, rubbing his chin, thinking over what she'd said. The sun had vanished, and the sky was deepening toward indigo. He looked at her. "I take it this mask would be more valuable than all the gold on the ship."

Veronica shrugged. "I don't care about that. I just want to find the mask."

"So you really *are* looking for a needle in a haystack."

"I guess so."

He shook his head, chuckling. "And I thought it was

going to be hard to find a whole boat. Now I'm looking for something hardly bigger than a human face?"

"It's bigger. I have a description of it. The face itself is surrounded by a halo of filigree that's supposed to represent the winds. The mask is supposed to be the face of the Storm Mother, the force that controlled the hurricanes. The story is that when the mask left with the priestess for Spain, the Storm Mother grew angry, wiping out both the island and the ship."

"How do you know that? I thought everyone was wiped out."

"Basically. There were a couple of survivors."

"Well, that's some story."

She watched him think about it, wondering what his impressions were. The story had become so familiar to her over the last six months that she had forgotten the freshness of it all when her father first shared it with her.

"It would be a real coup," he said presently. "A real coup."

"Yes, it would."

"However, when I consider the size of that mask and the size of the water out there . . ." He shook his head.

She didn't say anymore, because it really didn't matter what he thought. She was paying him to do a job, and he would do it. She didn't need his opinions.

"What the hell," he said finally, looking straight at her. "It'll be a fun way to spend a few months."

Fun? He thought this was going to be fun? She didn't know if she liked that. It indicated a less-than-professional attitude toward what was certainly a professional task from start to finish. This was an archaeological exploration. It had to be conducted methodically, painstakingly, with utmost care. Not like a beach holiday.

Remembering Tam's brief introduction, she felt her first serious qualms about the search. What had she gotten herself into?

Then he said something that caused her heart to sink to her toes.

"Lighten up, Veronica. We're going to have a great time."

She didn't want to have a great time. She wanted to get a job done as quickly as she could. Looking at the way he was grinning at her now, she realized she had made a huge mistake.

He was going to have *fun*. Whether she liked it or not.

Oh joy.

Chapter 5

Butch Wilson didn't look like a man who preferred life on the edge, but appearances could be deceiving. He was spreading slowly into middle age, and the only remnant of his sixties' rebellion was a gray ponytail. He was a soft-spoken man with a manner that didn't invite other men to play rooster games with him. Not that he needed to prove anything. From things Butch had said when he had too much tequila in him, Dugan suspected he knew more ways to kill a man than Dugan wanted to think about.

Before the flight, Veronica unrolled some charts and showed the two men the area she was particularly interested in.

"How did you come up with this area?" Dugan asked her.

"Drew made a computer model based on the eyewitness report of the ship's breakup. Assuming I'm right about where the witness saw the ship break up, and the conditions at the time, this is probably pretty close."

Dugan nodded, although he had some serious qualms.

There were a lot of assumptions in that statement she'd just made. But what the hell. It was *her* dime.

"Okay," said Butch. "Let's go."

"No barrel rolls," Dugan said as he climbed into the seat beside Butch. Veronica had opted to sit in the back, behind Butch, so she could perch her GPS receiver on the seat beside her. Butch had the same equipment on his control panel, so it was a definite redundancy.

"I wasn't planning any," Butch answered serenely.

"No nose dives, no sharp climbs, just make it straight and easy."

Butch laughed, and Veronica looked questioningly at them. Dugan turned on his seat to face her. "I told him not to give us a circus ride."

She nodded. "Thank you."

She took the headphones Butch handed her and put them on. "How can you hear?" Butch asked her in the microphone.

"Okay. Not perfect, but okay."

Dugan, watching her face, got the distinct impression she wasn't hearing well at all. Well, how could she? The headset wasn't going to help her hear consonants any better than her hearing aids could. He was going to get an awfully stiff neck from turning around to speak to her in this too-small plane.

"God," he said into the microphone, not caring who heard him, "this thing is a sardine can." Nobody responded.

"We're off then." Butch hit the ignition, and the plane's two engines started turning. A few minutes later they had clearance to taxi.

Secretly, Dugan liked this part of flying best. He liked the power of the takeoff and the way it made him feel.

But he'd have felt a whole lot better if he'd been doing the flying.

A few minutes later they were over the green waters moving in the general direction of the Marquesas. "It's better when you sail," Dugan couldn't resist saying into his mike.

"You're just attached to the ground, Dugan," Butch replied. "Got lead in your feet."

A snappy retort eluded Dugan as he thought about that. Some part of him agreed with Butch's assessment, he realized. His divorce from Jana had clipped his wings in a lot of ways. In retrospect he could see that he'd been too young to handle it.

But then, what was there to say in favor of getting old? Most of the people he liked were still kids at heart.

He glanced over his shoulder at Veronica, and saw she was intently looking out the side window. "We're not there yet," he said into his mike.

She nodded, but didn't say anything, and he found himself wondering if she had understood him at all. Probably not. And she probably wasn't at all interested.

From what he could see of her expression, he figured she was on tenterhooks, thinking of only one thing: what they might see from up here.

And, almost in spite of himself, he felt his own excitement growing. What if they saw something artificial down there? What if they saw a straight line in coral that could only be there because the coral had grown on something man-made? He'd seen plenty of that in his wilder, younger days when he'd dived the reefs. The wrecks he'd found hadn't been particularly interesting, but this time it could be different. Very different.

The water wasn't as clear as it had been a decade ago.

Runoff from the sugar cane farms that filled the Everglades had gradually clouded it, and he found himself thinking of the way it had been, when the water was so clear the bottom looked close enough to touch.

But cloudy or not, they could make out the major features of the sea bottom from this altitude, and he was beginning to get a kick out of it.

"Hey," he said, "this is neat."

"Yep," said Butch, "Never could understand the passion for flying high. You can't see a damn thing from way up there."

From up there, when he looked in the right direction, the reflections off the water weren't as obscuring as they could be from a boat, and he could see quite a large area of bottom. Not bad at all.

"Reminds me of my drug-running days," Butch remarked. "Flying below radar."

Dugan hoped Veronica couldn't hear that. He suspected she wouldn't at all approve. "Why'd you ever give that up, Butch?"

"Because the Colombians got involved. Used to be a friendly cottage industry. Then it got serious. No thanks."

About an hour into the flight, Veronica spoke for the first time. "Look! To the left. See it?"

Butch swiveled his head to the left, and Dugan tried to look across him. Being helpful by nature, Butch ignored his promise to fly straight and level and tipped the plane on its wing.

Dugan swallowed hard. "Where?" he said.

Veronica's answer was to point. Extrapolating as best he could, he picked out a spot of water. He couldn't see anything.

"Where?" said Butch. "Give me a direction."

"Ten o'clock," Dugan guessed.

"Let's go take a look."

Butch headed in that direction, blowing the search grid totally out of the water. Veronica practically had her face pressed to the window of the plane.

Then Dugan saw it. Long and narrow. A lump of mud, basically. A high point in the sand. Except . . . except that it looked a little too straight along one side. "Maybe," he said. "Maybe."

But Veronica was busy checking her GPS and scrawling coordinates down on a pad.

"Got it?" Butch asked.

"Yeah," Dugan answered. "Let's go back to the grid."

But they didn't see anything else during the rest of the flight. When they climbed out of the plane, Veronica was looking tired, and Dugan instinctively reached out to help her down. She accepted his hand readily.

"You sure you want to go again this afternoon?" Butch asked. Dugan noted that he was avoiding speaking to Veronica, but was treating Dugan as if he were leader of the expedition. It troubled him, and it if was troubling him, it must be annoying the shit out of Veronica.

He looked at her, catching her attention, noticing the pinched look around her eyes. "Do you still want to go out this afternoon?"

"Yes. The light will be different."

"Good point." He looked at Butch, but didn't reiterate what Veronica said. The man could damn well take his orders from a deaf woman. Especially when she was paying him.

"Okay," said Butch. "Three o'clock then."

Veronica nodded and turned abruptly to the car. Dugan wanted to follow her immediately, but he waited a moment, turning to Butch. "Ask *her* what she wants to do," he said.

"She can't hear me none too well."

"She'd hear you a whole lot better if you *looked* at her when you talk, okay? So from now on, you got a question, talk to *her*."

Butch held up a hand. "Okay, okay. Christ." He stomped off in the direction of the hangar, leaving Dugan to stare after him.

Jeez, he thought, Veronica may be deaf, and she may be stubborn, but she sure as hell isn't stupid.

Muttering under his breath, he went toward the car where she was waiting for him, wind blowing her hair about. She looked good in cotton coveralls, too, he thought irritably. And why the hell did he give a damn how some turkey treated her? It was her problem, not his.

He unlocked the car and threw the doors open, letting the heat out before he climbed in to turn on the ignition and the air conditioner. What the hell am I doing here anyway, he wondered. It was hot nearly all the time. Tropical breezes bedamned. Once, just once, he would like to be *cold*. It was as if his Yankee-raised body started screaming every now and then that there was supposed to be an occasional winter in life, goddammit.

And why the hell was he feeling so fucking irritated anyway?

Veronica slid into the passenger seat and closed the door. After a moment he closed his own. The air conditioner was still blowing warm air, but it was at least *dry* warm air.

He had planned to drop her off at her place and tell her he'd pick her up again at two thirty. But somehow he found himself driving right past her gate and finally pulling into his parking place at Green Water.

He turned to look at her and found her watching him with narrowed eyes. She must be wondering why he was acting like a jerk, grumbling to himself and taking corners like a madman.

"I'm hot," he said to her finally. He wasn't, really. Not anymore. And those few minutes on the hot apron at the airport didn't account for his mood either.

She nodded.

"Let's get lunch," he said finally. "We need to talk."

"I need some quiet," she said.

He opened his mouth to speak, then it struck him that was a remarkably odd thing for a deaf woman to say. She needed *quiet*? Didn't she already get too much of that? "What do you mean?"

"I'm exhausted from all the noise on the airplane. I want to take my hearing aids out and not hear for a little while."

"Oh." He didn't quite know what she meant, but he had a feeling this wasn't something she explained to everyone. "Okay. Tell you what. You take your hearing aids out, we'll go to lunch, I'll keep quiet, and then after lunch you put your aids in again and we'll talk."

She cocked her head, looking at him as if he were a strange puzzle. "Talk about what?"

"Nothing, really. I just want to talk."

She looked away, probably just thinking, but for the first time it struck him just how much she was shutting him out when she looked away. She wouldn't be able to understand a thing he said to her, so there was no point in even speaking to her.

He felt an urge to touch her, to make her look at him again, but he had no right to do that. He simply had to wait until she decided to come back. And that compounded his frustration even more.

But finally she did look at him again. Maybe just because he'd been so silent and unmoving for so long. Maybe because she was coming back from wherever she had gone to.

"Yes, I'd like lunch," she said. "And I'll leave my hearing aids in until afterward. I guess I need to get used to all the noise."

"Whichever way you want to do it."

They walked a short way up the street to the place he'd taken her for lunch the other day. For some reason, it was quieter. They got a comfortable table in a corner, away from everyone else.

"How's this?" he asked her.

She smiled. "Not bad. I'm sorry, but all the noise on the plane, and the static on the radio . . . my hearing aids make all that so loud, it starts to wear on me. It's not like before when I could hear. It's . . . different. Maybe because a lot of that noise is in ranges where I haven't lost much hearing, so it gets *really* loud."

"I thought they had hearing aids that could work in certain frequencies."

"They do. But they're not perfect. Just like my hearing."

She looked down, as if embarrassed, and he felt himself wanting to reach out to her. Uh-oh. Not a good response. Not a *safe* response. And God knew Jana had taught him all the reasons he shouldn't trust another woman.

"Well, when it gets too much, go ahead and pull them out. Not that I have any right to give you permission," he added swiftly, as her expression started to change. "I just want you to know it won't bother *me*. But let me know when you're doing it so I don't flap my jaws pointlessly."

A smile flitted across her face again, and he suddenly didn't feel quite so irritated.

They pored over the menus, Veronica finally settling on a baked flounder. He ordered a burger.

While they waited, he watched her relax, and watched the strain seep out of her face. Seeing the transformation, he got a pretty good idea of how stressful the noise had been for her. He kept silent, giving her time and space.

By the time their meals arrived, she looked much better. All the tension was gone from her face and body. She looked at him after the waiter departed. "What did you want to talk about?"

It burst out of him, almost before he was aware of what he was going to say. It was as if what had bothered him hadn't become fully conscious until this instant. "Does everybody treat you like you're stupid?"

She looked startled, then comprehension dawned. "You mean because I'm deaf?"

He nodded.

"Well . . . yes. A lot of people do. I probably wouldn't notice it as much if I'd been deaf all my life."

"You haven't been?" That bowled him over. He had just assumed she had been. "What happened? To your hearing?"

"I was in a car accident about a year ago."

He didn't know what to say. The words, "I'm sorry," just didn't cut it. Finally, he said, "That's rough. That's really rough."

"Other things were rougher."

"Well, you're doing remarkably well for someone who developed this problem a short time ago." Although even as he spoke, he realized he didn't have the background to say that with any certainty. He meant it only as a compliment.

Apparently she took it that way. Looking a trifle embarrassed, she said, "I've been really motivated."

"It must be irritating if people are treating you differently now."

"They are. But I kind of understand it. I won't say I never get annoyed, but basically I think people are just sure I won't understand them."

Or that because she was hard of hearing, she must be stupid. He remembered the way Butch had turned to him for the decision. But then, he'd known men who would never take orders from a woman, either, deaf or not. But Butch ought to be smarter. He knew who was paying for his time.

Finally, he said, "It would drive *me* crazy."

"It doesn't exactly thrill me, either."

They ate in silence for a while, Dugan thinking that he was getting too involved in what this woman thought about things, and how she felt. He needed to treat this like a straight business relationship. Her problems weren't his unless they had to do with their deal. Everything else was none of his business.

So why did he seem unable to do that? He gave a mental shrug and put it aside.

"When's the equipment arriving?" he asked her.

"I'm sorry, what?"

"The equipment. For the search. When is it arriving?"

"We have most of it here already. The metal detectors should be arriving tomorrow."

"What exactly do we have?"

"I think I told you. The metal detectors, the magnetometer, and some underwater cameras. You have the diving equipment, right?"

"Yeah. I have it. And what we haven't discussed is how you want to do this. I'm figuring we can save a lot of time if we go out for a few days at a stretch, rather than coming back to port every day."

She nodded. "So you think we should stay out for three or four days at a time?"

"Yes. I've got a cabin you can have to sleep in." It struck him then that she might be nervous about being the only woman on a boat with two guys. Come to think of it, he wasn't too thrilled with the idea himself. But how else were they going to do this? Her father had already said he wouldn't be joining them. "Can't your father come along? I'll give him my cabin, and Tam and I can share the V-berths."

"The what?"

"The berths in the bow of the boat. What about your father?"

"He's not well."

"So? All he has to do is sit in a deck chair and enjoy the view. The rest of us will be doing all the work."

"I'll ask him again."

Then she excused herself, saying she was going to remove her hearing aids. He watched her walk away to the bathroom, and wondered what he'd said wrong. Because he had a strong feeling she was bailing out on their conversation for some reason other than noise overload. And whatever it was had to do with her father.

But he didn't give a damn, he reminded himself. He absolutely, positively, did not give a damn.

* * *

Emilio Zaragosa was enjoying the late-afternoon sunshine in his hothouse. He puttered among the rosebushes he tended as if they were small children, humming quietly because he believed the plants liked music.

His pride and joy was getting ready to bloom, he noticed. The golden-edged pink rose that he intended to name for his first granddaughter, Emilia Maria. The bud was small yet, but the golden edging was already visible, a thin yellow line at the tips of the petals. Yes, the plant was breeding true to form. The first one had not simply been an accident.

He felt triumphant as he studied the bud, and considered whether he'd be ready to present it at a show soon. Or whether he wanted to keep it a delicious secret for just a little while longer. Emilio enjoyed secrets, as long as they were his own.

Feeling suddenly generous, he decided to cut a half dozen of his yellow roses for his wife to place on the table at dinner. He ordinarily waited to cut the flowers until they were on the verge of becoming overblown because he far preferred to see them on the bushes and watch them bloom at their natural pace.

But tonight he was feeling expansive and good, so he decided to cut some of the opening buds. His wife loved rosebuds, seeming to enjoy their perfect promise more than its fulfillment.

He thought about that sometimes, considering the differences between them, but Elena had always been something of a puzzle to him. He loved her heart and soul, and was sure she loved him equally, but on matters other than family their minds rarely met. He enjoyed their differences a great deal, probably because Elena always deferred to him when it was important. Otherwise he was quite content to let her have her head.

But it was only natural that they had different outlooks, he reminded himself. Elena hadn't been raised on the streets. She'd been a privileged child, and had been at university when he met her. She was also better educated then he, but he took pride in that fact. Pride in the fact that a woman who could have chosen any man had chosen him, uneducated child of the gutter though he was. Of course, by the time he'd met her, he'd been becoming relatively successful, but he didn't think that had weighed in her decision.

And if anything, Elena seemed to consider it every bit as important as he that they ensure none of their children or grandchildren ever do without.

Thinking of Elena always made him smile, and he was smiling as he cut the six delicate rosebuds and put them in a vase of water. She would like this.

Just then, Emilia came prancing into the hothouse, the door slamming behind her as it always did. Eight years old, she pranced rather then walked, her long dark hair bobbing around her shoulders.

"Abuelo?" she said. *Grandfather.*

"Yes, my child?"

"Grandmother wants me to tell you that Señor Gallegos is here to see you."

"He is, is he? Well, tell him to come out here, will you?"

"Yes, Grandfather."

"No, no, wait," he said, as she started to turn away. He clipped the last bud and put the stem in the vase. "Take these in to your grandmother for me. And be very careful."

Emilia beamed up at him, proud to have such an important task. She accepted the vase gingerly, then walked very carefully back to the door to the house.

He watched her and thought, as he did many times every day, that God had truly blessed him. He had so very much to be grateful for.

Five minutes later, Luis Gallegos joined him. Luis hated the greenhouse, complaining that it made him feel hot and claustrophobic, but Emilo ignored his complaints. If this was where Emilio was and what Emilio was doing when Luis came to see him, then Luis would just have to survive. And so far the man had managed to.

Luis always made Emilio think of a praying mantis, though the man wasn't particularly tall or long-limbed. He was slender, indeed, compared to Emilio's more comfortable bulk, but Luis wasn't that thin. It was something about the way the man moved that always made Emilio think of a mantis. Something about the way he moved and the way his jaw was always working.

"You see this rose, Luis?"

Luis, who was already sweating, obediently leaned over and gazed at the rosebud that Emilio touched with a gentle fingertip. "Unusual," he said, because he knew that was expected, not because he really cared.

"This rosebud will make me famous when everything else I've done in my life is long forgotten. It will make my granddaughter's name immortal."

Luis made a noise that indicated he was suitably impressed.

"Amazing isn't it?" Emilio said, caressing a velvety petal. "This simple act of nature will be as immortal as all the gold and art you and I worry so much about."

"It's . . . uh . . . pretty," Luis said, sensing that something was needed from him.

Emilio stifled a sigh and looked at his employee. "I take it you have something important to tell me?"

"Yes. Yes!" Luis looked as if he'd just remembered. But Emilio knew better then that. Dense as he might be about roses and plants, Luis was *not* stupid.

"Well?"

"Key West," Luis said. "I have news. The archaeologist hired a plane today and was flying low over the water to the northwest. I couldn't find out the exact coordinates, though, or what she learned."

Emilio didn't stifle his sigh this time. "Why not?"

"Because only three people know. And none of them are talking about it."

"We must remedy that, Luis. I need better information."

"Well, I hear she had hired a diver as well as the boat I told you about."

"Good. And maybe this time you had better take care of it in person. Whoever you're talking to in Key West doesn't seem to be very good at getting information."

"Me?" Luis wasn't fond of traveling outside the country, especially since there was a warrant out for him in the United States.

"Relax," Emilio said. "We'll get you papers. No one will know who you are."

Luis didn't argue. He knew better. "What makes you think they'll talk to *me*?"

"I think you have enough talent to persuade one of the divers to talk to you. For a reasonable compensation of course."

Luis's eyes brightened. He *was* good at buying information.

"So . . ." said Emilio, turning back to the roses. "You

go, you find out if you can get that diver on our payroll somehow."

"Somehow?"

"*Any*how," Emilio said firmly. "Whatever it takes. But I want a daily update on what that woman is learning. *Daily.*"

Whatever it takes. Emilio didn't say those words often. But when he did, he meant them. Fully. Completely.

And Luis knew it. "And if I can't?"

"Then arrange for an accident, Luis. So we can put our own diver in place. What do I care? The details I leave to you. But I want that information, and I want it every day."

Luis understood, and after a few minutes he left, grateful to escape the hothouse. But he had learned something, whether Emilio knew it or not, and Luis's stock-in-trade was information. Getting some on his boss was a bonanza.

Emilio Zaragosa was more than ordinarily interested in whatever the women archaeologist was searching for. This wasn't simply about artifacts and gold. This was about something more.

And Luis very much wanted to know what that was because information like that could be very useful. Very.

Espeically when it was about his boss.

Chapter 6

When Veronica returned to the cottage, Orin was sitting on the sofa reading a book. He had a blanket over his legs, even though it was warm in the room. He greeted her with a smile when she stepped in, and put his book aside.

"How did it go?" he asked.

"We found a couple of possibilities."

His blue eyes were shrewd. "But not what you hoped for."

"We knew the ship broke up. There can't be much showing after three hundred years."

"Probably not," he agreed.

She passed him and went down the small hallway that led to her bedroom. It was even warmer in there, away from the window air conditioner, and stuffy, too. She changed swiftly into a cool pair of white shorts and a royal blue polo shirt.

She needed to think about what she would make for dinner, but her mind wasn't ready to get off the plane yet, or to let go of the day's search. Yes, it had failed to show as much as she had hoped to see. She was only human, and tales of wrecks that were spotted from the air had whetted her hopes.

But she was also a realist, and she had grown up watching archaeologists dig in places where there was nothing but old tales to guide them. She knew how painstaking and slow the process could be. She knew that it might be years before she found the *Alcantara.*

But she was still disappointed.

And she didn't want to share that disappointment with her father. It was obvious to her that he disapproved of this quest, that he had disapproved of it when it had been her mother's quest. Why else would he have failed to mention it even in passing all these years?

She paused in the bathroom to freshen her face with cool water, then went out front to explore the contents of the refrigerator for something easy to cook. To her surprise, her father was just closing the front door, and in his hands he had a pizza box.

"This sounded good to me tonight," he said. "And I figured you wouldn't want to cook."

"Thanks." Disappointed or not, she couldn't help smiling in appreciation.

She helped him put out plates, napkins, and beverages, and they sat at the island on stools. He didn't say much and she found herself thinking how little they talked anymore.

There had been a period after he had first told her about the mask that they had talked constantly, she mastering her lipreading skills by picking his brain and discussing everything with him. But at some point in the last month or so, their conversations had grown briefer. And it wasn't just because he was so exhausted from his treatments.

It was as if he were withdrawing from her. And why wouldn't he, when she was withdrawing from him?

She felt a pang of regret and looked at him, wondering why she was doing this to them both. Why couldn't she forgive him? Why did she feel so angry at him all the time?

She watched him eating, his movements slow and almost heavy. The change in him during the last year was frightening, when she was willing to see it. He had grown so thin and frail-looking, and his beautiful gray hair was gone except for a pale fuzz. He had aged decades.

Something compelled her to speak to him, to share the truth for a change, instead of just guarded half-truths. "I *am* disappointed that we didn't find more."

If she had expected him to gloat, she was wrong. He looked up from his meal and nodded. "I imagine so," he said. "I know *I* would be."

"But I expected this."

"Of course you did. But we're only human, Veronica. We keep hoping things will leap out at us."

He was being so understanding, and she had to remind herself that he'd always been this way. Patient. Understanding. The problem between them was of her making, because she seemed incapable of understanding *him*.

"Why didn't you tell me, Dad?"

He paused, and finally put down the pizza he was picking at. She was convinced he'd ordered it simply so she wouldn't have to cook, not because he really wanted to eat it.

"Because," he said. Then he looked down, and she could no longer tell what he was saying.

"Dad, you have to look at me when you talk." She tried to keep the impatience from her voice, but wasn't sure she succeeded. How many times had she had to say that to him? How many times in every conversation she had did she get lost simply because people wouldn't look at her while they talked? With her father it was simply irritating to have to remind him. With other people it was embarrassing, and she resented the hell out of it.

He lifted his head, gave her a faint smile. "Sorry. I get lost inside myself when I think of your mother. She was so beautiful and . . . so obsessed. You remind me of her."

"What's wrong with being obsessed? That's how things get done."

His mouth twisted. "Perhaps. But it can also go too far."

"Too far?" she repeated, not certain she had understood him. The day had been incredibly fatiguing with all the noise, and the difficulty of trying to understand speech over headphones when she couldn't see the person who was talking, and the disappointment of not finding as much as she had hoped to. Her resources were rapidly diminishing, and she was torn between just withdrawing into silence and finding out what was behind her father's secrecy.

"Too far," he repeated. "It can go too far."

"In what way?"

"Your mother . . . she . . . well . . ." He hesitated and looked off into space. She had to watch his cheeks to be sure he was only thinking, and not speaking softly. After a minute, he redirected his gaze toward her.

"Your mother went too far," he said. "In some ways she was lost to me before she died."

Veronica heard the sorrow in his tone and felt sympathy for him. She knew what it was like to have someone you loved emotionally out of reach. Larry had taught her that bitter lesson.

"Anyway," Orin continued, his voice cracking, "it was all she could think about. It consumed her past the point of reason. I began to think of her as a wraith, a ghost flitting around the house, but not really there. When we first married, she was as interested in my work as I was in hers, but with time . . . with time there was nothing in her life except the search for the mask."

"It would be an amazing find."

"Of course it would. But her interest went well beyond that."

"But why?"

He shook his head, and for a moment she thought he wasn't going to answer. She held her breath, certain she was about to hear the real reason he had kept silent for so many years.

"Because," he said finally, "she was the descendant of Juan Bernal Vasquez y Maria."

The conquistador! Veronica's heart slammed. "I didn't know that."

"I haven't exactly been advertising it," Orin said wryly. "But yes, you're descended from Vasquez. Descended from the baby he carried on foot across Florida three hundred years ago."

Which meant she was also descended from the holy woman of the extinct, nameless tribe. Veronica suddenly understood her mother's passion and obsession for this search. Her heart was galloping, and dimly she was aware that she was breathing fast.

"Directly descended?"

"Oh, yes. The letter was passed down in the family. That's how your mother came by it. But there's more, Veronica. And this is where your mother became . . . misguided."

"Misguided? What's misguided about seeking such an invaluable artifact?"

"She wasn't just seeking an artifact. I would have had no problem with that. But she became obsessed with the fact that she was descended in the direct female line from this priestess. She came to believe that the mask was her birthright."

"Wasn't it?"

"No!" He was emphatic. "Not after all these centuries. Not when the people who made it are gone from the face of the earth. And not when—" He broke off sharply.

"Not when what? Dad, you can't stop there."

But his face had grown sad and closed, and the pizza sat between them, growing cold and congealing. The only sound in the cottage was the hum of the air conditioner as the minutes ticked by.

"Dad?" She saw him sigh, though she couldn't hear it, and she wanted to groan in frustration. "Dad?"

"She became convinced that as the female descendant of this priestess, as the last surviving member of this culture, that she was on a holy quest."

A holy quest. In that instant Veronica understood why her father had kept the secret for so long. He believed that his wife was more than obsessed; he believed she was delusional. And he feared his daughter would become prey to the same delusion if she learned the whole story.

She got up from the island and went to her room, where she removed her hearing aids. The story had unleashed a storm of emotions inside her, and she wasn't exactly sure what they all were. She was still angry that her father hadn't told her this years ago, but she was also saddened by the gulf that had existed between him and her mother. She felt sorry for him. But she also felt sorry for her mother, who must have felt so misunderstood.

And she was angry at her father for his attitude toward

the whole thing. Her mother had been right: the mask was her birthright. It might not matter much in this day and age when such things were best kept in museums and not in private hands, but it remained that it was still a vestige of Renata's heritage, the same as the letter was. She was entitled to her need to find it.

Entitled to be obsessed.

But *how* obsessed? Veronica struggled with that question for hours in the silence imposed on her by an accident. All she knew was that her father thought her mother had been delusional.

He'd probably had good reason to think so. Veronica herself had known a few people who were so absorbed in some idea or pursuit that they virtually shut out the rest of the world. To onlookers, they seemed crazy.

But it hurt to think her father had felt that way about her mother. She'd always assumed they'd had a great marriage, two archaeologists united not only by love for one another, but by love for their careers. But it seemed that might not have been the case.

But then, she reminded herself, her mother's death might have colored all of that for her father. Especially if he blamed Renata's search for her death. Of course he would twist the whole thing around in his grief.

Then she remembered how he had suggested Renata might have been killed. The thought chilled her, even though she didn't believe it. There would have been *no* reason for anyone to kill her. As far as she could tell, Renata hadn't even been close to finding the mask. Certainly not as close as she herself was. Assuming, of course, her interpretation of the available information wasn't totally off track.

It might be, of course. That was always a possibility,

but just then it was a possibility she didn't want to consider. She couldn't afford to consider it. It had been difficult enough to conclude that her mother had been searching in the wrong area, difficult enough to believe in her own reading of the information when it flew in the face of everything her mother had believed. Having come so far, she wasn't about to backtrack and reconsider yet again.

Besides, time was short. She needed to prove that her mother hadn't been crazy. She had to find the mask. She had to vindicate Renata.

And she had to do it before her father died.

Dugan decided to go out for a drink. He didn't hit the bars the way he used to, but after a day cooped up with Veronica Coleridge, he discovered he'd developed a mighty thirst. Well, okay, maybe a medium one. What he really needed was to be out among people who were having a good time just being alive. He craved it after spending all day with a woman who apparently wouldn't know a good time if it stood up and introduced itself.

Okay, so maybe he was being unfair, he thought as he slid onto a stool at one of the numerous bars along Duval Street and ordered a beer. She was deaf. Worse, she'd been deaf for only a year. That kind of thing would tend to put a damper on your zest for life. He didn't imagine he'd be the easiest person to get along with if that had happened to him. In fact, he might even be downright ornery for a while.

And she had more than that going on in her life. Her father was sick. Very sick. So there was that pressure. As far as he could tell, she didn't have a whole lot to smile about right now.

If that had been all that was going on, he might have

been more sympathetic. This three-month search thing . . . well, she was being unrealistic. And he kept getting the urge to grab her, tell her to relax, and ask her if she didn't have enough problems in her life without throwing this one in on the top of the heap.

Because the woman was a Type A personality looking for a coronary if ever he'd seen one. She reminded him of the people he used to work with on Wall Street, the driven, ninety-hour-a-week types who ate, drank, and slept their work, who would check on the international money markets in the middle of a social gathering, who never left their phones or pagers more than six inches away, and whose entire conversation seemed to be limited to options, currency fluctuations, buyouts, and takeovers.

Sometimes it appalled him to remember that, for a few years, he'd been one of them. And that was the primary reason that Veronica Coleridge was irritating him.

When he'd decided to bail out to Key West ten years ago, he might not have been thinking too clearly on some matters. Jana had really hurt him. The day he told her he'd been fired from the firm for refusing to invest his customers' money in a doubtful stock—a stock that a senior partner had a vested interest in—she'd told him he was a loser, that he'd always been a loser, and by the way, his best friend was a hell of a lot better in the sack than he was.

It was as if somebody had thrown a switch inside him, a switch that shut him down. Without a word, he'd packed and left, and he hadn't stopped driving until his Mercedes had nosed into Old Town. Then he'd sold the Mercedes, rented a shitty apartment, and settled down to drinking himself into a stupor.

Six days later he'd emerged from the bender a changed

man. He'd never gotten drunk again, but he'd sworn off anything remotely connected to his old life. He didn't care if he never "accomplished" anything again. Instead, he was hell-bent on wringing whatever pleasure he could out of life.

Looking at Veronica Coleridge was like looking in a mirror. Only she hadn't yet figured out that life was an apple to be enjoyed. And maybe she never would. But she sure as hell was going to drive him crazy.

Maybe he needed to get her drunk for six days. Take some of the creases out of her personality. Yeah. Right. She was starched past hope. Single-minded.

Wounded.

That resonated in him in a way he didn't like. The world was full of wounded souls; they were on every street corner. There was no reason she should stand out. But she did, and that scared him because he was by God *never* going to get close to a woman again. Period.

The bartender interrupted his gloomy thoughts. "Guy over there is looking to hire a diver."

"Tell him to look somewhere else. I'm booked."

"Have it your way."

Hah. He'd been trying to have it his way for the last ten years, and somehow it never quite worked out. And now, idiot that he was, he was going to spend three months getting wet. *Wet!*

A man slid into the barstool beside him, and with a South American lilt to his English ordered a cognac. Dugan glanced his way and found the man looking at him. "Hi," he said automatically.

"Hi," the man said. His cognac came and he nodded to the bartender. Then he turned back to Dugan. "You are Dugan Gallagher, no?"

"Yes." Cripes, the guy who wanted a diver. Probably couldn't take no for an answer.

"I thought so," the man said. "You work for the lady archaeologist."

"So?"

"I am only curious." He smiled. "My name is Luis Cortes. I am from Venezuela, and I am a bit of an archaeologist, also."

"Small world."

"Sometimes, yes." He sipped his cognac. "Buy you a drink?"

"I already have one. Thanks." He wondered how this guy knew about Veronica. She had said she wanted to keep the dives a secret, and he sure as hell hadn't told anyone except Tam about it. Butch wasn't a talker either. So maybe Veronica had told someone? Not likely.

Cortes smiled, not a very attractive expression, but still a smile. "So, this searching for treasure is a big excitement, yes?"

"Who said she was looking for treasure?"

He shrugged. "One assumes."

"One assumes too much."

Cortes shook his head. "In these waters? No, not too much. I am interested in wrecks, too. Would she like some more help?"

"Look, I don't know what you're talking about. We're just sailing, that's all."

"Mm." Cortes shrugged. "Okay."

Dugan turned back to his drink, hoping the guy would buzz off. But Luis Cortes kept sitting there, sipping his cognac. And Dugan was growing uneasier by the minute.

He told himself he was just being paranoid. And the fact was, anyone at his office might have overheard something from his conversation with Veronica and her father, or Ginny or Tam might have said something to someone, and on this damn island a secret was harder to keep than a bottle of booze. Still, the most anyone should know was that Veronica was chartering his boat. Unless Tam had been flapping his jaws.

He turned back to Cortes. "You live around here?"

The man shook his head and ordered another cognac. "Visiting," he said.

"How'd you hear about what I'm doing?"

Cortes shrugged. "As I said, I'm an archaeologist also. I keep, how you say, tabs? Tabs on the permits the state makes."

"Ahh." That sounded innocent enough. Dugan relaxed again. "Aren't there a lot of wrecks down in your neck of the woods?"

"Neck of the woods?"

"Your part of the world. Off the coast of Venezuela."

"Oh!" Cortes smiled. "Yes, of course. This is how I become interested. But I am interested in *all* wrecks."

But why this one? Dugan wondered. "Just a general interest?"

"Yes. I am here on a visit, I hear about this, I decide to ask. Curiosity, no more."

"Well, if you're curious, you'd better speak to someone else. I don't know anything about what you're talking about. I was hired to take a lady on a vacation."

Dugan wasn't sure, but he thought he saw an infinitesimal shift in Cortes's posture, something that enhanced his uneasiness. But it was gone so quickly, he wasn't sure of what he had seen.

"Well," said Cortes after a moment, "it is of no real significance."

"No?"

"No. I am on a holiday. If someone finds something of interest, I will read about it in the journals."

"I'm sure you will."

Cortes nodded and returned his attention to his cognac. A couple of minutes later, he bid Dugan farewell, and walked out of the bar.

It was nothing, Dugan told himself. Just some minor interest from a colleague of Veronica's. The man hadn't asked anything inappropriate, or pushed too hard for answers. It sounded like simple curiosity. He'd even had reasonable explanations for his interest and his knowledge. Veronica's permits were a matter of public record, after all.

That thought suddenly didn't feel too good either. She wanted secrecy, which now that he thought about it, bothered him. But she'd still had to get permits, which meant there was a public record, and any Tom, Dick, or Harry could have found out about it.

So why her insistence on secrecy? What the hell was she after? Something more important than a three-hundred-year-old gold mask? Because it seemed to him, if the mask was the thing she was after, she'd be better protected by publicizing what she was up to. The more people who knew, the less likely it was that anyone could pull a dirty trick.

And why the hell was he thinking about dirty tricks? A curiosity seeker had simply asked some nosy questions.

He ordered another beer and sipped it but hardly tasted it. All of a sudden he wasn't in the mood for the beer, the bar, or anything else.

Because all of a sudden it occurred to him that he might be thinking of dirty tricks because of Veronica Coleridge.

What if she were the one up to dirty tricks?

Throwing some money on the bar, he got up abruptly and walked out onto the crowded street. The nightly revelries were in full swing, the crowds thick on the sidewalk and spilling into the street. A few cars were inching by slowly, trying not to kill anyone.

This whole secrecy thing was bothering the shit out of him.

Having nowhere in particular to go, he allowed the swirling crowds to carry him slowly along. Music blared out of open doors from every direction, mingling with the laughter and chatter of the people. There was a festival feeling in the air, but he was so used to it he didn't notice that either.

Instead he found himself considering what ifs. What if the man who had just chatted with him was on the up-and-up. What if Veronica wasn't? What if she was insisting on secrecy because she planned to do something illegal . . . like selling her finds? He seemed to remember that under current law, the state had first crack at buying anything a treasure salvor found. What if she had other plans? What if that Cortes guy was actually some investigator for the state, trying to keep up with what she was doing?

And then he knew he was getting *really* paranoid. Too much beer, he decided. Entirely too much. He was beginning to sound like a conspiracy freak.

Half an hour later, he ran into Tam on the street, and allowed himself to be drawn into a crowd of Tam's friends. By the time he staggered home at one in the morning, he was convinced the wisest course of action was to ignore the whole thing. Veronica wouldn't have bothered with permits if she wasn't aboveboard, and that Cortes guy—well, he'd just been a curious tourist.

Maybe.

* * *

Luis Cortes, also known as Luis Gallegos, made two phone calls after he left the bar. The first was to Venezuela, to Emilio.

"Nothing yet," he reported. "I still have some other leads to check out."

A heavy sigh, then a *snip*. Emilio must be in the hothouse again, Luis thought, and gave thanks that he was on the other side of the Caribbean. "Very well," Emilio said. "But I want action, Luis. *Action.* I don't want to have to be wondering what's going on."

"I'm working on it."

When he hung up, Luis had a bad taste in his mouth, something coppery. Fear? No, he had bitten his lip. Besides, he wasn't afraid of Emilio. Yet.

But what he was about to do scared him. If Emilio ever found out . . . But he couldn't allow himself to think of that. Emilio knew only what Luis told him, and Luis was certainly not going to mention what he did next.

He dialed another number, one that had come to him through a circuitous pathway some months ago when he had started watching Veronica Coleridge's progress with the permitting process. A state employee, for a price, had given it to him, telling him that this man had also paid to know if anyone started searching for the *Alcantara*. Luis had paid the state employee even more to keep his silence and not pass the information to the other person.

He had squirreled the number away, planning to use it when the time was ripe. At the very least, he had figured then, it would be useful to get some more money out of Emilio.

But now he was going to use it to his own end, to get a small fortune for himself.

When the phone was answered, it was by a machine that said only in flat, accented English, "Leave a message."

So Luis left a message. "I have information about *La Nuestra Señora de Alcantara.* If you're interested, call my pager. I will call you back in five minutes." Then he left the number of the pager he had purchased only that morning. A pager Emilio knew nothing about.

The game was afoot. He'd expected to feel exhilarated. Instead he stood beside the pay phone and sweated more profusely than could have been explained by the humid night air.

He wished he knew something, anything, about the man he had just called. Instead, he had taken a leap into the dark unknown.

And just then he was sick with the awareness of it. What had he just unleashed?

Chapter 7

"You're hungover."

Veronica's tone of voice was scathing, and it was the last thing Dugan needed when his head was pounding like someone was using a jackhammer on it. He put his hands on his hips, feeling the boat sway beneath him, and swallowed hard. "So?" he said with all the belligerence he could muster.

It was one of those perfect Key West days. The sun was rising in a cloudless sky, the trades were blowing gently and steadily, and the water looked so clear it was like crystal.

Well, it would have been perfect except for Veronica, Dugan thought sourly. She was glaring at him across two feet of the polished wood deck of the *Mandolin*. Apparently they weren't moving fast enough for her royal highness.

"So?" she repeated. "So? I hired you! I have something to say about the condition you're in when you're working for me. We're supposed to get loaded today so we can sail this afternoon. How are you going to do that if you're hanging over the side of the boat?"

"I'm not hanging over the side of the boat. I have a headache. Take a chill pill, lady. It'll get done when it gets done."

"That's what I'm worried about."

She was shouting at him, and his ire was rising accordingly. He had to remind himself that she always spoke loudly, most likely because she was deaf, and at this moment in time she probably didn't even know she was shrieking.

But because she was, and because he was having an instinctive reaction to it, and because they were going to draw a crowd if their shouting match kept up, he turned his back on her and stalked to the other end of the deck.

The *Mandolin* was a beautiful ketch, forty-two feet long and lovingly crafted. Her hull was fiberglass, but her deck, rails, and other appointments were hand-polished teak and mahogany, giving her the grace of a more elegant age. It also meant a lot more maintenance, but Dugan found sanding and varnishing to be a relaxing pastime. He figured he easily spent more time taking care of the boat than he spent sailing her. And he didn't mind one little bit.

This was his haven, his private paradise, as sacred to him as his own mind. And now this woman was profaning it with her shrewishness. He resented the hell out of that.

"Where's the other diver?" she asked. "Wasn't he supposed to help?"

Dugan didn't bother answering, because answering would require him to face her. He didn't feel like doing that at the moment. Instead, he fixed his gaze firmly on the mouth of the bight, determined to pretend he was alone with the dawn.

But Veronica wasn't prepared to let him get away with that. He heard her footfalls on the deck behind him, then she was beside him, tugging his arm.

"Look at me," she said.

He didn't feel like taking her orders at the moment. But then he remembered her deafness, and realized the order had held a note of panic. A faint note, to be sure, but it had been there. She was getting edgy because he had cut her off.

So he looked at her, resentfully. "Tam will get here when Tam gets here."

"Is that any way to run a business?"

"It's the way I'm running *this* business. If you don't like it, hire someone else."

"What?"

Trying not to grit his teeth, he repeated his words, speaking slowly and very clearly. "I said, if you don't like the way I run my business, hire someone else."

"You're being unreasonable."

"No, I'm being entirely reasonable. You hired me to do a job. I'll do it my way. And while we're on the subject, are you going to tell me how to *dive*, too?"

She blinked rapidly, and he couldn't tell if she had understood him. He wondered if he even cared. The jackhammer was trying to put a crater right between his eyes, and the increasing brilliance of the sun wasn't helping.

She drew a breath, a surprisingly shaky breath that penetrated his misery and awoke his curiosity. "I'm not going to depend on a drunk," she said flatly. "I'm not going to let a drunk ruin any more of my life."

Warning bells started clanging in his mind, adding to

his unhappiness. There was something more here than a principled objection, and he found himself unsure of what to say. Finally, he said the only thing he could. "I don't drink when I'm going to be diving. Ever."

"You're going to dive today."

He shook his head. "It's not going to happen. We have to stow gear and supplies, sail out and start surveying the area you've designated. The likelihood that anyone is going to get wet today from anything except spray is slim to none." Which, now that he thought about it, was fine by him. His mood improved a little.

But hers didn't. He could almost see the impatience oozing from her pores.

"We don't have any time to waste."

"I didn't say anything about wasting time. But whatever happens today, we're not going to be diving, okay? And Tam will be here soon."

He hoped. Because Tam had been in even worse shape than he had last night, and when they'd parted after midnight, the guy had shown absolutely no inclination to head toward home. Dugan wasn't even sure he'd made it home at all.

He glanced at his watch and saw that it was still early, though. Plenty of time. And he hadn't exactly told Tam to be here at the crack of dawn, either.

He glanced at Veronica and saw her dubious expression. "He'll be here soon," he said again.

"Right."

The jackhammer in his head kicked up a fuss. Enough was enough. He left Veronica and descended the ladder below deck. In the galley he hunted around until he found a bottle of ibuprofen. He dumped three of them into his hand and downed them with water. It would get better; it always did. But he found himself remembering why it was he hadn't gotten drunk since his one bender ten years ago. It was no damn fun, when all was said and done, and he was devoted to fun.

Sort of.

He turned around and found Veronica standing in the doorway of the galley, watching him almost speculatively.

"I'll be fine," he said gruffly.

"Sure."

He hated her. He absolutely hated her. He wondered if he was going to make it through the next three months without killing her. And he wished to God she wouldn't fold her arms like that because all it did was make him aware that she had a really nice chest. Of course, the shorts weren't helping either, because she also had some very nice, very long legs. He'd always been a sucker for long legs.

"You'd better wear more clothes than that," he said irritably. "You're going to be a crispy critter."

"A what?"

"You're going to get sunburned!" Realizing he was on the edge of shouting at her, he bit his tongue, closed his eyes, and took a deep breath.

"I'm sorry I can't always understand you," she said acidly. "But you don't have to shout at me."

"Why not? You shout at me all the time."

He wanted to cut his throat. He wanted to grab his tongue and pull it out by the roots. Because as soon as the words were out, her face started to crumple and close, and her eyes, hitherto annoyed, were suddenly windows on a soul-deep hurt.

Without a word, she turned and headed up the ladder.

Oh, shit.

He stood there, wracking his aching brain, trying to think of something he could say or do to mend the hurt he had just inflicted.

Before he could think of anything, he heard a thud from the deck and Tam's not-so-cheerful voice calling out, "Permission to come aboard, skipper?"

Dugan climbed the ladder partway and poked his head out the hatch. Tam's duffel lay right in front of him, but Tam was still standing on the dock. Veronica had taken a seat on the stern bench and had her arms tightly folded, as she looked at Tam.

Dugan wished he didn't have to look at Tam himself. The man was red-eyed, pale, and none too steady on his feet. "Cripes, Tam, are you drunk?"

"Hell no," came the answer as Tam leaned to one side. "I'm sober. Mostly. Haven't had a drink in two hours."

"Can you even get aboard?"

"Sure. Make her stop moving." But Tam jumped onto the deck, and even managed to keep his balance. He only staggered two steps.

Veronica spoke. "He's drunk."

Dugan couldn't argue with her, so he didn't say a word.

Tam peered at her. "I said I'm not drunk."

"What is he saying?" she demanded.

"He says he's not drunk."

Tam squinted. "There's an echo. I already said that."

"Shut up," Dugan said. "You're supposed to be helping me load and store supplies and equipment."

"Sure. I said I would. I'm here, aren't I? I just need an hour."

"What's he saying?" Veronica said again.

"That he's going to go below, make some coffee and catch a nap while you and I go to the grocery store."

"The grocery store?"

"Why's she shouting?" Tam asked.

Dugan ignored him and answered Veronica. "Hell, yes. You want to eat for the next four days, don't you?"

Before she could explode, which she plainly wanted to do, he grabbed her arm, urged her up onto the dock, and dragged her toward his truck.

"Quit pulling on me," she demanded.

"Sure." But he wanted her in the truck with the air-conditioning on and the windows rolled up before she started shouting at him about Tam, because the honest truth was, he didn't want to spend the next five years being teased about how he'd been bitched out by a woman on the public dock. No way. The tale would be all over town by sunset . . . if it even took that long.

He revved the engine, waiting for the air to start cooling them.

"That man is drunk," Veronica said again. "You can't fool me."

"He sobers up fast. Lots of experience."

"What am I supposed to think? I hire two people to do a simple job and the very first day one shows up drunk and the other shows up hungover."

"Look, could you hold it down a little. Your voice is cutting through my aching brain like a buzz saw."

She glared at him.

"Listen, it won't happen again."

"It shouldn't have happened at all."

"Hey, it's an old sailing tradition. You get drunk the night before a voyage."

"Considering we're going to be setting sail every five or six days, this could get to be a real nuisance."

"Won't happen again. I'm considering the entire three months to be one voyage."

Her expression was dubious. "What about your friend?"

"Don't worry about him. Once we get near to diving, he won't touch booze. He won't even be in the same zip code with it."

Her brow was knit, as if she were straining to follow him, but finally, to his vast relief, she settled back with a sigh.

"That had better not," she said sternly, "ever happen again."

"It won't." He hoped. He knew he wouldn't do it again. Unfortunately, he wasn't a hundred percent certain about Tam. Only ninety-five percent. Well, maybe ninety. Eighty? Hell, he just wasn't as certain. Period.

He jammed the truck into gear and headed for the Publix supermarket at the east end of the island. Ordinarily he preferred to stay in Old Town and buy his supplies at the Waterfront market, but considering they leaned primarily toward an interesting collection of imported pastas, organically grown produce and expensive juices, he felt he'd do better stocking the galley at a regular supermarket.

Besides, it was farther away. Anything that would take a few extra minutes of time was fine by him, because every minute would bring Tam closer to sobriety.

Veronica didn't say a thing as they drove along North Roosevelt toward the shopping center. Traffic was stirring as the poor sods who actually lived there headed toward another day of taking care of tourists.

When he pulled into the parking lot, finding a slot near the door, he set the brake but left the engine running. Swiveling in his seat, he looked at Veronica.

She was staring steadfastly ahead, every line of her posture saying she was unhappy. Her hearing aids filled her ears, and he found himself thinking how uncomfortable they must be. And he still felt like a real crud for what he had said about her shouting. That had been a truly low blow.

He touched her arm, trying not to notice how silky her skin felt, trying not to notice how she flinched away from the touch. But she looked at him.

"I need you to help me pick out the kinds of things you want to eat for the next few days. Tam and I would probably settle for bread, cold cuts, and mustard."

She nodded, but didn't speak.

Then without thinking, he added, "Something strange happened last night."

"What did you say?"

He realized that he'd glanced away. He did it too often. He also noticed that she was trying to speak more quietly.

"I said, something strange happened last night."

"What?"

"Do you know a man named Luis Cortes?"

She shook her head, her brow knitting. "Who?"

He leaned across her, trying not to notice how good she smelled, and pulled a pad and pen out of the jumbled glove box. He wrote the name on the pad and passed it to her. "Luis Cortes," he said again. "Do you know him?"

"No. Who is he?"

"That's what I'm wondering. He says he's from Venezuela."

The look of perplexity was on her face again, so he reached for the pad. Apparently she still had some trouble lipreading, especially when it came to things she couldn't guess from context. He wondered how much of what he said she really heard, and how much she was interpolating. He scrawled, "He comes from Venezuela. Says he's an archaeologist."

She shook her head and passed the pad back to him. "I don't know him. Why?"

"I met him last night. He was asking about you."

"Me?" She turned her head, and Dugan wondered if she was shutting him out. But after a moment she faced him again. "What did he want to know?"

"He didn't exactly ask anything. He just sort of mentioned what you were doing, and that he'd learned about you because of the permits you got. Said he was just generally interested in wrecks."

Veronica nodded slowly, indicating she understood him. She didn't say anything immediately, but fell into a study of her hands. After a minute or so, she spoke, her gaze returning to his face. "What did you think?"

"Of him?" Dugan shrugged. "I was uneasy. But the questions seemed casual enough."

She sighed softly and gazed out the window for a while. When she finally spoke again, she didn't look at him. "My mother searched for this mask, too. She fell overboard and drowned."

"And?" He couldn't tell if she knew what he said, but she didn't seem to care because she didn't even glance at him.

"The coroner said it was an accident—that she fell, bumped her head, and drowned."

"It's been known to happen."

She continued as if she hadn't heard him. "My father believes she may have been killed."

The simple statement rocked Dugan. He stared at her, then looked out the window as if trying to remind himself he was sitting in a truck on dry land in front of a supermarket on another perfectly ordinary Key West day.

But he didn't believe it. "He thinks someone *killed* her?"

She didn't answer, and he supposed she hadn't been able to read his lips, considering he was looking the other way.

Indignation began to fill him. He turned to face her directly, and found her blue eyes were wide, unblinking. Almost distant. He didn't like that distance, not when a whole bunch of emotions were bouncing around inside him like a batch of Ping-Pong balls shot out of a cannon.

"You didn't tell me this was dangerous!" Which, it suddenly struck him, was a stupid thing to say because diving and wreck salvage were always dangerous, even when you didn't drag the possibility of bad guys into it.

"It's not," she said, forgetting her earlier attempts to keep her voice down.

"Your mother got killed!"

"I didn't say that."

He shook his head, hardly believing his ears. Miraculously, his hangover was gone, probably driven out by the anger he was feeling. "Look, maybe you're stupid enough to risk your neck hunting for a piece of gold that somebody is willing to kill for, but I'm not! I'm outta here. Now."

He waited, but she didn't say anything, just continued to look at him with those wide eyes. Anger and frustration seethed in him, but frustration was beginning to get the upper hand. Finally, unwilling to continue this standoff another minute, he said, "Get yourself somebody else, lady. You're more trouble than I'm willing to take on." Facing front, he reached to release the brake.

The touch of her hand stopped him. It was a light touch,

but strangely electrifying. He froze, then turned his head slowly to look at her.

"My mother wasn't murdered," she said. "The coroner had no reason to suspect foul play."

"Then why did you bring it up?"

"Because of what you said about this Luis Cortes."

"So it crossed your mind that your father might be right."

She nodded. "But that was a long time ago, Dugan. Even if my father is right, there's no reason to think that the same thing could happen after twenty-five years."

Probably not. However, life had taught him that lightning could indeed strike twice. "I don't know about this."

"What?"

"I don't like this. From what you said, this mask is extraordinarily valuable."

"Only from an archaeological point of view. The gold in it couldn't amount to all that much."

"You could say the same thing about a Van Gogh. It's valuable only from an artistic perspective. Otherwise, it's just a collection of paints and canvas."

He noted she didn't disagree with him. That didn't make him feel any better.

"Are you quitting?" she asked finally.

"No." No, he wasn't quitting, because he couldn't live with himself if he did. God knew who she might find to replace him. It wasn't that there weren't a lot of reputable boat owners and divers on the island, but there were a lot of the other kind too. And there was no way to be sure she didn't fall in with someone utterly unscrupulous.

God, he hated being a white knight. It always got him into trouble.

"Something else," he said, taking care to be sure that she could read him. "Why do you want to keep this a secret? Wouldn't it be safer if everyone knew what you were doing?"

"No. I've heard about what happens. There'll be a whole horde of searchers out there trying to undercut us."

She might have a point. Off the top of his head he could think of a number of people who wouldn't be able to resist the challenge.

"Okay, okay," he said finally. "But let's get a few things clear. You run the search. I run everything else. Because while you may have a clear idea what to look for and where, I'll bet you don't know diddly-squat about . . ."

"Don't know what?" she interrupted.

"I'll bet you don't know *anything* about sailing or diving."

"Not much," she admitted.

"So you leave that to me. Otherwise, there's going to be blood on the decks before a week is out."

He didn't know if she understood the last part of what he said. Probably not, because she stuck out her hand, and said, "Deal."

He wished he believed she was going to be able to stick to it. But he doubted it. She struck him as having exactly the driven, anal-retentive personality that was never going to be able to keep its mouth shut.

Oh, well, he thought philosophically. It was better than wondering what she was thinking.

As they walked into the store together, Veronica wondered about Dugan Gallagher. He was more volatile than the men she was accustomed to. More *immediate*. Whatever he was thinking apparently came out of his mouth. He seemed incapable of subterfuge or caginess. What you saw was what you got, evidently.

That could be a good thing, she supposed, but it wasn't going to make him easy to work with. She was still irritated that he was hungover this morning, and she found herself tensing when they passed the beer display, wondering if he was going to insist they had to buy a few six-packs for the cooler on the boat.

But he passed the display without a second look. Apparently he had meant it when he said he didn't drink when he was going to dive. And she found herself comparing him to Larry, who had believed that a beer or two after work, and a six-pack on Saturday, was his God-given right.

Funny, too, how that hadn't bothered her before the accident. She hadn't given it a second thought. Ever since that night, however, the mere whiff of beer made her stomach turn over.

She helped Dugan decide on a menu for the next four days. Lots of canned goods and other staples, and less of things that needed refrigeration. "It's a small refrigerator," he explained.

She was going to be missing salads an awful lot, and getting tired of canned stew. But these were normal deprivations on a dig, and she knew she could live with them. She just wondered why she had thought it was going to be any easier on a boat than in some remote part of the Yucatán.

Dugan bought far more than three people could possibly eat in a few days. Veronica looked at the mounting pile of cans and bottles, and finally had to say something. "We're not going to eat all of that before we come ashore again."

"No, we're not," he agreed. "But I learned a long time ago never to sail without additional provisions. You never know what might happen."

She hadn't thought about that, which in retrospect seemed foolish. There was an awful lot of water out there and even though the seas in this area were heavily traveled, there was no guarantee that another boat would pass within sight. It just wasn't the same as traveling along a major highway.

She threw three more cans of bartlett pears in the basket because she loved them. Why not? She was paying for the food.

Back at the boat they found Tam stretched out asleep on the stern bench.

"He's going to get a burn," Veronica remarked, envisioning all the delays that would cause.

"Nah," Dugan answered. "Not possible. His skin is galvanized steel."

It took her a few seconds to understand, then, reluctantly, she laughed. "Yeah? I still say he's going to make some dermatologist wealthy eventually."

He apparently appreciated her humor, because suddenly his dark eyes were crinkled in the corners, and his white teeth were gleaming. With a sense of shock, Veronica realized that she found him attractive, especially that smile. Unnerved, she took a half step backward, as if to escape what she was suddenly feeling.

"Come on," he said, "let's stash the groceries. Then I want to show you how to do a few things just in case."

"Just what?" God, how she hated asking people to repeat themselves. It was humiliating. Embarrassing. And she was sure every time she did so that it was going to be one time too many and that they were going to get impatient or frustrated. As a rule, she simply avoided dealing with people in order to avoid the entire problem.

He turned toward her so that he faced her fully. "Come

with me," he said, more slowly. "We'll put the groceries away."

She nodded. She'd already figured out that part because she'd understood "put" and "groceries" and had extrapolated the rest of it.

"I also want to show you some things about running the boat. In case something happens and you need to help."

"Okay."

He smiled, as if pleased that she understood, and she suddenly felt like a first grader who was getting a pat on the head. She didn't like the sensation at all. But maybe she had misinterpreted his smile. Even she was becoming aware that she had grown prickly, and apt to read negative things into innocent words and gestures. Even she had begun to realize that she was always on the defensive.

She followed him down to the galley and unloaded the bags while he put everything away, showing her where it all went. Then he led her up the ladder and into the control center, which he told her was a covered cockpit.

"Cockpit? Like on a plane?"

"Yup. Later, when we set out, I'll show you a little bit about driving the boat, okay?"

"I can't do that. I don't know anything about it. Besides, you're driving." The thought of having to do so herself made her distinctly uneasy. Since her deafness, she'd been uneasy about a lot of things, and no longer had the confidence that had once carried her into new situations.

He held up a finger. "Yes, you can do it. I can show you what you need to know. And yes, I will be driving most of the time. But what if something happens?"

"What could happen?" She hadn't even entertained the possibility that she might be alone on a boat in the middle of the water. "Dugan . . . if I have to drive this thing because something happens . . . I'm not going to know how to get home."

His mouth twisted. She thought he sighed, but she couldn't hear it.

"I'll show you everything you need to know," he said. "You're a smart woman. But you *have* to know how to take care of yourself out on the water."

She nodded, ignoring the whole childish feeling that was coming over her, a feeling of resistance and resentment. It was a mark of what had happened to her that she was feeling this way. A little over a year ago, she would have leapt into this eagerly, and she knew it.

She didn't like the change.

"The radio," he said. "Here." He pointed, then looked at her again. "Emergency beacon. You hit this switch . . ." He paused to point. ". . . and it will send an automatic distress signal until the batteries die."

She leaned closer and looked at the switch his finger was on. "Okay."

His finger moved to the next button, and she hastened to look at him, to read his lips. "This turns the radio on and off. You can leave it on speaker, so you can hear over the loudspeakers, or you can—"

"I won't need that," she interrupted, as her stomach began to burn. "I can't use that."

He looked at her, something passing swiftly over his face. "Okay, Okay. You're right. I thought you could send a message, even if you couldn't understand the response . . . okay. I'm sorry. Just remember the emergency beacon."

She nodded. "I will. But I don't know anything about sailing, or sails."

"You don't have to. This boat has an engine. I'll take

us out of the harbor using it, and you can see how it works, okay?"

An engine. She thought she could handle that, and it was a relief, because the ugly, bitter feeling was coming over her again, the resentment of what had been done to her. And she didn't like it. Because deep inside she knew she was never going to get any better, so it was time to start accepting her lot. Time to start learning to live with it.

She *knew* that, but she was still having a hard time with it. Part of her wanted to sink into bitter self-pity and never climb out of the hole again. But another part of her, a more adult part she sometimes thought, kept insisting that by doing so she could only cripple herself more.

Instinctively, her hand covered her belly, and she felt the emotional emptiness there. Deafness, she thought, at least managed to distract her from that.

Dugan reached out, taking her hand in his. His touch was warm, comforting, kindly, and it reached past barriers that he couldn't have crossed any other way. She lifted her eyes slowly to his.

"Are you going to be all right?" he asked.

She nodded, squaring her shoulders. "I'll be fine."

Just then there was a loud thud from the deck. They both turned and saw Tam peering into the cockpit.

"Hey," Tam said, and continued speaking. Because of his moustache, Veronica couldn't make out his words. She looked at Dugan, who was suddenly grinning. He explained.

"He wants to know if it's time to start loading."

Veronica managed a nod, and self-consciously pulled her hand from Dugan's. She couldn't afford weakness, she told herself. She couldn't afford to cling to anything, even something as small as the touch of another human being.

"It's *high* time," she said.

But this time, instead of getting irritated at her, Dugan simply grinned. "Let's go," he said.

Work, Veronica told himself. She needed to concentrate on work. She didn't have room for anything else in her life.

And she didn't want to.

Chapter 8

Luis Cortes showed up early in the afternoon, just as they were finishing loading.

The magnetometer was the last thing they brought on board because Dugan wanted everything else squared away before he figured out where they were going to put this piece of equipment, along with Veronica's computer.

It was early afternoon by the time they got around to it. Bringing enough compressed air for several dives a day proved to be quite a few canisters, and they all had to be secured so they wouldn't roll around. He had to rig a method of confining them, since he didn't ordinarily dive from this boat.

The metal detectors had to be secured, too, in a cargo locker.

"It's usually calm around here," he explained to Veronica. "Good sailing water. But you never know. A little bit of wind from a nearby storm can make it rough, so I don't want *anything* rolling around anywhere."

She nodded her understanding, but still found it a little daunting. She hadn't considered this either. In fact, she thought disparagingly, she hadn't thought of much. She had just assumed they'd pile the stuff on board the way she did in her trunk.

But Dugan didn't take such chances. He'd taken them once, and was never going to do it again. Some unexpectedly rough seas on a sail to Jamaica years ago had taught him the importance of securing things—and he still had the scars to prove it.

He decided to put the magnetometer on the table in the lounge. It was a black box, maybe half the size of most personal computers, with several cables and a couple of probes. The probes would hang out the porthole, trailing in the water, their purpose to measure the minute variations in the earth's magnetic field that would be caused by an iron deposit, such as a ship's gun.

He bolted the box to the table, figuring he could always get another tabletop. And they could eat standing up if necessary, but Veronica needed a place to work. This boat didn't exactly come equipped with office space.

Her laptop he wasn't worried about. She'd even had the sense to bring a converter so it could run on twelve-volt direct current. When things got rough, she could stash it in the locker under the bench beside the table.

But he *was* curious about why she needed it.

"Instead of recording the magnetometer readings to chart paper, I'm recording to disk."

"Sounds good to me." At least he didn't have to deal with some fancy kind of printer, too.

And that's when Luis showed up, just as they finished securing the magnetometer and were discussing whether to get lunch before they sailed.

"*Hola!*" he called from the dock.

Dugan poked his head out the hatch, then yanked it

swiftly back as he recognized the man. "Oh, Christ," he muttered.

"What is it?" Veronica asked.

"Luis Cortes. The guy I told you about."

"Oh." Veronica's mind began racing. The guy was being too persistent for someone with a casual interest, she thought. From what Dugan said he had told the man, Cortes should have lost interest. On the other hand, maybe Dugan hadn't done as good a job of putting the guy off as he thought. It wouldn't surprise her if he overestimated his impact on Cortes. Men had a habit of doing that.

"I'll go talk to him." She was out of the cockpit and on the deck before she could really think about what she was going to do. All she knew was she resented this stranger trying to horn in on her exploration.

He was a thin man, not too tall, giving the impression of being rawboned. And his jaw kept moving in the most disconcerting way.

"You want something?" she asked him.

He spoke, and she realized with a sinking stomach that she couldn't read him. The vowel sounds she could hear didn't match up with the movements of his lips in any way that made sense to her.

And she stood there with her heart plummeting, paralyzed yet again by her disability. Paralyzed once again with the realization of just how isolated and helpless she really was. Dugan had been making her forget that. He was so easy to read, and even when she couldn't she wasn't afraid to tell him so. But how many times was she going to ask this stranger to repeat himself before she totally humiliated herself or he gave up in disgust? Just how helpless did she want to show herself to be in front of an utter stranger?

Her eyes were suddenly burning, and she looked at Dugan. Worse yet, she realized, was that he understood what her problem was. She felt naked. Exposed. Hating it, she turned and hurried down the ladder, passing a startled Tam in the galley, where he was quenching his thirst with some orange juice. He said something that sounded questioning.

She couldn't understand him, either, because he had a moustache. Giving him no chance to discover that, or remind her yet again of how isolated she was, she pushed past him and disappeared into the aft cabin that Dugan had told her to use.

Then she threw herself facedown on the bunk, grabbing the pillow with her hands, and trying to fight down the rising tide of despair that threatened to drown her.

Sometime later, she heard something from above, heard the boat's engine begin to thrum, and felt a slight lurch. They were under weigh.

Ten minutes after that, there was a knock on the cabin door. She didn't answer it, but her silence achieved nothing. She felt someone sit beside her, and she lifted her head to look. It was Dugan.

He reached out and astonished her by stroking her hair. The sensation sent shivers of longing through her, and she bit her lip, resisting the effect of his tenderness.

"I told him to get lost," Dugan said. "I told him you're just taking a vacation and to go bug some treasure salvors."

She managed a nod, but her throat was so tight she couldn't speak.

"Are you sure your dad can't sail with us?"

She shook her head, and spoke thickly. "He's still too worn-out from the chemo. Being on a boat would exhaust him."

"Being deaf is a bitch, isn't it?"

The remark startled her, and all of a sudden all the emotions she'd been battling refused to be subdued any longer. Tears prickled her eyes, then began to run down her cheeks.

"Oh, boy," Dugan said. For an instant his expression was almost panicked. Then, astonishing her, he reached for her and lifted her until she was leaning against his chest.

Then he held her while hot tears burned her cheeks, and grief stung her throat, while broken, angry words tumbled out of her.

"I am so *sick* of being alone," she said, her hand crumpling the front of his polo shirt. "I'm so *sick* of it."

He said something, but she wasn't looking at him so she didn't know what it was. But she was past caring. The hurt inside her seemed determined to tumble out.

"I've been alone my whole damn life! And now I'm deaf, and I'm more alone than ever. I couldn't talk to that man! I couldn't talk to him, Dugan. Because I couldn't understand him. A year ago I'd have been able to go out there and talk to him in Spanish or English without a problem. But now . . . now I can't read his lips. I can't really hear him. Which means I can't do the simplest thing on earth for myself: talk to another human being!"

His voice rumbled in his chest, and it sounded soothing. She didn't care what he was saying. It didn't matter.

"My father's dying, my career's come to a halt, how am I ever going to teach again? And . . . and . . . I was married. I was married and I loved him, but he couldn't handle my deafness . . ." A hiccuping sob gripped her, and her words trailed off. She hated the way she sounded. Even in the midst of all the pain she was feeling, she hated the self-pitying way she sounded. But the simple fact was, she was never going to be close to anyone again because she couldn't talk to people anymore. Her friends avoided her, as if they were embarrassed by her deafness. Her father . . . her father was probably going to die even before she found the mask. She'd never had a mother, at least not one she could remember, and her father had even destroyed that little bit for her by telling her she had never known the woman who had given her life, that the woman she had known about, that he had told her about, had never really existed.

And all the things that made her hurt, all the things that made her angry, all the things she had resolutely been burying these past six months by focusing on this quest, had suddenly ballooned inside her, demanding to be let out. Demanding her attention.

She cried for a little while longer, but not too long. She hated herself for the weakness, and as soon as she could she sniffled her tears into oblivion. Then, wrenching out of Dugan's embrace because it felt perilously like something she could never have, she threw herself back on the bed and stared up at the ceiling.

Dugan sat beside her for a while longer. After a bit, he reached out and took her hand. She yanked it back. Finally, he called her name. Recognizing the vowel sounds, she looked at him.

"You're doing pretty damn good for someone who's only been deaf a year," he said. "Maybe you need to cry more often."

"What?"

But he didn't repeat himself. He seemed to know that she had understood him. "Tam's at the wheel. Wash your face and come up on deck. It's a beautiful day for a sail. You wouldn't want to miss it."

Then he got up and walked out, leaving her to wonder what he thought of her after her outburst. Then she decided it didn't matter what Dugan Gallagher thought of her. He was just a guy who owned the boat she was hiring.

But somewhere deep inside, she knew she was lying to herself.

Isolated. The word stuck with Dugan throughout the afternoon. Veronica came up on deck eventually and sat in the stern, watching the islands and water go by. After they got out of the channel into open water, Dugan turned off the engine, and he and Tam sheeted the spinnaker. The sail caught the wind and jerked them forward with a strong lurch, then settled them into a smooth ride over the gentle swells.

God, how he loved to sail!

Isolated. He hadn't thought of it that way before. He'd known she was deaf, but that was just a bit of difficulty in conversation. He supposed he hadn't really thought it through. She *was* isolated, probably in ways he couldn't even imagine.

Besides, she was communicating so well with him it hadn't occurred to him she couldn't do that with everybody. But today had shown him the truth of it. She couldn't read Tam and she couldn't read Cortes, and there were probably hundreds of other people out there she couldn't read either. People she ran into every day.

It struck him that simple things, like a conversation with a cashier, might be fraught with perils for her. What if the cashier looked down while speaking? Veronica might never hear what the person said. How many times a day did she have to explain that she was deaf and ask someone to repeat themselves? And how many times a day did she misunderstand something and get looked at as if she were stupid?

How many times a day did life make her feel inadequate?

He didn't want to think about it, but when he glanced away from the sun-dappled water to the woman sitting in the stern with her arms protectively folded around herself, he couldn't help but think about it.

So, to avoid following those paths, which weren't going to get him anywhere useful, he thought about Luis Cortes.

"We should get that guy checked out," he said to Tam.

"What guy?"

"The one who came to the boat just before we left. Cortes."

"Why? He was just curious."

"That's the second time he's been sniffing around what we're doing."

"Oh." Tam rubbed his moustache thoughtfully. "Okay. When we get back. I'll see what I can find out."

"Thanks."

Tam shrugged. "No big deal. So what's with Veronica?"

"She's deaf."

"Deaf? Well, that explains a lot. But she hears you okay."

"She can read my lips."

"Well, she can't read mine, apparently."

"You have to look right at her when you talk."

"Cool. Okay, I'll keep that in mind."

Tam as usual, Dugan thought. Everything rolled off his back. Dugan envied his attitude. He ought to be letting all of this roll off his back, too. After all, Veronica's problems were her own.

He couldn't help thinking about them, though. Including the ones she'd just revealed. Bad enough to be deaf, bad enough to be worried about her career because of it, but utterly unforgivable that her husband had ditched her because she couldn't hear. The guy was lower than rat shit.

Not his problems, he reminded himself yet again. But that didn't stop him from feeling an ache when he thought about all that Veronica had been through. He couldn't quite suppress the urge to go strangle the jerk she'd been married to. Nor could he quite shake the overpowering desire to rattle the bars of the universe and tell it to give this woman a little break here. God, her father, her husband, her hearing, maybe her job . . . Nobody should have to deal with all of that in such a short space of time.

How the hell was she holding it all together?

He glanced back again, and wondered, and couldn't quite ignore the feeling that there was even more wrong in her life than she'd told him.

After he left the dock, Luis drove back to Old Town. Finding a parking place was, as always, difficult, but he managed to squeeze himself into one. Then he wandered the streets, not really interested in the shops, bars, or restaurants.

He was waiting, just waiting. And he felt better in Old Town than he did elsewhere on Key West. But finally the warmth of the day began to wear on him, and he ducked into a restaurant where he ordered a seafood plate and a bottle of Tecate.

He was beginning to get nervous, he realized. Emilio was waiting for him to find a spy and start getting information. So far he hadn't managed to do that. And while his trip to the dock this afternoon had been designed to discover just exactly who was working with Veronica Coleridge so he would know who else he could approach besides Gallagher, he didn't think Emilio was going to be happy with the snail's pace. Now he knew about Tam Anson, but until he had Anson firmly in his pocket, he hadn't fulfilled his orders. Emilio could sometimes be an impatient man.

But the primary reason he didn't want to talk to Emilio was that he was feeling guilty, and he had an almost visceral belief in the man's omniscience. Which left him wondering why he had been so foolhardy as to call the other interested party. The party he was beginning, within the sanctity of his own mind, to call *El Desconocido*. The Unknown One.

Except that if Emilio was as much a mind reader as Luis sometimes believed, the sanctity of his mind was anything but, and he was going to be in serious trouble.

Luis simply wasn't cut out for the role of double agent, and thinking about it was beginning to make him sweat despite the blast of icy air from the vent directly over his head.

Ay Dios, what had he been thinking?

The shrimp, as fresh as any he had ever had, suddenly tasted like sawdust, and he put his fork down, signaling the waiter to bring him another Tecate.

What he needed to do, he decided, was remind himself of why he was doing this. Of what he hoped to gain. Working for Emilio was a good job, of course. He was fairly paid, and he'd seen quite a bit of the world. But what he didn't like was having to be at another man's beck and call.

And every time Emilio made him come into that hothouse, knowing full well that he hated it, Luis was reminded that he was little more than a servant.

He had bigger dreams than that. And if this mask was as important as Emilio seemed to think, then it was worth a great deal of money. *El Desconocido* was probably willing to pay well for it. Much more than Emilio would pay Luis for just doing his job as he always had.

And all of that money would mean that Luis could be his own man, not somebody else's employee. He could have a nice house—maybe not as nice as Emilio's, but Luis wasn't greedy—and not have to upend his entire life every time some boss wanted him to do something. He might even be home enough to make his wife happy again.

Thinking of Rosa made him frown. She'd been growing increasingly unhappy for the last several years, complaining that she was always lonely. Luis wasn't particularly moved by her complaints because she was happy enough to spend the money he made, a sum he couldn't have earned at an ordinary job. But . . . her misery made him unhappy because she made sure he knew she was miserable.

So, with more money, and the freedom not to work unless he might feel like it, he could see his entire life improving.

That was what he had to keep in mind: having his own villa, putting an end to his wife's complaints, and being his own master, which was something a man ought to be.

As he thought of those things, the shrimp began to look better, and he resumed eating as soon as his fresh bottle of beer and a glass arrived.

It would be okay, he told himself. Emilio would never figure out what was going on because he really couldn't read minds. That was just a stupid, superstitious feeling Luis had sometimes.

And *El Desconocido* would never know who Luis was. He would arrange it so that he would be anonymous, even when the payment was made. He had learned well from Emilio, and he had already set up an account to handle matters.

Burping with satisfaction—or so he told himself, even though he had a sneaking suspicion that his stomach was upset from nerves—Luis pushed the plate aside and reached for the beer. Life was good, he assured himself, and it was going to get much better. It *had* to. He deserved it.

He finished the Tecate and paid his bill, wondering what he was going to do next. He had initially been delighted with the idea of coming to Key West, but there was little to do that truly appealed to him. It was a place for couples, not a place for solitary men who were on business, unless they wanted to get drunk.

He sighed and looked up and down Duval Street. What now? He had no desire to buy a T-shirt or any of the other wares that were being displayed in shop windows. He decided to go back to his hotel room and simply wait. That's what his life had come to, he thought irritably. All he did these days was wait.

But when he was still a block from the hotel, his beeper chirped. All of a sudden he wasn't bored. All of a sudden his heart was racing and his palms were sweaty.

It was the moment of truth.

Hurrying now, he reached the hotel in a lather, and punched the elevator button impatiently. It seemed to take forever for a car to come down to the lobby, and forever for it to open its doors and spill out its occupants, a group of laughing women who all had short hair.

He sniffed disapprovingly, but they ignored him.

Inside the car, he punched the button for the fifth floor, but before the doors could close, a man stuck his hand in. Then Luis had to wait while the bellman loaded a middle-aged couple and eight suitcases into the car. The couple spoke French excitedly all the way up. Luis was relieved to escape.

He fumbled the card key into the lock and apparently didn't do it right because the green light didn't come on at the first try. He made it on the second and stepped into the cool, perfumed air of his room. At last!

From the phone on the bedside table, he called his pager for messages.

Then, despite being overheated, an icy chill ran down his back as he listened to a whispery, strangely accented voice say, "Call in fifteen minutes."

Luis had to play the message back three times to be sure he had the phone number correct, and each time he played it back, that strange, whispery voice, sounding as if it came from the bowels of hell, caused ice to run down his spine.

Luis glanced at his watch, comparing the time with the time stamp on the recording. Three more minutes.

He shouldn't do this, he thought with sudden fright. This was going to be the biggest mistake he could make. Emilio was going to find out, and have him beheaded.

And what about *El Desconocido*? He knew nothing about the man. He might be far worse than Emilio. At least Emilio was generally gentlemanly in his dealings unless he was thwarted. This unknown man might not have any reservations or inhibitions at all. What if he decided to use Luis to get the mask, then kill him?

He'd heard of such things happening. He had to be very careful that this man couldn't trace him. That's why the pager.

But just then, with a sinking stomach, he realized his mistake. He had purchased the pager with his own credit card. It was the only way he could get it activated immediately. He had lied about his name and address on the application, but there was still the credit card. What if *El Desconocido* was able to get that information?

Realizing he had made a serious mistake by not knowing anything about the devil he was planning to bargain with, he sat on the edge of the bed and seriously reconsidered what he was about to do.

He wouldn't make the call, he decided. No amount of money was worth getting tangled up with someone who might be more of a threat than he could imagine.

But then he thought how silly he was being. He was imagining devils from hell, not a human being who was probably very much like Emilio. He would direct payment for his services into a numbered account that couldn't be traced to him, and he wouldn't touch it for a while, not until he was sure it was safe.

And if the man found out his credit-card number—Luis swallowed hard. Well, he would just report it stolen after he made this phone call. And he would deny all knowledge of the person who had bought the pager with it. He would cover his tracks so thoroughly that no one could find out it was him.

Feeling better, he reached for the phone. Now. Punching in the number, he listened to the phone on the other end ring. Once, twice . . .

He heard the receiver lifted out of the cradle. The whispery voice said, "Yes?"

Luis had to clear his throat before he could speak. He felt his tongue sticking to the roof of his mouth. "Are you interested in the *Alcantara*?"

"Yes."

"How interested?"

"What do you have?"

Luis hesitated, considering how much to say. "I have a spy on a boat that is searching for the *Alcantara* right now."

It was a small exaggeration, one he fully intended to correct the instant the *Mandolin* returned to shore.

"Yes?"

It was not enough, apparently. "He is going to keep me informed."

"I see." There was a long pause. Then, "What is your interest in the *Alcantara*?"

Luis had no trouble with that one. "Money. My employer is paying me to keep him informed because he's interested in an, um, artifact on the sunken ship. I am interested in knowing if you are willing to pay me more."

There was a feathery laugh, little more than a few puffs of air. "Trustworthy, are you not?"

"Yes I am," Luis said, feeling his cheeks heat with anger. "To the highest bidder."

"Of course."

The unknown on the other end of the phone was silent for a while. Luis began to sweat profusely, rivulets running down his face, and wonder if he'd messed up somehow.

The man spoke again. "You work for Emilio Zaragosa, yes?"

Luis suddenly felt as if he were cased in ice. He couldn't move, couldn't speak.

"Do not worry," the voice said. "My agenda does not include exposing you. The mask is worth a great deal of money to me. I will pay you well if you deliver it. Keep me informed at this number. A machine will take your messages."

Then the call was disconnected.

And Luis sat frozen for a long time, because he was certain he had just spoken to the devil himself.

Ay Dios, what had he done?

Chapter 9

"This is boring," Tam announced to no one in particular.

They had been sailing back and forth across the area that interested Veronica for three days, and so far hadn't found anything. Tam had taken to sunbathing on the bow and reading a paperback thriller. Dugan sat hour after hour in the cockpit, keeping them on course, wondering how long he was going to be able to do this without going crazy. He liked to sail, yes. But he preferred to have a destination.

Just then Tam was standing at the stern, munching a peanut butter sandwich while they all took a break.

Veronica's brow furrowed as she looked at Tam. "What did you say?"

He turned to face her. "It's *boring*."

She shook her head slightly and looked at Dugan.

"He said it's boring."

"Cripes," Tam said. "You're translating English to English."

"What did he say?"

Dugan stifled a sigh, reminding himself not to get irritated by this. It wasn't as if Veronica could help it. He looked at her. "Why can't you read Tam's lips?"

She flushed. "He has a moustache."

Tam's hand flew to his luxuriant face hair. "No."

Dugan spared him a glance. "No what?"

"I'm not going to cut it off."

"Then get used to me translating English to English."

Tam looked at Veronica.

"Sorry," she said.

Tam shrugged. "You can't help it, I guess."

Veronica looked at Dugan.

"He said you can't help it."

"No, I can't." Then she turned her back on both of them.

Dugan was beginning to hate the gesture. There was something exceedingly juvenile about it. At the same time, every time she did it, he was beginning to feel an ache in his chest. Not because he minded being ignored by her—he kept telling himself that being ignored by her was what he wanted—but because it had begun to speak volumes to him after her use of the word *isolation* the other day.

He kept seeing her as alone and lonely. Alone was okay. He was alone himself, pretty much, and preferred it that way. But lonely was something else. He knew all about lonely, since he'd felt that way for months after Jana had dropped her little bomb. But lonely appeared to be a way of life for Veronica. And worse than that, he saw her keep widening the circle of emptiness around herself, as if she didn't know how to do anything else. In another person he would have assumed she wanted the solitude, but after her tears the other day, he had quite a different opinion.

But he didn't know what the hell to do about it. Or even if he *should* do anything about it. After all, as far as she was concerned, he was nothing but the guy she had hired to drive a boat and do a little diving for her.

He turned from her, not wanting to stare at her back any longer, because it was such a defensive, defenseless posture.

That's when he saw the clouds.

"Oh, shit," he said.

"What?" Tam asked. "Holy shit," he said a moment later.

Veronica, hearing their voices, turned around to look at them. "What?" she said. Apparently she'd picked up on their tones.

Dugan pointed to the west. The black squall line was clear, though it was nowhere near to blotting out the sun, and apparently not close enough yet to stir up the water.

"Oh," Veronica said when she saw the dark clouds, with their green underbellies. "That doesn't look good."

"No, it doesn't." Dugan hadn't been paying as much attention to the weather as he probably should have. The thing was, the weather in these parts was appallingly boring. Sunny, the trades blowing steadily, day after day after day. He'd gotten lax.

"Somebody kick my butt."

"Sure," said Tam. And obliged with a kick that just barely grazed him. They were both surprised to hear Veronica laugh.

"Well," Dugan said, "I'd better go see if I can get the marine forecast."

"What for?" Tam asked. "I can tell you already what it's going to say."

Dugan just shook his head. He already knew what Tam could tell him, but he wanted to know more. He wanted to know how strong the winds were, how high the seas might be, and which direction that squall line was moving. Little things like that.

But there was nothing on the radio. Apparently the storm was a localized one, probably caused by warm rising air off the water meeting a draft of colder air from the north. It might be nothing to worry about.

On the other hand . . .

Sticking his head out of the cockpit, he called to Tam. "Nothing on the radio. It must have just started building."

Tam nodded toward the west. "It's building fast, skipper. I think we ought to hightail it."

Looking at the clouds once again, Dugan had to agree. They were piling higher and taller, and he could already see the first chop on the waves. "Better pull in the sea anchor, Tam. Then let's sheet some sail and get the hell out of here."

Veronica was still standing where he'd left her, watching the storm clouds. Far from looking dismayed, she looked exhilarated. Her blue eyes were sparkling, and a smile curved her mouth. He decided she was too much of a landlubber to realize that she was in a small boat in the middle of nowhere facing the wrath of nature.

But her smile faded when she saw Tam pull in the anchor and start hoisting the sails.

"What are you doing?" she asked.

"We're going home," Dugan told her.

"We're not supposed to go until tomorrow."

"So we go one day early, miss the storm, and come back out here a day early. No time lost really." Then he went to help Tam hoist the sails.

He was going to enjoy this, he realized as the wind caught the sails and jerked the *Mandolin* forward. He was really going to enjoy this. It had been a long time since he'd had his baby under full sail, a long time since he'd let her fly at her top speed.

Veronica followed him into the cockpit when he resumed his place at the wheel. Tam took up position near the bow, also dearly enjoying the speed of their rush.

"I don't want to go back," Veronica told Dugan. "We were getting close to that other place I saw from the plane."

"If what you saw is part of the ship, it's been there for three hundred years. It'll still be there the day after tomorrow."

"But you don't understand."

He shook his head, forcing himself to keep looking at her so she could understand him. "I *do* understand," he said. "I understand that you're obsessed. We'll be back here the day after tomorrow. That's soon enough."

"Why couldn't we just ride the storm out?"

"Because it's not necessary. And if it's not necessary, there's no reason to risk all our necks to try to tough it out."

"I thought you were a bigger risk taker than that."

"Lady," he said sharply, "I've never been a risk taker. I prefer being smart. And right now, heading for port is the smart thing to do. You have no idea how small a forty-two-foot boat can feel when nature kicks up a fuss."

But before all was said and done, she got a taste of it. He was clipping along at a good twenty-five knots, but the storm was building faster. Before long, it was breathing down their necks, darkening the sun and roiling the water into choppy, high waves. The *Mandolin* began to feel as if she were skipping over the tops of the waves, each contact with the water causing the boat to shudder quickly.

Veronica stayed beside him in the cockpit, but Tam went below, saying something about better light to read by. That was okay by him. He was enjoying this run before the storm, and Veronica, at least, was being quiet. Tam seemed to have an aversion to quiet, needing to fill it with conversation.

Not that it was truly quiet. The sails were humming with life, the water was crashing against the bow, and from time to time he heard a distinct roll of thunder.

The ride was getting rougher by the minute. In the shallow water, it didn't take long for the wind to whip the waves up. He glanced at Veronica and saw her smiling, her eyes alight. She was enjoying it, too.

That surprised him. She had struck him as such a closed, crabby woman that he thought it amazing she liked staring into the teeth of a storm. He found himself grinning at her, enjoying her pleasure. Enjoying sharing this with her.

Just then a rogue wave came along, catching them from the stern. It lifted them up high, causing them to yaw to starboard, then vanished beneath them. The bow rose sharply, then plunged downward, nearly throwing him out of his seat. The wave had cost him control, and the *Mandolin* heeled sharply, tipping the world to port. He caught himself just in time, bracing himself against the side of the cockpit. When he found a moment to glance over at Veronica, she was gripping the console in front of her and laughing.

She looked his way, her face alight, and shouted, "It's better than an amusement park."

Tam stuck his head up through the hatch just then. "What the hell was that?"

"A wave," Dugan answered.

Tam rolled his eyes. "No shit, Sherlock."

He decided they had to reverse course. As the seas became rougher and choppier, battering them from aft, he realized it was foolhardy to keep trying to outrun the worst. He needed to have his bow into the waves before the boat heeled over. That meant bringing them around. Cautiously. The wave had started the process, and they were still rolling wildly to the side as each new wave hit them.

Dugan called below. "Tam?"

"Yo."

"Put out the sea anchor." It would drag from the stern of the boat like a parachute, and help turn and keep them bow into the waves. Much easier than fighting the wheel.

"Aye, aye."

Water was splashing over the gunwales now, and he decided it might be a good time to take down some of the sail. He turned to Veronica.

"I need to take in the sails."

"Okay."

"I need you to take the helm."

"What?"

He motioned her over. She came reluctantly, as if sensing she was being asked to do something she knew nothing about.

"Keep the wheel turned to the starboard," he said. "To the right, just about this much."

Her expression was dubious, but she nodded. "Okay. Why?"

"We need to be facing the waves. She'll roll until we do. Now, when you see we're facing directly into the waves, bring the wheel back to here. Got it?"

She nodded. He didn't wait to see if she had any further questions.

Just then, he felt the sea anchor catch, slowing them

down. The boat started to turn more swiftly. As it did so, the waves began to rock the *Mandolin* more wildly.

On deck, he waved to Tam, and between them they started to lower the sails. It was as he'd told Veronica earlier: there was no reason to take unnecessary chances. He'd have more control over the boat with the motor and less exposure to random wind gusts with his sails furled.

The storm wasn't that bad, but it was bad enough to pay attention to. The boat still hadn't fully turned into the waves, and when some waves hit them broadside there were a couple of moments when he was afraid he was going to lose his footing on the deck. But the sea anchor kept drawing them around, and finally they were nosing into the waves.

The *Mandolin* steadied. Apparently Veronica had understood what he wanted her to do. And Dugan felt enormous relief, because they'd just executed a tricky maneuver in one piece. Another one of those rogue waves might have capsized them, if it had hit them broadside. The gods were smiling, he decided.

But not for long, because then the rain hit, and it was heavy. He was almost drenched by the time he made it back to the cockpit and took over the helm.

Visibility was reduced to next to nothing, and he found himself relying on the sea anchor more than he would have liked to keep them pointing in the right direction, especially since it wasn't infallible.

But they seemed to be in the worst of it now, he thought. It was bad, but nothing the boat shouldn't be able to handle with proper seamanship, and it didn't seem to be getting any worse. There were a couple of bad moments when he felt the stern come out of the water, giving him no rudder control at all, but the sea anchor held them.

It was a hell of a good ride.

The rain let up suddenly, as if by magic. He could see the sea again, and the gray-green underbelly of the clouds. Lightning forked across the sky, pink and white. Dazzling. A few strokes streaked downward to the water. Man, it was beautiful.

He glanced over to see if Veronica was still enjoying herself, but she was gone. He hadn't seen her go below, and his heart clutched for an instant. What had happened to her?

Twisting, he saw her on the aft deck. She was standing there, looking upward into the clouds, her hands lifted in a pose that made him think of an ecstatic trance. Was she crazy? There was lightning.

He called to her, but she didn't hear him. She just stood there with her black hair whipping wildly around her, laughing into the teeth of the storm. Well, it looked like she was laughing, but he couldn't hear her over the noise of the waves and the thunder.

She was going to get herself killed.

"Tam! Tam, get up here."

After a few seconds, Tam's head appeared in the hatch. "What's up?"

"Take the wheel, will you?"

"Sure. Why not. But I was at a great part in the book . . ." His voice trailed off as he came up the ladder and saw Veronica. "What the hell is she doing?"

"She's crazy."

"That still doesn't explain what she's doing." He slammed the hatch shut and reached for the wheel. "I got it. But you better get her quick."

Dugan turned and saw what Tam meant. Some kind of strange aura seemed to be glowing around Veronica, a pale bluish haze. He'd seen that before, on masts of ships at sea in storms.

He instinctively glanced upward at the masts, to see if it was there, too. But it wasn't.

Oh, God, she was going to get hit by lightning. He could think of no other explanation. The possibility of it galvanized him, sending him at a dead run, out of the cockpit and across the wet deck. Spray stung him, but he ignored it, focused on only one thing.

In the instant before he grabbed Veronica, he wondered if he was going to get a shock. Even close to her he could see the blue shimmering, an electric light that would have prevented him from touching anything else on the planet.

But he couldn't leave Veronica to her fate. Grabbing her, he caught a glimpse of her startled face in the instant before he lifted her off her feet and swept her to the cockpit.

"What the hell are you doing?" she demanded, when he set her on her feet.

"Saving your life. You were glowing blue! Lightning was probably going to strike you."

She shook her head, looking angry and upset. "The storm won't hurt me." Then she turned, yanked open the hatch, and descended the ladder below.

Dugan looked at Tam, who shook his head and made a circle with his index finger by his head. "Crazy," Tam said. "She's crazy."

No, thought Dugan. *He* was the one who was crazy. Every damn time he tried to do the right thing, he got into trouble. The angry thought brought memories of Jana floating to the surface and with it a pain so old he was surprised to discover it could still feel fresh.

He turned from Tam, not wanting the other man to read

his face, and stared into the waves and clouds ahead of him. He ought to know better by now, he thought bitterly. He ought to know that people didn't want to be rescued, that they didn't respect you for doing what was right.

Jana had taught him that. He'd rescued her, too, from virtual poverty. An orphan, she'd been supporting herself waiting tables in a coffee shop across from Port Authority, getting paid less than minimum wage and picking up nickels and dimes in tips. She'd had dreams of going to school, but even with loans and financial aid she couldn't see how she could do it and still manage to live.

Well, he'd married her, after a courtship over the counter that had begun when he'd taken his ex-girlfriend to the terminal to catch a bus. He'd married her and paid her way through school and had evidently given her a taste for the finer things in life. Things she wasn't prepared to give up simply because he wasn't going to risk the funds of a lot of little investors who were counting on him to make their retirements happy. She hadn't even felt grateful enough to avoid getting in bed with his best friend.

The two of them had married, and now she was a stay-at-home wife with a Ferrari and a summer house in the Hamptons. No kids, but that somehow didn't surprise him. Neither Jana nor Mel had struck him as people who could make room in their lives for a child. In retrospect, he wondered now why he'd been so blind then. He'd been living in some kind of fool's paradise, envisioning kids and all the rest of it when Jana finished school. Hah!

But he was a wiser man now. Although apparently not as wise as he had thought. Like a fool he'd dashed out to save Veronica from the lightning, and all he'd gotten for it was her anger. In fact, this whole damn association of theirs was born of some misguided notion that he had to protect her. As if it were his responsibility.

Frowning at himself, he wondered when he was ever going to get his head straight. People were happiest when left to muck up their own lives without interference from well-meaning parties. He ought to know that by now.

Sighing, he tried to let go of his pain and anger, and focus on the storm. Tam and the sea anchor were keeping them bow into the waves, and the *Mandolin* was riding them like a trouper. In the distance he could see gray veils of rain, but they seemed to be sweeping to the east. He wondered how long they were going to have to ride this out.

He wondered just how angry Veronica was with him, and then he wondered why he should even care.

But he did, fool that he was. He turned to Tam. "I'm going below for a minute."

"No prob, skipper. And while you're down there, tell her she's a jerk. Being deaf ain't no excuse for being stupid."

Of course it wasn't, Dugan thought as he opened the hatch and descended the ladder. Of course it wasn't. But somehow he didn't think Veronica's action was simply stupid. Not when he remembered the look on her face as she stood out there, as if she were embracing the goddamn storm.

So, maybe he was losing his mind at last. The tropical sun had fried too many of his brain cells. Embracing the storm? Get real, man.

He half expected to find that Veronica had disappeared into her cabin. Well, his cabin. Another white-knight impulse. He should have kept his own cabin and let her share the V berths with Tam. That would have taught her a thing or two. Which thing or two he wasn't certain. But maybe it would have made her less likely to want to hang out here for three months.

Instead, she was sitting at the table in the galley, staring fixedly at her computer screen, which was full of wiggly lines that he supposed were the readouts from the magnetometer. The boat was still rocking quite a bit, so he passed on the possibility of coffee and settled for a plastic mugful of water. Then he sat across from her.

"Anything interesting?" he asked.

She wasn't looking at him, so she didn't hear exactly what he said, but he'd figured speaking would make her look at him. It didn't. She kept her gaze firmly fixed on her computer screen.

For somebody who hadn't been deaf all that long, he found himself thinking, she'd sure figured out how to use it as a weapon. He could have reached out and used touching her as a way to demand that she look at him, but he wasn't ready to sink that low.

Two could play at this game, he decided. He spoke again. "I didn't think so," he said, keeping his tone casual. "I doubt you'd have missed anything before."

He waited, but curiosity still hadn't gotten the better of her. He cast about for something else to say, hoping that if he talked long enough, eventually she'd have to give in and look at him.

Then he realized she'd taken out her hearing aids. Well, son of a bitch. How the hell was he supposed to get around that?

He sat looking at her, sipping his water, part of him paying attention to the *Mandolin*'s movements, part of him puzzling the mystery of the woman who sat across from him deliberately cloaked in silence.

And yet another part of him wondering why he gave a damn. He ought to just get up right now, head topside, and consign her to the devil. Why did he have this overwhelming feeling that he had to make this right somehow? Especially when she had so plainly blocked him out by taking out her hearing aids.

She wasn't his problem, so why was he acting like she was? It was that damned white-knight impulse again, that was what. He couldn't just let her be mad at him. He had to make things right. And he couldn't just accept that she'd had every right to get struck by lightning if she wanted to.

That last thought was so absurd it almost startled a laugh out of him. No, she didn't want to get struck by lightning. That wasn't what she'd been doing. Somehow, some way, she'd been feeling invincible.

He closed his eyes a minute, turning in to the boat, feeling her sink and then fly on the waves, listening to her slightest sound. Everything was okay. At least with the boat.

Then he recalled Veronica standing on the deck a few minutes earlier, arms raised as if to embrace the sky. Remembered the happy look on her face, the transported expression. Remembered the blue glow that had surrounded her.

Forgetting his resolutions, he reached over and tapped her arm. She looked at him, her gaze wary. "Tell me more about this mask."

"I can't hear you."

He nodded and pointed to his ear.

She sighed, hesitated, then finally picked up the case from the seat beside her and put in her hearing aids. He supposed he should have looked away, to give her privacy, but he didn't. Her blue eyes stared back at him defiantly.

"What?" she said, now that she could hear again.

"What were you doing out there?" He tried to keep any accusatory note from his voice, and thought he succeeded.

She shrugged. "I was feeling the storm."

"Feeling the storm?"

She nodded.

"Do you know why I grabbed you like that?"

She shook her head.

"Because you were glowing blue. I figured you were going to get hit by lightning any instant."

She didn't answer immediately, but looked down at her computer. He waited, restraining his impatience, wondering if she was going to shut him out again.

"I wasn't going to get hit," she said finally. "The storm wouldn't do that."

He gaped at her. "My God, you're crazy!"

"No, I'm not."

"No, you're right. *I'm* the one who's crazy. I ran out there, risking getting hit myself, to grab a woman who was glowing blue from the charge building up in her, and all the thanks I get is being told that the storm wouldn't hurt her and I shouldn't have done that? No, it's me who's crazy."

He didn't know how much of his diatribe she understood, but those blue eyes were looking at him again, wide-eyed and . . . haunted. They looked haunted.

She surprised him by reaching out to grip his forearm. "You don't understand," she said. "The storm was . . . it was . . . I could feel it. I was part of it."

"Yep, you sure were. The blue part of it. The lightning part of it."

"No." She sighed, and her face took on the frustrated expression he saw there entirely too often. It was beginning to irritate him, but not because he was getting impatient with her inability to understand. Because he was getting impatient that the two of them didn't seem to be able to communicate effectively. It wasn't just her hearing. They might have originated on two entirely different planets.

She spoke, still gripping his forearm. "It was . . . Oh, Dugan, it was wonderful. I could feel the storm. Feel the power. It was like . . . like . . ." After a moment she gave up, shaking her head. Then an idea struck her. "I think maybe it's like what you feel sailing this boat."

That silenced him, because he knew what she meant. It just surprised him that she was astute enough to have picked up on it.

This boat was almost a part of him, of his soul. Considering how rarely he managed to get out and sail her, it was amazing to realize that he never felt quite as alive as when he and the *Mandolin* were skipping over waves with the sails full of the breath of the wind. The humming of the sails and the creak of the rigging were almost a second heartbeat for him. It was as if, when he stood at the helm, he melded with the boat into one being.

Veronica had apparently picked up on that somehow, and he gave her high marks for being perceptive. But she had said she had felt the same way about the storm.

"You felt like you were part of the storm?"

She nodded, then gave an almost shy smile. "I had the feeling I could have clutched handfuls of thunderbolts."

"You almost did."

He was losing this argument, he realized. If it had been an argument. But when she put it in those terms, he felt kind of stupid for grabbing her. In those terms it made about as much sense as someone yanking him out of the boat's cockpit.

After a moment, he said, "I still think you could have been hurt."

"You could be hurt sailing this boat."

"It's not exactly the same thing as a thunderstorm, though."

"No?" She looked away from him, staring into the distance, giving him the feeling that she saw something he never would.

"Did I tell you I'm a direct descendant of the high priestess who went down on the *Alcantara*?"

His heart skipped a beat. This, he decided, was beginning to get spooky. He tapped her hand, making her look at him. "What are you trying to tell me?"

"Just what I said." She shrugged her shoulder. "Standing out there in the storm, it felt like I was . . . well, I felt more at peace than I've felt in a long time. I felt . . . at home. Connected."

This was getting too creepy to be believed. And it sounded crazy enough to merit a commitment order.

On the other hand . . . "So how did your ancestor survive?"

"The conquistador I told you about was her father. He saved her and carried her with him to St. Augustine. I'm a direct descendant of the female line."

He didn't know what to say to that. Finally, he said the only thing that occurred to him. "So I guess if this tribe had survived, you'd be the high priestess now."

She shrugged again. "I don't know. It doesn't really matter. But I'm wondering if maybe . . . maybe there isn't something in my bloodline that makes me feel a connection with storms."

"Have you always gotten . . . well, for lack of a better word—*high* during storms?"

"I wouldn't exactly call it a high. I've always loved them. They make me feel . . . good."

"Hmm."

Her expression became surprisingly shy. "I know it sounds crazy."

"That's one way of putting it."

"Maybe I just love storms. Maybe there isn't any connection at all."

"Maybe not." But something atavistic inside him kind of believed that there might be. "Is this why you're so hot to find that mask?"

"Partly. But mostly because my mother spent her life looking for it. It's something I need to do."

"I can understand that, I guess. But just do me a favor."

"What's that?"

"No more communing with storms from the deck of my boat. My insurance company would have a fit."

And much to his amazement, she laughed.

Okay, so maybe she wasn't that crazy after all. He could live with it.

But only for a couple of months.

Chapter 10

Tam was the first person off the *Mandolin* when they docked. Luis watched him leap off the boat with his duffel and set straight out for Old Town on foot, despite the rain and the darkening of the evening.

Luis, who was across the street inside a bookstore, watching the marina while he pretended to be perusing books, decided he might offer the man a ride.

Five minutes later he was in his car, driving down Truman Avenue a few feet behind Tam. Given local customs, it wasn't a problem to slow down, lower the passenger window, and call, "Want a ride?"

Tam bent down, looked in on him, and said, "Yeah, sure. Aren't you the guy who came out to the boat before we left?"

Luis didn't deny it. "Yes. I saw you get off the boat."

That seemed to be enough for Tam, who willingly tossed his duffel in the backseat and climbed in beside Luis.

"I'm on my way to get a drink," Luis said. This much had been easy, so he decided to go for the rest without beating around the bush. "Join me? I have a business offer to make."

Tam looked at him. "You need a diver? I'm booked for a while."

Luis shook his head. "Something much easier with better pay."

"Sounds good to me. Sure, let's have that drink."

Too easy, thought Luis. Either this man was stupid, or he was leading Luis on. He decided a little more caution might be in order.

So he didn't say much more until they reached the heart of Old Town and he managed to find a parking space. He let Tam pick the place, one that didn't even have any tables, just the long bar with stools, and doors that opened onto the street.

Luis ordered Tecate. Tam, who had more serious business in mind, ordered a Chivas. Why not, Luis thought. Tam wasn't paying for it. "How was your trip?" he said.

"Boring," Tam said. "I spent the whole damn time reading a book. We didn't do a thing."

Luis clucked sympathetically. "I wouldn't like that."

"Me neither. I only signed on because I thought I'd be diving."

"Why did you not dive?"

Tam opened his mouth as if to answer, then apparently changed his mind. Instead, he downed his shot of Chivas and sighed happily. "Damn, I missed that." Then he turned to Luis. "Why are you so curious?"

"I am an archaeologist. I understand Miss Coleridge is looking for a sunken Spanish treasure ship. So I am curious."

"Hmm." Tam stroked his moustache. "Wouldn't have anything to do with all that gold, would it?"

"What good would that do me? I could never get it out of your country. No, I'm just excited to maybe see an important wreck found."

"Well, you're going to have to wait a damn long time, because we didn't find anything at all. It's turning into the worst vacation I ever took."

Luis nodded sympathetically. He was good at looking sympathetic; the talent had been of great use to him over the years with Emilio. "It may be boring for a long time."

"That's what I'm afraid of. Oh, well, it's a job."

"Ah! You are getting paid for this."

Tam suddenly looked uneasy. "Well, yes."

Luis nodded again and took a moment to sip his beer so Tam wouldn't feel he was being pressured.

"I have always wanted to do what Miss Coleridge is doing," he said. "But I don't have the money."

"It can get real expensive," Tam agreed. He ordered another Chivas.

This was good, Luis thought. The more whiskey, the looser the tongue. Maybe he'd wait a bit, and let Tam have another shot or two. Then he decided, no, he would talk around the issue without pressuring. That would seem more natural.

"It has been my dream since I was a child," he told Tam. "To find a treasure ship. When I was young I dreamed of piracy, but as I got older I dreamed of fame as an archaeologist."

"Yeah?" Tam regarded him with interest. "I used to wish I could be a pirate, too."

Luis flashed a rare grin. "The thought of treasure makes me remember that."

"Yeah." Tam laughed and shook his head. "But I ain't

gonna touch it, man. The state would be all over my ass." His smile faded. "What are you after?"

"Just information. I just want to know what is happening, and what is found. Nothing more."

"Curiosity, huh?"

"Just curiosity."

"And you're willing to pay for that information?"

"I'm prepared to pay very well."

Tam pushed his glass aside. "Forget it," he said, his tone steely. "You're lying, and I don't sell out my friends."

Luis, quick as a snake, reached out and closed his hand around Tam's forearm. For such a slight man, he had amazing strength, and Tam looked shocked.

"Let me tell you, my friend," Luis said, his voice low and menacing, "I want information. That's all you have to do. Information. I pay for it."

"No."

"Well, then, I will have to get someone else on board that boat."

"There's no room for anyone else. There's two divers, and I'm one of them."

Luis shook his head. "You don't understand me. I will *make* room to put my own diver on that boat."

Tam looked dead into Luis's eyes, and he began to pale. After a moment he nodded. "Information only."

"Just information. Nothing more. I just want to know. What I do with that information needn't concern you. And your friends won't get hurt."

Tam gave another short, jerky nod. "Fair enough," he said finally. "Fair enough."

"Good. We understand each other." Luis smiled again and took a roll of bills out of his pocket. He put them on the bar in front of Tam. "Your down payment."

Tam took the money and stuffed it in his pocket. As Luis had suspected, the other man liked easy money.

"Okay," said Tam. "I can do that."

"Of course you can. It's only a little thing."

"Yeah," said Tam. "Yeah." And after another shot of Chivas, he looked as if he thought it was a pretty good deal.

But after that, Tam seemed eager to get away from him, and Luis was glad enough to let him go, once they had worked out arrangements. Tam would call Luis's pager when he came ashore, then Luis would call him to get the information. The business was settled. Well, except for the phone calls.

The first one he made to Emilio, then waited impatiently for the man to come to the phone. Emilio often kept him waiting. It seemed he was watching a videotape of *Die Hard* and didn't want to interrupt a riveting action scene, at least according to Elena Zaragosa, who answered the telephone. Luis reminded himself that this call was on Emilio's bill.

At last Emilio picked up the phone. "*Digame,*" he said. Tell me.

"One of the divers has agreed to keep me informed," Luis told him. "But so far they have found nothing at all."

"They might find nothing at all for years," Emilio said philosophically. "I'm a patient man."

Luis was not nearly so patient, probably because he was the one who was going to be expected to spend the rest of his life in this godforsaken little town, checking in with Tam Anson until the ship was found. This, thought Luis, was beginning to feel like a sentence to life in prison.

Emilio evidently sensed his employee's discontent. Things like this had Luis nearly convinced that Emilio was a mind reader. "It won't be so bad, Luis," Emilio said sympathetically. "You don't have to stay there."

"No?"

"Of course not. You can have this man of yours call you with the information. And, once in a while, you can return to Key West to check up on him."

Luis's life suddenly looked brighter. "Thank you."

"I am not a heartless beast."

But then there was the call to *El Desconocido,* to tell him things were going well. He fretted over that one, wondering what he would do if *El Desconocido* thought Luis should stay in Key West. How would he explain that to Emilio?

But he didn't have to answer that question right away, because all he got was an answering machine, and the whispery voice saying, "Leave a message." So he left a message, making no promises about when he would call again, or how he was going to keep on top of the situation. It wasn't the man's business, after all, because he only wanted to know when the ship was found.

After hanging up the phone, Luis decided that this arrangement might work after all. No contact between them, other than messages, and eventually a huge check to be deposited to his anonymous account.

Yes, it would work. Emilio would never know what happened. And no one would ever know that Luis had been involved.

Life was good. He decided to treat himself to the most expensive meal in town.

Unlike Tam, who had climbed off the boat like a jailbreaking prisoner, Veronica remained to help Dugan with the chores, such as emptying the perishables from the rerigerator and securing all the hatches and tarps. By the ime they were done, they were both soaking wet from the ain.

Dugan never understood the impulse that made him then ay, "Want to come to my place to dry off?"

Her eyes widened, and for a moment she didn't say anyhing. Then she said, "Pardon me?"

He was already regretting the impulse that had made him speak, but he had a sneaking suspicion she had understood him perfectly and was just buying time. So he repeated the fateful words.

"Want to come to my place to dry off? I can make us some dinner." Her father wasn't expecting her back until the next day, but he wondered if she would use that as an excuse. Part of him hoped like hell she would, while another part of him was reluctant to say good-bye to her. Between her remark about being isolated and her reaction to the storm, he discovered he was fascinated by her. As fascinated as a moth by a candle flame, knowing full well he could get burned, but unable to help himself.

She finally nodded, almost hesitantly. It amazed him that she hadn't found a reason to say no. But maybe she was tired of her isolation and had decided to reach out.

He wasn't sure, though, that he wanted to be the one she reached out to. However, it was too late now.

He loaded their duffels into the back of his truck and drove them to his house. The rain was beginning to lighten, but the evening was dark and gray, and passing swiftly into night. He pulled off the street and into his driveway, which was just long enough and wide enough for him to park without blocking the sidewalk. Tam's motor scooter was there, but that didn't mean anything since Tam had walked to the dock. But the upstairs windows were all dark, and

Dugan felt surprisingly relieved. For some reason he didn't feel like dealing with Tam tonight.

"Home sweet home," he told Veronica as he ushered her inside and flipped on the lights.

Rugs were scattered over gleaming wood plank floors darkened from age and layers of varnish. The room was filled with old furniture, some of which had come with the house, some of which he'd picked up secondhand. The effect was to make it seem that the house and furnishings had been passed down through generations.

It was no decorator showpiece, but it suited him, probably in part because it would have appalled Jana. There had been a time when that seemed like a good enough reason to do anything.

Veronica stood right inside the door, looking about uncertainly. He caught her eye and pointed. "Bathroom's in there. Feel free to freshen up and change. Want some coffee?"

"Yes, please."

"I'll go make it." He waited a moment, to be sure she headed for the bathroom, then made his way to the kitchen.

The kitchen was the one place where he ceded space to the current century. Every appliance was new; there was a dishwasher and a trash compactor, and nearly every kitchen gadget known to man from a drip coffeemaker to a food processor to a pasta maker. And he used every one of them.

The pot was just finishing brewing when Veronica joined him. She had changed into white shorts and a loose red shirt with long sleeves that she had rolled up. Her dark hair was still damp, pulled out of the way in a ponytail that somehow emphasized the gray streak. Something deep inside Dugan stirred, but he ruthlessly stamped it out.

"Coffee?" he asked, holding out a mug. After the last few days, he knew she took hers black.

"Thank you." She pulled out a chair at the round oak table in one corner of the kitchen and sat, looking around curiously. "What a contrast," she said. "All the old cabinets and all the brand-new appliances."

He smiled and sat in the chair facing her. "This is one place I need my conveniences."

She smiled and nodded. "And in the bathroom."

It was true, his bathroom was as modern as his kitchen . . . except for the tub. It was a huge, claw-footed tub that he wouldn't have parted with for a fortune, because it was big enough for him to stretch out his legs in. "What do you think?"

"I like it. It feels homey."

That's what he thought too. For an unwanted bachelor he'd done pretty damn good at making a home.

"So you cook?" she asked.

"Sometimes."

She lifted an inquiring brow.

"Well, when I need to get away, but I can't sail away because of business, I sometimes go on a cooking spree."

"I'm sorry?"

He repeated himself more slowly, and saw her understanding.

She glanced at his flat stomach. "What do you do with all the food?"

"It's easy to get rid of. I pick up a phone and call Tam and a few other friends. Next thing I know, the house is overrun with people, and we're all eating and having a party."

The look she gave him just then was so wistful that he felt his heart ache.

"Don't you ever have parties?" he asked.

He could tell that she understood him, but for an instant he had the feeling that she was going to pretend she didn't. But then she answered.

"No."

"Why not?"

She shrugged. "No time, I guess."

"Aw, come on, you can't possibly work that hard."

This time she didn't answer, and he knew she wasn't going to. What was going on here?

Leaning back in his chair, he sipped his coffee and considered going to change. He was getting chilly in his wet clothes with the air-conditioning on. But something made him reluctant to leave Veronica at that moment. He had the feeling that she was struggling with something, not quite ready to speak about it or admit it even to herself.

And hadn't he just warned himself for the umpty-umpth time not to play the knight-errant? So what was he doing sitting there waiting for her to spill her guts?

"I'm going to change," he said. He realized she hadn't been looking at him when her eyes suddenly leapt to his face, and she said, "Sorry?"

"I'm going to change."

"Okay."

He rose and headed for his bedroom, wondering how she could stand not being able to hear, and how other people could stand repeating things so often. And then it suddenly struck him . . . he actually didn't mind it that much. He was getting used to it.

God forbid. No way. Life insisted on sending enough hassles his way. He didn't need to ask for any more.

He stripped his clothes and hung them to dry over a wooden rack he'd purchased for the purpose. Living in such a humid climate, clothes were apt to be damp more often than not when you took them off, and he'd learned his lesson about mildew his first week there.

Still feeling chilled, he changed into jeans and a yellow polo shirt, then returned to the kitchen. He found Veronica sitting hunched over her mug, staring into her coffee as if it were a crystal ball.

"Reading the tea leaves?" he asked.

She didn't even look at him. That's when he realized she had removed her hearing aids. The waterproof pouch was beside her on the table.

Great. What were they going to do? Sit and stare at one another?

He touched her shoulder and she jumped, looking up swiftly at him. "Sorry, didn't mean to frighten you. Can you hear me?"

Apparently she couldn't, because she shook her head and pointed to her ear. "I took out my aids."

He pushed the pouch toward her. "Put them in. We can't talk without them."

He knew she didn't understand a word he was saying, probably couldn't hear his voice at all. But talking was a habit, one he couldn't break over night.

She had understood the gesture, though, and for a few seconds he saw mulishness in her face, a stubbornness that reminded him of a recalcitrant child. Oddly enough, it made him want to laugh. She was cute when she stuck her chin out like that.

But finally she reached for the pouch and with irritated gestures put her aids back in her ears.

"Thank you," he said.

Her blue eyes regarded him resentfully.

"Why are they bothering you?" he asked. "It's quiet in here."

"I've had them in all day. My ears feel sore."

"I'm sorry."

She looked as if she didn't believe him.

"How can we talk if you can't hear me?"

"What do we have to talk about?"

Good question. But he had an answer for it. "Would I have invited you here if I didn't want to talk with you?"

"Yes."

He felt his jaw drop. Certainly she hadn't thought... hadn't expected... Hell's bells! If that's what she had believed, why the hell had she come with him?

"I'm insulted," he said sharply.

"What?"

"Insulted. Offended." He found himself jabbing at his chest.

She shrugged one shoulder. "Sorry."

He pulled out the chair across from her, swung it around, and straddled it. He was still annoyed. "What kind of men do you hang around with?"

"What?"

But before he repeated his question, he felt the wind go out of his sails. What kind of men? What kind of stupid question was that? He'd been around enough men to know that most men were that kind of man. He passed his hand over his face, wiping away his anger and frustration. This woman could madden him more quickly than any woman he'd ever known. Not a good thing.

"Let's start again."

She cocked her head. "Start what again?"

"This conversation."

"Oh." She shrugged again. He was beginning to hate

that shrug. It kept making him feel as if nothing he said or did mattered, as if she were utterly indifferent to him. And why *that* should be bothering him was something he didn't want to examine too closely just then.

"Lady, for someone who claims to feel isolated, you sure do your best to keep everyone at a distance."

She understood that. He could see it in her eyes, could see the way they shadowed with hurt, then flared. She jumped to her feet and wrapped her arms around herself, then began to pace the kitchen.

"You don't know anything about me," she said.

He didn't bother to reply. She wasn't looking at him, and anyway, he didn't think she wanted to hear anything he had to say.

"If you're going to keep throwing that moment of weakness up at me, we're not going to be doing business much longer."

He was tempted; he was sorely tempted. But some lingering remnant of moral fiber wouldn't let him take the easy way out. So he waited. Finally, she started talking.

"All my life, I've been alone. When I was little, and made friends during the school year, summer would always come and we'd leave to go on a dig somewhere. And when I came back in the fall, my friends would have found new friends. Or I'd come back to a different school because my father had taken a position at a different university."

She shrugged, but this time the gesture didn't irritate him, because it was plainly directed at herself. "It was no big deal. I had a lot of advantages other children didn't have. I visited places some of them can only dream about. And as I got older and could start participating on the digs, I learned a hell of a lot."

She faced him then. "The point I'm making is that I

prefer being alone. It's served me well. And the one time since childhood that I let somebody get close, it proved to be the biggest mistake of my life."

He suddenly had the worst urge to go to her and hug her, because he knew in his gut what he was hearing was bravado, and not a word of it was true.

"I've learned a lot of things that some people never learn," she went on forcefully—which also meant louder. He had to remind himself that she wasn't consciously shouting. "I learned to be self-reliant, to get by on my own resources in almost any situation. I learned to take care of myself."

He nodded, not knowing whether she cared what he thought, and not sure what he thought of this proud little exposition except that it was making him feel very sorry for her.

"Anyway," she said, "when I was talking about being isolated earlier, I was talking about being deaf. And all I meant was that it makes conversing so difficult."

Bullshit, he thought. If that was what she had meant, then he was the Pied Piper of Hamlin. He was tempted to tell her to get a shovel, but he resisted the impulse. She had a Ph.D. all right, in horse manure. But maybe the worst of it was the sneaking suspicion that she really believed all this rationalization.

She was looking at him, as if waiting for his response. Trouble was, he was a lousy liar, and if he said what he was really thinking, they'd only get into an argument.

So he hid behind a question. "Who was the person you let get close to you?"

"Which person?"

"The one who hurt you."

She turned her back to him and he felt a spark of anger.

He'd been ignored before in his life, but there was something especially annoying about the way this person ignored him by turning her back. The urge to turn her around and make her face him nearly overwhelmed him.

But then she surprised him by speaking. "My husband," she said presently, repeating what she had told him before. "My *ex*-husband. He left me after I became deaf. He said he couldn't handle it."

There had to be more to it than that, Dugan thought. Because any guy worth his salt who loved a woman would have stuck around if that's all there was to it. Of course, there were plenty of guys who weren't worth their salt. Some were something you wanted to scrape off your shoe. But how had a woman like her become involved with such a slug?

"What else happened?" he asked, even though it was useless because her back was to him. But the sound of his voice had the effect of bringing her around, and it was less intrusive than touching her.

Although he was beginning to think that he needed to avoid touching her for reasons other than not wanting to offend her. Mostly because the thought of touching her was beginning to sound too good.

"What?" she asked.

"What else happened? There was more than your deafness, wasn't there?"

Her face darkened. "It's none of your business."

"No? Well, here you are, dripping your angst all over my kitchen floor, telling me I don't know you at all, but I *do* know you were crying earlier about being isolated, and I *do* know you said someone hurt you and it was the biggest mistake of your life. Now, since we've come this far, why don't you just tell me all of it? Then I'll shut up and leave you in your isolated ivory tower."

He didn't know if she understood a tenth of what he'd just said. He wasn't exactly sure what he meant by it himself. What he did know was that he wanted the whole story, not just the antiseptic bits and pieces she had shared with him.

"I'm not in an ivory tower! I'm deaf. It cost me my husband. He couldn't handle it even though he's the one who made me—"

She broke off sharply and whirled around, giving him her back.

But this time he was having none of it. He rose and went to her, taking her by the shoulders and turning her to face him. She stiffened and glared up at him. "Let me go."

"No. Not until you answer me. Your husband made you deaf? How'd he do that? Tell me, Veronica."

She looked up at him, a mixture of emotions racing across her face. Then, in a burst she cried, "You want to know? It wasn't really his fault. He'd had a couple of beers, but it was the other driver who caused the accident. And I lost my hearing and our baby."

Then she pulled away from him and hurried out of the kitchen. A few moments later he heard the front door close behind her.

He thought about going after her; she was upset and raw. But it wasn't raining anymore, and she was staying only a couple of blocks away. And because she was raw, he didn't think she could handle any more of him just then.

So he quelled his impulse to rescue her. He knew at least some of where she was coming from, because he'd been there himself, and he remembered how having other people around had sometimes made his nerves feel scraped.

He found himself wishing he hadn't pressed her for answers, not because it had been painful to hear, although it had been.

But because it made her seem too much like a kindred spirit.

Chapter 11

Orin wasn't feeling well. He insisted that the doctor said he was doing just fine, that his cancer was still in remission, but Veronica had a hard time believing it. In the two months since they had arrived in Key West, he seemed to have shrunk.

"It's just age," he told her. "Honestly. There's nothing wrong with me."

"You ought to go back to Tampa and have another scan."

"I'm supposed to do that in a month. That's soon enough."

But she didn't believe it. Fear was nibbling at her heart constantly, and every time she got aboard the *Mandolin* to sail out for four or five days, she wondered if he would be gone when she returned.

She was supposed to leave again in the morning, but her heart was beginning to go out of the whole process. The magnetometer had found some anomalies early in the game, and Dugan and Tam had been doing an awful lot of diving ever since, going over huge areas of the seafloor with the metal detectors. Nothing. Not a thing, except some rubbish and a rusty propeller.

Day after boring day they sat out there on the water. Or at least *she* did. Tam and Dugan at least seemed to enjoy diving, if not the painstaking sweeping of the seafloor. Tam was a natural talker who tried to turn every evening into a party, but she still couldn't understand what he was saying most of the time, which left her feeling cut off and cut out. Sometimes he'd break out his harmonica, though, and would play sea chanties and other haunting bits of music that she recognized. And sometimes Dugan would sing along.

She didn't have enough confidence to do that, but she did enjoy listening. A lot of evenings, though, she just pulled out her hearing aids and hid in the silence. And Dugan never said a word about it, as if he no longer minded when she put up her walls of silence. In fact, ever since she had told him what had happened to her, he seemed to have pulled far away, so far away that she didn't feel as if they were even casual acquaintances anymore. Now she felt as if they were utter strangers, even though they saw each other every day and talked quite a bit—but always about business.

She told herself it was no big deal; he was just an employee. But their three months were running out, and she wasn't sure she could persuade him to extend their agreement. Tam, she gathered, kept talking about being done with the whole thing. Dugan didn't say a word one way or another.

Now there was her father. She looked at him again, taking in the dark circles under his eyes and the lack of color in his face. He wasn't healthy at all.

"I'm taking you back to Tampa," she announced. "You need to see your doctor and get another CAT scan."

He shook his head. "I'm fine. Just a little under the weather. Besides, you don't want to give up your search. You need to prove me wrong before it's too late."

Something inside her flared. That bone of contention had been lying between them for many months, and they ordinarily avoided mentioning it. But now he had thrown it up in her face. "What is the matter with you?" she demanded. "You can't possibly think this search is more important than your health."

"Actually," he said mildly, "I think your emotional health is more important than anything, including my physical health."

"I'm just fine."

"Are you?" He shrugged. "It's possible, I suppose, but I don't see it. You're angry with me, you're driven, and you're absolutely convinced that I committed a mortal sin by not telling you about the mask and your mother's search for it. Never mind that I did it for your own good."

"How could it possibly be for my own good to lie to me about what mattered to my mother? Were you ashamed of her? Damn it, Dad, it's not as if she were a prostitute. She was an archaeologist searching for a lost artifact."

"I wasn't ashamed of her, Veronica. Never, ever. I think she was obsessed, but she wouldn't be the first person in our field to be obsessed by something like this. And she had the added motivation of being related to the last surviving priestess. I could understand that."

"Then what was it you couldn't understand?"

"Nothing. I told you. I didn't tell you about this because I was *afraid* for you. I knew it would consume you. And I feared you'd get hurt the way your mother did."

She shook her head angrily. "Her death was an accident."

"I disagree. But the facts are neither here nor there, Veronica. The fears I had kept me from telling you about it. In the long run, what does it really matter? Everything else I told you about her was true, and I told you *everything else* about her."

"But you left out the single most important thing, Dad. You left out the quest that defined her. And you lied to me. I don't like being lied to. Larry lied to me when he said he loved me. I don't like liars."

"I never lied."

"Except by omission."

"That's not the same thing."

She knew they were going to get nowhere with this discussion. He was convinced he was right; she was convinced he was wrong. And she couldn't even find words that could adequately explain to him just how wounded she felt by his "omissions" all those years. Couldn't explain how betrayed she felt by his unwillingness to trust her with the truth.

She also couldn't escape the notion that he'd felt her mother's quest had been insane. He kept calling it an obsession, and she didn't think he meant that in the casual sense. He hadn't trusted her mother's judgment.

"You don't think the mask existed, do you?"

His eyebrows, just beginning to grow back some hair, lifted. "I don't doubt that it existed."

"Then why do you think she was wasting her time? Why did you think she was deluded?"

"I never said she was deluded."

"You imply it with everything you say. What's at the root of all this, Dad? What?"

He sighed and looked away, staring out the window into the sun-drenched garden. Minutes passed while Veronica grew impatient and began to wonder if he was ever going to tell her the whole truth and stop treating her like a child who needed protection.

Why he felt a sudden need to protect her was something she couldn't understand. He certainly hadn't protected her from much when she'd been a child. Living at archaeological digs had taught her a lot about the rougher side of life, especially in small, impoverished towns, and *cantinas* and bars all over the world while her dad and his colleagues had a drink or two. She'd nearly been raped at the age of twelve, rescued only by a Mexican woman who'd heard her cries and had come running with the *metate* she used for grinding corn, to beat the man around the head. She'd been robbed in the market, had witnessed brawls and knife fights, and knew what a prostitute was by the time she was eight. Protect her from *what*?

Orin finally turned back to her. "I know I haven't been the best father. I know you have a lot of difficult feelings about me right now. But don't add that resentment to this discussion, Veronica. Let's have this one as adult professionals. Colleagues."

"We can't discuss my mother as colleagues."

"Of course not. I'm not talking about your mother here. I'm talking about the disagreement of professional opinion she and I had."

This was certainly a new tack, Veronica thought. But her curiosity was aroused and she forgot her anger with him, at least for the moment. "What difference?"

"She believed Bernal's account that the mask was taken aboard the *Alcantara*. I never did. Think about it, Veronica. Would that tribe really have let something so important to them be taken from the island? They believed that mask protected them from the wrath of hurricanes and waterspouts. Would they really have let anyone, even the high priestess, take it away?"

"If it didn't go down on that ship, then what happened to it?" But she already knew the answer. It followed logically.

Orin spoke her thought. "It vanished in the hurricane that wiped the tribe out."

It was the one question she hadn't asked herself over the last months of preparation. Even as she had questioned the conclusions her mother had drawn about where the *Alcantara* had sunk, she had never questioned whether the mask was aboard.

She felt her stomach contract as she considered the possibility. "Why didn't you tell me this before?"

"Because I needed anything that would get you out of that rocking chair and back into life. I'd have lied, cheated, and stolen to get you back, Veronica."

"Did you?"

"Lie?" He shook his head. "No. But I didn't tell you my doubts."

She was feeling unpleasantly manipulated, but she couldn't seem to get angry about it. Only sad. Depressed. She sat for a few minutes, wondering why she hadn't just killed herself after Larry left her. There'd been nothing left to live for, so why had she hung around? Why had she given anyone the opportunity to manipulate her the way her father had? And now he was trying to rip it all away from her.

Her eyes felt hot and swollen as she looked at her father. "Why are you finally telling me this?"

"Because you wanted to know the truth of what I thought

about your mother's search. I told you. I disagreed with her on purely professional grounds."

There was more to it than that, Veronica thought. More to his telling her this now. He was still afraid that her mother had been murdered, and she suspected he was still afraid that she might get hurt.

She closed her eyes, shutting him out, closing herself inside her own head and forcing herself to be objective. He might be right. Would the tribe have allowed the priestess to take the mask to Spain with her, leaving them unprotected? Would she have been willing to do that to her people?"

So little was known about the tribe, their beliefs, or what they might have done about this, though. All anyone knew about the mask of the Storm Mother and the tribe was what Bernal had recorded. And he might have lied, or simply not known the truth.

But she couldn't imagine any reason why Bernal would have lied. A storm had destroyed the *Alcantara,* and there was nothing to be gained by lying about what was aboard her. Nothing at all.

But he might have lied about how the mask came to be aboard. Maybe his wife, the priestess, hadn't been willing to leave her island. Maybe he had forced her to come along, and had brought the mask himself as a prize. There was no way to know what kind of man he had been, and what the circumstances were.

But there was absolutely no reason she could imagine that he stood to gain anything by lying about the mask being aboard the galleon.

She opened her eyes and found her father watching her. "Bernal didn't lie. The mask was aboard the *Alcantara.*

How it came to be there may be open to question, but he can't have had any reason to lie about its being there."

Her father gave her a half nod. "Perhaps not. So you're going to continue the search?"

"Yes."

"Then be very, very careful, Veronica. More people than you think know what you're doing."

"What do you mean?"

"Some of our colleagues have mentioned your search to me. They've heard whispers of it in the community. There's actually a great deal of interest. Which could put you in danger."

"Just rumors," she said. "I haven't told anyone what I'm doing. Have you?"

He shook his head. "It doesn't matter. *Someone* knows. There are rumors. Most of the people I talk to simply shake their heads as if they don't believe it, and I don't say anything to change their minds. But it remains: People are interested."

As an archaeologist, she was accustomed to the interest of her colleagues in what she was doing. Usually it didn't trouble her, but this time . . . this time it made her uneasy.

There was supposedly ten million dollars in bullion on the *Alcantara*. Her head wasn't so far in the clouds that she didn't know what a temptation that kind of sum would be to almost anyone. But she didn't care about the gold; she only wanted the mask. It was *hers*. Her birthright. And even though she was going to put it in a museum, she still wanted to hold it in her hands and feel a connection with an ancestor who had been dead for three hundred years. A connection with her mother.

"All I want is the mask," she said. "I don't care what happens with the gold. The state can have it."

"They'll certainly try to take it," Orin said drily. "But the mask—my dear child, you *do* understand that the mask is probably worth as much as the bullion. Maybe even more?"

No, she hadn't thought of it in those terms, stupid as it made her feel now. She was an archaeologist. She thought of artifacts in terms of the knowledge they would provide about the cultures they represented. As far as she was concerned, the mask's greatest value would be realized when it sat in a museum. She hadn't been thinking about collectors whose sole interest was possession of the rare and beautiful. Dollar value didn't matter to them, nor did knowledge. Owning something unique was all they cared about.

And the mask would certainly be unique. "I don't have anything to worry about until I find the mask. And no one will know about that except Tam, Dugan, and me. They'll keep quiet." She was surprised to realize that she trusted Dugan that far. Apparently even with the strained distance between them, she had come to trust his word—and he had vouched for Tam.

"I'm worried about you," Orin said.

"Me? I can take care of myself. *You're* the one with cancer. And I'm going to take you back to Tampa for a checkup."

"No. You stay here and continue your search. If it'll make you happy, I'll call my doctor and make an appointment. But you stay here. Just be careful, Veronica. There are all kinds of sharks in the water."

She didn't for a minute think he meant sharks that swam.

"So this mask," Dugan said to Veronica. They were sailing out toward the search area, Dugan at the helm, Veronica beside him. Tam was on the bow again, getting even browner as he read yet another paperback thriller. It was a windy day, with choppy waves, as a dry front passed through.

She'd had her head averted as she watched the water, hoping to spy a dolphin. Hearing his voice, she turned quickly to him. "I'm sorry?"

"I was asking about the mask."

"Oh. What about it?"

"What if it never existed?"

She felt her mouth twist wryly, and was surprised that she wasn't getting even a little annoyed. For some odd reason it just felt so good to be sailing today that she couldn't take offense. "It's mentioned in more than one source. A friar who recorded something about the people during the conversion process mentioned it."

"So it wasn't just this one guy, this great-great-whatever-grandfather of yours."

"No. But why would he lie about it anyway, Dugan?" The same question she'd had to ask herself just the night before with her father.

"I don't know. To make it sound more dramatic? To make himself sound more important? What if his wife wasn't the high priestess? But after learning that the island was wiped out by the same storm, he decided to invent a tale that would give him more of a cachet. More importance than just being a soldier who happened to have a native child."

That was another possibility she hadn't considered, and her stomach lurched. It was beginning to occur to her that her father knew what he was talking about when he called this an obsession. Even a modicum of objectivity would have made her consider all these questions months ago. Instead, she had accepted her mother's quest as her own, and had never considered a thing except that Renata might have been wrong about the location of the wreck.

She spoke, the words heavy in her mouth. "It's possible, I guess. But I'm still going to look. What I have to go on is more proof than you have for what you're suggesting."

"Oh, I didn't mean you should stop looking. I just meant what if. What if you never find it?"

"That's not an unusual state of affairs in archaeology. It's something I have to live with." Never mind that the possibility sometimes kept her awake at night, reviewing all her deductions about where the wreck lay.

"But it strikes me that this mask is more important to you than the average clay pot or whatever. You've got more hinging on it."

That was true, but she wasn't about to admit it. "No, not really. I just want to recover it because it would be such a singular find."

"Hmm." His tone told her that he didn't really believe her, and she didn't have the heart to keep on lying more forcefully.

The hum of the rigging and the slap of the bow against the waves was growing louder, as was the whine of the wind in her hearing aids, making it more difficult for Veronica to sort Dugan's voice out of the cacophony. She was aware that he said something else, but other than a few vowel sounds, she missed it.

She turned toward him. "What?"

He raised his voice. "I just said I hoped you . . ."

The rest vanished in the background noise. Instinctively, she leaned toward him, bringing her ear closer to his mouth. At that moment, a wave unbalanced her, and Dugan grabbed her arm to steady her.

For Veronica, it was as if some hidden place inside her suddenly burst open, splitting her psyche. Some part of her was aware of the boat, of the wave, of the sharp rocking of the deck beneath her feet, but another part of her focused on something utterly different. The dry warmth of Dugan's hand on her arm. The sprinkling of golden hairs on his legs. The closeness of his mouth to her ear. The sensation that she was playing out a plan as old as time. An almost mystical sense of emotional and sexual connection to him. A strange feeling that was almost déjà vu, but larger somehow.

A wild vortex of panic suddenly rose in her.

She jerked her arm out of Dugan's grasp and stepped backward, as if burned. Her eyes flew to his face, fearing he'd sensed what she had been feeling, terrified that he would realize just how vulnerable she was.

But all she saw there was genuine concern. "Are you okay?" he asked.

His voice twined with the sounds of the *Mandolin*, the restlessness of the sea, seeming to be part of them, making it seem to her that the boat and the sea were alive, too, and that he was part of them. Something similar to what she had felt with the storm.

She blinked and dragged her gaze from him without answering, trying to grasp reality again, trying to escape the strangeness of what she was feeling.

"Veronica?"

His voice came through clearly, past the breath of the wind that hummed in the sails, past the ceaseless whisper of the waves as they struck the boat. Reluctantly, she turned toward him, wondering if she would once again feel that unwanted connection.

But the world seemed to have returned to normal.

"Are you okay?" he asked.

"Fine. I'm fine. I just lost my balance." In more ways than one. She wondered why her mind was playing tricks on her, making her feel as if she were tapping into something larger than simple reality. Making her feel as if she were tapping into some power larger than she could imagine.

Maybe her father was right. Maybe this was some kind of obsession. She wondered if her mother had felt this, too, this sense of connection with something beyond. If the search for the mask had been fueled by that as much as an archeologist's desire to find a unique artifact.

Or was this quest tapping into something in her blood, something that had made her ancestress a high priestess. Was she experiencing some sort of genetic memory?

But how did Dugan fit into that, she wondered. Why her awareness of him so suddenly, and why had it felt so much like her awareness of the power in the storm?

But no matter how many questions she asked, there were no answers. The sun must be getting to her, she decided. It kept dazzling her eyes when it bounced off the waves, and maybe it had caused some kind of seizure. She'd read somewhere a long time ago that anyone could have a seizure induced by the proper frequency of strobing from a light source. Anyone. Maybe that's all this had been.

She had to believe it. Anything else was unacceptable.

Dugan said something, but she wasn't looking at him. When she did, he repeated himself.

"You'd better go below for a while," he said. "The sun must be getting to you."

She nodded and did as he said, glad to escape him. Glad to escape the feeling that the sea and the wind were trying to tell her something. Glad to leave her madness behind.

But a little while later he followed her. She was sitting in the galley on the bench, staring at her computer, pretending to review the squiggles that represented information from the magnetometer. She might as well have been blind.

He sat on the bench perpendicular to hers, and reluctantly she looked at him.

"Tam's at the wheel," he said. "We should be there in an hour."

"Okay."

"What happened up there?"

"What do you mean?" She didn't want to admit anything.

"You looked terrified for a couple of minutes there. Dazed."

She wanted to tell him he must have imagined it, but she couldn't bring herself to lie. "I don't know. Some kind of weird déjà vu."

"That's always fun." He smiled, then surprised her by reaching out to cover her hand with his. She knew she should yank away from his touch, because it felt too good and she couldn't afford that, but she didn't. "Sailors hallucinate sometimes, you know."

"Really?"

"Yup. I guess the mind gets bored with the endless sameness of the waves and sky after a while, and starts supplying interesting images. It doesn't usually happen if you're really busy and there are a lot of other people around, but it can. Just staring out there for a long period of time seems to make the brain misfire."

She appreciated his attempt to soothe her, but she didn't

know how to tell him so. She didn't want to admit that she'd been hallucinating feelings, not images. That seemed worse somehow.

"I was on a long trip once, and during the heat of the day, I swear I saw a guy on a green surfboard skimming over the waves and giggling hysterically. Couldn't have been real. Nobody can do that with a surfboard, and besides, he wouldn't have been doing it fifty miles from the nearest land. But I saw it as clearly as I'm seeing you right now."

A reluctant smile began to lift the corners of her mouth. "A green surfboard?"

"Green as new grass. It was wild."

"I can imagine." Her smile deepened at the image, then faded as she recalled what she had experienced. "I didn't see anything. I just . . . felt it. Like I did in the storm. It was some kind of connection."

"To what?"

"The water, the wind, the boat." She didn't mention the connection she had felt to him. "As if it was all alive."

"I feel that all the time. It's Gaia."

She somehow didn't think they had felt the same thing. Because what she had felt had been powerful. It had been *other.*

Apparently he sensed her disagreement, because he squeezed her hand, and said, "Maybe I don't feel it exactly the way you did."

"I don't know."

He said something she couldn't make out, then added, "Maybe you've got something in your blood."

It so closely paralleled the thought that had crossed her mind that she felt a shiver of surprise. "What do you mean?"

"Well, you're descended from that priestess, right? Take

me. I'm one-eighth Native American. My granddad was a half-blood Cherokee. Anyway, he told me a lot of stuff when I was little about how the whole world was alive. As if the whole Earth, the planet, the atmosphere, the oceans—as if all of that is part of a living being. The ancient Greeks called it Gaia. My granddad called it something else, but I can't remember the word he used. Anyway, I don't worry about it when I feel it, because I was lucky enough to grow up with a man who considered that to be real. It's different for you, I guess."

It was very different for her. She'd been raised by a man who respected science, and there wasn't any room in her life for the kind of mysticism he was talking about.

Not that there was anything wrong with it—for other people. But not for her. She couldn't afford to let that kind of thinking cloud her mind.

But hadn't she already done that to some extent? Just last night her father had made her aware that she had neglected to ask some very important questions, questions that would have occurred to her on any other exploration.

But feeling as if she were somehow connected to the power of the storm, or the wind, or the sea—she didn't want to allow herself to feel that. And she wasn't comfortable with blaming what she had felt on some kind of genetic memory. In fact, the whole idea of genetic memory left her cold.

"Look," said Dugan, snagging her attention and making her look at him, "why is it so impossible to think there's something in the genes that predisposes some of us to feel these things? It's not so crazy, Veronica. Something has to set a shaman apart."

"Maybe." But the word came reluctantly. She'd lost too many of her moorings in the past year to be willing to cut loose from any more. She needed to believe the world was objective, quantifiable, inanimate. She didn't want to be listening for voices on the breeze or in the storm. She didn't want to let go of hard-edged reality.

"I need a nap," she announced suddenly. "I need some quiet time."

Dugan didn't say a word as she pulled her hearing aids out and stuffed them in the waterproof pouch that was never far away. Then, without another word, she got up and went back to her cabin.

It was safe in there, she found herself thinking, like a small child scared of the dark. She couldn't hear the wind in the rigging or the whisper of the waves. And the creak of the boat as it skimmed the waves was inaudible to her.

It was silent. And she was beginning to believe that in silence lay safety.

Chapter 12

Luis had come back to Key West because nothing had happened. That sounded ridiculous, but the simple truth was, even with all he had read about these explorations for sunken ships, he found it hard to believe that Veronica Coleridge had found nothing at all after two months. Tam had told him all about her preparation and planning, the way she had even had an oceanographer determine which area she should look in.

It impressed Luis enough that he was actually troubled that so far nothing had been found. He knew it was possible that the assumptions on which the oceanographer's calculations had been based might be wrong. Perhaps the *Alcantara* hadn't gone down between the Marquesas and Key West. It was entirely possible that it had gone down in the reef to the south of the Keys, where most of the treasure ships had sunk. Apparently that was the official view of the archives in Spain. Tam had told him that, too. But Veronica had made a different determination based on some ancient letter from the lone survivor.

All of this Luis had passed on to both Emilio Zaragosa

and *El Desconocido.* He saw no reason not to share equally with them at the present time.

But uneasiness brought him back to Key West. Because it was entirely possible that Tam was lying to him. Only with his own eyes would he be able to be certain that nothing had yet been found.

So he was back in the hot, humid streets, thinking longingly of the mountains of his native Venezuela, where it was cooler and dryer. He had, of course, through miscommunication, managed to arrive the very day the *Mandolin* put out for sea again. Which meant he would now have to cool his heels for four or five days before he could have a face-to-face conversation with Tam.

Sometimes Luis felt cursed.

He felt even more cursed that evening when he called to tell Emilio that he had just missed Tam, so wouldn't have any word to pass along for at least the next four days.

"That is all right," Emilio said. "I have a feeling."

"A feeling?" *Por Dios,* he hated Emilio's prescience. His stomach sank sharply, and he felt another attack of heartburn coming on. "What feeling, *señor*?"

"I have the feeling that they are about to find something of importance. So I will be there next week, Luis."

No. *No! Madre de Dios,* wasn't his life difficult enough without Emilio on the spot, breathing down his neck? He cast about wildly, trying to find some reason to prevent Emilio from coming. "Why hurry?" he finally asked. "You can fly up here in a few hours if they find something."

"Ah, so true, my faithful Luis. Except that I don't want to fly up there. I can hardly supervise affairs from land. No, I will be sailing up on the *Conchita.* I need to be in place when they discover the *Alcantara.*"

He was cursed indeed, Luis thought bitterly when he

hung up the phone. Damn Emilio and his uncanny knack for sensing things. Because he didn't for a moment believe Emilio felt it necessary to be present personally to oversee what Veronica Coleridge did. Not unless Emilio, for some reason, no longer perfectly trusted Luis.

Beginning to feel as if eyes were boring into his head, watching his every movement, Luis slunk out to a bar. He thought about phoning *El Desconocido* with the lack of news, then decided against it. The Unknown One was simply going to have to wait a long time for an update, at least until Luis had figured out how to communicate without giving himself away to Emilio.

He didn't believe that Emilio had proof of Luis's infidelity. No. That was impossible. But Emilio sensed it. Which was why he had so steadfastly been trying to avoid Emilio these last two months. And perhaps that was what had tipped off Emilio?

Luis slapped his forehead in anger as he entered the bar, then gave thanks for the cool waves of air-conditioning that washed over him. Maybe he should simply stay in his hotel room for the next four days. Order room service—Emilio could afford it—and just hole up until he sorted his way through the awful tangle his life was becoming.

Instead he ordered a Tecate and considered drowning his sorrows.

What was he to do? He supposed he could drop all contact with *El Desconocido,* get rid of the pager, and hide his tracks. At least then Emilio would never find out. But the problem was—and he wasn't stupid enough to underestimate the possibility—*El Desconocido* might have figured out who Luis was.

Careful as he'd been to leave no trail, he'd been working for Emilio long enough to know how difficult it was *not* to leave a trail. There was always something, like a loose thread on a shirt, that could be found if someone looked carefully enough.

He had canceled his credit card two months ago, claiming it had been stolen, but only after he had paid for six months use of the pager in cash. That little attempt to hide his connection to the pager had seemed wise at the time. It had even seemed brilliant. Now he wasn't so sure.

Maybe, and this was a distinct possibility, there was no way to hide his duplicity from Emilio indefinitely. Maybe he just needed to resign himself to the fact that sooner or later Emilio was going to find out. What he needed to be doing, instead of covering his tracks, was preparing his escape plan, to be ready to disappear on a moment's notice.

The trouble was, he couldn't think of a way to do that. Not if Emilio was going to be aboard the *Conchita*. Because if Emilio was aboard the boat, he was going to insist that Luis be there as well, no matter how seasick Luis became. After all, if Emilio didn't care that the humidity and humus smell of the hothouse made Luis sick, he was unlikely to be more sympathetic about seasickness. And how was Luis supposed to escape a boat on a moment's notice?

His life was cursed. There was no doubt about it.

They were dragging the magnetometer again, extending their search to the southwest, moving into the area which Drew Hunnecutt had designated as the next likeliest location of the wreck. Dugan was unable to believe that any man, even an oceanographer, could have realistically figured out the conditions during a hurricane three hundred years ago, at least not well enough to know where a galleon had sunk. But he supposed Drew's suggestions at least gave them an excuse to narrow the search to a reasonable area.

They were motoring along at a lazy pace, bobbing gently on soft swells. Tam had finished his book, pulled yet another out of his duffel, and retreated to the stern bench to read through his mirrored sunglasses. His skin was nut brown now, and his hair and moustache were bleached almost white. Dugan, who stayed mostly in the shadier cockpit, had darkened, too, from the light reflecting off the water. Even Veronica, who slathered sunscreen all over herself and stayed below most of the time, using her computer, had picked up a healthy glow.

And Dugan was bored out of his gourd. He liked sailing, but not this much. Maybe it was time to put the boat on autopilot and do some fishing. Maybe then he'd at least feel as if he was accomplishing *something*.

Less than a month left, he reminded himself. Just a little over three weeks. Then she could find someone else to drive a boat for her.

Just then the motor kicked out. It died. A sputter, and it was gone. Dugan tried restarting it, but the starter ground uselessly.

"Oh fucking great," he muttered under his breath. The fuel gauge said they still had plenty of gas.

"What happened?" Tam called from the stern.

"Engine died."

"I'll take a look." He jumped off the bench and opened the stern hatch, then slid down into the hold.

Dugan considered running up some sail and continuing that way, but then decided not to. He was more concerned about the engine problem. It was probably some minor thing, but he could think of a few major things that he wouldn't want to wait to discover.

They were drifting east, slowly but surely. He shrugged it off—what were they going to run into?—and locked the wheel. The boat was rolling more since they were without power, but it wasn't anything to worry about.

He turned to go help Tam just as Veronica's head popped up through the hatch.

"What's wrong?" she asked.

He paused to look down at her. "Engine died."

"What?"

"The engine died."

"Oh. Can you fix it?"

"I don't know yet."

"We're not stuck, are we? I mean, we have the sails."

"No, we're not stuck."

"Then put up the sails and let's keep searching."

He stifled a sigh and squatted down so he was closer to her face. "I need to make sure there's nothing serious wrong with the engine first."

"Serious?"

"Something that could endanger us."

"Oh."

Tam called from behind him. "Dugan?"

"Yeah?"

"We got a broken gas line."

He straightened and turned to look back at Tam. "Did much spill?"

"Nah, the shutoff worked. I'm going to try to jury-rig it."

"Okay." He looked back at Veronica. "Broken gas line. Tam's going to try to fix it."

"How long will that take?"

All of a sudden, Dugan was angry. For weeks now this woman had been pushing him on this search as if he were nothing but a mule to be goaded, and he was getting mightily tired of it. Christ, she hardly even talked to anyone anymore.

He squatted and faced her. "Do you give a damn about anything except finding that damn mask?"

She blinked, and her head pulled back a little. "Of course I do."

"Then act like it for the next five minutes. Or maybe the next hour or two, because I'm getting tired of crisscrossing the same piece of empty ocean all day every day looking for something that probably doesn't even exist."

"It *does* exist!"

"You have only one conquistador's word for that. How do you know he didn't make up the tale to cover the fact that he kept the damn mask and melted it down so he could live a life of luxury?"

She gave a little gasp, then disappeared swiftly down the ladder. Good riddance, he thought, and went to help Tam. Only he really didn't mean it. That woman just got under his skin faster than chiggers on a hot summer afternoon. And he didn't want to think about why that was.

It took them only ten minutes to repair the gas-line leak. Tam returned to his reading, and Dugan went below to tell Veronica they were ready to get started again. He found her glued to her computer screen, a frown knitting her brow.

"Veronica?"

Several seconds passed before she looked up at him, her gaze almost vague.

"We fixed the problem. We're ready to start again. I'll take us back to where we left off."

"No!"

"No?"

"No." She shook her head, her face tight. "There's something . . . I'm getting an anomaly. Can you take us a little further in the direction we've been drifting?"

In spite of himself, he felt his pulse leap. "Yeah. Sure. What is it?"

"I don't know," she said impatiently. "But something's disturbing the magnetic field not too far from here."

He climbed back up into the cockpit and turned the engine over. It responded immediately, telling him all was well. Then, slowly, he began to take them in the easterly direction they'd been drifting.

After about five minutes, she called up to him. "Stop. It's starting to taper off."

He obeyed, calling to Tam to get ready to put out the anchor. Tam jumped up quickly, glad of the change of pace apparently. Then Dugan took them back to a point about midway between where Veronica had first noticed the anomaly and where she said it had started to taper off.

"Lower the anchor, Tam."

Veronica came surging up the ladder, her face as excited and happy as Dugan had ever seen it. "It might be a cannon," she said. "It's a big enough anomaly."

Then she threw her arms around Dugan and hugged him. The gesture surprised him, but it felt good, too, so he hugged her back, finally lifting her right off her feet. She laughed, and he found himself thinking that she ought to laugh more often.

Such a serious little puss. The thought, coming out of nowhere, disturbed him, and he quickly set her down again.

"We'll go down now," he said, when he had her attention.

"Yes. Yes, please!"

Tam came up behind him. "About damn time," he muttered. "Action at last."

"What did he say?" Veronica asked.

"You don't want to know."

A shadow passed over her face, then she laughed. "Okay, I don't want to know."

He and Tam climbed into their wet suits and gathered up their gear.

"It's probably a spittoon from the late nineteenth century," Tam grumbled as he pulled his flippers on, then reached for his air tank. "How much you wanna bet? Or some old iron bathtub somebody dumped out here."

"Can you be any more positive?"

"I don't think so."

At least Veronica couldn't understand him. She was standing at the side of the boat, looking down into the water as if she hoped her gaze could penetrate the thirty feet below them and see what the magnetometer had detected. He didn't think it would, because they'd have seen it from the plane, if that was possible.

He checked his regulator and waited until Tam checked his. Then he lowered the dive platform at the stern and picked up his metal detector.

"Okay," he said to Tam. "You take starboard, I'll take port. Let's do a longitudinal sweep, starting right under the boat, for about a hundred yards fore and aft, then move out another ten yards and repeat. If we don't find anything, we'll put out some buoys and guide ropes and do it the intelligent way."

Tam laughed. Veronica looked perplexed, as if she hadn't understood most of what he said. But that was okay. He'd explain later if she wanted to know. For right now, his pulse was hammering, adrenaline was filling him, and he couldn't *wait* to get down there and see if they could find something.

And to think he'd been wishing he'd never agreed to do this.

He wet his mask, pulled it on, stuck the regulator in his mouth, and stepped into the water. He heard Tam jump in right behind him.

God, he hated to get wet. But he loved to dive. He headed straight for the bottom, where he could see mud and some seaweed beds. No coral, at least not there, which was a good thing. Searching in coral could be an unpleasant experience.

The metal detector was a small instrument, not much bigger than an Uzi, with a pistol grip, a dial on top for him to watch, and a six-inch detector plate on a short rod sticking out of it. He didn't bother sweeping it around because he needed to read the dial, and anyway, it would detect metal within a few feet in all directions.

Visibility was excellent, and he found himself almost wishing there was a reef nearby. It would have been great to enjoy the fish and all the color. Instead, he had crystalline water and a muddy bottom with occasional patches of growth. Oh well.

Ten minutes passed, then fifteen as he swam slowly, keeping his attention on the meter. Nothing, and more nothing. Then he turned around and headed back, feeling a growing sense of impatience. The magnetometer hadn't imagined it. But of course, they didn't know exactly where it was. They were probably going to have to survey the whole area to pinpoint whatever it was she'd found, then he and Tam were going to have to get serious about crisscrossing the area using guidelines so they wouldn't miss anything. Painstaking, but instead of dreading it, he was actually anticipating it.

Because all of a sudden, he thought it might well be

the highlight of his life if he discovered a three-hundred-year-old cannon.

That's when the dial on his meter jumped. Digging his fingers into the mud to hold himself still, he swept the meter around, looking for the point at which it peaked. When it did, he set it down and reached for his diving knife.

Pulling it out of the sheath, he began to dig into the mud. Unfortunately, digging kicked up enough debris that the clarity of the water was lost, and his vision began to be obscured.

But not so obscured that he failed to see the glint of metal. Digging around, he found a coin, partially encrusted, then another, and another. His heart was beating rapidly by then, so rapidly that he was concerned about his air consumption. His pulse was pounding in his ears.

They'd found something.

Veronica remembered other times in her life when seconds and minutes seemed to drag, but she couldn't recall anytime when they had dragged this badly. She counted them off, pacing the deck of the *Mandolin,* while the minutes stretched into a half hour.

Her mind was springboarding between painful hope and the absolute conviction that they couldn't have found the *Alcantara.* Even when she had so bullheadedly set out on this three-month exercise, she hadn't really believed that they would find the ship. The possibility seemed as remote to her as winning the lottery—and she never bought lottery tickets.

But she had bought this lottery ticket despite the huge odds, and had pressed forward as if she were convinced that she was bound to win. Even in her own mind she had realized there was something not entirely rational about her behavior but she had refused to back off. She knew she was acting out of emotion rather than scientific objectivity, but vindicating her mother had become paramount in her life.

Now, as she paced the deck, waiting to discover whether they'd found a cannon or some piece of junk dropped off a boat of much later date, she found herself wondering why she had assumed such an immense burden. What she was doing bordered on the insane. People didn't just get into a boat and look around for several months and discover a specific three-hundred-year-old wreck. It didn't happen. Oh, they might easily find *a* wreck. The waters were littered with them. But a specific wreck? With as little information as she had? Not likely.

But still she hoped. Even if she couldn't find the mask, finding something that would substantiate that she had located the *Alcantara* would be a major achievement. Even if it didn't prove to her father that he had been wrong.

Peering over the side, looking through the polarized lenses of her sunglasses, she tried to see the shapes of the divers below. But she could see nothing except murky hints of the bottom below the boat.

Then there was the question of why she felt she had to prove her father wrong. Why she felt this almost childish need to look at him, and say, "So there." The truth of it was, she was doing exactly what he had feared she might do if she learned about her mother's quest. Not that what she was doing really deserved that level of fear. It wasn't so very different from the things Orin had done in his life.

Unless you believed, as he did, that her mother had been killed because of it.

Veronica couldn't believe it. Her mother had taken a terrible risk that day, setting out alone in a boat to dive the reefs. She should never have done such a thing. And alone on a boat at sea, or diving alone, there were dozens of things that could prove fatal. Veronica had no difficulty believing the coroner's determination that Renata must have been leaning over the side when a wave caught the boat, throwing her out and causing her to hit her head as she fell. The scenario was well within the realm of possibility. And the sorry fact was, people died from such senseless accidents all the time.

Orin's refusal to believe it probably had more to do with his refusal to believe his wife could have been so foolhardy. He probably believed some sinister force was at work.

She looked over the side again, then reminded herself she was probably doing exactly what her mother had been doing. A chill passed down her spine, and impulsively she went to get a life jacket and strap it on. Her mother might still be alive today if she had followed this one simple precaution.

Some puffy popcorn clouds were appearing in the sky, and she tried to amuse herself for a few minutes by imagining what animals the shapes looked like. But that didn't distract her for long. Soon her eyes were glued to the swells again, trying to pick out the shapes of Tam and Dugan from the splintered light.

When she saw the first head, she almost doubted her eyes. Then she was sure it was Dugan, his brown hair darkened by the water. He was only twenty feet from the boat, to the stern. He lifted an arm and waved to her, then disappeared again beneath the waves.

What had that meant? Was he in trouble of some kind? Her heart slammed into high gear, and she made her way to the stern, standing near the diving platform, wondering what she should do. Take out her hearing aids and dive in? But her eardrums were perforated, and she wasn't supposed to get in the water without earplugs. Fool that she was, she hadn't brought any with her because she hadn't expected to need to get into the water.

Just when she thought she was going to fly apart from the tension, Dugan's head popped out of the water again, just a couple of feet from the platform. He pulled out his regulator, then grabbed the ladder and climbed aboard.

"Thank God!" The words burst out of Veronica before she could stop them.

Dugan pushed back his diving mask and looked at her. "Thank God?"

"I didn't know what it meant when you waved. I was afraid you might be in trouble."

"Sorry. I just wanted to see exactly how far from the boat I was. It looked like about twenty feet to me. You?"

She nodded and stepped back, making room for him to climb off the platform onto the deck. "That's about what I thought."

"Get a GPS right now, will you?"

Wondering why, she went to the cockpit and checked the reading on the Global Positioning System. Pulling a small memo pad out of her shorts pocket, she scribbled it down.

Turning, she saw that Dugan was pulling off his fins. He'd already set his air, harness, weight belt, and regulator aside, and his mask was on the bench. The wet suit fit him like a second skin, and she found herself thinking that he had a damn good body for a man who appeared to spend his whole life lazing around at a desk or on the deck of a boat.

"Where's Tam?" she asked, but he was too far away and

she couldn't read his lips. She went back to the stern and found a dry patch of bench to sit on. "Where's Tam?" she asked again.

"Probably still following his search pattern."

"Why'd you stop?"

He perched on the other seat and grinned at her while he toweled his hair dry, but he didn't say anything.

Hope began to grow in her, and with it came unbearable anticipation. "Dugan? Don't tease me."

He shrugged, tossed the towel aside and reached down for his belt. Hanging from it was a large black pouch. He disconnected it from the belt and handed it to her.

"You might want to take that below before you open it."

"Why?"

"Less chance of an accident."

Rising, she hurried forward and down the ladder to the galley. Dugan was right behind her, and he switched on as many lights as he could while she struggled to open the pouch. Her fingers were too eager, making a hash of it, and finally Dugan took it from her.

"Here, let me," he said, his grin growing even wider. He pulled the pouch open, then upended it on the table.

Veronica stopped breathing as she looked at the pile of disks, some of them green or gray with oxidation, some crusted with calciferous deposits. Coins, she thought, her heart slamming.

Then she saw the gold. It glinted still, undamaged by its sojourn at sea. With a trembling hand she reached out and lifted it, turning it so the light would highlight the pattern on it.

"Oh my God," she said, lifting her eyes slowly to Dugan's. "This is a royal. A Spanish eight-*escudo*. My God, do you know how rare these are? One of these would fetch more than a hundred thousand dollars on the open market."

Dugan sat with a thud. "You're kidding. That little thing?"

"That little thing."

They sat staring at it for a few moments. "God," sad Dugan. "It's hard to believe."

She didn't really hear him, because she wasn't looking at him, but she picked up on the sense of what he said. She was more interested in searching for some indication of the coin's age.

But then she flipped it over and gasped. "Sixteen ninety-two," she said, lifting her gaze to his face. "It's old enough."

Dugan's grin split his face. "Maybe you aren't so crazy after all, lady. What about the rest of them?"

She set the gold coin down and touched the others with her fingertip, sorting them. "Copper and silver, it looks like. Valuable, but not as valuable. I'll need to wash them in an acid bath to clean them."

"We can't do that here, can we?"

"I didn't bring the stuff. I didn't want to disturb the site too much."

"You mean you don't want to start digging stuff up?"

She shook her head. "We've got to do this right. That means surveying the whole area around this find before we do any more. Then, when we get ready to start excavating, we'll need to be able to document what we do, mark our finds, handle discoveries appropriately so they don't deteriorate . . ."

His eyebrows lifted. "We're not just on a pillaging expedition for one item then?"

"God, no! This is a major archaeological find. I may

want to get my hands on that mask, but that doesn't mean I'm going to destroy the rest of it looking. We have to do this responsibly."

Something in his face softened a little, and he nodded. "Sounds good to me. But a word of advice?"

"What's that?"

"I'd put that royal someplace very safe. And I wouldn't mention it to Tam."

Her heart skipped. "You don't trust him?"

"I trust him plenty. But that's a hell of a lot of temptation in one tiny little package."

She nodded slowly; she could understand his point. "Where should I hide it?"

"Stuff it in with your panties or your bras." He winked, making her blush. "I don't know. Just find a good place in your cabin. He won't be looking for it if we don't tell him about it, so it'll be safe anywhere."

Taking his advice, she tucked the royal in her breast pocket. "The rest of this stuff is pretty valuable, too. There might be silver *reals* in there . . . they can be worth thousands."

"Maybe it would just be best if we didn't discuss the potential value of these coins."

"Okay. That makes sense."

"The less anyone knows about it, the safer we are."

Her breath caught again, and her gaze drifted down to the pile of tarnished coins. Her father had warned her about this possibility, but she'd dismissed it. After all, she'd been on plenty of digs where no one tried to steal their discoveries.

But the reality of the value of the gold coin in her pocket, and the fact that Dugan evidently felt there might be some risk in this, made the possibility seem a whole lot more real.

"Better yet," said Dugan. "Hide all but a couple of these coins. We'll tell Tam I found one or two copper ones. The less anyone knows about this, the better until we can get a crowd of people working on it with us."

"But why keep it a secret if we're only going to tell a bunch of people anyway?"

His gaze seemed to bore into her. "Safety in numbers. Until you're ready to bring numbers out here, we keep mum. That's it."

Another chill ran down her spine, and she found herself thinking of her mother. "You don't think someone would kill over this?"

He shrugged. "Probably not. But they sure might horn in. Unless you want to see a dozen boats out here getting in your way, the less we say the better. And that includes Tam."

Just then, there was a thud from the deck of the boat.

"Must be Tam," Dugan said. "Put the coins away, except for a couple. I'll go see if he found anything."

Veronica went to do as he'd suggested, leaving only a couple of green-tarnished copper coins on the table. The thought flitted across her mind that Dugan was being paranoid, and that they were hardly going to be able to keep the secret from Tam for long.

Then she wondered why in the world she should trust Dugan any more than Tam.

Just as she was mounting the ladder to the deck, Dugan stuck his head through the hatch.

"Tam thinks he found a cannon."

Chapter 13

"I'm going back with him to check it out."

Veronica forgot all about the coins, forgot about Dugan's paranoia and what might happen if word got out. Excitement filled her and she rushed up the rest of the ladder and onto the deck. Dugan was pulling on his fins again, and his air tank. Tam mounted a fresh tank into his harness, then pulled it on. He grinned at Veronica and said something.

"What?" God, how she hated this.

Dugan turned to her. "He says it won't be long. We're going right to it."

"Okay." She managed a smile for Tam, who winked and gave her an "okay" sign with his thumb and forefinger. And Veronica found herself thinking that there might be some advantage to learning sign language. She'd been avoiding it, wanting to appear as normal as possible, and besides, the counselor who'd worked with her had advised her that learning sign was extremely difficult for adults.

But a beard or moustache wouldn't prevent her from reading sign the way Tam's moustache kept her from reading his lips. On the other hand, Tam didn't know Ameslan anyway. There was no way, she thought with sudden glumness, no way she would ever be able to talk to some people.

But before she could sink too far into self-pity, Dugan and Tam moved to the diving platform and jumped into the water. A cannon. Maybe they'd found a cannon.

Hope suddenly filled her, so strong that she could hardly stand it. She found herself crossing her fingers like a child, and she finally gave in and crossed her arms, too.

The soft swells were growing a little bigger, she noticed, and a glance upward showed her that the little fluffs of popcorn had turned into large, puffy cumulus clouds. Rain? She hoped not. She wanted to stay right there and survey the entire area around them, because in her heart of hearts she was convinced they'd found the *Alcantara.*

Somewhere below them lay the rotting timbers and precious cargo of a ship that had vanished three hundred years ago. A ship that had borne her ancestors.

Possibly, she thought with an unexpected catch in her throat, the bones of the priestess lay beneath her. She might only be thirty feet from her final resting place. It amazed her how strongly that affected her.

But this whole exploration had made her emotional, she realized. It wasn't like any other archaeological expedition she'd ever gone on. This one meant something to her in terms of her own family history.

It was almost as if a circle were closing at last, a circle made up of the female line stretching from an ancient priestess to her, spanning the centuries. And it was, she realized for the first time, so incredibly appropriate that she was using her inheritance to fund this exploration. The fortune, after all, had been passed down through generations of the Bernal and Escobar families until it had come to rest in the hands of their sole descendant, Renata Coleridge. In the hands of her only child, Veronica.

It was as if some cosmic plan were coming to fruition.

Then she cautioned herself not to be so fanciful and mystical about this. For heaven's sake, she didn't even know if they'd actually found the *Alcantara*.

Twenty minutes passed while she watched the cumulus pile higher and the day grow hazier. Finally, she went to check the barometer, but it was still holding steady from this morning. For now there was no problem. Whatever was happening overhead was probably localized.

Finally, when she was just about ready to jump in the water to ease her impatience, Tam and Dugan bobbed to the surface a few feet from the boat. Dugan grabbed the ladder, spat his regulator out of his mouth, pulled his mask back and called to her, "It's a cannon. It's a by-God cannon."

Tam yanked out his own regulator and let out a *wahoo*. The rest of what he crowed was lost on Veronica.

Dugan pulled himself up the ladder to the platform, then stepped onto the deck. Tam wasn't far behind. The two of them shed their gear, then Tam began doing a little jig. Dugan laughed at him, then did a strange thing.

He turned to Veronica and held out his arms.

Heedless of the water still dripping from his wet suit, she practically launched herself at him. He caught her and swung her around in circles, both of them laughing. She knew that moment, that very instant, was going to be etched in crystalline clarity in her memory forever. The clouds above, the aquamarine of the water, the way the sun prickled on her skin. And the way Dugan's arms felt around her.

Tam started clapping his hands, then broke into something that resembled an end zone victory dance. Dugan set her on her feet and gave her a high five. She returned it willingly, feeling a smile that was stretching her face from ear to ear.

"We did it," Dugan told her, catching her hand with his. "We did it. And I gotta tell you, Veronica, I never thought we'd find a thing."

"I was beginning to doubt it myself."

His eyes were dancing. "I guess it's pretty clear now. There *has* to be a ship down there somewhere."

"What did the cannon look like?"

Tam said something.

Dugan turned back to Veronica. "He's going to go back and take some pictures a little later. Right now we've got the mud all stirred up from digging around. Let's go below, and I'll draw you a picture of what we saw, okay?"

She nodded, then waited as he stripped his wet suit. Beneath it he was wearing swim trunks, and at that moment in time, with all the joy she was feeling, she thought he was as beautiful as any Roman god. Then he pulled on an oversize T-shirt and the image was lost.

He stowed his equipment, then signaled her to follow him below. Tam remained behind, still wearing his wet suit, busy switching his regulator to another bottle of air.

The lounge seemed dim after the brightness outside. Dugan pulled back some of the short white curtains to let more light in through the portholes, then grabbed Veronica's legal pad and her gold Cross pencil and sat at the table.

She sat across from him, waiting impatiently while he flipped to a blank sheet of paper and began to sketch.

"I'm not the world's best artist," he said, catching her eye. "But this I think I can do."

She couldn't repress a smile. "Hurry. Just hurry."

He obliged, drawing a long cylindrical object, larger on one end than the other, that was mostly buried in sand. He added a few details, suggesting a wide ridge around the mouth of the cylinder and belling. At the other end, the carabel was unmistakable.

"It's a cannon," she said, her heart leaping.

He nodded and looked at her, making sure she was watching his lips. "No doubt of it."

"What kind of shape is it in?"

"It looks pretty rusty and I didn't want to scrape any of it away to see what was underneath."

"No, oh no! I'm glad you didn't do that. There are special treatments for getting the rust off without damaging the cannon. Besides, not knowing how badly rusted it is . . . well, you could tap on it and watch it disintegrate."

"I don't think so. Not this one. It was buried in more than a foot of sand, so I imagine Tam must have dinged it a few times while digging it out. So what now, boss? Do we raise it? Not that I think we can without some additional equipment. Those old cannons weigh between two and four tons, don't they?"

"No, let it stay. I don't want to disturb anything yet. First we continue our survey of the area, until we have a pretty good map of how the wreck scattered, and where we need to look. Then we'll go over it with metal detectors and see if we pick up anything else."

"And then?"

"I want to check any metallic finds for evidence that this is the *Alcantara*. If it is, I'll set up an excavation."

"You mean hire more people and all that?"

She nodded. "And probably a bigger boat with some serious salvage equipment. Depending on what else we find out here, anyway."

"Okay."

"You look disappointed."

He shrugged, then said, "Maybe I am a little."

"Why?"

"Because . . . well, because today was just so damn much fun." He flashed her a wry smile. "A real adventure. I don't know why, but it won't seem as exciting with a dozen divers and a big boat. Maybe because it'll seem more like a commercial enterprise."

It was the child in him speaking, and she knew it. But the child in her identified with what he was saying. It would have been nice if they could have kept the crew limited to the three of them, and kept their secret. But she didn't see how that was possible, not if she was going to do a serious excavation with an eye to the archaeological value of the site. If she were just treasure hunting, that would be different, but . . .

"You know the state insists this be done right. We can't just go around digging things up and keeping only what we want. We have to consider the archaeological value of the site."

"I know that. But it sure is fun this way."

She almost agreed, but then had to laugh. "Oh, I don't know. We've been bored to death for weeks now."

"That changed radically, didn't it?"

She didn't answer, but pulled his sketch of the cannon closer to her. "You're sure it's iron?"

"Yes."

She looked down at it, studying what he had drawn. "Then it had to have been a cargo ship."

He said something that sounded inquisitive, so she assumed he was asking why.

"Spanish warships carried bronze guns almost exclusively. Anyway, iron guns would fit with what I know about the *Alcantara.* Apparently she had picked up a shipment of goods from Manila that had been delivered 'round the Cape and transferred to her at Veracruz. While there, she also traded ballast for gold bars out of Peru."

"Wouldn't she have been with a fleet, carrying that much gold?"

"That's the interesting part. She wasn't. There were two other cargo ships sailing with her, but the word was all that they carried were textiles and spices. Apparently this shipment of gold was something unusual. And from what Bernal recorded in his letter, it was hush-hush. Nobody knew it was on board until the captain wouldn't let them dump ballast to lighten the *Alcantara* when the seas became rough."

"Geez." He rubbed his chin and considered the image. "Wouldn't you like to know why they made a secret of the gold? Maybe somebody was stealing it."

"I've wondered about that. Considering how it was being shipped, it certainly might have been contraband. But we'll know that if we find any of it."

"How so?"

"Contraband wasn't usually marked with all the stamps of the legitimate bars."

He shook his head slowly. "It must have been such a temptation back then. All that gold being plundered from every corner of the Americas. Why wouldn't a conquistador or an administrator figure he could siphon off a little for himself with nobody the wiser?"

"But then he had to get it back home where it would do some good for him. Imagine how many people he'd have to pay off to get it there. Unless he carried it personally."

His eyes took on a gleam. "I wonder if we'll find out

what your conquistador was carrying apart from a mask, a wife, and a child."

She often wondered the same thing. "We probably won't be able to tell."

"I know, but I'm still going to wonder. It's more fun that way."

Tam took the pictures with the underwater camera. By then it was late afternoon, but they decided to continue with the survey. All of them were high on the excitement of the discovery.

But that evening, after they'd towed the magnetometer probe for another three hours without finding anything, Veronica sat alone in her cabin, thinking about the coins they'd found.

The gold royal was tucked into her toiletries case, wrapped in layers of tissue, under a pile of cotton balls. The rest of the coins, much dirtier with tarnish and deposits, were hidden in a drawer, not far from the bed, under an old pair of coveralls.

The act of hiding them had brought home to her the reality of her father's warnings. She'd been dismissing them as exaggerated, but Dugan's reaction, telling her he didn't even want his friend Tam to see the coins, had cut through her denial.

What she was doing was dangerous indeed. If Dugan thought there was sufficient temptation to be worried about Tam, then maybe she was foolish to dismiss her father's concerns. One woman, two men, and a small boat were hardly safe from the unscrupulous. People sometimes got killed in those waters just because someone wanted their *boat,* never mind millions of dollars in gold. And while it didn't happen often, it still happened.

Her mother's death had probably been accidental. She

still believed that because Renata hadn't found anything, so unless someone wanted to *prevent* her from finding something, there could have been no reason to kill her.

But this was different. She'd been so focused on finding the mask, to complete her mother's quest and to convince her father that her mother hadn't been deluded, that she'd been dismissing the sheer value of the find.

Rising from the bunk, she went to open the drawer where the silver and copper coins were stashed. Some of them were stuck together by the crust that coated them, but some were still individual. On them, even through the tarnish and deposits, she could see some of the patterns underneath. The hint of the royal crest, the suggestions of markings around the edges, probably the name of the king at the time of minting, and the year.

There was a knock on the door, and she hurriedly covered the coins and closed the drawer. "Yes?"

She recognized Dugan's voice, even though she couldn't make out what he was saying. "Come in."

He stepped into the room and closed the door behind him. "I was wondering if you still had your hearing aids in."

She nodded. "I was just thinking about taking them out for the night."

"Give me a few minutes?"

"Sure." She took the bench, and he perched on the bunk.

"What exactly are your priorities here?" he asked.

"What do you mean?"

"Are you here to find the mask, or to do a complete excavation?"

The questions surprised her. "Why do you ask?" She thought she'd made that clear earlier today.

"Well, when we talked at the outset of this venture, you

said you wanted to find a wreck. That was tough enough. Then you said you wanted to find this mask. You might as well search for a needle in a haystack, and I kind of thought the whole thing was insane."

"Maybe it is."

"Come on, you know it is. We've found a wreck, but you could spend years salvaging and never run across that mask."

"I know that. What's your point, Dugan?"

"Just that I'm wondering what your plans are. Up until this afternoon, I figured you'd found your wreck, we'd go stumbling around for a while trying to find the mask, then you'd pack up and go home. Now you're talking about doing a major archaeological excavation."

"What difference does it make? If I found a vessel, I was naturally going to excavate. I don't see where the problem is."

He blew air between his lips and looked down at his hands. She waited, telling herself that whatever he was hedging around didn't matter, but she felt her stomach sinking anyway. She didn't want to have to continue the venture without Dugan.

The thought opened another door inside her, one that gave her a jolt as she realized how dependent she had become on him. She read his lips easily, often more easily than she read her father's. There was something about the way he enunciated that made conversing with him easy. With other people, it was not so easy. In fact, it could be overwhelming. And all she had to do was miss a key word to be totally lost.

Dugan had become her buffer. She could talk to him, and he would make it all happen. It was the same with her father. She talked to him, and he made arrangements for her. If she lost either one of them, she was going to be alone in a hearing world that she couldn't fully understand, amidst people who might not care that she couldn't hear.

Disappointment started edging on panic. These past weeks Dugan had, all unintentionally, wrapped her in a safe cocoon where her disability was all but insignificant. She had even gotten used to not being able to understand Tam, and he had gotten used to not being understood. He either used gestures, or Dugan told her what she needed to know.

And if she lost Dugan, all of that was going to go away. She was going to have to hire another boat, one that might be captained by a man who wouldn't care about her disability, who might only get annoyed if she didn't understand him—or who, worse yet, might use her hearing problem against her.

She would have to deal with divers and crew members and God knew what else, with no one to buffer her against all the misunderstandings. With no one to be her trustworthy ears, the way Dugan had the past months.

She shouldn't have allowed herself to become so dependent, but she had. And worse yet, she knew she always would, because she had become terrified of the world. She no longer felt confident of herself in dealing with other people, even friends. Most of her friends had drifted away anyway, reluctant to deal with her disability, and those few that hadn't utterly vanished hardly came around anymore.

Some of that was surely her fault. But not all of it. She had good reason to be scared of the world. Most of the world had become opaque to her.

Dugan looked up. "I have a business to run," he said slowly. "I don't see what part I would have in all of this."

Her heart plummeted. "Are you sure you can't continue?" She didn't know how she was going to get along without him, and some childish part of her wanted to tell him so. But she didn't want him to stay because he felt obligated by her deafness. That would be the only thing that could be worse than being on her own in a hearing world. She'd feel so awful about that, so guilty, that she didn't think she could live with herself.

"I don't know," he said finally. "Funny, isn't it, how things change."

"What's changed?"

"My involvement in all of this." He gave her a sad, wry smile. "It wasn't what I had in mind when I agreed to contract with you for three months."

"No? What did you have in mind?" Should she tell him how wonderful it was for her to be able to converse with him this way, almost as well as she would have been able to before her accident? No. That would obligate him.

"I don't know. Three months of sun and sea looking for a needle in a haystack. I didn't really want to do it."

"Then why did you?"

"Because I didn't want you to fall in with someone less scrupulous who might take advantage of you."

"So what's changed?"

"That I have a business to run. I can't let my business manager fill in for me indefinitely."

She felt her throat tighten. "Do what you have to."

"That's usually the way, isn't it? But it's not what I *want* to do."

Her heart skipped a beat. "What?"

"It's not what I want to do. Today . . . well, today reminded me just how fun and exciting life can be. But you need a bigger boat."

"And you need to run your business."

He nodded.

"But we still need to finish the survey."

"I can do that." He sighed and rubbed his chin. "Hell, maybe I can make . . ." His words trailed off, vanishing in the veil of her disability.

"What? I'm sorry. You said . . . ?"

"Ginny. My business manager. Well, she's really just an office manager. I guess she could run things for a while. If I raise her salary."

"Would that make her happy?"

"Ginny would do it for nothing if I asked her to. I'm the one who has to be comfortable with this. I don't want to take advantage of her."

Veronica couldn't argue with that.

"But I'll need to spend a little more time on shore. I'm having trouble keeping up with the stuff she *can't* handle while we're away. We'll need to take two days between outings."

Veronica was only too willing to do that, if it would keep him from abandoning her. "We can do that," she said.

"You won't get too impatient?"

"No. I promise. I . . . like working with you. You understand me." In more ways than one, she found herself thinking. Dugan had been like a balm to her soul these past weeks. Even though they'd been a little distant, he'd still been there whenever she needed him. And he seemed to understand her frustration and anger with her current situation, enough so that he didn't become impatient with her on the occasions when she couldn't understand him. He seemed to know that it had to be worse for her than for him.

"Okay, then. I'd like to continue." He suddenly flashed a wide smile. "Hell, I want to be here when they start bringing stuff up. It'll be like reaching three hundred years back into history."

"There've been some really exciting finds," she told him, wanting to keep his enthusiasm up. "On one wreck they even found a book that was still readable after three centuries. In fact, wrecks are actually better than land sites for making discoveries."

"How come?"

"Because they're a perfect capsule of a single point in time. And everything on them was usable and valuable. A lot of what an archaeologist does on land is dig through people's garbage pits and try to ascertain time periods from how deep the find is. This is different. Instead of finding only discards, things that are broken and unwanted, we find all kinds of things that are still in good condition, things that would never have been thrown away whole. It's a wonderful opportunity."

"But still a very limited time period."

"Well, yes, around here at any rate. The Mediterranean is a different matter. There you can find wrecks going back thousands of years, with all the same advantages. Those ships carried things that were considered valuable in their time, but more than that, they carry the daily implements and tools of life. It's like getting a huge snapshot of an instant in time that tells you nearly everything about how people lived and worked, and what they valued."

He was smiling, she saw, and afraid that he was laughing at her, she fell silent.

"Don't stop," he said. "You have a lot of passion for your work, don't you?"

"I guess so."

"It's a good thing."

She felt herself flushing with pleasure. Impulsively, she

turned and opened the drawer containing the coins and took some of them out. She passed a couple to him, and kept one for herself.

"I've been looking at these, thinking about the fact that my ancestors could have handled these very coins." She rubbed the one she held gently between her fingers. "It gives me chills."

He nodded and held up one of the coins, studying it. "It makes you wonder, doesn't it? When I was looking at that cannon down there today, I found myself wondering where it had been. How many ports, how many stormy seas before it wound up buried here. Then I got to thinking about the people who sailed these ships and had to rely on cannons for safe passage against pirates. It must have been one hell of a wild time."

He laughed. "Well, hell, I'm a wild guy myself. I've been getting too stodgy running the business. I've forgotten that I always wanted adventure."

"Did you?"

He pressed the coins back to her. "I sure did."

"Then how did you come to have a business?"

"Life takes some crazy turns sometimes. It sure wasn't my plan when I came to Key West."

"What was?"

"I was going to be a drunken beach bum."

The words startled a laugh out of her. "I thought you were kidding when you said that."

"Nope." He shook his head, a twinkle dancing in his dark eyes. "Keep in mind that I was only twenty-six."

"Ahh. That explains a lot. But what happened to make you feel that way?"

He looked almost embarrassed. "Well, I had a helluva bad day."

"Just one?"

"One was enough for a lifetime."

"What happened?"

She heard his sigh, which was long and heavy. For a minute he looked down, hiding his mouth from her. But then, as if he remembered her hearing problem, he raised his head. "I lost my wife and my job in the space of two hours."

"That's awful!"

He shrugged, as if to say it wasn't the biggest deal in his life anymore, but Veronica somehow doubted it. Measuring it against her own loss, and how she could still barely think about it, she suspected he was far more wounded than he was willing to admit, even to himself. "How did it happen?" She imagined a terrible accident.

"I got fired from my job because of a little scruple. Well, okay, it was a big scruple. Remember that scruples are bad things."

She wasn't sure she had followed him correctly, then understanding dawned. "They *can* get in the way."

"And how. I vowed never to have any again, but . . . well, you know how that goes. Somehow they just keep cropping up."

"What was your scruple?"

"I was running a mutual fund for a lot of small investors. You know, silly things like the entire savings of some little old lady in Des Moines. Chicken feed in the world of high finance, but that's what mutuals are for. Anyway, my boss was really high on one particular electronics stock and kept pressuring me to put a significant amount of my fund into it, talking about its great growth potential. On paper it looked okay, but maybe a little mediocre. I was bothered mainly because the company wasn't that old. You get just a little cautious when you're handling the little old lady's money."

"I can imagine. I know I would."

"Yeah." His mouth twisted. "So I kept hesitating, and the pressure kept getting stronger, and finally it dawned on stupid me that there had to be a *reason* my boss was so insistent. That's when I discovered he owned a significant chunk of the company. If I'd bought as many shares as he wanted me to, the price would have gone up and he could have sold at a pretty good profit. Alternatively, he could have bailed himself out of the arrangement by selling all his shares to my fund. Either way it stank, and I flat-out refused."

"Good for you."

His smile was wry. "Yeah. But to make matters worse, I accused him of being unethical. He, of course, painted it in a different light, telling me that he was only recommending a stock he believed in. As proof of that, he waved his shares in my face, telling me he wouldn't have bought the stock if he didn't think it was a damn good investment."

Veronica didn't know what to say to that.

"So I was a little hot. And I was in trouble. And I got fired. You gotta play by the rules. Never mind that the company in question folded three weeks later. When I heard about it, I thought of making a big stink, maybe suing the firm, then I decided it was too damn much trouble and a waste of time. Especially since I made enough of a stink when I got fired that the boss stopped pushing the stock, so none of my little old ladies got burned,"

"Thank goodness for that." Veronica was feeling a surprising sense of indignation. It had been so long since she'd felt anything on behalf of anyone but herself that the feeling seemed almost alien. Then she welcomed it. It was a sign that her life hadn't been completely blighted.

"Anyway," he said slowly, "I guess I may as well finish the sordid tale. I went home, told my wife what had happened, she called me seven kinds of fool—or maybe more. I didn't keep count. Suffice it to say, there was enough invective flowing to fill an Olympic pool. She got nasty. I started to get nasty. I mean . . . stupid as it sounds, I felt betrayed. Felt like the money I was making was more important to her than I was."

Impulsively, Veronica reached out to take his hand and squeeze it. He squeezed back. "I'm sorry," she said.

"Hell, I got off lucky. What if I hadn't found that out until after we had kids? I wouldn't have been able to drop out and become a beach bum."

"Did you? Did you really?"

"Yeah, I did." He gave a short laugh. "Juvenile angst, that's what it was. I let her keep everything except my car—a Mercedes, so I wasn't completely stupid. I packed up, drove down here, sold the car, and proceeded to get drunk for a week."

Veronica felt something inside her curdle a bit. She tried to withdraw her hand, but he wouldn't let her.

"That hangover nearly killed me," he said. "I don't drink a whole lot anymore. Anyway, I had all these grand ideas of just hanging around, working only when I had to, and wasting my life away on the beach or on a small boat. Just totally blowing it all off. But . . . I kinda got bored."

She felt herself relaxing again, and a reluctant smile lifted the corners of her mouth. "You did, did you."

"I sure did. Somehow I fell in with Tam, he was having trouble with his diving business—"

"What kind of trouble?"

"Uh . . ." He hesitated, then gave her an amused look. "Laziness trouble. Tam has a tendency to work in spurts and he likes easy money. Running a business full-time required a little too much. So I started helping out, and finally just bought the business."

"Which ended your beach-bum days."

"Aw, it was a lousy idea anyway. I hate to get wet."

Veronica stared at him, then started laughing helplessly.

"Hey, what's so funny?"

"You hate to get wet. You're kidding, right?"

"No, I'm not kidding. I think I'm a reincarnated cat. I'll do it if I have to, but I absolutely hate getting wet."

"But you run a diving business."

"There is that little problem."

"And you have a boat."

"Who says I have to make sense? Besides, on the boat I don't get all that wet."

"Except when you dive."

"Can't be avoided then. I happen to like to dive."

She laughed again. She couldn't help it and hoped she wasn't offending him, but the whole idea was so funny. He hated to get wet, yet here he was surrounded by water and diving off the back end of this boat whenever necessary . . . although, come to think of it, she'd never seen him jump over the side for a swim in the evening the way Tam did. He preferred to take a quick shower on board.

"I don't get it," she said breathlessly. Her sides were beginning to ache from laughing. "Dugan . . . you've built your whole life around water."

"I know. I guess it's my karma."

She went off into another peal of laughter, and he grinned with her. In the past year, she had forgotten how good it felt to laugh, and it felt so good she didn't want to stop. But after just a few moments, it began to sound a little hysterical, even to her. She was laughing too hard and too long.

Dugan tugged her hand, pulling her out of her chair until she perched beside him on the bunk. The action had the effect of stilling her laughter, and she looked at him resentfully, as if he were the one who had put her on the edge of such a mix of wild feeling. And she could feel tears hovering just behind her eyes, tears that had no reason. What was wrong with her?

"It's good to hear you laugh," he said, his tone surprisingly gentle. "You should do it more often. But not like this, Veronica. Not like this. . . ."

What did he mean? Had he picked up on her near hysteria? But before she could gather herself enough to say anything at all, he took her by surprise.

He kissed her.

Chapter 14

He had meant it to be a gentle kiss. Just a reassuring, affectionate touch. When he'd heard the hysteria edge into her laughter, he'd recognized what lay behind it: all the feelings she hadn't dealt with in the past year. Ever since she'd told him how she'd lost her husband and her unborn child, his every survival instinct had been warning him to keep clear. It would be entirely too easy to get tangled up with this wounded, lonely woman.

He knew his own weaknesses. He had a fondness for sensual pleasures—oh, hell, he *liked* sex, and since Jana he preferred to keep sex and his heart utterly separated. Hence, he rarely allowed himself to acknowledge a sexual attraction unless he was sure the rest of him would be safe from involvement. He'd been putting a big mental off-limits sign on Veronica almost since the moment he met her. And everything she'd done to irritate him had, perversely, pleased him, because it raised barriers between them.

But then she'd told him about her husband and child,

and his defenses had started crumbling faster than he could patch them. Instead, he had retreated behind distance.

Until then. Something deep inside him ached, and he could no longer deny that he was concerned about this woman. Concerned and attracted. A deadly combination.

So he meant it to be brief. He told himself it was something like getting wet. He needed to comfort her somehow, but he didn't want to get past that. Ever.

Except that when their lips met, he might as well have put a match to kerosene. Without intending to, he'd crossed the barrier and landed on the other side, and all it had taken was the velvety feel of her lips and the gentle whisper of her ragged breaths.

He felt the tension in her, the reluctance to accept his touch. It was a good excuse to pull back. But the part of him that had never been able to resist a challenge wouldn't let him do it. He went from wanting to comfort her to wanting her to kiss him back.

He lifted a hand and ran it from her bare shoulder down her arm. It was a light touch, hardly more than the whisper of a butterfly's wing, but it had an amazing effect on her.

She shivered. She whispered, "No . . ." And then her mouth pressed closer to his and she twisted toward him as if she couldn't help herself. He got what he wanted. She kissed him back.

As their mouths came hungrily together, as their tongues met, his mind filled with all the questions he'd been steadfastly refusing to consider for the last two months. How smooth was her skin? What did she taste like? How did she quiver and move when touched? Were her breasts soft or firm, would they respond quickly or slowly. . . .

And now he not only wondered, he craved the answers.

Once again he passed his hand down her arm, barely enough to brush the fine, almost invisible, golden hairs that dusted them. Once again he felt a shiver pass through her, and some part of him realized this woman was as hungry for his touches as he was for hers.

Then her arms wrapped around his head and his around her waist, and they fell back on the bunk, drinking from each other as if they were long-sought oases in the desert.

Her musky woman-scent began to fill the air around him, and an ache in his groin answered. He pressed his hand against her bottom, dragging her closer until he could feel the firmness of her belly against his hardness. Too fast, too hot. A warning bell clanged somewhere in the dim recesses of his mind, telling him he was being overwhelmed by something unique, and by something that was going to shame him later.

He was past caring. Having Veronica in his arms was like hearing a siren's call. She was irresistible.

He dragged his mouth from hers at last, gasping for air. Before he could regain his senses, her hips rocked against him almost demandingly, begging for his touches. She was panting, her eyes closed, her lips swollen, her entire body pressing against him.

He rolled over on top of her, capturing her beneath his weight, and pleasure exploded in his mind when her legs opened to bring him closer. Her hands reached for his shoulders, tugging him closer, and he was lost.

He spread kisses on her skin, finding it every bit as soft as he had hoped. A pulse pounded wildly in her throat, and he kissed it, drawing a faint moan from her. His hands, as if they had a life of their own, slipped up beneath her tank top and cupped her breasts. Her bra was thin, little barrier to his touches, and he felt, at last, just how soft and full she really was. Felt her nipples pucker eagerly in response to the brush of his fingers through the tricot.

Her hips arched up against him, and the sensation jolted him with pleasure, causing him to press harder into her, negating the layers of clothing between them. With each motion of his hips, she rose to meet him.

He was swamped in desire, heat pounding in his veins, driving the last sensible thoughts from his head.

With a twist, he opened the front of her bra and drew her nipple into his mouth, sucking in rhythm with the movement of her hips. A soft, keening cry escaped her, and her movements became almost frantic, her hands digging into his shoulders. His response was explosive. Her passion was infectious, pushing him to the very top in moments.

Then he felt her stiffen and rise up hard against him, finding her satisfaction. With one more hard movement, he took his own, spilling over the crest of the wave, and crashing on the other side.

It was not the crash that hurt. His brain reawakened, and it was not happy with him. He might be a quasi beach bum, but he prided himself on the idea that the years had given him at least a little maturity. Instead he'd just acted like a sixteen-year-old in the backseat of Daddy's car. Christ.

He had a wild, juvenile urge to erase the last ten minutes from memory. A case of amnesia would do fine just about now. But only if he could give a case to Veronica as well.

He pried open an eye and looked down at her. Her lips were swollen, her chest was heaving . . . although he refused to look too closely. With a sudden feeling of tenderness, he pulled her tank top down, covering her. Then he rolled off of her and, since amnesia wasn't going to cooperate, he drew her into his arms.

He wasn't the world's best lover—Jana had certainly made him aware of that—but he'd also figured out a long time ago that the worst sin a man could commit was to fall asleep, leave, or light a cigarette right after. Hold her. That's all you had to do. Just hold her.

But in this situation, he was glad there wasn't a weapon nearby, because he had a feeling that as soon as she came down off her high, Veronica was going to want to cut out his gizzard.

Which was a damn good reason not to get involved with nice women. Not that he could blame her if she did get mad. Why wouldn't she? He'd come on like a rutting animal and had taken advantage of a moment that should have been kindness and nothing more. But if you were going to act like a jackass, it was generally better to be a jackass with someone who was prepared for it. Not with someone who'd probably lived her life on a straight and narrow path the way he suspected Veronica had. Hell, if she told him she'd been a virgin on her wedding night, he'd believe her.

As the minutes ticked by with her snuggled into his shoulder, his anxiety grew. Was she planning the most cutting thing she could possibly say? Was she feeling too ashamed to even look at him? The latter possibility concerned him far more than the former. He'd hate himself if he'd made her feel ashamed.

She stirred a little, and a soft murmur escaped her. Hesitantly, he looked down at her and met her sleepy gaze. Then he saw the soft smile on her mouth.

"Mmm," she murmured quietly. "That was nice."

Nice? *Nice?* Her words were so far removed from what

he had expected that his brain was suddenly in free fall, and he couldn't think of a thing to say.

Then, stunning him even further, she tipped her head and kissed his cheek. Panic of a new kind began to fill him. He had to get out of there now. This could lead to things he'd sworn off for the rest of his life. This could get him emotionally involved in the way he had been with Jana.

He wished he'd never touched her. He wished he'd never discovered that behind that prickly, determined, rather depressed facade she wore there was a sensuous woman who wasn't ashamed of her needs. Who wasn't embarrassed by the things men and women did together. A decent woman who could also be an uninhibited lover, something he'd always believed couldn't go hand in hand.

This was quicksand.

But needing to get away and actually doing it were two separate things. He wasn't cruel enough just to get up and walk out, as if what had just happened was no more important than sharing a cup of coffee. He'd learned from Jana just how vulnerable a person was when it came to making love. He didn't want to wound Veronica.

But hanging around was apt to wound *him*. And maybe her eventually, because he didn't want her to misinterpret this interlude as meaning something more than it had.

Although just what exactly it meant he didn't want to think about too hard just then.

Finally, combining imperatives, he kissed her forehead and said, "I have to go above. I've left things unattended too long."

Then, before she could react, and before he could say anything that might cause more trouble, he slipped his arm from beneath her, got up, and left.

He didn't look back. He didn't want to see the shadows creep into her fantastic blue eyes. He didn't want to know what he'd done.

He found Tam above decks, standing at the rail puffing on a cigarette. Tam was the only person he'd ever known who could have a cigarette every now and then but no more.

"How do you do that?" Dugan asked now, wanting to get his mind off Veronica.

"Do what?"

"Smoke just one cigarette every few days or weeks."

"Oh." Tam laughed and tossed the butt overboard. "Sometimes it just tastes good. And it's a good rush. But if I smoked all the time, I wouldn't get the rush, and I'd blow out my lungs."

"But people get *hooked.*"

Tam shrugged. "I don't. I've never gotten hooked on anything."

Dugan wisely avoided asking Tam to enumerate the things he'd never gotten hooked on.

Tam turned, leaning his hip against the rail so he faced Dugan. "So, how come you came up early today?"

"Huh?"

"From the dive. You were already up here when I surfaced to tell you guys about the cannon."

"Oh." How to explain that one without lying? He hated to lie. "I found a copper coin," he said finally, remembering the coin he'd been playing with only a short while ago. "But it's so corroded we couldn't really tell anything."

"Did they have copper coins back then?"

"Apparently so. But Veronica said she'd have to use special stuff to clean it before we'll know anything. Now that cannon," he said, swiftly changing the subject, "that cannon is something else."

"Yeah." Tam laughed. "Man, I could hardly believe it when I started burrowing. I honestly thought I was going to find some kind of trash, you know? The propeller off somebody's boat. An old tackle box. I gotta tell you, Dugan, I didn't think we were going to find a damn thing on this wild-goose chase."

"Me, neither."

"So there I am, scooping mud away, expecting to find something that was obviously from the last thirty years, and instead, all of a sudden, I'm looking at this huge rusty thing. Man, my heart started hammering. I had a feeling what it was gonna be. I had a feeling." He shook his head and folded his arms, turning his attention out to sea. Moonlight dappled the water and created a silver path toward the east.

"It's incredible, isn't it?"

"Incredible?" Tam looked at him. "Man, we found the pot of gold at the end of the rainbow."

Dugan felt a shiver of unease creep down his spine. "We might not ever find anything else. And it might not be the *Alcantara*."

"Don't you get it? Just finding that cannon was like finding the gold at the end of the rainbow. The odds are incredible."

Dugan's uneasiness faded. "That's a fact."

"And wow, what a head rush it was." Tam laughed. "I could do with a jolt of that every so often. I can't remember the last time I had so much fun."

Dugan had to agree with him there. It was as if he'd been spending his life in some kind of limbo these past ten years. For all he'd told himself he was doing exactly what he wanted, the simple fact was, he'd been waiting, just biding his time. For what he hadn't known. But finding the coins today, and then the cannon, had told him. He'd been biding his time, waiting for this. The treasure hunt to end all treasure hunts.

Tam pulled a pack of cigarettes out of his breast pocket and lit another one. "Celebrating," he said by way of explanation. "I suppose tomorrow we'll go back into boring survey mode, and I'll be climbing the walls again. But I'll tell you, Dugan, I won't be climbing 'em quite so fast, not if there's a chance to make another find like this."

They were infected with the treasure-hunting bug, Dugan realized. Both of them. He had a feeling they now had it every bit as bad as Veronica. Tam was right. It was a great head rush.

And he was already hooked.

Three days later when they sailed into harbor, the three of them were as high as kites. They'd mapped out an oblong area where they'd gotten a number of interesting readings on the magnetometer, and Veronica had decided it would be a good place to start diving to check out the more interesting anomalies. They had a plan of action.

And Tam hotfooted it right home to call Luis's pager.

Luis was a man in hell. The way he figured it, Emilio would be showing up any day, and interfering in everything he had planned. Worse, as the days passed, Luis became more and more convinced that Emilio had somehow figured out what was going on.

Then there was *El Desconocido*. Unknown in more ways than Luis wanted to think about. As the days passed and he didn't call the man to give him an update, Luis became increasingly paranoid. Sure that he was being watched. Sure that the man knew who he was. The man's unknown nature had grown in Luis's mind to be a dark, looming threat, almost supernatural in nature.

Rosa, Luis's wife, had always said he was superstitious. As if Rosa wasn't. She insisted on having a crucifix in every room of the house, she kept the votive-candle industry in business, always tossed salt over her shoulder when she spilled it and knocked on wood when she felt someone had tempted fate. Luis had always scorned such silliness, but Rosa threw his contempt back in his face by pointing out that he had virtually demonized Emilio in his mind.

But she didn't know Emilio the way Luis did. The man was entirely too knowing. Too perceptive. And there was no reason to think *El Desconocido* wasn't at least as uncanny as Emilio.

Of course, there was no reason to think he was, and Luis kept trying to tell himself that, but the paranoid part of his mind wouldn't listen.

He felt threat closing in on him from all quarters, inchoate and dark. And it was all his own fault for trying to deceive Emilio.

By the time his pager beeped, Luis was half-convinced he was a dead man. The chirping snagged his attention, but he broke into a sweat when he thought of looking at it to see the number of the caller. He was afraid that it would be *El Desconocido* asking why he hadn't called with information. But he was terrified that it might be Emilio, letting him know the game was up.

Finally, he dragged himself across the room, and with a trembling hand he lifted the pager to look at the display.

It was Tam. His relief was so great that he dropped the pager with a clatter. Tam. Now he would have some information to use to appease Emilio. And maybe he would use it to appease *El Desconocido* as well. Just to assure the man he was delivering on his promise.

Not that they really had a deal, he reminded himself. He hadn't exactly promised anything, and the man hadn't made any demands. He had simply said he would pay well for the mask.

That wasn't exactly betraying Emilio, Luis told himself. He had made no commitment to anyone else.

Feeling a little better, he picked up the phone and called Tam.

"We need to meet," Tam said. "I've got something."

Luis's heart quickened, and his fears dimmed as excitement poured through him. He named a place, and Tam said, "Fifteen minutes."

When Luis hung up the phone, he realized he was no longer shaking. His fears were imaginary, he told himself. They had been born of too much inaction, that was all. He would get Tam's information, then would decide what to do with it.

He left the hotel, hurrying at a quick pace to the bar just off Duval Street, where they could sit in the dim recesses at the back and be observed by no one on the street.

The late afternoon was hot, the crowds were already building for an evening of revelry. On the one hand, the crowds exacerbated Luis's paranoia because it would be so easy for a spy to follow him. On the other hand, they made him feel safer, because no one could hurt him with so many people around.

When he stepped into the frigid interior of the bar, he felt a strong qualm. It was so dark after the brightness of the outdoors, and anyone could be hiding way at the back. Even *El Desconocido.*

He told himself he was being foolish, though, and made his way to the small table all the way in the back. It was rarely occupied, because most people seemed to like to be able to watch the street through the open doors. Luis paused at the bar long enough to order his Tecate, then slipped into a chair to wait.

He felt safer then. There was a wall at his back, and he could see everyone who came into the bar before they could see him. And not even Emilio, he told himself, could possibly see what he was doing there, not even if he walked in that very minute.

It was right about that time it dawned on him that he wasn't cut out to play a double agent. He didn't have the temperament for it any more than he had the temperament to gamble. He worried too much.

But then he reminded himself how much money might be involved. Emilio would pay him only a bonus for his work on this matter. *El Desconocido* might pay him millions. It was worth the risk.

If he didn't have a heart attack from stress first.

Tam was a few minutes late, but not so late that Luis started worrying about it. Of course, the Tecate—of which he was drinking a little too much lately—helped relax him. By the time Tam arrived, he was actually bobbing his head in time to the reggae blaring from the overhead speakers.

Tam ordered a double scotch on ice and carried it back to the table. He turned a chair so that he, too, could sit with his back to the wall.

"Worried someone will find you?" Luis asked, even though he was concerned about the same thing.

"I know half the people who live in this damn town," Tam said. "And I don't want to be overheard."

"It would be hard to hear over the music." It was one of the reasons he had chosen this place to meet.

"Maybe."

"So you have news for me?"

"Yep." Tam tossed back about half his whiskey and let out a satisfied sigh.

"You found the *Alcantara*?"

"Maybe. But maybe not. We found a *cannon*. There's no way to be sure where it came from. Anyway, we did a survey and came up with an area to explore, based on magnetometer readings."

Luis didn't want to admit that he didn't know what a magnetometer was, so he nodded sagely. "So a wreck is there."

Tam shrugged. "Damned if I know. Nobody knows for sure. All we know is there's some iron down there. We're going back to dive and see what all of it is. It might be a wreck. It might be the *Alcantara*. It also might be another ship, or just a seagoing junkyard."

"That's all you found?" He had the feeling Tam was withholding something.

"That's it." Tam stared at him through narrowed eyes. "Hey, man, what's the rush? It takes years to find and salvage these wrecks. A cannon is a cannon. We're lucky we found it."

"But the Coleridge woman, she thinks it is the wreck?"

"She's hoping it is. Aren't we all?"

Tam took his money, five hundred dollars, drained his glass, and departed, leaving Luis sitting in the dark corner by himself.

This was entirely too vague for his liking. Entirely. He wanted action soon.

But he didn't have any idea how to get it.

Forty minutes later he called Emilio. His boss was in a jovial mood, enjoying a sail across the Caribbean. "It's beautiful, Luis," he said expansively. "I wish you were here."

Luis thanked all the gods in the universe that he was not on the *Conchita*. It was easier to deal with Emilio on the phone, and besides, he would only get sick. "I have news," he said, his mouth suddenly dry.

"Yes? What?" Emilio's excitement was unmistakable.

"They found a cannon," Luis said.

"A cannon?"

"A cannon. They are not sure if this is from the *Alcantara*, but my informant says they have mapped an area to begin diving. They used a magneto."

"A magnetometer, Luis," said Emilio, who was far more well versed in the methods of archaeology. "Fascinating. If they've mapped out an area to explore, then they have probably found the remains of a ship."

"But they don't know what ship."

"No matter. I'll be there when they discover it, and that's all that concerns me."

That was exactly what concerned Luis, too. Having Emilio breathing down his neck. And having Emilio nearby when the mask was found.

He debated for more than an hour about whether he should call *El Desconocido,* and finally decided he had to. He had begun to play with fire, and if he stopped juggling it now he might get burned. But he decided to add another piece of information to this phone call, a piece that might help protect him.

He left a message, and twenty minutes later the unknown man called him back at his hotel.

"You say you have information?"

"I do," said Luis. "They found a cannon, and have mapped an area for exploration. They think they have found the ship."

"Excellent. Anything else?"

Luis hesitated, unsure whether to say more.

"When will your employer arrive?"

The words struck terror in Luis's heart. How had the man known Emilio was coming? "Uh . . . soon."

"Keep me informed." There was a soft *click*, then *El Desconocido* was gone.

And Luis realized he had made a bargain with the devil.

Chapter 15

The deck of the *Mandolin* was scattered with small treasures: encrusted coins, tools, and even some iron ship's fittings. The biggest treasure yet found was a Ming Dynasty jar, not even chipped from its journey to the bottom of the sea.

"It must have been packed in sawdust or something," Veronica told Dugan as she gently brushed damp mud from it. "The years in the water ate away the crate and the packing material and left the jar untouched."

"It's fabulous." He'd just found it, and was still smiling with pleasure. "This is it, isn't it, Veronica? The *Alcantara*?"

"I think so. She *was* carrying treasures from the Orient. I need to check this jar against what's on the ship's manifest, but I seem to remember there were some jars like this on it."

It amazed him that records of such things had survived all these years, but Veronica had told him about the archives of the Indies, stored now in Seville. Bean counters had been bean counters even back then, and meticulous records had been kept of nearly every jot and tittle aboard these ships. Not the hammers, of course, or even the plates the crew ate off, but of the cargo—yes, of the cargo.

There was a lot more below them. He and Tam had been scouring the bottom, marking places where treasures existed, only bringing a sampling to the surface.

"Well, we've established it was a cargo ship," Veronica said, sitting back on her heels. "We've now established it was carrying goods that had been shipped out of Manila. I'd say I'm ninety percent certain we've found the *Alcantara.*"

He crouched beside her. "So what now?"

"We take this stuff back to shore, hire a few more divers, get a bigger boat, and start salvaging in earnest."

He couldn't stop himself. "What about the mask?"

Her gaze shadowed. "If we find it, we find it."

They'd been keeping a careful distance ever since their encounter in her cabin, dancing around one another as if one of them had something contagious. But all of a sudden that distance irritated him all to hell. So he tried to cross it, but safely. "How's your father doing?"

"I don't know. He's up in Tampa having another scan."

"You're worried about him." He didn't mean it as a question.

But she took it as one anyway. "I guess."

Her answer bothered him. "You *guess*?"

She shrugged.

Dugan had his share of faults, but he loved his parents deeply, and even if he only saw them once a year, he'd *never* say he *guessed* he was worried because one of them had cancer. Especially if it was as bad as Orin Coleridge's appeared to be. "What's with you two?" he asked.

She acted as if she didn't hear him. He knew better than

that because he was staring right at her hearing aid. But she had turned her face away, so she probably hadn't understood him. And the only reason she had looked away was because she didn't want to discuss this with him.

He was getting damn tired of being tuned out like this. Tired of her rudeness.

He tapped her shoulder. She looked at him.

"Being deaf," he said flatly, "doesn't give you the right to be rude, or to use your lack of hearing as a weapon."

She gasped, anger sparking in her eyes. "Who are you to tell me how to behave?"

"Another human being. Damn it, Veronica, if you don't want to talk about something, just say so. But ask yourself how the hell you'd feel if I turned my back on you so I couldn't hear what you have to say."

"Where do you get off talking to me this way, you . . . you dropout!" This time when she turned away, she gave him the full brunt of it, dragging the jar around with her so that she could busy herself with it while showing him nothing but her rigid back.

Violence was always an option, he found himself thinking. She was making him that mad just then. Unfortunately, it wasn't his style. The last time he'd resorted to it, he'd been thirteen. Jesse Calisto had been making his life hell for weeks, shoving him around and making sport of him. And one day, much to his own amazement, Dugan had thrown a punch that had given Jesse a bloody lip. The detention had been worth it, especially since nobody ever messed with Dugan again.

But that wasn't his usual way of handling problems, and it sure as hell wasn't the way he wanted to handle Veronica, even if he *was* savoring an image of shaking her until her teeth rattled.

He stared at her back for a minute, then moved, grabbing the jar from her and putting it behind his back, forcing her to look at him.

She glared at him. "Give that back! You might damage it."

"You'll get it back as soon as we're done talking."

"We *are* done talking."

"I don't see it that way. And I don't like you turning your back on me. It's rude. It's juvenile. And I deserve to be treated with more respect than that."

"You don't have any right to lecture me!"

Her voice was a hell of a lot louder than usual, and he found himself thinking that he was glad they were at sea, where no one could hear. And Tam was still in the water. "Have I told you lately that you're a shrew?"

"So what?"

"Christ. Look, all I did was ask a question. All you had to do was say, 'Dugan, I'd really rather not discuss that with you because I don't think it's any of your business.' What you *don't* have the right to do is turn your back on me, tune me out, and treat me as if I don't exist. And quite frankly, lady, I am getting really tired of you turning your back anytime you don't like something."

"And you're so much better?"

"I may be a *dropout,* but I sure as hell don't treat people rudely."

"What do you think you're doing right now?"

Helluva good question, he thought. It was hopeless. He started to laugh.

Her glare didn't last another thirty seconds. He saw the twitch hit the corners of her mouth, and moments later she was laughing, too.

"Okay," he said when he could breathe again. He handed

her the jar. "I'll make you a deal. I won't lecture you if you won't turn your back on me."

"Why is that so much worse than telling you to get lost?"

The question caught him sideways. He squatted in front of her and thought about it. "It just is. Maybe because when you turn your back it's a complete dismissal. Because it removes me from your universe as completely as if you'd dropped me off the edge of the planet. When a hearing person turns her back, you can still argue with her."

"Get the last word, you mean."

Another laugh escaped him. "I guess. It's just different. It's rude when anybody does it, but it bothers me a hell of a lot more when you do it. Because it cuts us off completely."

She nodded slowly, thinking about what he was saying. He gave her credit for that. But then, he liked Veronica. She wasn't a bad person. She just had a few . . . behavior problems. But hell, who didn't. He knew he drove her up the wall sometimes with his laid-back approach to things. He just couldn't see getting in a sweat about much. But this woman put him in a lather faster than anybody he'd ever met.

She studied the jar, absently wiping streaks of mud off it. "This is the *Alcantara,*" she said. "I know it is."

Her voice was unusually quiet, so much so he wasn't sure she was talking to him, so he didn't answer.

She lifted her head and looked at him, her expression strained. "I've got to find that mask, Dugan."

"I thought you said . . ."

"I know what I said. But I've got to find that mask. My dad says he's doing okay, but I can tell he's not. He's lying to me. I've got to find that mask before he dies."

"Why?"

"To prove to him my mother wasn't on a wild-goose chase. To prove to him that she was right. He didn't even tell me about this quest of hers until six months ago. He kept the secret from me all through my childhood. So no matter how much he told me about her, I never really knew her. Hell, I didn't even know what she was doing on a boat when she got killed."

"Whew. I'll bet that made you angry."

"It did. It still does, but . . . not as much. The anger's going away. Now I just feel cheated. But . . . oh, I don't know how to explain it. It's like I *have* to vindicate my mother before he dies."

"I guess I can see that." His knees were starting to kill him from squatting, so he stood up, gently drawing her to her feet. "It may be an impossible task."

"I know that!" Anguish filled the words.

"Veronica . . ."

"Don't you see?" She held out her hands to him, her eyes swimming with tears. "Can't you see how much it hurts? I never knew my mother, and now I'm losing my father, and all I can do, the *only* thing I can do, is try to find that mask before it's too late! Oh, God, make it go away!"

He was holding her hands so she couldn't turn away, and the rawness of her pain lashed at him. In that one plea, *God, make it go away,* she conveyed to him exactly how much she was suffering. How trapped she was, and how helpless. And all she could do . . . His chest tightened in sympathy.

"We've got to hurry," she said, yanking her hands from his, and dashing away the tears. "There isn't much time. . . ."

"But if we hurry too much . . . well, you're an archaeologist. You know better than I do what happens to archaeologists who trash excavation sites. You could ruin your entire future."

She nodded jerkily, but he could see the sheen of tears in her eyes. "I've got to find it, Dugan. Soon."

He thought she was being a little irrational, but emotions were rarely rational. She had a feeling biting her on the tail, driving her, and trying to be reasonable about it wasn't helping. She saw her time growing shorter by the day.

He wasn't used to thinking in those terms. Excited as he was about their finds, it wasn't his nature to get impatient about most things. If it took twenty years, fine. The fun was in the journey anyway.

But he didn't have a dying father he needed to prove something to. He suspected that Veronica didn't begin to realize why this was so important to her emotionally. He had a gut feeling that it had more to do with proving herself than proving something about her mother. More to do with proving she was as good or better than her mother.

He looked over her head, out at the endless expanse of blue-green water and sky, and thought about that. He'd never been particularly driven to prove anything to anyone, but that didn't mean he couldn't understand those who were.

And Veronica . . . he suspected that the death of her mother had deprived her of something more than a mother's love. He wondered if, all those years her dad was dragging her around the globe, he hadn't made her feel inadequate simply because she wasn't her mother. And maybe, along the way, she had nearly busted herself on the shoals of trying to replace her mother for him. Maybe that's why she had become an archaeologist.

Orin probably hadn't meant to make Veronica feel lacking. He'd naturally been grieving, and Veronica may have interpreted that, in a child's way, to mean she wasn't good enough for him. Maybe she constantly felt the lack because she wasn't able to perform as an adult for him, either as an archaeologist or as a housekeeper, cook, and God-knew-what. He could see that happening.

But this was awfully deep, and he wasn't a psychologist. He had no way of knowing if he was on the right track or miles off course. But this made a whole lot more sense to him than that Veronica wanted to vindicate her mother.

"What are you thinking?" she asked.

He looked down at her. "I'm trying to figure out how we can hunt for that mask without making such a hash out of this whole thing that you can never again show your face at a professional meeting."

The corners of her mouth lifted, and the shine of tears in her eyes stayed dammed behind her lids. "It's tougher than it sounds."

"So is everything in life. Doesn't mean it can't be done."

She was close, and he was a fool, so he drew her closer. Well, maybe not so foolish, because it occurred to his dim-witted brain, even as he knew he was making a big mistake, that there seemed to be a cord or a current running between him and Veronica, and it kept tugging him close to her no matter how he tried to stay away. Since the time they'd made out, he'd found himself actually craving to feel her close again.

So he pulled her close, hugging her, promising himself he wouldn't do any more than that. And when she came into his embrace he knew a feeling of satisfaction that went soul deep. But before he could start noticing things like how her breasts felt against his chest, or how her hips seemed to fit his exactly, Tam bobbed to the surface.

Dugan let go of Veronica instantly and stepped back. She looked questioningly at him and he pointed. She turned and saw Tam, and said in a plainly disappointed voice, "Oh."

He wished she wasn't so disappointed. Being strong and smart and wise would be a hell of a lot easier if she weren't so plainly hankering after him the way he was hankering after her. If she'd put up a little fight and tell him it wasn't good for either of them. If she'd even been a little bit pissed by the way he had treated her that evening in her cabin. Instead, she had acted like a cat who'd just had a bowl of cream.

And even while they'd been keeping a cautious distance ever since, he still caught her giving him . . . well, for lack of a better word, *hungry* looks from time to time. Which wouldn't have been a problem if they hadn't reflected his own internal longing so well.

Hell's bells.

Thank God for Tam, who climbed onto the diving platform, shoved his mask back, and crowed.

Veronica looked at Dugan. "What did he say?"

"Something approximating *cock-a-doodle-doo.*"

She looked perplexed, so he repeated it. She laughed. Quit laughing, he thought. When she laughed he always wanted to kiss her.

"Yeehaw!" Tam said, pulling loose the pouch that was fastened to his diving belt. "Come take a gander."

He pulled open the Velcro fastenings, reached into the

bag, and pulled out a golden cross, about three inches long, that was encrusted with emeralds.

Veronica caught her breath. Dugan stared in amazement. Winking in the strong sunlight for the first time in three hundred years, the cross seemed to blaze.

"Ain't she pretty?" Tam asked. He passed it to Veronica, who took it with a trembling hand.

"It's fantastic," she said reverently. "Fantastic. Look at the delicacy of the work."

Dugan thought it wasn't quite as fine a piece as you could find in most jewelry stores, then reminded himself it had been made by hand. The gold looked like gold wires twisted together in intricate knots, making the mountings for the emeralds. And the emeralds . . . the stones alone, if they were unflawed, were probably worth a small fortune.

Her hand still shaking, Veronica slowly turned the cross over. The back of it was flat gold onto which the wire and stones had been laid. Dugan heard her catch her breath again.

"There's an inscription," she said. "Oh my God, there's an inscription."

"What does it say?" Tam, still dripping, crowded in with them.

"It's worn, hard to make out . . ." She held it closer to her eyes, squinting, trying to twist it so that shadows fell into the engraving and the glint of the sun didn't blind her.

"It looks like . . . Felipe . . . Carlos . . ." Her voice trailed off and she looked at Dugan. "Felipe Carlos Lorca. The captain of the *Alcantara*."

Tam let out a whoop of joy, but Dugan hardly heard him. His gaze fixed on the cross, and his heart almost seemed to stop. Then slowly, he lifted his eyes to Veronica's, and saw the same feeling of awe in them.

Slowly he reached out and took the cross from her. Holding it in the palm of his hand, he stared at it, thinking of the man on whose chest this cross must once have ridden, about a man who wouldn't throw the gold overboard to save the ship. About a man who had met his Maker in these very waters. Had this been around his neck when he went down? Had it been pressed in his hand as he prayed mightily for salvation from the storm?

He raised his gaze again, wanting to say something of this to Veronica, wanting to share this incredible moment with someone he was sure felt exactly the same thing, unlike Tam who was thinking only of excitement and riches.

But when he lifted his eyes, he saw something behind Veronica. His heart stilled.

"We've got company," he said.

Tam immediately fell silent and turned to look. A huge white yacht was sailing into view over the horizon.

"Just a pleasure tripper," Tam said.

"What?" Veronica asked. Turning, she saw the boat.

Dugan spoke. "Just do me a favor, Tam."

"Sure. What?"

"Get out of your diving gear and put it away. Veronica, let's clear this stuff off the deck and put it below."

Tam frowned. "Why? It's just somebody out for a sail."

"Just do what I said," Dugan said shortly. "Damn it, Tam, we don't want any questions. Got it? That boat will probably sail on without even really noticing us. But if it decides to get close and friendly, I don't want to have to explain what we're doing. Okay?"

"Okay, okay." Tam started stripping his wet suit.

Veronica tugged on Dugan's arm. When he looked at her she said, "You don't think we're in danger, do you?"

"Probably not. But out here you can't dial nine-one-one,

so it's best to play it safe. Before that boat gets any closer, I want us to look like we're out here to fish. I sure as hell don't want to have to explain what we're doing with a Ming Dynasty jar on our deck."

Speaking of which, he grabbed the jar and carried it below, stuffing it into a locker with the spare blankets he rarely needed. In moments Veronica followed, her hands full of coins and a hammer. Those he stowed in the locker in the cabin she was using. Then came the corroded eating utensils. As for the cross . . . the cross he tucked into his duffel bag in a roll of socks. He saw a smile flit across Veronica's face as he did it.

Fifteen minutes later, they were sitting on deck, trailing a line in the water. It was impossible to hide the air tanks since they'd had to lash them to the deck, but that was easy enough to explain, even though there were an awful lot of them. He just put a speargun in plain view. Spearfishing. Diving for fun and pleasure.

The yacht was closer now, giving them all an appreciation of its size.

"Some rich dude for sure," Tam remarked. "Bet he's got a crew of six."

"Probably."

Veronica was sitting in a canvas director's chair, sipping a soft drink. "I can't imagine owning a boat that big. What's the point?"

Dugan kind of agreed with her.

"I get the point," Tam said. "The lap of luxury is the point. Your own private floating hotel, getting away from it all and not having to deal with the unwashed masses unless you want to go ashore somewhere."

Dugan translated for Veronica, who nodded. "I guess. I seems sinful, somehow."

Dugan had to laugh. She gave him an annoyed look, which he ignored. "What's sinful about it? The guy has money to take floating vacations. How is it more sinful than taking a cruise? Or going to Disney World?"

"I don't know. It just is. Maybe because you can't use it all the time. So you spend huge amounts of money on something you might only use for a few weeks a year."

"I guess that does seem a little wasteful. But it's really on the same order as the guy who owns a car but only drives it once a week."

"Not really. Because you *need* a car."

Dugan laughed again, thinking she was being a little puritanical about this. "Who's to say the guy doesn't give a fortune to charity every year?"

"Maybe he does. But he could have given another six or seven million if he hadn't bought that yacht."

"Come on, admit it. Wouldn't you love to have a boat like that?"

Her disapproving expression suddenly melted into a smile. "Of course I would."

Both he and Tam laughed. "So it's just envy?"

"You bet it is. But I like your boat better."

So did Dugan. He was very closely attached to his *Mandolin.* She was a sweet boat, the sweetest he could have asked for, and just right for one man. One man or a couple.

He didn't know where that last thought came from, and he refused to look at it too closely. Instead, he returned his attention to the boat.

"They must be turning," he remarked after a few minutes.

"Turning?" Veronica asked.

"Either that or they're slowing down. I'm hoping they're turning."

"But why would they be slowing down?"

"That's a question I'd rather not have to answer."

He felt her look at him, but he'd already looked away, and he refused to meet her gaze. He didn't want to see what he knew he was going to find there: worry and a dozen questions.

"Tam?"

"Yo."

"Keep playing with that fishing rod. Make it look good. I'm going below to get my gun."

"Might be a good idea, skipper."

Boats could, it was true, slow down and pull alongside just to be friendly. But they didn't do it very often. Veronica started to follow him, but he waved her back into her chair.

"Look like we're all just out here to get a tan and catch a fish, okay? Don't follow me below. Don't act like we might be worried."

"You *are* worried, aren't you?"

"Just a little bit."

She searched his face, then nodded and relaxed in her chair.

Below, Dugan unlocked the drawer where he kept a Glock 9mm. He'd never needed it before, but you didn't sail in these waters alone without a little protection. Not if you were in your right mind. Because every so often—not very often, mind you—somebody would decide to steal a boat on the high seas. And like he'd said earlier to Veronica, out here you couldn't dial 911.

The Glock was in a drybag, and he kept it in there. He didn't want anybody to see it. But when he came back up on deck, he kept the bag beside him on the bench, unsealed so he could get the gun quickly.

"They're slowing down, Dugan," Tam told him.

"I can see that." They were still a fair bit away, still beyond hailing distance, but getting closer. "I don't like this."

"Me neither."

So Dugan pulled another soft drink from the cooler and popped the top on the can. Tam reeled in his line and replaced the bait on his hook. Veronica drummed her fingers nervously.

"They've stopped," Tam said after a while.

"It looks like it."

Dugan squinted into the sun, trying to make out details, but the boat was still too far away. It was a funny place to put down an anchor. Of course, they might be having some kind of trouble.

"Want me to get the binoculars?" Tam asked.

"Not just yet."

"What are you two talking about?" Veronica asked.

Dugan turned to her. "The boat has stopped, and we were discussing whether to get binoculars. I said we'd wait a bit."

"Why?" she asked. "If we weren't all so paranoid, we'd get out the binoculars, wouldn't we?"

She had a point.

"And why are we so paranoid anyway? It's just another boat, and it's not getting too close."

"Well," said Dugan, "I kind of get paranoid when I'm sitting on top of ten million dollars in gold bars, not to mention the value of the other treasures."

"Oh." Veronica subsided, but by way of making peace, Dugan got the binoculars from the cockpit and trained them on the other boat.

"*La Conchita,*" he said, reading the name on the boat's bow. "Venezuelan."

From the corner of his eye, he saw Tam start. Lowering the binoculars, he looked at his friend. "You know that boat?"

Tam shook his head. "Never saw it before in my life."

But it seemed to Dugan that Tam's gaze slid away too quickly, and he felt his scalp prickle uncomfortably. "You sure, Tam?"

"Of course I'm sure."

Veronica spoke. "Will you two *please* tell me what you're talking about?"

"The boat is out of Venezuela," Dugan told her. "I just asked Tam if he knew anything about her." He took another look at the yacht through the glasses, but didn't see anything interesting one way or another. Somebody sunning on the deck, no unusual activity.

He put the binoculars down and resumed his seat on the bench. Then he had a thought. "Remember that guy who was hanging around when we first got started, asking questions about what we were doing?"

"What guy?" Tam asked.

"That Hispanic guy. Luis something-or-other. Wasn't he from Venezuela?"

Tam said nothing. Veronica's lips pressed together.

And Dugan felt a sinking sensation in the pit of his stomach. This wasn't a coincidence.

Chapter 16

"I think we ought to just go back to diving," Veronica said.

They'd been sitting on deck for over an hour, and time was dragging for them all. The other boat hadn't moved any closer; in fact it hadn't moved at all. From time to time Dugan looked through the binoculars, but saw nothing unusual on deck.

"No," he said.

Tam stirred, reeling in his line once again. "Why not? They're not doing anything."

"That's just it. They're not doing anything. If they've got an engine problem, they should either move in the next hour or two, or they ought to be sending out a distress call." He pointed to the radio in the cockpit. "I don't hear anything."

Tam sighed. Veronica, who'd only caught part of what passed between them, wiggled irritably in her chair. "This is ridiculous. What if they've decided to park there to fish, too? We could spend days here doing nothing at all."

Dugan turned to face her. "Are you in such an all-fired

rush to find that mask that you're willing to risk your neck?"

"I don't see what I'd be risking! So what if we do a little diving. They probably won't think that's any more unusual than if we sit here fishing. They couldn't possibly know what we're out here for."

"I wouldn't be so sure of that. That Luis what's-his-name knew what you were doing here. And even if they don't know, what if someone is sitting over there in the covered bridge with a pair of binoculars trained on us watching every move we make? If we start hauling up interesting stuff from below, they'll know exactly what we're up to."

Veronica swore softly but didn't press the issue. "I'm going below," she said finally. "The sun's giving me a headache."

Down in her cabin, she removed her hearing aids and rubbed her ears, erasing the feeling of them from her skin's memory.

The sun was giving her a headache, but so was that other boat, and so was Dugan. Dugan most especially. After what had happened between them in this cabin such a short time ago, she could hardly believe he had retreated into a purely business relationship. Apparently he regretted the entire encounter.

She didn't know whether she did. For one thing, it had taught her that her feelings weren't as dead as she had believed. She could still feel attracted to a man, still get sexually aroused.

On the other hand, she wasn't sure that was a good thing. Since Larry, she'd told herself she wasn't ever again going to let a man get within ten feet of her heart. Hah. Apparently she had already done that.

Not that he was too close, but the distance they had between them was really troubling her since their encounter. It bothered her no end that he seemed able to encapsulate her, to put her away on a shelf, with such ease after such intimacy.

Stretching out on the bunk, she gave the pillow one frustrated punch before she rolled onto her back and stared at the ceiling. Or the deck above, or whatever it was called on a boat. She was having trouble absorbing the terminology and at the moment she didn't especially care what it was.

Dugan was irritating her with his detachment and careful distance, and no matter how much she told herself that it didn't matter, that it was for the best, and that she was safer this way, she was still irritated.

Because the passion that had erupted between them was as addicting as cocaine. Heady and sweet, it had suffused her, made her feel alive, made her feel desirable—all things she hadn't felt once since Larry had deserted her. She wanted to experience it again, wanted to test herself and see if the awakening was real or if it had been some kind of illusion.

And that was dangerous to her peace of mind—such peace of mind as she had anyway. It was like opening a door into a place where she might get hurt. A place where terrible dangers lurked. Never again did she want to feel what Larry had made her feel when he left her, and the only way to avoid that was to avoid men. All men. Any man.

So why was she feeling this way?

Annoyed with herself, and finding no answers to her confusion, she turned her thoughts to the yacht that was anchored maybe a half mile away. She couldn't give up her quest just because some jerk with too much money had decided this was a nice place to take a rest. Surely Dugan couldn't be proposing to cancel their work indefinitely?

What were they supposed to do? Pack up and go home? Not likely. She had a job to finish. But more than that, she wasn't going to abandon the site to a possible treasure hunter. No way.

But her thoughts kept straying back to Dugan, and her body kept insisting on remembering how his weight had felt pressing her into the bunk. She even remembered the quick, short gasps of his breath, and the memory made liquid heat pour through her and settle heavily between her legs.

She had it bad.

Finally, realizing that staying below by herself was only making her more frustrated, she got up, put her hearing aids back in her ears, and went above deck.

As far as she could tell, nothing at all had changed. Tam was still fishing over the side, Dugan was still sprawled on the bench drinking cola from a can, and the boat was still out there.

"No change," Dugan said to her.

"I can see that. What are we going to do? Pull up anchor and go home? That would be stupid. If they *do* know what we're doing, they'll just move in and try to steal things. We have to get back to work."

Dugan sat up straight. "Not yet."

"How long is not yet?"

"Until I say so."

She put her hands on her hips. "Just who is paying for this expedition?"

"You are. But hiring me doesn't require me to do anything I consider foolish."

"Look, if those people out there meant us any ill, they'd have already done something, wouldn't they? Tried to get closer? Talked to us? Threatened us? They're just sitting there, doing nothing at all. They're probably doing exactly what we're doing. Fishing over the side."

"I don't see any fishing poles. Look, Veronica, just say they *do* know what we're doing out here. Maybe they just want to keep an eye on us until we bring up something really spectacular. Or maybe they're watching us to determine how many of us there are, or whether there's another boat working with us."

"But we haven't even told a soul that we've found anything! They might know we're looking, but they won't know we've found anything."

"Exactly. And I suggest we keep it that way."

"For how long?"

"As long as it takes."

Tam said something that sounded disgusted, and reeled in his line. Then he set his rod down with a thud and disappeared below.

Veronica watched him go, then turned to Dugan. "What's his beef?"

"He says he's tired of listening to us argue."

Stifling a sigh, she sat down in the director's chair again. "This is insane. We can't stay paralyzed like this."

"Just for a while."

"Could you please be more definite?"

"Unfortunately, no. This is one of those times you could do with a little beach-bum mentality. Relax, Veronica."

"Relax." She blew a frustrated sigh between her lips. "Relax, he says. My entire life is on the line, and I'm supposed to relax."

"Yeah. Enjoy the sun, the water, the beautiful day. We'll

wait them out. And if they're up to something, and we don't do anything at all, eventually they'll have to show their hand."

"When?"

He shrugged.

She didn't say another word for a while. The heat was getting to her, and despite her desire to remain irritated with Dugan, she found herself growing drowsy. As the sun changed position, she shifted her chair, keeping her back to it. A little shade would have been useful just about then, but the only shade on deck was in the covered cockpit.

"We could move," she said finally.

"Move?"

"Sure. To another place in our search area."

"Hmm." He seemed to be thinking about that. "See if they follow us, you mean?"

"Yes. We were thinking about changing our position in the morning anyway."

He nodded slowly. Then he picked up the binoculars and looked toward the other boat. "Uh- oh," he said.

That was perfectly understandable to Veronica, even though he wasn't facing her. "What's wrong?"

He faced her. "There's a launch headed this way."

She turned, squinting into the sun, and saw a speck of white on the water heading toward them. "Is this bad?"

When she looked at him again, he asked, "Do I look like a mind reader? Tam? Tam, get your butt up here now."

There was a muffled answer from below, then Tam bounded up the ladder. "What's . . . oh." He shaded his eyes and peered toward the launch, which was growing rapidly larger. He said something else.

"What?" demanded Veronica. Suddenly she was very impatient with her hearing loss, more impatient than she had been in weeks, with Dugan buffering her against the world.

Dugan turned to her. "Tam asked if they radioed for permission to come over. They didn't."

"That's bad?"

"At sea, it's bad form." He reached for the drybag and pulled out the Glock, checking the load.

"What's that for?" Veronica asked.

"Emergencies."

To Veronica it seemed as if the day had suddenly turned cold. The sun was still shining, and its light was still sparkling off the water like diamonds, but she couldn't feel the heat anymore. Goose bumps rose along her arms.

She tried to tell herself that Dugan was overreacting, but she didn't believe it. She found herself remembering how her mother had died, and her father's persistent suspicion that she had been killed. Had it happened just like this? Somebody approaching in a launch, with a friendly face, getting aboard, maybe chatting for a few minutes before hitting her over the head?

Unconsciously, she moved closer to Dugan. He was holding a gun, and that gun suddenly looked like a nice thing to be near. He put his left arm around her shoulder.

The launch pulled up alongside. There was only one man in it, a small man wearing a sort of sailor's uniform.

He called to them, but Veronica couldn't read his lips. She heard Dugan answer, but didn't know what he was saying because she couldn't tear her eyes from the launch long enough to read him.

Her deafness closed around her like a muffling cloak, cutting her off from the world. And with the cutting off came a fear, a fear that she had felt intensely during the first months of the accident, but one which she hadn't felt as much since Dugan had become her anchor.

It crept through her, reaching every cell in her being, reminding her just how helpless she was in a hearing world. That man could be making all kinds of threats, and she wouldn't even know it.

It was a panicky, sickening sensation, making her feel as if she were somehow cut loose and in free fall. Mouths were moving, voices sounding in her hearing aids, but all she could make out was a stutter of vowel sounds and tonalities. Nobody sounded upset, she realized. Dugan, his side against hers, his arm around her shoulders, didn't seem tense. He even seemed more relaxed than he had just been a minute ago. She told herself she was imagining threats simply because she couldn't make out the words that were flying back and forth. Her panic eased a little, but not her essential fear. How was she ever going to get through life like this? For the moment she was leaning on Dugan, letting him shelter her from the world of misunderstandings that she would experience except for him and his patience. But what was going to happen to her when she no longer had Dugan at her side?

How would she be coping with this problem if Dugan weren't with her? She wouldn't be able to understand the man on the boat at all. And having to tell people she was deaf . . . that always made her feel stripped naked and vulnerable. It was knowledge about her that could be used against her, and she was painfully aware of it.

She heard the launch's motor rev, then it pulled away and headed back to the yacht. She looked up at Dugan, pulling on his shirtfront as if she were a child trying to get his attention.

He looked down at her. "We've been invited over for dinner."

Tam said something explosive behind them, and they both turned. Dugan dropped his arm from Veronica's shoulder, and she found herself missing his touch as if some part of her had been torn away.

Dugan said something. Tam spoke again, his voice tense.

"Jesus Christ!" Dugan snapped.

Veronica understood that from the angry tone and the vowels. Unnerved, she stepped away from Dugan. "What's going on?"

He looked at her. "Let's go below. I don't know how much they may be able to see over there, but I don't want to give anything away."

"Give what away?"

"Let's go below. Tam, too."

So they all descended to the galley and sat in the lounge on the bench around the table. Veronica could see the two men's faces clearly, but that wouldn't help her to understand Tam. "Why don't you shave your mustache," she said. "It'll grow back. But I can never understand what you're saying."

He shook his head, putting a protective hand over his mouth.

"Veronica," Dugan said to get her attention.

She looked at him. "What happened up there?"

"We've been invited for dinner on the yacht."

"I got that part."

"Tam says we shouldn't go."

She looked at Tam. "Why not?"

"Veronica." Dugan drew her attention back to him. "Tam says . . . Tam says . . . You remember that guy who came by the dock asking about what we were doing. That Luis guy?"

She nodded. "Is he on that boat?" The thought made the back of her neck prickle. "Is he?"

"I don't know. But Tam said the guy paid him for information."

The news struck her like a bomb. It exploded inside her head, and for several seconds there was nothing but a whiteness in her mind, and a hot-cold feeling in her body. Anger swelled in her until she wanted to scream. When her vision cleared, she looked at Tam, speaking through her teeth.

"You sold information about what we're doing?"

Tam nodded slowly. He said something rapidly and Dugan spoke again.

"The guy told Tam if he didn't give him the information, he'd arrange an accident so we'd have to take on another diver."

Veronica could scarcely believe what she was hearing. Her mind rebelled, refusing to accept this as truth. They had to be kidding. But as she searched their faces, she knew they weren't.

"My God," she whispered. "My God, I trusted you. And Dugan told me I could." Something very close to hatred began to seethe in her. Betrayed again. By a man. Naturally. She should have known better than to trust *any* man. Ever. About anything.

"I trusted him, too," Dugan said. "And right now I'd like to rip his head off and feed his entrails to the sharks. But that's illegal. So." He passed a hand over his face. "Keeping in mind that this guy has already threatened an 'accident,' Tam thinks it would be a big mistake to go over to that yacht tonight."

"But we don't even know if they're associated with that creep Tam is consorting with."

Tam said something protestingly. Dugan told him to shut

up. "He says he wasn't consorting with the guy, just trying to keep his legs from being broken."

"Well, big hairy deal," Veronica said acidly. "Look at us now. We *all* might have broken legs by midnight, thanks to you and your big mouth. Why didn't you just come to Dugan or me and tell one of us what was going on?"

Tam said something heatedly.

Dugan translated. "He said he figured that then he'd be dead."

"God Almighty." She was past knowing what to say. "So now we have thugs breathing down our necks? How fucking wonderful."

Unable to breathe the same air with Tam, she got up and left the galley, heading back to her cabin, where she closed the door with more force than usual.

What the hell was she going to do? If people were threatening to break Tam's legs just to find out what she was doing, what might they do now that she had found the wreck? Millions of dollars in gold bars, which didn't interest her at all, were for some people sufficient motivation to commit murder.

And those might be the people on the boat anchored a short distance away.

But would murderers invite them to dinner? Well, yes, now that she thought about it. It would be far easier to kill them over there on the other boat. Or poison their food.

The extremity of her own thoughts caught her, snapping her back from her worry just long enough that she realized the utter absurdity of what she was thinking. They had no proof that the people on the other boat were anything but wealthy vacationers who might be looking for a change of pace in their dinner companionship. They might just be eccentric but harmless.

But she didn't quite believe it. Not when she was floating thirty feet above a treasure trove. It was just too unlikely.

There was a knock on the door. Reluctantly, she called, "Come in."

Dugan entered, closing the door behind him. "I'm tempted to sail back to Key West right now and dump Tam."

"What good will that do? The damage has been done. How much did he tell this guy?"

"That we found a cannon and a couple of coins."

She nodded, then waved in the general direction of the boat. "And a week later we have a boat anchored a quarter mile away. Coincidence?"

Dugan shook his head. He started to perch on the edge of the bunk, apparently thought better of it and sat on the chair. Veronica took the bunk.

"I was thinking about radioing for the Coast Guard," he told her. "Two problems."

"What are they?"

"First, I don't really have a problem. What am I going to do? Tell them a strange boat has anchored five hundred yards away and the owners invited us to dinner? That'll get them out here really fast."

"But maybe if you tell them what we're doing?"

He shook his head. "That's the other problem. If I radio, the other boat might hear it. And if they're here to make trouble, the Coasties couldn't get here fast enough."

She nodded slowly, her head feeling heavy, her neck aching with tension. "And maybe they're just perfectly innocent travelers."

"I can't quite believe it."

"Me neither. So what are we going to do?"

"I'd suggest running for shore, except I don't think we can outrun them if they decide they don't want us to. From the looks of that boat, I'd be willing to bet he's got some really powerful engines. We'd be tacking, which would lengthen the distance . . ." He trailed off and shook his head. "No, I don't think that would be wise."

"Besides, if we leave the site, they might start salvaging it. Making a mess of it." Her hands curled into fists on her lap. "They could ruin everything."

"I suppose so. Well, I guess that leaves only one option."

"Which is?"

He looked ruefully at her. "You and Tam stay here. He can handle the boat and get you home if necessary. I'll go over for dinner tonight, claim you two are sick with something, and see what's going on."

"No." She was unable to restrain the hand that reached out and gripped his arm. "No, Dugan. If they're up to something, you'll be all alone."

He shrugged. "Somebody has to go. I'm sure as hell not going to send Tam because I can't trust him. And we can't all go together because that would make it too easy if they want to pull something."

He didn't define "pull something," and she didn't ask. Her imagination was already vivid enough. "Then I'll go," she said. "This is *my* expedition. I can't let you risk your neck in my place."

He just looked at her. He didn't say a word, just looked. And she knew what he was thinking. She was deaf. She couldn't go over there and be sure of having a conversation she could understand.

Her heart sank, killing her anger and fear, and replacing it with despair. She'd been living in a fool's paradise this last couple of months, feeling capable and in charge, mostly thanks to Dugan. But now, faced with a crisis, she was totally incapable of dealing with it because she couldn't hear.

The black cloud she had left behind months ago when her father had awakened her interest with his story of the mask descended on her again, suffocating her. She was handicapped. She was disabled. She was incapable. Someone else would have to front for her because she couldn't do such a simple thing: have a conversation with a stranger.

Oh, she might be able to understand the people on the boat. If they didn't have strange accents. If they didn't have face hair. If they were sure to look at her when they spoke. But Dugan wasn't willing to trust that. Wasn't willing to trust her.

And when she came right down to it, she wasn't willing to trust herself.

"I'll think about it," she said, her mouth feeling heavy, her lips and tongue unwilling to form the words as depression enveloped her. Turning from Dugan, she twisted around and lay down on the bunk with her back to him.

What was the point, she wondered dismally. She should have just stayed in her rocking chair at home and watched the seasons pass outside the window. Because here she was, trying to do something that mattered more to her than almost anything else in the world, and she wasn't even able to deal with a potentially serious threat because she couldn't hear.

Instinctively, her hands went to her belly, pressing where her baby had once been growing. She hadn't been able to do that right, either. Hell, she hadn't even been able to do marriage right. She was a dismal failure at *everything*.

She ought to take her hearing aids out and throw them overboard. When push came to shove, they didn't do her any good at all, and just then they were irritating her. Irritating her because she could hear Dugan every time he shifted in his chair. Irritated her because when she was above deck, the wind in them was sometimes so loud that she couldn't hear anything else. Irritated that they didn't help her hearing enough to go have a conversation with a stranger.

All they were was ugly, flesh-colored plastic blobs that irrevocably marked her as defective.

Turning over, she pulled her aids out of her ears, gripped them in her right hand, and started to throw them.

Before she had even completed the swing, Dugan caught her hand, stopping her. She opened her eyes and looked at him. He shook his head, then gently pried the devices from her hand and set them on the desk.

Then, utterly amazing her, he stretched out beside her on the bunk and drew her into a warm embrace. He murmured things she couldn't understand, couldn't even hear, but that didn't matter. All she needed was his hug. His fingers combed gently through her wind-knotted hair and rubbed her scalp, working out the tension that had it screamingly tight.

He was telling her it was going to be all right, she was sure of that, but she didn't believe him. She couldn't believe him. How could she believe him when she knew her hearing would never come back. She was always going to have a gaping hole in her abilities, a huge stumbling block between her and other people that would prevent her from doing things that others took for granted.

No, it was never going to be all right again.

She didn't know when the tears started leaking from her eyes but her face grew wet. The tears, though, far from worsening her mood, seemed to snap her out of it. This was no way to behave when she was facing a crisis, hearing or not.

She pulled her head back and looked into Dugan's eyes. "Nobody's going over there for dinner."

He lifted his brows questioningly.

"We can't meet them on their turf. They have to come to us." She hoped she was being clear, because her own voice sounded like a distant trumpet to her, so far away that it might be coming from the other end of a large building.

But he nodded, and held up his hand, making the okay sign. He understood her, and he agreed with her, and what's more, he was talking to her without demanding she put in her hearing aids.

Something in her melted, and the tears began to flow again. He drew her head onto his shoulder and let them wet his shirt. They healed nothing, but their flow and his embrace brought her a vast sense of relief.

Somebody, at least, wasn't overwhelmed or offended by her deafness. Somebody, at least, still cared enough to comfort her.

Somebody cared enough to reach across the yawning chasm that silence had put between her and the rest of the world. The realization gave her a sense of safety. And even though it was illusory, she clung to it.

These might be her last minutes of safety ever.

Chapter 17

The witching hour had passed. The sun was getting low in the sky, and the westerlies had kicked up, blowing a steady fifteen to twenty knots. Waves were rocking the *Mandolin* and had swung her around so that the *Conchita* was at ten o'clock. Dugan didn't want to tear his gaze from the other boat, but Veronica kept shifting around so much that finally he did.

"What's wrong?" he asked.

"The wind's whistling in my hearing aids. I'm trying to find a position to stop it."

He was touched that she had shared that. She'd rarely confided the difficulties she faced. Then he decided that he didn't want to feel touched. Things were in danger of getting out of hand again. He returned his gaze to the yacht.

"What do you think they're going to do?" she asked.

"I haven't a foggy."

"What?"

He turned so he faced her and repeated himself. She shook her head. "I'm sorry, the wind's drowning you out."

"Be right back." Rising from the bench, he went below

and got out his diver's slate and marker. Sitting beside her again, he wrote it down for her.

"Foggy," she said, reading it. "I thought it was, 'I haven't the foggiest idea.' "

He wiped out the words on the slate and wrote new ones. *Just an abbreviated version.*

She nodded. At least she wasn't going to lecture him on the proper use of the language or something. But the fact was, after this afternoon, he was braced for trouble from her. He'd reminded her she was deaf, making her cry, and then he'd had the awful temerity to hold her. Yup, he was in for trouble.

But he was more concerned about the yacht, and whether the owner was going to make even bigger trouble. Veronica he could handle. A bunch of goons he wasn't so sure about.

Sure enough, about a half hour after they were due across the water for dinner, the launch set out again from the yacht.

"Here they come," he said needlessly. "Tam?"

Tam was at the bow again, trailing a line in the water and keeping to himself.

"We're about to get company. Whose side are you on?"

"Yours, of course. Hey, these guys threatened me. I don't feel very safe with them."

"You better not double-cross me."

"I won't. I swear."

Dugan wished he felt more confident of that.

The launch drew steadily closer. He felt the tension growing in Veronica, and he had to resist an urge to take her hand. This wasn't the time. Hell, this lifetime wasn't the time. Instead he reached out and felt the Glock beside him.

The sun was beginning to paint the thin clouds vermillion. There was nothing quite like a tropical sunset.

He reached for the slate again and scribbled across it, *Sit so you can see my face.*

"Why?"

If trouble, you can see it in my face. You can read me too.

She nodded and moved from the bench to the director's chair, which had slid forward a few feet from the rocking of the boat in the increasingly choppy water.

The launch was closer now, and Dugan didn't need binoculars to see that there was more than one person aboard it. There were, in fact, three. Not exactly a threatening group, he thought, and relaxed a little. Then he had another thought, and picked up the binoculars.

No guns. At least none he could see. So unless they were carrying pistols under their shirts or behind their backs, this encounter shouldn't be too difficult. Unless, of course, they had Uzis or something in the locker under the stern seat. Shit. The possibilities just didn't get any better.

When the launch pulled alongside, he saw there were two sailor types and a small man in a riotous tropical print shirt. He had gray hair and a round, friendly face, and Dugan found himself thinking he might have been wrong about all this.

The small man looked up at him. "*¿Con su permiso?*"

Dugan hesitated, not sure he wanted to let anyone board his boat. On the other hand, the guy had asked nicely, and trying to conduct a conversation over four feet of water in two boats that were starting to rock like a roller-coaster ride could get a little ridiculous.

"Just you?" he asked. "*¿Solamente usted?*"

"Just me," the man agreed in accented English.

Well, Dugan thought, if the little guy was up here, the big guys down in the boat were less likely to start shooting this way. Under the circumstances, his paranoia seemed extreme, but he wasn't prepared to let go of it yet. Whatever made him feel safer was good.

He noted Tam was standing in the bow, watching events closely. Presumably he had both a flare gun and a speargun at hand.

"Okay," Dugan told the little man. He got the ladder and hung it over the side. The man made the crossing with athletic ease, as if he did it often. Then he was standing on the deck of the *Mandolin,* adjusting his clothing and smiling on the world in general.

"I," he said in accented English, "am Emilio Zaragosa."

Dugan nodded. "Dugan Gallagher. My friends Tam Anson and Veronica Coleridge."

"My pleasure," Emilio said, making a courtly little bow in the direction of the others. "I was concerned when you did not accept my dinner invitation."

"We were feeling a little seasick."

"Really? You don't look at all . . . green."

"We're starting to get over it. Look, we really appreciate the offer of hospitality, but we came out here to get away from it all."

"So?" Emilio sat, putting himself between Dugan and the launch. Dugan took that as a good sign. Apparently they weren't getting ready to break out weapons. He sat facing Emilio. Veronica remained seated in the director's chair, her gaze flying between the two men.

"Look," said Dugan, "Why don't you cut to the chase? Inviting us to dinner was hospitable. Tracking us down when we don't show is something else."

Emilio waved a hand. "I'm sorry. I was concerned."

"Really." Dugan's voice dripped disbelief.

Emilio sighed. "Are you going to be difficult, Mr. Gallagher, or can we handle these matters like civilized men?"

"What matters?"

"The matter of *La Nuestra Señora de Alcantara.*"

Veronica had evidently understood that much of what the man said, because Dugan heard her gasp softly. He didn't think Emilio heard it, though. Between the wind and the waves, hearing was getting difficult even for him.

"What's that?" he asked blandly, pretending he didn't know.

"Why dance around?" Emilio asked. "We both know what you're doing out here. We both know about the ship."

"We do?"

Emilio shook his head. "Games, Mr. Gallagher. Let's not waste each other's time."

"Fair enough," Dugan agreed. "So what is it you want from us?"

"To participate in the salvage."

"Really. To what extent? And what are your qualifications?"

"I've brought divers with me. I'll pay them."

"And what do you hope to get out of this?"

"The joy of discovery."

Yeah, right, Dugan thought. "Very magnanimous."

Emilio looked embarrassed. "No, no, this is something I have always dreamed of doing."

"Well, I think you'll discover that Ms. Coleridge wants only trained personnel working on this problem right now. It would be too easy for treasure hunters to mess up the recovery and ruin the archaeological value. Sorry to disappoint you."

Emilio placed his hands on his thighs and looked up at

the sky, as if seeking patience. "Perhaps I have not made myself clear. I am *going* to help you."

"Really."

"Really. It will be to the advantage of both of us."

"How so?"

"I will bear the expense of the additional divers. Work will proceed more quickly."

"I'm not sure that speed is of the essence."

Emilio frowned at him, and Dugan began to get a measure of the man. He didn't like what he saw. There was a coldness to Emilio's dark eyes, belied by the joviality of his face. He was a man who did not like to be crossed. What now?

"All right," Emilio said. "Let me tell you what is going to happen. You are going to sail this boat out of here. I am going to conduct the salvage. And if you do not do this first thing in the morning, I am going to ram your boat, and all that will be found of you is little pieces of flotsam. Is that clear enough?"

"Very clear. I'll need to discuss it with Ms. Coleridge."

"What is there to discuss?"

"Whether we're going to run or be rammed."

Emilio's eyebrows lifted, as if he could scarcely believe his ears. "I am not joking."

"Neither am I. Now will you kindly remove yourself from my boat?"

"Wait." Veronica spoke, surprising them both. They immediately looked at her. Dugan tried to signal her to be quiet, but she wasn't paying attention.

"You want the gold, right?" she asked Emilio.

He didn't answer her.

"You can have the gold. You can have *all* the gold. I

only want one thing from this wreck. If you give me what I want, you can have all the rest."

"How are you going to stop me from taking whatever I want?"

She looked at Dugan, and he realized she didn't understand Emilio clearly, but had apparently picked up the substance of their conversation from what he had said to Emilio. So he told her what Emilio had said.

Emilio interrupted. "Why are you repeating me?"

"Ms. Coleridge is deaf."

"Ahh." Emilio looked at her and gave her a charming smile. "How sad."

"It's not sad." she said sharply. "It's irritating. So you want to know how I'm going to stop you?"

"Yes, please."

"It's really very simple. These are U.S. coastal waters. They're patrolled regularly. I have a permit to excavate this site. You don't. So if you don't keep me around, the next time the Coast Guard passes through here, they're going to take action against you. You need me. You need *us* if you hope to salvage much at all."

"I don't care about your Coast Guard."

Dugan translated again.

Veronica looked at Emilio. "You will when you find yourself staring down the barrels of their guns. And what's more, if I disappear, everyone's going to have a pretty good idea of what happened to me. So you don't want to kill us. You don't want to hurt us at all."

Emilio nodded slowly. "Perhaps you have a point."

Dugan couldn't tell if Veronica had understood him, but she didn't look at Dugan for a translation.

"All I want is one piece," Veronica said again. "You can have whatever else you want."

Emilio nodded. "I will think about it. We will talk again in the morning."

Then he stood up, gave Dugan a mocking salute, and climbed back into his launch. Moments later, he was on his way back to his own boat.

Dugan looked at Veronica, and saw that she was pale and shaking. Whatever had impelled her to stand up to Emilio that way had deserted her. He was tempted to reach out for her, but first he had another more important task.

"Tam, you son of a bitch!" he shouted toward the bow.

Tam faced him and held up both hands, as if to say, What could he do?

Then Dugan knelt before Veronica, taking her icy hands in his. "Are you okay?"

She didn't answer. Instead she tugged her hands from his and reached up, pulling her hearing aids out. "God, the wind is shrieking in my ears. I can't stand it anymore. I could only hear a few words of what you said, it's so loud."

"Well, you did pretty damn good for someone who couldn't hear a thing."

Her blue eyes, as bright as sapphires, met his. "I'm sorry. I can't hear you. If you want to talk, we'll have to go below."

He wanted to talk about all of this, but first he wanted to do something else. Wrapping his arms around her, he hugged her, feeling her fragility, feeling the tremors that shook her. And it felt so damn good when, after a few seconds, she hugged him back.

He was glad Tam had the sense not to come aft then, because he was feeling an urge to strangle him. If Tam had just told them what was going on from the outset, they could have done something to prevent this. Now they were miles out at sea with no help in sight. Not a great position to be in.

Veronica was still shivering, so he decided to take her below. Once there, he started brewing a pot of coffee. No one was going to sleep that night anyway, so the caffeine didn't matter.

When he joined her at the table, she obliged by putting in her hearing aids again.

"How much of that did you follow?" he asked her.

"Not a lot. I got the sense that he was threatening us. Something about ramming, right?"

"Yeah, he said that. Basically he wants to take over the salvage."

"That would follow from what he said about ramming."

"I guess so." They sat in silence for several minutes, sipping coffee, listening to the creaks of the boat as she rocked on the waves.

"What now?" Veronica asked.

"I'd suggest hoisting anchor and getting the fuck out of here, but I suspect he's going to be watching for that."

"Could he catch us?"

"Probably. My engine isn't likely to be as powerful as his, and if I sail, while I might go faster, I'll have to tack while he can go straight. Yeah, he could probably ram us. On the other hand, I can maneuver faster. Hmm." He started thinking about the possibilities of escape.

"It doesn't matter," Veronica said. "I'm not going to abandon the site."

He looked at her. "Are you crazy?"

"Maybe. I don't care. I'm not going to let him take this away from me."

"Woman, you're out of your mind! There is nothing down there worth our lives."

"Maybe not to you."

He decided that he was the crazy one. Given his philosophy of life, that he was here to have fun, why had he gotten tangled up in this mess in the first place? He should have flat-out said no instead of rushing to the aid of a perceived damsel in distress. A damsel who, by the way, was in distress of her own making, and rapidly digging the hole deeper.

He was sure she must have a few ounces of common sense left in her brain. The problem was how to reach it. "Look, Veronica, maybe you're willing to risk your neck for that mask, but *I'm* not. And neither is Tam."

Her mouth tightened, drawing into a thin, harsh line. But her eyes held something else, a haunted look that made him squirm where he sat.

"Okay," she said. "Take me over to the guy's boat. I'll work with him, and you both go home."

Yup, she was crazier than a loon. "Don't be ridiculous. The guy has no intention of letting any of us live to tell the tale of this. How could he? I'm surprised he hasn't already blown us out of the water."

"He's probably not a murderer. Just a thief."

"I should be so lucky. If he's not a murderer, then how come he was threatening to ram us? No, he's probably figured out that keeping us alive will prevent the hue and cry being raised. I mean, if we don't go back to port on a regular basis, sooner or later someone is going to come looking for us. And that might get in the way of his salvage job."

"Exactly." Her eyes were alight again. "That's exactly why I tried to make the deal with him. He needs us, at least for the time being. He'll keep us alive as long as we cooperate."

"To what end?"

"Maybe I can get the mask."

"Fuck the fucking mask!"

She blinked and drew back a little. "Will you let me finish? Maybe I can get the mask. But at the very least, we'll have more time to find a way out of this mess. We *have* to cooperate."

He sat there drumming his fingers, turning the conundrum around in his mind. Discussing things with Veronica wasn't wise, he decided, because she had a very narrow perspective on events: getting the mask. He, however, had a much broader perspective: saving his neck, and, whether she liked it or not, saving *her* neck. He didn't give a flip about Tam's neck.

Looking for hints, answers, ideas, or even a grain of hope, he replayed his conversation with Emilio in his mind. "You know," he said suddenly, engaging Veronica's attention, "Emilio started off by saying he wanted to help us with the salvage."

"So?"

"So then, when I said you probably didn't want any help because the salvage had to be done with care, he announced that we could either sail away immediately and leave the site to him, or he would ram us."

"He was going to let us leave?"

"That's what I don't get. Letting us sail away would probably only mean that we'd come back with the big guns to drive him away. So why did he say that?"

"Probably to encourage us to cooperate with him. Which, as I said to him, is distinctly to his advantage. I've got the permits, Dugan. He doesn't. I've got a contract on this area of water with the state of Florida. Nobody else can salvage this wreck."

"Like he cares."

"But he *will* care if the Coast Guard comes out here and finds an illegal salvage going on. It's not like he can get what he wants overnight. This is going to take months, probably years. He needs us."

"Well, I feel a little better," he said sarcastically. "I guess I can count on breathing for the next few weeks."

She ignored his tone. "As long as we don't cross him. I've got a feeling he could get very ugly."

"No kidding. Okay. So we do the deal with him in the morning. Tell him we want his help. Tell him even *I* agree with that. Then what? Is he going to let us go back to town every few days for supplies? I doubt it. Man, I just can't see how this is going to work unless he kills us."

Veronica frowned and traced the rim of her mug with her index finger. "He'll let us go back to town. He has to. Because I'm going to explain to him that my father will raise the dead if I don't show up when I'm supposed to. So he's going to have to let us go. He probably just won't let us go alone."

"I don't see it. He can't let you have time alone with your father, and if you ask me, Orin's going to get very suspicious if you have some thug glued to your side while you talk to him. It'd be easier just to make you gone."

"I don't know." All of a sudden she rested her forehead in her palm and closed her eyes. "I'm so tired. So confused. There's got to be a way to handle this."

He didn't say anything. She wouldn't understand him anyway, with her eyes closed. So, against his better judgment, he reached out and laid his hand on her shoulder.

It was odd, but he'd gone from trying to find some way to outwit Emilio to trying to find a way to keep the two of them alive as long as possible. Ten minutes ago he'd been swearing he was going to haul up anchor and head for home as fast as the *Mandolin* would take him. Now he was trying to find ways to stay here and stay alive.

Veronica. It all had to do with Veronica. She was making him crazy. If he had two ounces of common sense, he'd hog-tie and gag her and head for home lickety-split, taking his chances with getting rammed.

But she wasn't going to cooperate with that, and she was going to be very angry with him if he went ahead and did it anyway.

He didn't want to make her mad at him, which just went to show that she'd softened his brain. Turned it to mush. For his own sake, he needed to get as far away from her as possible as soon as possible, before all he had between his ears was Jell-O.

But there was no place to go, and the big problem of Emilio still existed, and Veronica was clearly not going to vanish from the planet anytime soon. Not if he had anything to say about it. So instead of keeping his distance, he reached out and pulled her against his side, hugging her tight.

Somehow they would get through this. They *had* to.

"Dammit," Tam said to Dugan, "I've got as much to lose as either of you right now. Do you think they have any use for me now that they're here?"

Dugan looked at Veronica, wondering if she'd followed what Tam had said. But she didn't look questioningly at him, so he let it go.

"So I'm supposed to trust you now?" Dugan asked.

"I don't know if I'd call it trust. But you can believe I want to get out of this alive as much as you do, and cooperating with them isn't going to save me, because they don't need me. What can I possibly do for them that they can't do for themselves, now that they're here?"

"Well . . . you could tell them about the things we discuss. Our plans for getting away."

Tam's lips whitened as he tightened them. "I want to get away as much as you do. I never would have told them anything at all if they hadn't threatened to hurt me."

"Yeah? So what happens now if they threaten to hurt you if you don't tell them everything we say over here?"

"This is different."

Dugan leaned toward him threateningly. "How so?"

"Because before all they wanted was some information. I didn't think it was that big a deal. For Chrissake, Dugan, everybody on Key West would have heard about what we're doing out here before long anyway. Keeping a secret in that town is like trying to hold water in a sieve. I didn't think it was any big deal to let them know we found a cannon."

"Well, it turned out to be a big deal, didn't it. Just what did you think they were going to do when they found out? If they were threatening to hurt you for not cooperating, what did you think was going to happen when they learned we'd found something? Did you think they were going to put on tutus and dance a congratulatory *Swan Lake*?"

Tam threw up his hands. "Okay. Okay. I didn't think far enough in advance. I never do. You've been telling me that ever since you bailed the diving business out of trouble. So I'm not the world's greatest prophet."

"That's an understatement."

"Yeah. Well." He jerked his shoulders back and rotated his head as if his neck were stiff. "Still, this is different. They're here now, they threatened to ram us, and I'm not going to do one damn little thing that might get any of us hurt or killed. This is *different,* man. Totally."

Maybe it was. Maybe Tam was smart enough to see that his best chance at self-preservation didn't lie with Emilio and his henchmen. On the other hand, that could change in an instant, couldn't it? And Dugan wasn't the kind of person who found it easy to trust again when he'd been betrayed once.

"I don't know, Tam."

"Look, I swear, all I want is for us to find a way out of this. *All* of us. I was a jerk, and I know it. But I learned my lesson."

It was possible, Dugan supposed. Tam had never been stupid; he just wasn't the kind who could see very far beyond his own nose.

"Look," said Tam. "I'll make you a deal. I'll do my part. Whatever you tell me. And I won't ask why. I'll just do it. Fair enough?"

"I guess so," Dugan agreed reluctantly. "So . . . do you think you can take the first watch? And will you wake me up if you see anything suspicious at all?"

"I can do that. You *know* I can do that. I won't let those guys within a hundred yards of the *Mandolin.*"

Dugan had decided that they needed to keep watch through the night. He hadn't told Veronica that yet, and he didn't know how much of this conversation she was following, but he felt that they shouldn't dare lower their guard for a minute. If Emilio Zaragosa really wanted them out of the way, what better opportunity than to ram them in the middle of the night? No one would see, and no one could even start looking for them before dawn. If anyone bothered, because he figured that it would be at least three days before anyone would report them missing.

"This sucks," he said to no one in particular. But Veronica nodded.

"Okay," he said to Tam, "you take first watch. Wake me at two." It sounded good, though frankly he didn't think he was going to sleep a wink.

"You got it." Tam climbed the ladder and closed the hatch behind him, leaving Dugan alone with Veronica.

"We're taking watches," he told her. "I'll take over at two."

"I gathered that."

"So you can go to bed and sleep without worrying."

She shook her head slowly. "I'm not going to sleep, and I don't want to go to bed alone."

He didn't know if she meant that the way it had sounded. Probably not, he decided. She just didn't want to be alone.

"Fine," he said. "I'm not going to sleep either. So we can just sit here and play cards or something."

She made an exasperated sound.

"Why? What?"

"Is playing cards all you can think of doing?" she asked.

There was no mistaking the look in her eye. He felt his mouth go dry. "Now?" he asked. "With death breathing down our necks?"

"Can you think of a better time? We'll probably be dead by this time tomorrow, and all you want to do is play cards?"

One of them was crazy, but he wasn't sure which. What she said made a kind of perverse sense. After all . . . Well, hell, he couldn't get himself into any trouble if they were going to be dead this time tomorrow. On the other hand, if they survived . . .

"Why?" he asked. He had to know why.

She shrugged. "Because I've been wondering what it

would be like to be with you without all our clothes on. Because you attract me. Because I'm damned if I want to spend the next eight hours crawling up the walls with my nerves screaming."

"So I'm like . . . an antianxiety pill?"

She would have laughed, he thought, if she hadn't been so tense, and if her eyes hadn't held a dark sorrow in them. But she didn't laugh, and all she did was shake her head.

He didn't want to know what that meant. It was safe to be an antianxiety pill for her. For them both. But anything more, he couldn't handle.

Or thought he couldn't, until finally she said, her lips quivering, "Dugan, I'm scared."

Why the hell hadn't she just said that in the first place?

Without another word, he took her hand, tugged her to her feet, and pulled her back to the cabin.

All of a sudden, this seemed like absolutely the sanest thing they could do.

And he would brook no other opinions on the subject.

Chapter 18

Dugan turned on only one light in the cabin, a small bulb in a wall sconce. It was enough light for the minutes to come. He had a feeling that neither of them would welcome harsh reality just then. This was an escape, a journey into a dream territory where there weren't any villains.

He could hear Veronica's rapid breaths. He wondered if she could hear his. He wondered if she would hear anything at all, or if she would take out her hearing aids and make these moments utterly silent.

She did. He watched her put them away, and felt a pang that she was putting that barrier between them. But maybe she didn't see it that way. Maybe for her the hearing aids were more of a barrier, bringing her sounds he wouldn't even notice, sounds that might trouble her. Or maybe by cutting off her hearing she could concentrate more on other sensations.

It didn't matter.

Because she was reaching for the hem of her shirt, pulling it up over her head. He liked this in her, he realized, her lack of shyness, her lack of reluctance. Finding a lover who was willing to take full responsibility for what she was doing, a lover who came as an equal . . . that was pretty special. It was also something he'd never experienced before. Most women wanted to be coaxed and seduced, at least the first few times.

Veronica was so different.

He found himself wondering if she had really meant what she said about being dead this time tomorrow. And he discovered that he hoped she hadn't really meant it, that it had just been an excuse for the next few hours. Because if she *had* meant it, then these moments would have to be locked up forever in memory as if they had never happened, if they survived. That thought saddened him. What she was offering was another kind of death.

His hands were shaking. He hadn't allowed himself to realize just how much he wanted to make love to her. He'd been skating away from the feelings for weeks, pretending they didn't exist, refusing to acknowledge them even when they tried to force their way to his attention.

Now he could evade them no longer. He wanted her. He wanted her as much as he had ever wanted anything in his life. His mouth was dry with longing. His body felt heavy with building desire, like the air right before a thunderstorm.

She stripped off her shorts and stood before him in nothing but panties and bra. She looked at him then, her face revealing an insecurity, a fear of what he might think that swept past all his defenses and buried itself in his heart. Yet there was something else, he realized. Without her aids, she never took her eyes from his face. He watched every emotion play through her heart: hope, longing, need, and fear. She couldn't turn away, and the intensity of her gaze left him nowhere to turn either. He hadn't yet taken off a stitch of clothes, and he felt more naked than ever before in his life.

He looked down to unbutton his shorts, but she crossed the cabin in an instant, her hands on his face, turning his eyes back to her. "Here," she whispered soundlessly, locking him into her world of silence, bringing him closer to her by making him read her lips. "Let me. Let me."

He nodded and felt his entire being sink into those luminous eyes as her fingers worked the button, then the zipper, then slid his shorts over his hips. He wiggled them down, thinking for a moment that it was a wasted gesture with their eyes locked together, but her hands told her what he was doing. She smiled softly and let out a silent giggle. "Nice buns."

"Ummm . . . yours, too," he answered. It felt so out of place to say such a thing at such a moment. For in the unbroken contact of their gaze, he was finding an intimacy that went far beyond anything he'd ever known with a woman, an intimacy that was almost reverent. And yet words tumbled out. "Very, very nice," he added, his hands trailing over her body like a blind man reading braille.

Hills, valleys, hollows, and curves, they became his as his hands wandered over them, learning them, memorizing them. He watched the play of response in her eyes and on her face, reading her as he had never read a woman before. Feeling her as he had never felt a woman before.

Her hands found the bottom hem of his shirt and lifted, peeling it off of him. He felt a pang in his soul as the fabric neared his chin. If only for an instant, he would lose her eyes. Only for an instant, but for an eternity too long. He raised his arms to make it easier for her, and tried to tell himself it was only a blink. Just a second. Maybe less.

Yet as soon as the shirt slipped past, his eyes shot open

and searched for hers. Just a second. Maybe less. Far too long. She seemed to recognize the moment and paused with their hands upraised and touching, the fabric still at his wrists. She studied him, and he her, renewing a contact that reached to the ends of time and space. "I need you," she mouthed.

"I need you, too," he mouthed back, now with equal silence. For his world had gone silent too. The creak of the boat, the susurration of the sea, the rustle of cloth on skin, all of these were lost to him. He was drowning in the depths of her passion, her joy, her need. She was all that existed. She had become the entire universe, and in that universe, sound was irrelevant. In that universe, there was only the soft, shared, longing gaze of lovers, and the connection of two souls. "You are perfect," he said soundlessly.

For a moment, she nearly lost sight of his eyes again. Seconds ago it had been his T-shirt that took him away from her. Now it was the fast-rising film of her own tears. She hadn't imagined it. *You are perfect.* He'd said it, and in the reflection of his eyes, for just an instant, she had felt it. And then her body betrayed her, her eyes welling with the echo of a need that ran to the core of her being. And in the sweet caress of his soundless words, in the echo of that need, in the release of her tear, her vision dimmed, and she lost him. She blinked, but her body seemed determined to win this race of eyelids and tears. She felt a tug from his hands, still held over their heads, and she knew what he wanted. She shook her head. She needed his face again first. It was utterly inexplicable, but seeing his eyes had become the single most important thing in the whole world. She needed to see into his soul again. And in his soul, to see the reflection of her own, as he saw her.

Even with tear-dimmed vision, she could see and feel him moving closer. Now lips brushed against eyebrows and lashes. Gentle kisses, so soft she could barely feel them, wicked away moisture. The soft scratch of his cheek against hers. The warmth of his breath on her ear. She tipped her face backward and opened her eyes. Her vision was clear enough to see what she needed, for his face was strong and soft and open and near.

Now their hands lowered. Underwear slid away, and fingertips searched. Eyes remained locked together, windows on souls that were about to become one.

They slid onto the bunk as one being, a silent sigh as heads rested onto the pillow. Her hands grew bolder, and her fingernails scraped delicately along his belly, then his chest, circling closer, teasing the moment to agonizing frustration.

It was almost as if he were blindfolded, for he was so lost in her eyes that only the scintillating echoes of nerve endings told him where she had been, and only his aching need could predict where she would go next.

Finally . . . was it? Had she? It was too faint to be sure, and he felt a plea deep within him. She must have seen it, for she answered it with a wicked smile and another too-faint-to-be-sure touch. Then another. His back arched as if reaching up for her, but her deft fingertips rose with him and continued their patient work.

Two could play at this game, he realized, and his hands began to explore her with equal playfulness. Her eyes grew wide as he traced a slow circle around her areolae, contact so faint it nearly buzzed at the very tips of his fingers. He did it again, and then again, watching her face go soft and dreamy. He wanted to close his eyes and sink into her touches. She no doubt wanted the same. And yet, on this night, there would be no comfortable distance behind closed eyelids. Their passion and need and joy would play out in the full light of each other's eyes.

Then he saw doubt and the flicker of fear in her blue gaze. It was as if he could feel her thoughts deep within his heart. She was wondering, what if she disappointed him? What if she did not respond to his most intimate touches? There would be no hiding in this moment. Or perhaps they were his own thoughts, for he feared the same things.

He reached out to reassure her, and in her response to his touches, he found his own reassurance.

One of his hands took hers and slowly pressed it down his belly to his manhood, firm and ready. She pulled his fingertips to her delicate tuft, already damp to the touch. She seemed surprised at her body's own readiness, as if she hadn't realized how far they had come. As if she had lost track of her growing passion in the intimacy of their connection. The thought swelled his heart, because he knew he hadn't come to this place alone.

"You are perfect," he mouthed again.

Now the delicate touches played over new nerves. Hips began to rock gently to the mounting rhythms of passion. His pupils dilated, huge black pools that beckoned her. She started to kiss him, then pulled back, clinging to his eyes with hers.

He saw the almost-kiss form, and echoed it with one of his own. She was amazing. Exquisite. He had never before imagined, let alone experienced, so complete a connection with another human being. Just as his need began to ache, her legs began to open, and they slowly rolled into union. Union. As if a completing a circuit, for now they were joined twice.

Joined twice. In his eyes, and in her womb. It was impossible to say which touched him more. Deep within her, muscles clenched in welcoming caresses, drawing him deeper into her heart and soul. Gentle. Their union was gentle. Gentle of heart. Gentle of spirit.

It was difficult to keep his eyes open. This was a time when he went away into himself, rising the sea of raw sensation, letting the waves carry him. But he could not let go. She needed him, now. Her eyes and her body spoke that need. And he needed her. He needed her trust and her soul and her heart. And her body. That need pulled him to her yet again, grinding slowly, feeling her grip him from within, until it seemed his entire body was ready to rise out of itself. Up, up, up to the edge, and if only he could close his eyes, he would tumble over. If only.

She felt the electric sparkles building along every nerve ending in her body. Her breath was ragged, as if there were not enough oxygen in the room. Every flex of their hips spurred her higher, higher, higher. With just a moment of total darkness, free to plunge into the sea of sensations that rolled over her, she could crest and ride that wave. Just a moment.

His eyes were growing distant, but they found hers for one more split second. "Perfect," he mouthed.

The wave took her on its own and she rose up to meet it with raw, naked, exposed joy. He saw it happen and his own face froze for a second, as if an electric shock had passed through him. She felt him pulsing within her, and matched his pulses with her own, their eyes locked, looking deep into each other's souls in that most ragged and vulnerable of moments. Connected in body, heart, soul, and trust.

The clenching seemed to go on forever. He felt as if his

body were alight, her eyes alone fanning the flames. On and on and on until every bit of him was spent, every muscle exhausted, every nerve numb.

And, for the first time, their eyes closed for a kiss.

Perfection had a price. Dugan stared up at the roof of the cabin, listening to Veronica's soft breathing beside him, and realized that he was going to have to pay the piper. Wherever he'd gone in those otherworldly minutes with her, in that incredible free fall of lovemaking when he had surely tumbled through an abyss right into the heart of her, the fact was, reality had returned, and perfection always had a price.

The only question that still had to be answered was what was the price going to be. Best-case scenario: She thought of this as a fling, an adrenaline-induced affirmation of life in the face of death that she would want to forget as quickly as possible.

Yeah, that would work. That would hurt only a little bit. A wound to his pride. A small wound to his heart that wasn't quite as indifferent to her as he kept telling it to be. But it would be survivable.

The other best-case scenario was that they'd all be dead within twenty-four hours, and none of this would matter a hill of beans anyway.

God, he was getting morbid.

But what he feared, really feared, was that this hadn't been a fling, that he was more deeply involved than he realized, and that this was going to become something with the potential to rip his heart out by the roots. Jana had turned him into an Aztec sacrifice once. He didn't want to volunteer for a repeat performance.

But what you wanted and what life doled out weren't always the same thing. He had plenty of scars to prove it.

Idiot. He needed to stop thinking about this and start thinking about what they were going to do about Emilio Zaragosa. Because, regardless of the extravagant statements he was making to himself, the best-case scenario was that he and Veronica both survived long enough to have to decide how to treat what had just happened between them.

Being dead wasn't an option.

It might be unavoidable, but he sure as hell wasn't going to do anything to encourage that outcome.

He glanced at his watch. The luminous dial told him that he'd need to relieve Tam in a few minutes. He'd think better above deck anyway, without Veronica's closeness to distract him. Without the incredible scent of their love-making thick in his nostrils. Without the awareness that if he just rolled over and touched her he could probably lose himself in her all over again.

It was definitely not the time for that.

Easing away from Veronica, he dressed as quietly as he could, then remembered she wouldn't be able to hear him anyway. Which reminded him of the hours just passed, when she had drawn him into her silent world, making him share it with her.

Something about her doing that had left him with an ache in the vicinity of his heart. As if she had shared some ineffable part of herself with him.

And he had to stop thinking this way before he seriously messed something up. Or before he got any more messed up than he was right now.

He shoved his feet into his deck shoes and closed the door soundlessly behind him. While she might not be able to hear it close, she could feel the vibrations, and from watching her over the past few months, he knew she was extremely sensitive to such things.

In the galley, he made a pot of coffee. When it had finished brewing, he took two mugs above deck and handed one to Tam, who was sitting in the director's chair with his feet up on a bench.

"Quiet," Tam said, accepting the mug. "Not a peep."

"Hmph." Dugan sat on the bench, resting his elbows on his knees, cradling the mug in his hands. The difference between the daytime temperatures and those at night couldn't have been much more than ten degrees, but he still felt the night air like a chill.

"Weird, huh?" said Tam. "It's almost like the Keystone Kops. Do these guys even know what they're doing?"

"I suspect Emilio isn't usually a hands-on sort of thug," Dugan replied. "He probably has people do the dirty work for him."

"Or maybe he's a thief who's never needed to kill before."

"Don't say that word."

"Okay. But maybe he's not."

That was a possibility, Dugan thought.

"Maybe there's a language problem," Tam said. "Maybe he didn't really mean to threaten to ram us."

"Are you prepared to wager your life on that?"

"Uh . . . no."

Dugan shook his head and sipped his coffee.

"It's still weird," Tam said. "They're sitting over there, and we're sitting over here, and how are they going to stop us if we try to sail away right this minute?"

Dugan was thinking the same thing. For all he felt the other boat must have far better engines than his there was still a reasonable chance that if they could pull away they could keep ahead.

Tam spoke. "Veronica doesn't want to leave, does she?"

"No."

"I heard some of what she said about abandoning the site. And she's probably right. They'd trash the whole thing. But what's more important, Dugan? Us or the damn wreck."

"I know, I know." But the simple truth was, if he were to be brutally honest about it, Veronica was more important to him than any of it. And if he took off from the site, she'd probably never forgive him.

"Why are you letting her push you around like this?" Tam wanted to know. "She's crazy. I figured that out months ago. Got her head fixed on this search until there's no room for anything else."

It was true. "On the other hand," he reminded Tam, "Zaragosa wasn't making a whole lot of sense earlier. First he wants to join our expedition. Then he's going to ram us if we don't cooperate. Then he wanders off and just leaves us. I'm not sure he isn't just blustering."

"So we're going to hang around and find out?"

"It looks that way."

"Why? Why for God's sake? Just because Veronica's afraid he might mess things up a little?"

"There's a lot at stake for her in this." And he was surprising himself by defending her stupidity. Not too long ago, he'd been telling her she was crazy, too.

Tam jumped up from his chair and pointed a finger at Dugan. "You, my friend, are being led around by your nose by a little bit of pussy."

Then Tam disappeared down the hatch, slamming it behind him.

Maybe he was, Dugan thought, looking up at the stars.

Maybe he was. But the simple fact was, if he couldn't get away without someone on the *Conchita* seeing him go, then he probably wasn't going to get away at all. His belief in that had been bolstered by the way Emilio seemed utterly unconcerned that they might try to sail away.

He looked at the yacht again, and realized it had moved a lot closer since sundown. It was no longer a quarter mile away. Not even half that far now. Which meant that Zaragosa had no intention of giving them a head start.

"They're closer."

The sound of Veronica's voice startled him, and he swung around. She was half out of the hatch, looking toward the *Conchita.*

"Yeah," he said, wondering if she could hear him.

"Who slammed the hatch?" she asked.

"Tam." Damn his eyes.

She came the rest of the way up the ladder and closed the hatch, then came to sit beside him. "What now, skipper?"

It was the first time she had called him that. He wondered if it was deliberate.

"I vote we get the hell out of here now. We can be back with the Coast Guard by late tomorrow afternoon, Veronica. He can't do much damage by then."

"You're sure we can get away safely?"

No, he wasn't sure. He sure as hell wasn't. But he wasn't sure either if he wanted to hang around to discover that Emilio wasn't as much of a turkey as he seemed. "I don't know."

She cocked her head toward the other boat. "He doesn't seem to think so. If he did, we'd have a guard on us."

He nodded, agreeing with her assessment. "Probably."

"On the other hand," she continued, "maybe that's what he wants us to think."

He sighed heavily. "You know, I'm getting tired of trying to second guess that slimeball. That entire conversation with him didn't make sense. And I know he couldn't be that stupid or impulsive because he managed to get information out of Tam for weeks. Which means the guy *does* think ahead."

"Most likely."

"And that means his entire visit this afternoon was nothing but a delaying tactic of some kind."

"A delay for what?"

"Damned if I know." It still didn't make any sense, and the more he thought about the whole thing, the less clear it became. There was something he didn't know about what was going on here.

In fact, the more he thought about it, the more ridiculous the entire pseudoconfrontation had been early that evening. Almost as if Zaragosa had simply been buying time.

But for what? All he had succeeded in doing was keeping them from diving all afternoon. Hardly a major accomplishment.

"We've got to go for help," he said.

He expected Veronica to argue with him, to cling to her insistence that Emilio could have whatever he wanted if only she could have the mask. But she didn't say anything.

"Look," he said, "I'll hightail it for shore, and we'll get the Coast Guard out here right away. He can't possibly do that much damage in a few hours."

"You mean go right now?"

"Yes. We'll pull into port before sunrise. We can have a cutter out here by noon."

She nodded. "But . . . don't you think he's thought of that?"

"I don't know what he's thought of. And considering that the more I think about it, the more nonsensical that whole conversation becomes, I'm not sure the guy isn't a few bricks shy of a load, if you follow me. Maybe he's just a dingbat."

"A dangerous dingbat."

"All the more reason to get the hell out of here now."

"Okay."

"What?" He could hardly believe she was capitulating.

"Okay," she repeated more forcefully. "Okay. Let's get out of here now."

Determined not to give her a chance to change her mind, he headed for the cockpit.

Luis decided that life was a living hell. He hadn't called *El Desconocido* in a week, not since he had learned that Emilio was sailing toward Key West. He might be able to carry off his duplicity with Emilio safely stashed in Venezuela, but not with Emilio right on the spot. So he had made no more phone calls, and had written off his dreams of a better life . . . for the moment at least.

And he had decided to be grateful that Emilio hadn't insisted he join him on his yacht. Luis hated boats. The mere thought of being on one made him violently seasick.

But now he wished he were on the yacht, because his pager was flashing *El Desconocido*'s phone number at him. Apparently this mess wasn't going to be as easy to walk away from as he had hoped.

He considered not returning the call. Then he considered all the possibilities that could arise since the man seemed to have an idea who Luis was . . . and none of those possibilities was pleasant. What was it American mobsters said? Fish food with cement shoes?

That possibility seemed very real to Luis as he stared at his pager. Nor did he feel very confident that if he headed back home right this very instant that he would be any safer.

Finally, aching from tension and sweating profusely, he took the pager and went to find a pay phone. He was caught in the middle, he realized unhappily. Emilio sensed something was going on, even if he hadn't found out exactly what Luis was up to. And the Unknown One . . . he knew too much indeed.

Luis found himself wishing he had never gotten his bright idea.

Standing in the humid night air at the outdoor pay phone, Luis dialed the number. When the whispery voice answered, he felt his spine turn to ice.

"I have no information," he told the man, his voice quavering.

"You lie."

He lied. And the man knew it. "What do you want?"

"I want you to make very, very sure that Emilio Zaragosa doesn't get the mask of the Storm Mother."

Luis's breath locked in his throat. The mask? This man and Emilio both wanted the mask? Oh, this was bad indeed. For Luis. "I can't . . . I'm not out there . . . How am I supposed to prevent this?"

"Find a way."

"But . . . Look, what's so important about this mask anyway? There are huge amounts of gold on that . . . "

"I don't want the gold. I want the mask."

"But *why?*" Luis very nearly wailed the question as he faced the likelihood he would be dead before long. "Why?"

"Because it belongs to me. To my people. I want it back."

Then the Unknown One hung up the phone with a sharp click, leaving Luis standing in the dead of a Key West night with sweat dripping down his face, his hands shaking, and his knees feeling like rubber.

It belonged to *him?* To his *people?* Suddenly Luis knew he was dealing with something far worse than a criminal. He was dealing with a fanatic.

Ay Madre de Dios, what was he going to do?

Chapter 19

"I hate getting wet," Dugan said. Even more, he hated going into dark water in the middle of the night. He stared down at the inky blackness from the stern of his boat, and cursed quietly.

When he had turned over the engine and hit the throttle, the *Mandolin* had leapt forward as she always did . . . then she had slowed down and drifted while the engines strained. It didn't take Einstein's IQ to know there was something wrong.

"Are you sure the propeller's fouled?" Veronica asked.

He nodded grimly. Not that it really mattered. They didn't have a rudder either. They weren't going anywhere.

He straightened and looked at her so she could see his mouth. "I've got to check it out. But I think we've been sabotaged."

Her lips formed the word *sabotage* soundlessly, and her eyes grew wider. "Tam?" she asked.

He didn't know. It might have been, because Tam had taken the first watch, plenty of time to mess things up. "Go wake him up, will you?"

Veronica nodded and headed for the hatch, but before she had moved two steps, Tam came up the ladder. "What's going on?" he asked. "We pulling out?"

"Not fucking likely," Dugan said. "The propeller's fouled." And Tam couldn't have faked that look of astonishment in a million years, he decided.

"How?" Tam asked. "There's nothing in the water to get tangled up on."

"Well, the rudder's gone, too."

"Jesus Christ." Tam sat with a thud. "I don't believe it."

"Me neither. I'm going to check it out." Get wet. In dark water. Christ Almighty.

On the off chance that he could fix the problem, he stripped to his shorts and donned his breathing apparatus. The air through his regulator tasted stale, but he was used to that. Grabbing the underwater light, he stepped off and felt the cool, dark water close over him. He felt the air bubbles trapped against his skin letting go. It was the sensation he hated most, as if something were crawling all over him.

He forced himself to ignore it. There were more important problems than his dislike of being in the water at night.

And a few moments later he discovered them. The propeller was fouled, all right. Fouled in something that looked like heavy-duty chicken wire. The stuff was wrapped so tightly around the propeller and shaft that he figured it would take him days to cut it all off.

Then there was the rudder. It had fouled, too, and in the process had broken. They wouldn't be going anywhere anytime soon.

After a moment, he kicked his way to the surface and pulled himself up on the diving platform. The night air chilled him immediately, but he didn't care. He was just glad to be out of the water. He pulled his regulator and mask off and dumped the diving rig into Tam's lap.

"Jeez, thanks," Tam muttered.

"What's wrong?" Veronica asked him. "What happened?"

"Sabotage. We have been royally sabotaged. We're not going anywhere."

"So call the Coast Guard."

He looked toward the *Conchita,* and saw activity on the deck. The launch was being lowered again. "I'm not sure we'll live long enough for them to get here."

Then he sat down to wait.

Veronica watched the launch approach and could hardly believe this was real. It was three in the morning in the middle of nowhere basically, and she was watching a boat approach bearing what could only be more bad news. Instinctively, she eased toward Dugan and tucked her hand in his, taking what comfort she could from the way he squeezed her fingers.

But there was no comfort. She had barreled ahead on this insane search despite her father's warnings that it could be dangerous to discover a treasure ship. She had insisted they stay in the face of threats, and only now that they could not escape had the reality of all of this come home.

She had been a fool. She had been worse than a fool, she had been a self-centered bitch. She'd been angry at her father for no good reason, and now she might never again have the chance to tell him that she loved him and that she understood why he'd kept the story of the mask from her all these years. She'd dragged Dugan and Tam into a mess that might well get them killed, and had refused to listen yesterday when Dugan had suggested they just clear out. She'd been full of herself.

No, not full of herself. Driven. Driven to a point past common sense. If she had just agreed to leave yesterday afternoon, they wouldn't be sitting in a disabled boat watching the approach of doom.

"Well," said Dugan, looking at her She turned her attention to him, reading his lips. "Now we know why Emilio was making so little sense when he was here. He was just buying time for his diver to disable our boat."

Her heart lurched. He was right. "Call the Coast Guard now," she said. "Please."

He shook his head. "I'm telling you, if we do that, we might be signing our own death warrants. Cooperation is all we have left. Until I think of something."

He squeezed her hand again. She nodded reluctantly and turned her attention back to the launch. It was only a few yards away now, and slowing down. It bore three men, she noticed. None of them was Emilio Zaragosa.

"Ahoy," said the man in the bow of the boat as they pulled alongside. He said something else, but Veronica couldn't make it out, especially since it was so dark she could barely see his face.

Dugan answered, but he wasn't looking at her now, and she couldn't understand. God, she *hated* this. *Hated* it.

Then Dugan looked at her. "We've been invited aboard the *Conchita.*"

"No," she said, feeling her whole body tense. "No."

"Yes," he said. "We don't have any choice. Time to negotiate."

Finally, she nodded. "I need the bag for my hearing aids. In case . . ."

He turned, said something to the man in the boat, then faced her. "Go get it."

She went below, her mind working at top speed, trying to figure out a way to avoid going with the men. But what difference did it make? They were sitting ducks anyway, miles from shore. Maybe they *would* be safer on the *Conchita.* Emilio probably wouldn't want to dirty his decks with their blood.

She got the waterproof case and put her hearing aids in it. With the noise from the launch's engine, and the wind blowing in her ears from their speed, she wouldn't be able to hear anything anyway.

She hesitated, thinking of the Glock. But there was no way she could fit it in her case, which was just big enough to hold and cushion her hearing aids. Nor could she hide it on her person, not when she was wearing a tank top and shorts.

So what was she going to do? Go above deck and point the gun at the men in the launch? Men who weren't waving weapons at them? If she, Dugan, and Tam started waving a gun, things might get really ugly. At least as it stood now, they hadn't reached that point. And they might not ever reach it if everyone kept a level head.

Still, she opened the drawer to look at the Glock, only it wasn't there. Dugan must have it up above.

Back on deck, she found that Tam had already climbed into the launch. Dugan indicated that it was her turn. He helped her over the side and steadied her until Tam caught her waist. Then she was sitting on one of the bench seats, watching Dugan climb aboard. Moments later the launch pulled away from the *Mandolin.*

She noticed no one was talking as they made their way to the yacht. She also noticed that the three sailors in the launch with them were armed. The guns were visible now, and the gloves were off, it seemed. Now they would find out the real story. She was suddenly grateful she hadn't tried to bring the Glock, not when she looked at those guns. One little pistol wouldn't stand a chance.

Ten minutes later they were all standing on the deck of Zaragosa's yacht, being watched by armed men. It was a luxurious boat, Veronica noticed. The kind of thing she had hitherto only seen in movies. Upholstered chairs, tables with glass tops, even a Jacuzzi on deck.

She opened the bag to take out her hearing aids and insert them, but as soon as she started to reach into the bag, Dugan's hand shot out and stopped her.

She looked at him, and he shook his head.

"Why? I need my aids."

He jerked his chin, pointing and she looked, discovering that she had two gun barrels pointed directly at her. They thought she might be armed.

A sudden chill made goose bumps rise on her arms, but she refused to stop. Reaching into the bag, she pulled out one of the flesh-colored devices and showed it to them. Then she put it in her ear. A moment later she inserted the other one.

Sound returned to her, none of it useful. She could hear the whistle of the wind and even the restless movements of the people around her, but that was all. No one was talking.

Then a small man appeared. He resembled Emilio with his round friendly face, although he was considerably plumper and much younger. Unfortunately he also had a thick moustache, and Veronica couldn't understand him at all when he spoke.

Dugan turned to her. "He says we should sit and make ourselves comfortable. His father will be here soon."

"His father?" A family affair. Somehow that didn't reassure her. "Sit? When I'm this nervous?"

"There isn't much choice when you're at the wrong end of a gun barrel, sweetie."

Sweetie. She didn't know if she liked that either, but she promptly sat on a tube chair that was upholstered in blue-cotton duck. A few minutes later another man appeared, this one wearing a short white coat. He offered them iced drinks.

As if it were a social call. Veronica passed on the drink, and on the plate of crackers and caviar that appeared next.

"What is this?" she asked Dugan. "Our last meal?"

Despite the tension in his face, she caught the glimmer of laughter around the edges of his eyes and mouth. "Try to be positive," he suggested. "It's caviar."

But she couldn't laugh with two guns aimed in her general direction. "This is surreal."

Dugan nodded, and for that matter, so did Tam. Tam who had brought all this trouble on them. She supposed she ought to be angry with him, but she couldn't muster the feeling. She had no difficulty believing that he had been scared into cooperation. And if they'd disabled Tam somehow, there would have been another diver, and the same problem.

Emilio joined them at last, wearing a silk smoking jacket over slacks. He greeted them all warmly, as if they were his welcome guests and not his prisoners. And Veronica still couldn't understand a word he said. She had to twist to watch Dugan just so she could piece together what was going on.

Dugan reached out and took her hand. Trying to help

as much as he could, he framed everything he said to Emilio in a way that would keep her fully informed.

"So," said Emilio, "your boat is disabled, eh?"

"Funny, funny. That was pretty slick, keeping us occupied while your diver set us up."

Emilio spread his hands. "Of course. I am not a fool. Did you really think I was going to let you run for help?"

"In retrospect, no. I was the fool to think you'd ever let us leave."

"Ah, but I *will.* Once I have accomplished my task. I have no desire to hurt anyone."

Dugan believed that about as much as he believed he could dig a hole to China. There'd be too many international complications if Veronica reported that a major archaeological find had been looted by this man. No, Emilio would have to get rid of them sooner or later. But he wasn't going to let Emilio know he realized that. It was better to make the man believe that they would cooperate to save their lives.

"So," said Emilio, "the lady had offered a deal. I'm interested. Why don't we discuss it?"

Dugan looked at Veronica, squeezing her fingers. "He wants to discuss the deal you offered."

She nodded and looked at Emilio. She looked as cool as a cucumber, Dugan thought. Nobody would guess how uptight she was. He could tell only because her hand was so icy.

"The deal is exactly what I said," she told the man. "I have no interest in the gold. There may or may not really be ten or twenty million dollars in bullion down there. I don't know. But you can have it all. I'm more interested in the artifacts. Specifically, a gold mask."

Emilio nodded slowly. "What is this mask?"

Dugan relayed the question, but he couldn't quite escape the feeling that Emilio already knew the answer.

Veronica spoke. "It's the one remaining artifact from a dead culture, an article of great religious significance. To me that makes it worth more than anything else on the *Alcantara.* If it's even there."

Emilio sat up a little straighter. "You have doubts?"

Veronica nodded. "My father very wisely pointed out that an item that was so precious to a culture would hardly have been allowed to sail away to Spain. At least not voluntarily. And the story goes that the priestess carried it voluntarily."

Emilio shrugged. "And maybe someone lied about how it came to be on the ship."

"Perhaps."

"But that is all you want, this mask?"

Veronica nodded.

"Then we have a deal. We will work with you. You get the mask, I get whatever else I want, yes?"

Veronica nodded, but from something in her expression, Dugan got the strong feeling that she felt she was selling her soul. "Whatever you want."

"Fair enough. And I can trust you not to go to your Coast Guard?"

Veronica hesitated, then said, "Yes." Dugan wondered if she was lying, or merely out of her mind.

Emilio smiled. "Good. That is good. Because you see, I have a man in Key West. And if you call down trouble on my head, you will call down trouble on your own. I know who your father is, and I know where to find him."

Dugan felt the jaws of the trap snap shut. They were done for.

* * *

Emilio offered them beds aboard the *Conchita,* but the three of them refused adamantly, so the launch carried them back to the *Mandolin,* where they gathered in the lounge and stared glumly at one another.

"We're all running on adrenaline," Dugan said finally. "Let's be careful we don't get punchy from lack of sleep."

"Who can sleep?" Veronica asked. "My God, I've got to find some way to warn my father. Some way to get him to go into hiding until we find a way out of this mess."

"He was bluffing," Tam said. "I'm sure he was bluffing."

Dugan repeated his words for Veronica, then asked, "How the hell can you be sure of that?"

"Because if he's talking about that Luis guy, I can tell you right now the man's no killer."

"He scared you enough to convince you to cooperate."

Tam subsided.

When Dugan had caught her up, Veronica said, "Maybe he's talking about someone else. He could have more than one man in Key West."

"Great. This is just fucking great." Dugan, a laid-back guy to the bone, felt a totally uncharacteristic urge to smash something. He didn't like feeling boxed in with no way out.

"I've got to figure out how to warn my father," Veronica said. "There's got to be a way. Then we find the mask and get the hell out of here."

"Sure," said Dugan sarcastically. "We'll just sail off into the sunset on our broken boat."

She turned on him. "You can give up if you want, but I'm not going to. There's too much at stake. I'm not going to let that man hurt my father, and I'm not going to let him have the mask. No matter what it takes."

Dugan admired her spunk, if not her brains. "Let's hold it right here. We're not making sense. We've got two problems, and instead of making grandiose statements about what we will and won't do, we need to work the *problems*. First, we need to find a way to warn Orin so he can get out of the way. Then we need to find a way to get ourselves out of here."

"With the mask."

Dugan frowned at her. "With or *without* the mask. The important thing is getting out of this alive."

She looked at him, her face tight, her eyes suspiciously wet. "I'm not going without the mask."

"Two hours ago you said—"

"That was before he threatened my father. That was before I realized that he wants the mask, too."

Dugan opened his mouth to argue, but snapped it shut. She was right. He'd had the feeling when Emilio asked about the mask that he already knew what it was. And more, his question about it not being on the boat had seemed too . . . interested. If all he wanted was the gold, he wouldn't give a damn whether the mask was there.

"Hold it," he said finally. "If Emilio wants that mask . . . Honey, it's the last thing on earth you want to get your hands on. He's willing to kill for what he wants."

"But don't you see? If I can find it and hide it, he can't kill us without losing it forever. So we can use it as a bargaining chip. We can promise to give it to him if he lets us go safely home and leaves my father alone."

He nodded slowly. "Well, that's a decent possibility. Except for one problem."

"What's that?"

"How likely is it that we can find the mask in the next four days?"

"What do you mean? Why does it matter how long it takes?"

"Because if we don't reach port by Friday at the latest, my office manager is going to call out the dogs."

"But why? We haven't exactly been regular about our comings and goings."

"No, but she knows I have five days' provisions. She won't worry until she knows we're out of food and still haven't shown up. Then nothing short of an aerial bombardment is going to keep her from going to the Coast Guard."

"Oh." Her tone sank.

"Then there's your father."

"He won't worry. Not for a while. He's in Tampa and won't be back until after his last test on Monday."

"That leaves Ginny. And believe me, Ginny is enough of a problem. Once she gets a search going, Emilio's going to know it. It's kind of hard to miss the choppers. And then . . . well, I'd be surprised if we weren't dead meat. Because he's not going to give us a chance to tell anyone what he's up to."

She nodded slowly. "The mask is our only chance, then. We've got to find it. It's the only chip we have."

Dugan knew unyielding stubbornness when he saw it. She wasn't being entirely rational, but then he realized she hadn't really been rational about this from the beginning. Maybe it had something to do with the loss of her hearing, and maybe it had something to do with feeling that she'd been second best her entire life. Or maybe it was something else. But he had the feeling that Veronica's entire future depended on finding this mask. That without this, she would exist as a shell of the woman she could have been.

As for using it as a bargaining chip—well, maybe. It was a slim hope, worth pursuing if they could find the thing. But he wasn't going to hold his breath. For now, he just had to concentrate on using every minute to try to figure out an effective way out of this mess, no matter what it cost him.

The mask might be more important to Veronica than her life. She certainly gave him that impression sometimes. But she was more important to *him* than life.

The feeling hit him sideways and made him angry. He tried to dismiss it, telling himself that was just a wild-eyed overdramatization of what he felt, which was that she was a nice lady who deserved to live, but was in serious need of a brain tune-up.

Because nothing, but nothing, was more important to Dugan than his own skin. He'd made that mistake once, and wasn't dumb enough to repeat it.

Regardless of what he really felt about Veronica, he knew one thing for certain. He wasn't going to bail out on her. If she was going to stay and hunt for the mask, then so was he.

In the meantime, he'd pray to all the gods, past and present, that something would turn up to get them out of this mess.

Chapter 20

Dugan had to hand it to Veronica: over the next two days, she conducted the excavation as if it were an archaeological dig under her total control. And the interesting thing was, Emilio Zaragosa let her do it.

She took command, telling everyone how it was going to be. Instead of the almost haphazard search Dugan had expected with metal detectors and divers digging up things only to abandon them when they appeared to have no intrinsic value, they followed a careful, methodical plan and all of Veronica's salvage instructions.

While the *Mandolin* sat disabled, a line with six colored buoys attached was run out from the *Conchita* to the launch some sixty yards away. Yacht and launch paced each other while six divers used the line as a guide and followed their marker buoys, ensuring they searched every square inch along the path designated by the boats.

It was pretty effective, too. They brought up a lot of interesting stuff, all of which was dumped in a rubber raft. And by the end of the first day, they brought up some gold bars.

Everyone got excited about the gold. Except Dugan. He was personally disappointed in the bars. He'd been expecting something like the gold bars he'd seen in photographs of Federal Reserve vaults. Instead these bars were thin, uneven, narrow little strips of gold.

And they were unmarked. That got Veronica really excited because they were contraband. Even Emilio seemed rather tickled by the development as they all had dinner aboard his yacht.

Like a goddamn social gathering, Dugan thought as they sat around a table with a snowy white cloth and dined on exquisite delicacies served by a white-coated waiter. Emilio Zaragosa was a strange man.

But Veronica amazed him. She seemed to be totally absorbed in the search, seemed to have completely forgotten that her father was in danger, and that she might be dead in a matter of days.

But that was all show. He saw it in her blue eyes from time to time, as darker things flickered there in quiet moments. She was, in short, doing a damn good job of convincing Emilio they were on the same side. He wondered if the guy was falling for it.

The second day they used the dredges. Dugan hated that. The damn things blew away the muck at the bottom to reveal treasures, and it made things a whole lot quicker, but he still hated it because it muddied the water until visibility was limited, and made him feel as if he were locked in a dimly lit closet.

But they found a lot more gold bars, and some jewelry: gold chains, another jeweled cross, a pair of heavy earrings. They also found more fittings from the ship, cannons, and a brass bell that finally, beyond any doubt, identified the ship, for it was engraved with her name.

Dugan found the bell. He was at the bottom in murky water, his ears filled with the sound of the dredge a dozen feet away, when he saw the glimmer of metal.

His heart nearly stopped, and for a wild moment he thought maybe he'd found the mask. He'd already figured out how he was going to conceal it if he did, even though it had to be as large or larger then a human face and he felt to be sure the bag was still hanging from his belt. All the divers carried the bags for small finds. Unbeknownst to anyone else, Dugan had a second bag tucked inside the first.

If he found the mask. He was beginning to wonder if he even wanted to. Once he found it, Veronica would have satisfied her quest, and would vanish, either back into her own world, or at the end of one of the guns aboard the *Conchita*. He decided he hated the damn mask.

He brought the bell up at the end of his dive and dumped it into the rubber raft, where they were placing all their finds. Then he swam over to the *Mandolin* and climbed aboard.

Veronica was there, but Tam still hadn't surfaced yet. She was hunched over a notebook, writing furiously. Expedition notes, he supposed, as if they'd ever be of any use. He wondered if she'd utterly disconnected from reality.

After he'd gone below to get himself something to drink and eat, he went to sit on deck with her. Tam still wasn't up. Instinctively, he looked toward the *Conchita*, and could see binoculars trained on them. They were being towed behind the yacht, and watched constantly. He shifted so his back was to the guy who was watching them. After knowing Veronica, he no longer underestimated people's ability to read lips.

"You okay?" he asked her.

She looked up, her gaze blank. "Fine."

"What are you writing?"

"Notes. On the off chance that I might get my excavation back."

So she hadn't totally lost touch. She sighed and put the pad aside. "I know I'm probably wasting my time, but it's easier than thinking about all this."

"I can understand that. Any bright ideas?"

"No. Only that we'd better find the mask quick."

"Yeah. I wish."

Neither of them said anything for a few minutes. Then he asked, "I guess we're supposed to dine with our captor again tonight?"

"That's what he said."

"I don't get the guy. He keeps treating us like guests all the while he's pointing guns at us."

Her mouth twisted. "He's a civilized criminal."

"Ahh. That explains a whole lot."

A while later, her face thoughtful, she said, "He really *is* a strange man."

"How so?"

"He seems genuinely excited about the finds we're making, even the ones that have no monetary value."

"So?"

"I don't know. It just doesn't fit with my idea of a guy who's willing to kill for money." She waved a hand as if she couldn't quite find a way to say what she meant.

He found himself remembering his boss at the brokerage. "He certainly doesn't act like your standard archvillain. But then I've learned something about bad people over the years."

"Which is?"

"They don't think they're bad. They generally think they have good reasons for what they're doing."

"That fits Emilio. I keep getting the feeling he's trying to prove to us that he's really not a bad guy."

"You mean the fancy dinners and all that? Yeah. We're getting treated like honored guests."

"So maybe he won't really kill us."

Dugan tensed. "Don't start fooling yourself, Veronica. Whatever his motivation, he'll do whatever he considers necessary to get what he thinks he's entitled to. He may feel bad about it, but that won't keep him from doing it."

She looked away, staring toward the *Conchita*. After a bit, she nodded. "Have you got any ideas?"

"I'm still thinking like mad. Give me a little more time."

She glanced again toward the *Conchita* and waved at the man with the binoculars. "That's Tomás. I'm being very nice to him."

"Wise." He watched as Tomás waved back. "He seems to like you."

"I'm working on it. He's the one who's usually guarding us."

And to think he'd believed she had totally spaced the whole situation.

"I found something interesting," he said, and pointed to the rubber raft. "I suppose you'll get to see it this evening after we *dine*." He couldn't help lacing the word with heavy sarcasm.

"What is it?"

"The ship's bell. Engraved with her name. It *is* the *Alcantara*."

For an instant her face lit with excitement, and he felt a pang, realizing she hadn't looked like that for a while.

Not since they had made love. Then the expression slid away, replaced by something dark and despairing.

After a few moments, she said, "I know it's childish, but I feel like throwing a temper tantrum and screaming that it's not fair."

He nodded. He kind of felt like that himself. "Stupid me. I thought when I agreed to work with you that I was buying myself a three-month, all-expenses-paid vacation at sea."

"Yeah?" A short laugh escaped her. "Funny how things turn out."

"I suppose you would know."

"Meaning?"

He shrugged. "The accident, losing your hearing."

"Losing my baby." She said it, her tone full of a sorrow that he could only imagine. "I think that was the worst part. I mean, I know she wasn't born yet, and I never got to hold her, but there's this emptiness . . ." Her voice trailed off and she shook her head.

"You'll have a child someday." He knew it was probably the wrong thing to say, but it was all he could think of.

"No, I never will."

The words jolted him, though he wasn't sure why. "Why not? Did something happen to make it impossible?"

"No. But I'm not stupid enough to ever let a man that close to me again emotionally."

"Because one guy was a jerk?" He wondered why he was defending men to her, and why it mattered. It just did.

Her mouth twisted again, and he thought she was going to say something angry, but instead all she did was say mildly, "Because one woman was a jerk?"

"Who? What? Me you mean? Because of Jana?"

She nodded. "It's been ten years, hasn't it? You don't look like someone who's in a rush to get attached again."

The instinctive response, "That's different," rose to his lips, but he managed to swallow it before he made himself look like an ass. Especially since she was right. And that made him feel even more foolish because he was offering advice he wouldn't take himself. "So all right," he said finally.

She surprised him with a laugh. "It's okay. I'm just not in any rush to feel that kind of pain again."

"Well, look at it this way. Any guy who falls for you now won't be upset because you're deaf."

"That's true."

But her smile faded a little, and he decided it was time to change the subject. "So, what have you been thinking about, apart from the wreck?"

"Thinking about?" She appeared surprised by the question, then shrugged. "My father. Quite honestly, Dugan, I've got to see him at least one more time. I've got to."

There was something desperate in her tone that told him they'd moved into some really deep waters here, and that she wasn't going to be jollied past this. "How come?"

"Because I've been so rotten to him." She put her pen down on her notebook and twisted her hands together. "I haven't been fair to him. After my accident, I went into a rock-bottom depression."

"Not surprising."

But she wasn't looking at him, and he wasn't sure she heard him.

"It was like I'd fallen into this dark pit. Everything hurt. It was almost too much effort to breathe. I got out of bed every morning only because Dad insisted on it, then I sat in a rocking chair and stared out the window all day. I don't even remember if I thought about anything at all. I just sat there and rocked and hurt too much to bear. All I wanted was to die."

He reached out, covering her hands with his, squeezing to offer what sympathy he could. He'd met that black dog once, in the weeks after Jana had ditched him, so he had at least a small idea of where she'd been.

"Anyway, I lost about six months that way. There was a therapist coming in who was helping me to lipread, but I only went through the motions. And I never really practiced what she taught me. I just didn't care.

"Then my father learned he had terminal cancer. At the time they told him he had only about six months to live." She turned and looked at Dugan. "He's beaten the odds. He's still around, and he's in remission. Or at least he was. God, I hope he doesn't get bad news in Tampa."

"Me too."

"Anyway, I guess when he learned he was sick, he got even more worried about me. That's when he decided to tell me about my mother and the quest. I was so damn angry at him that I could hardly see for days. He gave me this long, typewritten letter, telling me all the things he'd never told me about my mother when I was growing up. God, I hated him for keeping all that from me."

Dugan made what he hoped was a sympathetic sound, but he wasn't quite sure why she had been so angry with her father.

"It sounds stupid, doesn't it," she continued after a moment. "I look at the whole thing now and I can't seem to remember why I felt so angry with him. Why I felt so betrayed. I kept thinking that his secrecy had kept me from really knowing my mother. But all it kept me from knowing was part of her work. Her obsession."

He tugged on her hand, turning her attention to him so she could read his lips. "I can understand being angry because you felt he had been lying to you."

She nodded.

"But maybe it was more, Veronica."

"How so?"

"Maybe you hated him for dragging you out of your depression."

"What do you mean?"

"Well, I felt pretty bad after Jana. I think I told you. I had some idiotic notion of drinking myself to death or wasting the rest of my life on a beach. I was going to quit life."

"So?"

"So, learning to live again hurts. It's a lot easier just to give up. I imagine that made you as angry as any of the rest of it. Maybe more so. He didn't leave you in your safe little corner in your comfortable little pity party. He told you something that forced you to face life again."

She nodded slowly, and for several moments closed her eyes. "Maybe you're right. All I know is, I've been so angry and hateful to him since then that I don't think I'll ever be able to forgive myself."

"Well, the good news is, you might not have much time to worry about it."

She looked astonished and then laughed almost helplessly. "You're terrible, Dugan."

"Nah. I'm just a guy. And I don't believe in guilt. Which isn't to say that I never suffer from it. But what good does it do? The deed's done, so get on with picking up the pieces."

"If I have the opportunity to pick them up."

He heard the thickening in her voice which told him she

was on the edge of tears. He slid over until he was beside her, and put his arm around her. She turned toward him, burying her face in his shoulder, despite the fact that his wet suit offered little comfort.

She didn't cry. He didn't know whether that was good or bad, but the tears never came. Little by little she relaxed against him, as if letting go of a terrible tension.

Then she said, without looking at him, "We're going to die, aren't we?"

He didn't know how to answer that. In forty-eight hours, Ginny would start thinking about calling the Coast Guard. He had no idea how long she would wait after that, but he figured not too long. Saturday morning, maybe. At the outside. Then the search would begin. And then Emilio Zaragosa was going to do whatever he believed necessary to protect himself.

Which probably meant getting rid of the witnesses.

Looking across at the *Conchita,* he saw the rubber raft tethered to the yacht's side. It was his own raft, co-opted by Emilio, probably so that he couldn't use it for its intended purpose: escape. And he wondered if there was some way he could get ahold of it.

Veronica stirred and straightened. "Sorry," she said, wiping her eyes. "I'll be okay."

"Sure you will." But the urge to get her out of this mess was growing stronger by the minute. He figured he had thirty-six hours left. "Listen, I'm suffocating in this wet suit. Let me go make my last dive."

"Sure." She gave him a smile, a smile so brave that in spite of himself, he leaned over and kissed her.

"I'll be back," he said a là Schwarzennegger. It broadened her smile, and it was her smile he remembered as he went over the side again.

He was feeling fed up even before he even submerged. He hated getting in the water as always, but he hated it a hell of a lot more with the dredges. Impatient with the mud they raised, and tired of feeling boxed in, he finally swam away from the guide buoys to the far side of the launch. The water cleared up a little, and he began to run his metal detector around, something to keep himself occupied while he thought about their situation. Something to do in case one of the other divers saw him, an excuse for being so far away from the buoy.

A glance at his watch told him he had to stay down another thirty minutes to satisfy the watchdogs, but he was damned if he was going to do it over there. It would have been different if this had been for Veronica, but it was galling him to be doing it for Emilio.

Besides, he needed some time to think. To think about ways he could get that raft. If nothing else, he might be able to get them away in it after dark. The problem was, Emilio kept a guard on deck all night, and the guard kept an eye on that raft. Taking it would be inviting big trouble.

But they were already in big trouble, he reminded himself. And the trouble was going to get even bigger when Ginny reported the *Mandolin* missing. Maybe they were getting to the point of having nothing at all to lose. How many more hours was he going to bide his time, hoping some brilliant scheme occurred to him?

On the other hand, how likely was it that he was going to persuade Veronica to leave without the damn mask, unless they were within minutes of being killed? Thinking back to the conversation they had just had, he got even more uneasy. Did she really think Emilio was going to have a change of heart and not kill them?

His estimate of the man was entirely different. He figured Emilio would genuinely prefer not to have to kill anyone, but that wouldn't stop him from doing what he believed necessary to protect himself . . . and to protect his son. *Let us not forget,* he told himself, *that the man's son is aboard that yacht.* Dugan wasn't one to underestimate the protectiveness of a parent.

Cripes. It was late Wednesday afternoon. Somehow he had to get them far enough away from here by Friday afternoon that Emilio couldn't touch them, or he had to find a way to keep Ginny from sending up flares. And Ginny was no dummy. Lies weren't going to work too well. The woman was an ace at reading between the lines.

Then, of course, even if they got away, what was to stop Emilio from rubbing them out once they got ashore? He'd said he had a man in Key West who would kill Veronica's father. And Veronica believed that if they found the mask, they'd have the necessary bargaining chip to protect them.

As if they were likely to turn that mask up in the next twenty-four hours. God Almighty, he had to find a way to get them out of there that night. He had meetings on Friday. Ginny might be sending up flares tomorrow night.

Time was closing in on him like the muck raised by the dredges. Veronica believed that safety lay in finding the mask. Without it, she might well refuse to leave. Emilio was going to get pissed if the Coast Guard started searching for the *Mandolin,* and there was no telling how he might react. On the other hand, if they got away, Emilio still might take revenge on them at some later date.

And he was getting sick of running over and over this ground again. Every time he made up his mind that there was only one way to handle this situation, it would occur to him that he might only be making things worse.

But regardless, the clock ran out tomorrow night.

That was when he noticed that the dial on his metal detector was peaking like mad. Probably another cannon. They'd already found three.

He almost ignored it, but then he remembered Veronica and the *real* reason he was staying wet for hours every day. Blowing a sigh through his regulator that sent up a spume of bubbles, he homed in on the signal.

Setting the detector aside, he began to clear away the muck with his hands. Twelve inches down, he found an iron band attached to some rotting wood. Clearing away as much of the mud as he could, he thought he might have found a box of some kind. Cargo? Not gold bars, certainly. All those they had found had been in heaps, the way they had been stashed in the cargo holds.

Expecting to find tools or something equally prosaic, he tugged at the ironbound wood. It came away in his hands easily, rotten as it was. Below he found more silt and after clearing away several inches of it, he was about to quit.

Then he saw the glimmer of gold.

Dinner that night was the same as the night before. Snowy white tablecloth, impeccable service, jewel-toned glasses of wine. Except for the man with the gun standing just inside the door, it might have been any elegant dinner on an elegant yacht.

The entrée was Beef Wellington served with baby peas. Dugan passed on the wine as he always did because alcohol and diving didn't mix well. Veronica sipped hers, but only lightly. Basically, Emilio and his son Teo were the only ones eating and drinking with genuine pleasure.

And the big brass bell that Dugan had found was the centerpiece on the table. Veronica's gaze kept straying to it, her eyes reflecting something between longing and disappointment. Even Emilio noticed it finally.

"Take a look at the bell if you wish, Veronica," he said. "It's a beautiful specimen."

She looked at Dugan, who repeated what Emilio had said, then smiled faintly at Emilio and reached for the bell.

"Doesn't that annoy you?" Emilio asked Dugan.

"What?"

"Having to repeat everything for her."

Dugan felt a flicker of something hot in the pit of his stomach, something a lot more vital than the fear, worry, and bouts of despair he'd been having for the last two days. Something closer to killing anger. "No. It doesn't annoy me at all."

Veronica reached out and touched his arm. "Dugan, what's wrong?"

"Not a damn thing." For all he played the dapper gentleman, Dugan thought, Emilio didn't understand the most basic elements of courtesy. Or decency. And they didn't have much time left to escape his clutches.

Veronica looked down at the bell she held. "It's beautiful," she remarked.

It was. Shiny and bright, except for a single long dent on the side, it might have been new. Her fingers traced the engraving along the lip: *La Nuestra Señora de Alcantara Deo Gratias 1696.*

"It's amazing, isn't it?" she continued, her voice hushed as her fingers caressed the brass. "Imagine how it must have been ringing in those last hours."

Then, carefully, she put it back on the table. "I wonder who wore those earrings we found today."

Emilio shrugged. "We will never know. Nor does it matter."

Dugan saw the flare in Veronica's eye as he told her what Emilio said. She turned to their captor, and said firmly, "It's all that *really* matters, the lives these items can tell us about. Their value lies in the stories they have to tell, and that's beyond price."

He shrugged, apparently not caring to argue with her. The waiter soundlessly began to remove their plates while another man brought in a dessert cart.

"I have no history," Emilio said. "I was orphaned by the age of seven, and I lived in the streets. By eight I had learned how to feed and clothe myself without help. Stories are nice to listen to, but all that matters is money. Money is security."

When Dugan repeated what he said, Veronica shook her head. "I feel sorry for you, Emilio. You don't understand the magic."

"Magic? Pah! Magic is for fools."

Dugan didn't bother repeating that, because he sensed that Veronica had gotten the gist of it.

"I have money," she said. "My mother's family left me a wealthy woman. But my life would be meaningless without the magic."

"There is no magic."

"Yes, there is. What do you think makes the mask of the Storm Mother so important? The little bit of gold in it? No, Emilio. Its value, both monetary and otherwise, arises from what it represents. And what it represents is elemental magic. More than three hundred years ago, a woman donned that mask to control the power of the storm in order to protect her people. She put it on, and in doing so, she and her people believed she became one with the Storm Mother, the hurricane. If those people hadn't believed that, if that woman hadn't worn that mask for that purpose, it would be just another trinket, nothing particularly special. If some artisan made one today, what would it be worth, Emilio?"

"It's valuable because it's unique."

"Only partly. There are many unique things in the world that aren't that valuable. This is valuable because people want it. And people want it because of what it represents. Because of what it once was."

He shrugged. "And you want it because of the story," he said.

Dugan quickly repeated his words. Veronica listened soberly, then shook her head. "No, I want it because it belongs to me. Because it is my heritage. Because my mother died looking for it. Because of the story it tells, and the magic it bears. Because someday I hope to be able to put it on and feel the connection with my forebear."

Emilio sighed. "Have it your way. If we find it, I'll let you put it on."

For all of thirty seconds, Dugan thought. If *he* had anything to say about it, Veronica was going to get to wear that mask until she'd gleaned everything from it she'd ever hoped to. Hell, if she wanted to stand out in a storm and wear it and chant to the Storm Mother, then he was going to make sure she could. Because he was damn well going to get them away from here.

Yeah, right. It was an impossible list of things to do when he had a gun aimed at him. Which reminded him.

"Emilio? We have a small problem."

"What's that?"

"If I don't sail back into Key West by Friday, my secretary is going to call out the searchers."

Emilio frowned and sat back in his chair. "Use my radio. Tell her not to."

"It's not that easy. She knows how many days of provisions I'm carrying. By her reckoning, I'm going to be out of food by tomorrow night. She'll give me one day after that. Besides, I have business meetings scheduled on Friday with some out of towners. I can't skip them. I can't call them off."

He waited nervously while Emilio mulled this over. He was well aware that by telling the man that there was a clock ticking, he might be unleashing the unthinkable. On the other hand, maybe it would pressure Emilio into taking a different risk.

"You know," Emilio said presently, "I can finish this excavation without you."

The implied threat was chillingly clear. "I know that. I'm just warning you what's going to happen."

"So I remove you, let the Coast Guard look high and low, and come back in a few weeks to finish the task."

Veronica spoke. "You keep forgetting, Emilio. I have the permits. You can't conduct an excavation out here without me. Not for long. And after we disappear, everyone's going to suspect it had something to do with pirates or looters because it'll be inexplicable otherwise."

Emilio looked at Dugan. "She understood me."

"Sometimes she can."

He sighed. "All right. I admit it is a convenience to have the protection of your permits. But that is all it is, *comprende*? Keep that in mind. If you become too inconvenient, I can always resume my search in a year or so."

There was a hardness in Emilio's eyes, a hardness that made Dugan distinctly uncomfortable. "Well," he said, "I guess I can radio my secretary, but I don't think it'll work. I've never been able to lie to her. It might just set her right off."

His hands were right on the arms of his chair as he waited. The ticking clock in the back of his mind seemed to be ticking faster than ever. But he had to focus Emilio on something else, on another apparent plan to escape.

"I'll think about it," Emilio said finally. "I'll have a decision in the morning about what we will do. In the meantime, I'm going to put a guard on your boat."

His plan had backfired. All he had done was make the situation worse.

Chapter 21

It was late by the time they returned to the *Mandolin*, but that was expected. Emilio very much followed the Spanish custom of a late meal. It was nearing midnight, and the three of them were feeling pretty tired as the launch returned them.

And, unhappily, a guard came to stay on the boat with them. Apparently Dugan had made Emilio uneasy by talking about what his secretary might do, and, fearing that the Coast Guard might have already been alerted, he didn't want the three of them to have a chance to say anything that might cause trouble if a search vessel came upon them.

Dugan wanted to kick his own ass for not keeping his mouth shut.

The guard stayed above deck with his gun and an ugly knife for company while the rest of them went below. The hatch, they were told, had to stay open, which made it hard for them to talk.

"I'm going to bed," Veronica said wearily.

Dugan didn't like the way she looked. Where earlier a whole gamut of emotions had run through her, something about the guard on deck seemed to have left her whipped, as if she couldn't imagine any hope remaining.

"We need to talk," Dugan said. Tam perked up immediately, looking at him eagerly. Veronica hadn't made out his words, and she said, "What?"

He laid a finger across his lips and pointed above. While he'd gotten used to Veronica's habit of talking way too loudly, he was also well aware that she might easily be heard from above, especially with the hatch open.

She didn't take his caution amiss. She simply nodded and spread her hands questioningly.

One of her notebooks was on the galley table. He grabbed it and a pencil, and scrawled quickly, "We need to talk. Quietly. Your cabin."

She nodded and turned immediately, the two men following her.

Once there, Dugan closed the door quietly and again laid his finger to his lips. On the pad, he wrote, "We've got to talk quietly or the guard will hear us."

Veronica nodded. Taking the pad, she wrote, "I'll just write what I have to say."

"Good," he said quietly. "Can you hear me?"

She nodded.

"Okay. We've got to get out of here tonight."

Tam spoke. "No shock there, man. I don't like the guard. That's a major bad development. They're getting ready to off us."

"If something happens to make Emilio think it's necessary," Dugan agreed. "Unfortunately, I screwed up."

Veronica made a quiet, questioning sound.

"I miscalculated. I'd made up my mind we had to get out of here tonight, and I was trying to make him think he was safe at least until Friday."

Veronica nodded, but Tam said, "It didn't work."

"No. Apparently all I did was make him think we were going to try to pull something."

Veronica shrugged and scrawled, "Doesn't matter. We can't leave without mask. It is only protection against him later. And we have no *way* to leave."

She passed the pad to Dugan, who scanned it quickly. "You're a sweetheart," he said. "But I fucked up. The last thing I wanted tonight was a guard on this boat."

"So okay," Tam said. "Let's cut to the chase, huh? How are we going to get out of here?"

"We're going to go swipe the raft."

"No." The word came out of Veronica, and she caught herself. Taking the pad from Dugan, she wrote. "*No*! Too dangerous!"

Dugan took the pad and wrote on it in large, firm block letters. "WHATEVER YOU DO, DON'T MAKE A SOUND."

She nodded and placed a hand over her mouth.

"Okay. I found the mask."

Both Tam and Veronica were apparently so stunned that neither of them moved for several seconds. Then Tam let out a low whistle, and Veronica made a squealing sound that was smothered by her hand.

Then she shook her head. "Don't kid me," she said.

"Shh!" He laid his finger over his lips again. "Veronica, you're the sweetest thing since honey, but you talk too loud. Especially for right now. Watch it, okay?"

She nodded. "Tell me," she whispered. "For God's sake, tell me."

"I found it on my last dive. I kid you not. I wandered away from the others because I was feeling kind of pissed off, and I was thinking about how we could get out of this mess. It was underneath some wood with iron bindings, sort of like a chest. And it's definitely the mask you wanted."

"Draw it. Please." Her whisper was strained.

He obliged her, taking the pad to do a rough sketch, a mask with big eyeholes, a pronounced nose, and a small hole for the mouth. And radiating from it were cyclonic shaped spirals.

"That's it," Veronica whispered reverently. "Oh, wow, that's it." Her fingers traced the drawing almost lovingly. "Can I see it?"

"I hid it."

"Where?"

"Under the boat in all that crap we're fouled in."

She looked down at the drawing again. "My God, do you know what this means?"

"Later," he said. "We'll worry about that later. For right now, we've got to get us and the mask out of here. The way I figure it is this. We'll wait another couple of hours. What I'm going to do is try to get the guard a little drunk. Tam, you've got a bottle with you, haven't you?"

"How'd you know?"

"When did you ever travel without one? I'll need it. I want this guy to drink enough to get sleepy. Then I'm going over the side to get the raft. It'll be your job to keep the guard occupied if he wakes up, okay?"

"I can do that," Tam agreed.

"We may have to disable him," Dugan continued.

"Disable?" Veronica repeated the word with distaste, but at least she kept her voice way down.

"Tie him up so he can't raise the alarm. But I don't want to do that unless we have to, because he's carrying a radio, and I'm willing to bet he's supposed to check in regularly."

"Probably," Tam agreed. "Otherwise, they wouldn't be comfortable putting one guy over here with the three of us."

"Anyway, I'll get the raft over here, we'll get the mask and get the hell out of Dodge. Once we're out on the sea somewhere in the dark, we can set the emergency beacon going and the *Conchita* won't have a hope in hell of finding us before the Coast Guard does."

Because the Gulf of Mexico was a big body of water, and a raft drifting on the currents for even a couple of hours could get helplessly lost. The Coast Guard would be able to triangulate on the emergency beacon, but the *Conchita* wouldn't. The way Dugan felt, he didn't especially care whether anyone found them. He was perfectly prepared to paddle the whole distance to shore. Anything was better than hanging around like sheep being used for their wool before being taken to the slaughterhouse.

He sent Tam to get the bottle of booze and take it above deck. Before long, he and Veronica could hear the sounds of Tam and the guard laughing. So it was working.

Half an hour later, Tam came below again and gave the report. He'd offered the guard a couple of swallows from the bottle, and the guard had taken them. Then he'd left the bottle above where the guard could get it. All they could do now was hope the man would drink some more. A lot more.

Veronica was too wound up to sleep, but Dugan made her stretch out on the bunk anyway, on the off chance that she might drift off. Then he changed into his wet suit, hot and uncomfortable though it was out of the water. At least it only covered him to a few inches above his knee.

He sat beside her, keeping an eye on the luminous dial of his watch. All the lights had been turned off, to make it appear they were all in bed and allow his eyes to adjust thoroughly to the dark. The *Mandolin* rocked gently on the waves, making him feel almost like a baby in a cradle.

She was a good boat, he thought. And if he managed to survive this mess, he was going to get her fixed up and take a long sail, just for himself. No archaeological problems, no bad guys, just one man and the sea.

"I can hardly wait to see the mask."

Veronica's whisper came out of the dark. He didn't know how to respond to her, because she wouldn't be able to read his lips. Finally, he settled on a sound of agreement.

"Is it really beautiful?"

"Mmm." Although actually, he didn't think so. It was kind of chunky, and the artisanry wasn't exactly overwhelming. But he supposed, given the tools its makers had to work with, it was probably pretty good.

She reached out, and he sensed her hand was trying to find something. Then it landed on his bare knee, sending a pleasurable shiver through him. This was not the time, Dugan, he told himself. Not the time at all.

"Thank you for finding it."

He wanted to tell her it was just dumb luck, but then he decided it didn't really matter anyway, because she didn't really give a damn about him or how he had found it. All she was interested in was the mask.

And if they survived this mess, she'd take the mask and vanish from his life as if she'd never been.

He tested the possibility, sort of like testing a sore tooth, and found it made him ache a little. Oh, well, people had walked out of his life before.

The minutes were creeping by rather slowly, and he had

to force himself to pay attention to the sounds from above rather than allowing himself to be lulled by the boat's rocking . . . or distracted by Veronica's hand on his knee.

It would be so easy, so easy, to while away the next hour by making love to her. But he couldn't afford to do that for a lot of reasons. First, he didn't especially care to have the guard overhear them and get his jollies from it. Secondly, it would distract him from important things that might develop over the next hour. And finally . . . finally, he didn't think he dared to let Veronica get that close again. What had happened to them before . . . that had been intoxicating. Too intoxicating and too intimate. He wasn't prepared to risk it again, because each time it was as if she sank little hooks deeper into him. He could still tear away without mortal damage, but not if he let those hooks get much deeper.

He glanced at his watch again. Fifteen more minutes. Veronica had been sleeping restlessly for a little time now, soft little snores escaping her every now and then. The guard above hadn't moved in a while. He wasn't sure, but he thought he might have heard him talk into the radio around one, and he wondered if the man was on an hourly schedule. It might be best to wait until shortly after two before trying to go over the side.

But he figured one thing for sure. The man must be getting awfully tired. Emilio's thugs didn't have the earmarks of highly trained personnel, the kind who could go for two days straight without sleeping if necessary. And most ordinary people were getting pretty drowsy by two in the morning.

He wasn't a man who prayed often, but he found himself praying that the guard was helping himself to the bottle. Why not? The man must be wondering why he'd been set to guard three people who couldn't possibly have anywhere to go in the midst of all this water in a boat that was hopelessly fouled. Why would the man even think that nipping into the bottle would cause him any trouble?

At two, he heard the guard talking again, probably radioing to someone on the *Conchita.* At about the same time, Tam came aft to the cabin.

"Ready?" he asked in a whisper.

"Not yet. The guard just radioed in. Let's wait a few."

Veronica stirred, her hand slipping from his knee, and he felt the lack of her touch deep within him.

"Dugan?"

Reaching out, he grabbed her hand. "Shh," he said, hoping she could hear him.

"Dugan?"

Squinting in the darkness, he found her face and silenced her by the simple expedient of kissing her. It nearly killed him when he felt her go soft beneath his lips. Soft and inviting. And it was hard, so hard to back away.

But he made himself do it, and she sat up, a shadow in the dark cabin. This was no good, he thought. She couldn't see well enough to understand anything he might say. But he needed his night vision.

"Christ," he muttered. Not knowing what else to do, he leaned over to her and wrapped an arm around her, pulling her close and putting his mouth right by her ear. "Quiet. Don't do anything."

Apparently she got most of it, because she nodded.

"Wait," he said.

She nodded again.

They waited. Another fifteen minutes passed by with nerve-shrieking slowness, but finally Dugan admitted he couldn't wait any longer. If they waited too long, the guard would need to report in again, and someone on the boat would get nervous if he didn't.

"Go look," he told Tam.

Tam nodded and slipped away silently. They had agreed he would check the guard first because he had an excuse to go on deck: his whiskey.

Then, leading Veronica by the hand, Dugan followed, waiting at the foot of the ladder. Three endless minutes later, Tam's shadow appeared above.

"He's asleep."

Dugan turned to Veronica and signed with his hands that she was to stay right there. She nodded understanding. Then he pointed to her ears, and imitated putting her hearing aids in her waterproof pouch. Again she nodded.

Thank God, he thought, for starshine, magnified by the reflections off the water, or they'd be sunk, with Veronica unable to hear. As it was, she could just make out his gestures.

Then he climbed the ladder. Moments later, he went swiftly and silently over the side, leaving Tam sitting on the bench not too far from the guard, the bottle in his hands as if he was just there for a drink.

The water was warm, as the water always was there, but still chilly by comparison to his body. The first few seconds as it seeped into his wet suit were uncomfortable, but then the layer of water between him and his rubber skin became the same temperature as his body. By then he'd already struck out toward the *Conchita,* which was brightly lighted enough to be an easy beacon.

At least the raft was black. Had it been yellow, he'd have had a serious problem on his hands because with all the light from Emilio's yacht, it would have been too obvious as he dragged it back to the *Mandolin.*

Five minutes later, he was cutting the line that tied it to the *Conchita* and dragging it back toward his own boat. If anyone was guarding Emilio's deck, he hadn't done anything to make himself obvious. Thank God. Thank God. Prayerful words kept running through his mind in time with the beating of his heart.

Dragging the raft through the water was more difficult than simply swimming over to the yacht. The waves weren't bad, but the chop kept trying to pull the towline out of his hands. And the raft, light as it was on the surface, was still heavy, and still resisted his forward pull every time that meant mounting another wave.

Ten minutes to get back. Everything was still quiet. He towed the raft to the stern of his boat, as far from the yacht as he could get it.

Tam leaned over the side, taking the line attached to the raft and tying it to the stern cleat. Then Tam passed him an underwater light. Holding his breath, Dugan submerged to rescue the mask from its hiding place.

Veronica felt as if she were going to crawl out of her skin. She couldn't hear a thing because she'd followed Dugan's direction to put her hearing aids in their waterproof pouch, which was attached to her belt. She knew he was right to tell her to do that. It would be all too easy to ruin them in the splash from a wave once they were in the raft.

If they ever got into the raft. If they got away.

Horrifying possibilities kept creeping into her mind, kept sending icy tendrils of fear along her scalp and spine. Nothing in her life had prepared her for that night, and being cut off because of her hearing scared her even more.

She wouldn't know if something went wrong. She

wouldn't be able to hear if someone tried to give her a warning. Every single inadequacy, real and imagined, began to hammer at her, undermining her.

But what choice did she have? she kept asking herself. What other options were there? Emilio had threatened her father, had threatened her and Dugan. And if she had doubted his intentions even a little, those doubts were answered by the guard on deck.

Nervous, she climbed up the ladder a little to look out. The guard was still dozing, and Tam was still sitting on the bench. Where was Dugan? Had he brought the raft back yet?

Then she felt, rather than heard, a thud in the hull of the boat. Oh, God, what now?

She didn't have long to wonder, though. The bump woke the guard, who jumped to his feet. Tam stayed sitting on the bench, and she could see him making placating gestures with his hands, and he seemed to be talking. She ducked back down the ladder, afraid the guard might see her, then peered cautiously over the lip of the hatch.

Tam and the guard were looking toward the stern of the boat, away from her. Something was going on, and she didn't like the look of it. Tam's gestures were becoming more rapid, as if he was arguing. God, she wished she could hear.

Worrying that Tam might need some help, she climbed up the ladder into the cockpit, bumping the radio on her way.

Tam jerked around, staring at her in horror. The guard turned, too, and grabbed his gun.

Then all hell broke loose.

* * *

Through the water, Dugan could hear muffled sounds. His heart went into overdrive as he struggled to tie the bag holding the mask to one of the straps around the inflated tubes of the black raft. After what seemed like an eternity, he managed it.

Then with a kick of his powerful legs, he surfaced beside the boat. He could hear shouting, and, more chillingly, he could hear the radio crackling quietly, and a voice, which identified itself as the Coast Guard station in Key West, asking what the problem was.

Kicking, he pushed himself around to the rear of the boat and saw Tam struggling with the guard. There was a shout from the direction of the *Conchita,* and he knew the seconds were numbered. With another powerful kick of his legs, he launched himself far enough out of the water that he was able to grab a stern cleat and pull himself onto the boat.

Chaos reigned. In an instant his eye took it all in. Tam was fighting with the guard; there was a flash of steel, probably the guard's knife. Veronica had picked up a boat hook and was crossing the deck toward the struggling men. And the voice on the radio kept asking for information.

The struggling men suddenly moved, staggering toward the port side near the raft, then, with a yowl of pain, Tam staggered, gripping his side, and went overboard.

Dugan heard no splash, realized Tam must have fallen into the raft. The guard, apparently oblivious to anyone else, was struggling with the line tied to the stern cleat.

Veronica raced forward at the same time Dugan did, the boat hook aimed at the guard. The guard saw her coming, jumped to the side, and the boat hook slid past him. Veronica, at full tilt, came up hard against the gunwale and lost the boat hook over the side.

Which left Dugan, who was unarmed except for the small diving knife he carried. The guard was waving a much larger knife, a knife that Dugan noticed was darkly stained. Tam's blood.

To his left, he could hear shouts from the *Conchita.* The night brightened as more lights came on aboard the yacht. Any minute now, he thought, and there would be gunfire. Or the launch would head toward them. Time was running out.

In that instant, as if he were somehow lifted out of himself, he felt an immense infusion of power, felt a narrowing of focus that cut out everything except the knife and the man before him. He didn't have the time for the circle, feint, and parry of a knife fight. Tam must have managed to get rid of the guy's gun, but that wouldn't matter at all if the man from the yacht had time to get there.

He had one move, maybe two. If he couldn't get rid of this guard in one or two moves, they were screwed.

But he didn't feel the fear, didn't even feel the tension. He had gone beyond that. All he could think was that this was his last chance to save Veronica.

As if his body belonged to someone else, he felt himself lunge forward, felt his left hand latch onto the man's right forearm, turning the knife away. As if his hand belonged to someone else, he felt his own diving knife sink home in the guard's side as if layers of skin, muscle, and bone were made out of soft butter.

He saw the guard's eyes widen, saw the man begin to collapse. As he did so, the guard pulled his right hand around, unwittingly pointing his own knife at himself. Whether he fell on it, Dugan didn't wait to see.

Crossing the deck in two strides, he grabbed Veronica. She'd apparently gotten the wind knocked from her and was gasping it back into her lungs. He lifted her, tucking her into his side, glancing back at the yacht. Men were climbing into the launch. Their time was up.

"We've got to go into the water," he told Veronica, pointing at the yacht.

She nodded.

"Ready?"

"Tam?"

"He fell into the raft."

She nodded again and he guided her to the side.

The raft was gone. The line had come loose from the stern cleat.

Chapter 22

The raft was nowhere to be seen. It had vanished off the stern of the *Mandolin* into the night as if it had never been.

Veronica felt Dugan squeeze her fingers. She looked at him, wishing she could hear something. Anything. All she knew was that Emilio's men were going to be there in a few minutes, and they had nowhere to go.

"In the water," Dugan said. She could read his lips, though she couldn't hear his voice at all. He was enunciating very carefully, though.

"They . . . kill us," he said.

She nodded. "They'll kill us. Yes."

He said something else, but his gestures indicated they were about to go over the side. She nodded, kicking off her useless deck shoes, hoping that her T-shirt and shorts wouldn't drag her down. She had a fleeting thought of her ears, of how she wasn't supposed to get water in them, but ignored it. It didn't matter now.

He pulled a life jacket out of the stern locker and helped her put it on.

"What about you?" she demanded. He just shook his head.

Then, holding hands, they jumped off the stern of the boat. It was cold, but not that cold. For an instant she panicked because it was so dark and she couldn't see anything. Where was up? Down?

But Dugan's hand never let go of hers, and a second later she popped to the surface. She looked at him, but he was looking past her toward the yacht. Without a word, he tucked her hand into the belt at the waist of his wet suit, a webbed belt that sometimes held diving weights, but tonight held only a knife sheath.

Then he started swimming away from the *Mandolin*. She understood that she was supposed to hang on to him so they wouldn't get separated. Kicking her feet and stroking with her free arm, she helped as much as she could. And little by little, they moved away from the light cast by the yacht into the darkness of an endless sea.

She heard the launch motor start up, and it surprised her that she could hear it so well. It was the water, she realized. It was as if the water transmitted sounds through her body.

Then she heard something else. A bigger, deeper motor.

She tugged on Dugan's belt sharply, once, twice. He stopped swimming and turned to face her, treading water.

"Do you hear it?" she asked. "There's a big boat coming."

He scanned the sea in every direction, but all he could see was the brightly lighted *Conchita* and the smaller shadow of the *Mandolin* in the distance.

He looked at her, hoping she could read him in the dimness. "Are you sure?"

But apparently she couldn't, because she merely pointed in the general direction from which they had come.

Another boat, he thought. It was possible. But would it be useful? The odds that they would even be spotted in the darkness on the water was so slim it hurt even to contemplate it. They had to find the raft, both because Tam might well be bleeding to death, and because they needed a way to stay afloat. He'd passed on a life jacket for himself because it would have slowed their escape. But he honestly didn't know how long he was going to be able to tread water. And even so, the chances that two people bobbing in the sea would be discovered even in daylight were slim to none. So they had to stay near the *Mandolin*. She had sent out a distress call—why Tam or Veronica had done that, he didn't know—but it had been sent and the Coast Guard would be looking for them at first light.

But Tam . . .

He turned, trying to see the raft, knowing the chances were small. The blackness of the raft that had been a blessing when he was snatching it was now a curse. It was invisible out there, bobbing on the waves. It might only be twenty yards away, but they'd never see it.

Facing Veronica, he said as clearly as he could, "We've got to find Tam."

She nodded. Maybe she understood. Maybe all she'd read was Tam's name and had filled in the blanks.

But now he heard it, too, the sound of a boat's engine. A large boat. His heart leapt as he wondered if there might have been a Coast Guard cutter in the vicinity that was now responding to the distress call.

"Do you hear it?" Veronica asked. "Do you?"

He nodded. A wave slapped him in the face just then,

and he had to spit brine out of his mouth. The water was getting choppier, he thought.

Suddenly Veronica pointed. He turned and felt his heart slam as he saw a large, dark boat emerging from the night, headed straight toward the *Conchita.* Veronica raised her hand, as if she were going to shout and wave, but Dugan grabbed it, shaking his head vehemently.

It was no Coast Guard cutter. It was somebody's yacht, and it was running without lights. Like a pirate.

Oh, Jesus, he thought, what now?

The unknown vessel began slowing down, and a short time later it was pulled up alongside the *Conchita.* More of Emilio's henchmen?

Then, across the water, he heard shouting. It didn't sound pleasant. A gun was fired. Another. A short time later, the *Conchita* hefted anchor and sailed away into the night, followed by the dark boat. The *Mandolin* was left behind.

All too soon, Dugan and Veronica were alone in the vast expanse of an empty sea.

Veronica's ears sometimes rang. Usually she heard almost nothing at all, but occasionally her ears would begin to chirp, almost like a telephone. So when she first heard the sound, she thought it must be her ears ringing.

It was a faint sound, a very high-pitched squeal that lasted only a second or two then stopped. It might be nothing at all. But then again . . .

It was almost beyond the range of her hearing, the sound. Up in the frequencies where she hadn't lost her hearing, but almost beyond them. And entirely too regular.

That was what got to her finally, the regularity. The sounds in her ears, when she had them, didn't keep time. They came randomly. This was like . . . She tried to think of a comparison. She knew she had heard something like it before, but she wasn't sure what it was.

Dugan pulled her close. Now that they were alone with nothing for miles around them, he shouted to be heard.

"We have to get back to the boat," he yelled.

"Tam."

"We can't find him from here. We're too low in the water. We need lights."

She nodded slowly. But then something clicked in her mind. "I hear the raft."

"What?"

"I hear the raft!"

Even in the dimness of the starlight, she could see the disbelief on his face. She was deaf. Why would he believe her?

"I hear something electronic, switching on and off," she told him. "Strobing. I recognize the sound."

"But how can you hear it? I don't hear anything except the waves."

"I can't hear the waves, Dugan. The electronic sound is *all* I can hear except when you shout."

"But . . ."

She shook her head impatiently. "Listen to me. I've lost the whole middle range of my hearing. All the usual day-to-day sounds are pretty much gone unless they're really loud. But I didn't lose my upper range. The really high sounds."

He nodded slowly. And finally he shouted, "But the raft wouldn't be making any sound."

"Unless Tam turned on the emergency beacon."

She saw realization dawn in his face. "Where?" he demanded.

She pointed to her left, somewhere behind the *Mandolin,* which was still drifting helplessly. "That way."

He nodded, tucking her hand through his belt again, and began swimming in that direction. Waves slapped her in the face repeatedly, and she realized that she could feel a storm building somewhere. The knowledge hummed in her, as if the sea were transmitting a message. They had to find Tam before the water became too rough. Before the storm arrived.

After a short eternity, Dugan stopped swimming, catching his breath. Veronica took the opportunity to listen. The sound was still there, the only thing she could hear. A whine, repetitious. Louder.

"We're closer," she said. "Dugan, we're closer." She pointed in the general direction she heard the sound from.

He nodded, still gulping air, and peered in that direction. He spoke, but she didn't hear him.

She was concentrating on the sound, annoyed when a wave would slap her in the head and drown it. But little by little, she focused in on it, narrowing the direction down.

And then she saw the faint light. It was blinking off the water vapor that covered the sea like a blanket, casting the faintest of haloes. "There," she said, excitement welling in her. "There. The light. You can barely see it!"

Seconds ticked by while he stared into the night, trying to see it. Then he nodded and turned to her with a big smile. He spoke, but she still couldn't hear him.

"Louder," she said. "Shout at me."

"Can you swim to the boat?"

She looked back over her shoulder. It wasn't far. Maybe a hundred feet. "Yes. But what about the raft?"

He pointed at her, then pointed toward the *Mandolin.*

Then he pointed at himself and pointed toward the dimly strobing halo of light.

"But . . ." Fear filled her. "Dugan, you could get lost out there! I can't let you go alone."

"You *have* to. I can't pull you both!"

The justice of his words hit her hard. She could swim, but not nearly as well as he, and the paddling she'd been doing for the last half hour had left her feeling drained already. She didn't have a wet suit, either, and even though the water temperature was probably eighty degrees, it was sapping her body heat, and she was beginning to feel cold. She would only hinder him.

He caught her chin with one hand, while with the other he continued to tread water. "Turn on all the lights."

"Okay."

"If anybody but the Coast Guard comes, jump overboard."

"Yes."

He was shouting, and she could hear the strain in his voice. He had to get Tam, she understood that. But, oh, God, she didn't want to lose Dugan.

Then he kissed her. It wasn't much of a kiss, when he was trying to keep his head above water, but it touched her to her very toes.

Then, with a little wave, he swam away into the darkness toward the faint, pulsating halo of light. Veronica stared after him, aching and afraid. If Dugan never came back . . .

But she couldn't allow herself to think about that. Instead, trying to force some energy into muscles that were beginning to feel rubbery, she reminded herself that a shark might find her at any minute. Then she started swimming toward the dark shadow of the *Mandolin*.

But thinking about sharks had been exactly the wrong thing to do, because it reminded her that a shark might find Dugan as well. Almost without realizing it, she began to pray harder than she had ever prayed in her life.

She was able to climb the ladder on the starboard side, a ladder that was permanently attached to the boat. But when she hit the deck at last, she collapsed, exhausted, feeling like she couldn't move another inch.

Then she saw the body. She had completely forgotten that the guard was still lying on the deck on the port side. A feeling of instinctive revulsion filled her, forcing her to her feet. Trapped on a disabled boat with a dead body. Her skin started crawling.

But she had to turn on the lights for Dugan. Forcing herself to ignore the guard, she turned on all the running lights and the cockpit lights, and even some of the lights down below, opening curtains so the glow could reach out the portholes.

Then, reluctant to remain below where she was completely cut off, she returned to the deck and tried to ignore the dark shape of the dead guard.

If he *was* dead. That thought seemed to clutch her throat and squeeze it. Staring at the man, she froze and tried to think what to do. She didn't want to touch him. She didn't want him there. But what if he wasn't dead and needed help? Could she just leave him there bleeding?

Remembering Dugan's Glock, which he had hidden once again in the galley drawer, she went down to get it. She had no idea if the safety was on or off, or if it was even loaded. She just had to hope that it would fool someone if necessary.

When she came back above, shock hit her like an icy

fist. There was another shadow on deck. A man was standing there. A man she had seen before.

Luis Gallegos saw the gun in her hand, and raised his own.

"Don't shoot," he said.

But Veronica couldn't hear him. Her hearing aids were still in the pouch hanging from her belt. With her trembling left hand, she opened the bag and pulled one of them out. She fumbled around, and finally got it into her ear. Then she put the gun in her other hand, pulled out the other aid, and pushed it into place.

The night was suddenly alive again. She could hear the keening of the wind, loud in her hearing aids, could hear the slap of the rising waves against the boat.

"Sit down," she told Luis. "What are you doing here?"

He said something, but she could only make out a few words. Finally, she nodded toward the guard. "Is he dead?"

Luis nodded. He was keeping his hands where she could see them, looking as frightened as she felt.

And there she stood, with her back to the radio, which she could now hear was on. She must have bumped the switches when she came up earlier, and the sound must have been what startled the guard and gotten Tam into all the trouble.

A wave of crushing despair washed over her as she realized she might have cost Tam his life because of her disability. And with that wave of despair came more self-doubt. Who was she to think she could hold a man at gunpoint when she didn't even know if the gun would shoot if she pulled the trigger?

And now, because of her, Dugan was out there swimming across the darkened sea, looking for his friend who might be dying.

No. She couldn't afford to think this way. Absolutely not. She'd messed up. She'd bumped the radio and turned on the distress signal. It was an accident.

But in her heart of hearts, she couldn't quite forgive herself.

The minutes crept by. The Glock was growing heavy in her hand, even though it was plastic. Luis kept trying to talk to her, and she kept telling him to shut up. She couldn't understand enough of what he said, and right now she didn't want to expend the effort of trying. God, she wished she could use the radio, talk to the Coast Guard, tell them what was happening.

When Dugan came back. *If* Dugan came back . . . The wind was picking up, and the sea was growing rougher, and he was out there in it.

And she was terrified for him.

Chasing a moving target was never easy, and the raft was a moving target, being carried by the choppy seas. When he paused to get his breath, Dugan looked up and saw that the stars were vanishing in the west, erased as if by a giant hand. A storm was coming in. Time was getting short.

But it was much easier to see the pale, flashing glow of the beacon. Much easier. He was getting closer. He glanced behind him and could still make out the lights aboard the *Mandolin.* With the beacon on the raft going, and the *Mandolin* sending its automated distress call, the Coast Guard should arrive shortly after dawn. Maybe.

He couldn't afford to think about the alternatives.

His muscles were still fatigued, tired of the seemingly endless swimming they'd been doing, but his breathing rate had steadied and slowed. He drew some deep breaths and began to swim toward the faint beacon on the raft, a beacon that would be far easier to see from above.

Thank God Tam had been conscious enough to start it. He just hoped Tam hadn't bled to death.

How long he had been swimming, Dugan had no idea. There was still no light on the eastern horizon, so it hadn't been as long as it felt. How far away was dawn? He had no idea. It was like being trapped in the darkness with no idea when he might escape. And oddly, he was beginning to feel a little claustrophobic, as if the darkness and the sea were closing in on him. God, he was stupid to have swum out here alone at night.

At one point, he lost the beacon. For an instant, panic started to rise in him, but he battled it down. He had only the lights of the *Mandolin* behind him to give him a sense of direction, and the *Mandolin* was drifting, too.

His chest squeezed, and he wondered if Veronica was okay. He should have waited to make sure she was able to board the ketch. Hell, there were a lot of things he should have done differently. He was no superhero, and tonight had proved it.

Then he caught the faint flicker again and struck out once more, forcing his arms and legs to propel him as if he were doing the hundred meters for the Olympics. Only an Olympic swimming pool didn't have waves like this that insisted on slapping him in the face and throwing him around like a cork.

But the light was getting brighter. Then, finally, he thought he glimpsed the raft, a dark, nonreflective shape against the starlight-sprinkled waves. A jolt of adrenaline rushed through him, renewing his strength.

Minutes later, just as his muscles were beginning to turn into burnt rubber, his head bumped something hard. Dropping his legs, he lifted his head from the water and saw the raft inches away. Before it could escape again, he latched on to one of the side straps and clung for dear life.

"Tam? Tam?"

No answer. Gasping for air, Dugan waited to catch his breath, waited for one last trickle of strength to return to his limbs. Then, gracelessly, he heaved himself up into the raft.

Tam was there. Unconscious. Breathing shallowly. A sticky pool of wetness testified that he was still bleeding. With hands, more than eyes, Dugan searched his body and found the seeping wound in Tam's side. Unable to do anything else, he ripped Tam's T-shirt off of him, and jury-rigged a pressure bandage, hoping to stop the bleeding.

There was nothing else he could do. Ten minutes later, as recovered as he would get, he picked up the paddle.

He wondered if he would be able to do it. The lights of the *Mandolin* were a long way away. And if it started to rain . . .

But thinking about it wouldn't help. He dug the blade of the oar into the restless sea, and started paddling.

The storm struck before dawn. Bringing tall waves and battering winds, it swept in over the water like the hurricane of centuries ago, buffeting the helpless *Mandolin*, spinning it like a cork in a whirlpool. Lightning forked down from the sky, and Veronica could feel her hair standing on end.

Luis grew violently seasick, and finally wound up huddled on the deck, clinging to the edge of the bench, no longer a threat.

And Veronica grew strangely unafraid, at least for herself. The power of the storm seemed to hum through her, filling her with wild power that made her feel almost invincible. She looked at the cowering Luis and felt pity for him.

But then she looked out to sea, and in the flickers of brilliant lightning, she saw the waves. Dugan was out there. What rose in her then was not fear but anger. Reaching out with both hands, as if she wanted to grasp the lightning bolts, she raised her voice and shouted into the storm.

"He's *mine*!"

She could barely hear herself over the shriek of the wind in her hearing aids, but she felt the shout rise from the pit of her stomach, a roar that was lost in a crack of thunder. A wave caught the *Mandolin,* tossing it to one side, nearly knocking her out of the captain's chair. She ignored it. Inside, in a dark, still place in her soul, she willed the storm to spare Dugan. But the storm only seemed to shriek louder.

And the night seemed to be endless.

Mexican standoff, Veronica thought. Her eyes were gritty as she sat in the captain's chair in the cockpit, facing backwards, trying to keep the gun trained on Luis. The man was sitting on the stern bench, his hands long since fallen helplessly to his lap, looking as exhausted as she felt.

The body still lay on the deck between them.

The pink streamers of dawn were making their appearance in the east, lightening the world enough that she could see the fading storm. Fear was chasing along her nerve endings, fear that Dugan hadn't survived the storm, fear that she and Luis would be stuck out here on a disabled boat.

The wind was humming in her hearing aids, sometimes shrieking. The battering of the waves against the hull was loud, too, a constant background noise that drowned any other sounds. In effect, even with her hearing aids, she was deaf.

Luis looked as if he were sleeping. Taking a chance, Veronica left the cockpit and looked around. All of a sudden, her breath locked in her throat. There, a small speck in the sky, was a helicopter. Watching it approach, Veronica's eyes clouded with tears. Rescue was at hand, but what about Dugan?

The helicopter approached swiftly, and not five minutes later it was hovering over her, a man leaning out the door looking down at her. She waved, forgetting she had a gun in her hand.

A few seconds later, the helicopter lifted abruptly and flew away. That's when she noticed she was still holding the Glock. God, they must think she was a madwoman.

Then, her hopes sinking, she turned and saw that Luis was awake, staring after the chopper with as much dismay and longing as she was feeling.

They'd come back, she told herself. They had to. Even if she *had* waved a gun. Exhausted, almost hopeless, she returned to the cockpit and sat, watching Luis, wondering if somewhere along the way she had gone crazy.

When the cutter finally pulled alongside the *Mandolin,* Veronica found herself staring down the barrels of rifles from the ship's deck above her. A loudspeaker was booming something she couldn't understand. Her mind groggy with fatigue, it took her a minute to realize why they were pointing those rifles at her.

She tossed the Glock down onto the deck and put up her hands.

Twenty minutes later, she and Luis were aboard the

cutter, sitting in a small gray cabin and being questioned by two men in uniform. She couldn't understand them, couldn't understand what Luis was saying, and she was past caring. Where was Dugan?

But finally their attention focused on her, and she could ignore them no longer. Drawing herself up as straight as she could despite her fatigue, she looked one of the men in the eye. For the first time she spoke the words without any sense of shame or embarrassment.

"I'm deaf," she said. "If you want me to understand you, you need to talk slowly and clearly so I can read your lips. Did you find the raft?"

The two men exchanged looks. Then one of them said, speaking almost too slowly, "What raft?"

So she told them. Without giving them a chance to ask any questions, she let the whole story tumble out of her, everything about her expedition, Emilio Zaragosa, the strange boat that had come in the night and driven Emilio away, about the guard who had stabbed Tam, and how Tam had drifted away on the raft and Dugan had swum out into the night sea to find it.

And when she was done, she put her head down on the table and began to cry.

They asked her questions, when she stopped crying. Some she understood, and others she didn't, but she wasn't prepared to give any ground. When she couldn't understand, she made them write it down.

It seemed like hours later before the questions began to run out, before they stopped covering the same ground over and over. It probably wasn't that long, but it seemed to Veronica to be an eternity. Her heart was beating painfully out of fear for Dugan, and her hopes for his safety were growing dimmer by the minute.

Needing to distract herself, she turned to Luis. "How did you get on my boat?"

He spoke, but she couldn't understand his words. They tumbled too rapidly over his lips, and his accent made them even harder to follow. Finally, she shoved a pad over to him and said, "Write it down."

He wrote.

"Some unknown man wants the mask you were looking for. He made me tell him where you and Emilio were, and he made me come with him when he came to face Emilio. Then he made me get off his boat and onto yours. I don't know why."

One of the Coast Guard officers took the pad and scanned it. There was a hurried conversation, then one of the men left the room.

Luis looked at her and spoke, and this time she read his lips without any trouble. "I'm sorry," he said.

She didn't know how to respond, and didn't have time to, because just then the door opened and Dugan entered the room. He looked pale and fatigued, and was still wearing his wet suit. But he carried a bag with him, and without a word he opened it and pulled the mask of the Storm Mother from it.

Then he put it in Veronica's trembling hands. "For you," he said simply. "For you."

She hardly looked at it. Instead she pushed it aside on the table and jumped to her feet. A moment later she was in Dugan's arms, holding close the most important thing in her world: him.

Chapter 23

"I'm sorry, Daddy." Veronica had spoken the words a dozen times since her father's return from Tampa yesterday. Orin, who was still in remission, seemed to be growing stronger by the day and was even thinking about joining Dugan, Tam, and her on the *Mandolin* for the next trip, once the ketch was fully repaired, and once Tam was fully recovered.

In the meantime, the tropical days hung heavily on Veronica's hands. The mask, the cause of so much trouble, had been sent to the university in Tampa for safekeeping. Veronica hadn't even tried it on, and Orin didn't especially want to see it.

He turned to her now and held out his arms to give her a hug.

"It's okay," he said, smoothing her hair. "It's okay. I understand what you were going through. And you were right that I made a big mistake by withholding the whole story. Sweetie, I understand."

But she still wasn't prepared to fully forgive herself, and sometimes she thought what a fool she'd been, to have wasted so much precious time, time that could never be recovered, by being angry with her father. "You were trying to protect me," she said. "I understand that now."

"Well, I don't seem to have saved you any trouble at all," he said ruefully.

He said something else, too, but his head had turned away a little too much, and all she could hear was the cacophony of vowels. She didn't feel angry about that, though. Not this time. Orin tried hard not to forget her deafness, but he was old and tired, and sometimes forgetful. She loved that in him as much as she loved everything else.

He looked at her again. "Dugan's here. I just saw his car. Have a good time."

She gave him a quick squeeze and a kiss on the cheek, then went out to meet Dugan, who was just getting out of his car.

"I like that," he said, smiling at her over the top of the car.

"Like what?"

"A woman who's on time."

She laughed for no special reason, other than that she felt really good. The past week had been difficult and exhausting. She'd had to talk to many strangers to get the whole matter sorted out, most especially explaining the dead man on the deck of the *Mandolin,* but that was behind her now, and she felt free.

"You're sure you want to do this?" he asked before pulling away from the curb.

"Absolutely."

"Let's go then."

He was going to teach her to dive. Once she had realized that she could hear better when she was submerged in the water, it had occurred to her that in the water she was at no disadvantage at all. She might never be able to teach again at the university—although she was beginning to think about ways to get around her hearing problems—but she could at least participate fully in her archaeological work the way she would have on dry land. She was even envisioning focusing her entire career on salvaging ships from the past.

Dugan took her to a quiet, deserted bay, where the voices and noises of other people wouldn't make it difficult for her to hear him. After an hour of instruction, they took a break to picnic on the narrow strip of sandy beach.

"We can go again next week," he told her. "The *Mandolin* will be ready."

"Great." She sighed and looked out over the water. "What if Emilio comes back?"

He drew her attention back to him. "I don't think he will. From what Luis said, there's someone else in the mix now, someone who was willing to drive Emilio off."

"But what if *that* guy comes after us."

"Luis said all he wanted was the mask. The mask is safely in a museum. Honestly, honey, I don't think there's anything to worry about."

He was calling her honey more and more often, and every time he did, her heart gave a little leap, only to crash in despair. No man would want her. She was deaf. And while Dugan seemed to handle it with grace and ease, she figured it had to annoy him at times, It certainly annoyed *her,* and it was her problem. Why would he want to take it on?

Besides, he'd barely touched her since the rescue. Once or twice he'd touched her hand, but that was it.

He touched her now, his fingertips lightly caressing the back of her hand as she leaned on it.

"Are you sure you want to keep helping with the excavation?" she asked. "I know you have your business to worry about."

"Of course I want to keep helping. I haven't had this much excitement in years. I'm not about to go back to being a mole."

She couldn't resist. "But you hate to get wet."

He waved a dismissing hand. "The wet suit helps. Besides, after swimming all those hours in the dark water that night, I figure getting wet is a minor thing."

Then his fingers wrapped around her wrist and tugged gently. Everything inside her seemed to go soft and weak as he drew her down to lie facing him.

"Besides," he said, looking right into her eyes. "I don't want to be away from you."

Her heart seemed to stop, then it fluttered wildly as hope and disbelief filled her. "What?"

"I don't want to be away from you," he repeated more firmly. "Look, I know I'm a quasi beach bum with a tiny diving business, and I know you're a high-powered Ph.D. with a whole life back in Tampa but . . . well . . ." He sighed and closed his eyes a minute. When he opened them again, he sighed ruefully.

"I swore I'd never do this again."

"Never do what?" Hope had her heart beating so painfully she thought it was going to burst from her chest.

"I swore I'd never get involved again. Swore I'd never love again. Just goes to show, if you say you'll never do something, life will make you eat your words."

"Dugan?" She was afraid to believe what she was hearing, and his name passed her lips sounding like a plea.

"How about you?" he said. "Are you still resolved to avoid getting involved?"

It was a straightforward question, one she felt she must answer. But the words were so difficult to find, so at last she said only, "No." Because she was already involved, and she knew it.

"Great. So if I hang around a while, there might be a remote possibility that you could come to love me? Just a little?"

Her breathing had become rapid as her heart pounded madly with excitement and joy. "Umm . . ."

"I know, I know, I'm asking a whole lot." Some of the hope left his face, and he started to look away, but before he could, she caught his chin and kept him turned toward her.

"I'm already involved," she said, her voice trembling. "I already love you."

He looked almost skeptical, even as hope filled his eyes. "Really?"

"Honestly. I didn't want to but . . . I did. I fell in love with you."

He let out a whoop what was loud in her ears, then dragged her closer until he was holding her so tightly she could barely breathe. And she loved it. She loved every blessed second of it. It was like waking from a nightmare to a sunny morning. The past year slipped away like fog before the sunrise.

Dugan was the light in her life, and the way he was holding her told her she was the light in his.

And never had a morning been more beautiful.

Epilogue

Gold mask stolen

TAMPA—A priceless gold mask, the only remaining artifact of a lost Caribbean culture, was stolen over the weekend from the new Antiquities Museum at the University of South Florida. Police have no suspects at this time.

The mask was the museum's first acquisition. It was donated by Dr. Veronica Coleridge Gallagher, who discovered it and subsequently endowed the museum at the campus where she is a professor. . . .

The news clipping, which had tumbled out of an envelope with a foreign postmark, fluttered to the table as Veronica dropped it. She had just gotten back from another week at sea excavating the *Alcantara,* and this was the first she had heard of the theft. Grabbing the envelope the article had come in, she pulled a sheet of folded notepaper out of it, fearing that she was going to find a mocking note from Emilio.

Instead, she read, "The mask has returned to its rightful owners, the descendants of those who created it, those who know and cherish its power. We bless you, Daughter of the Storm, for helping to return it."

It should have mattered to her that she would never see it again, but somehow it didn't. The mask seemed like the remnant of a nightmare, and it had lost its hold on her when she had awakened. She had other things to worry about, other discoveries to make and a whole new life to live with Dugan and a baby on the way.

But for an instant she felt an overwhelming sense of completion and satisfaction. Turning, she tossed the article and the note in the trash.

It was over.

Dear Reader:

Somewhere deep within me lies a frustrated fantasy writer. I have a strong attraction to stories of myth and legend that offer teasing glimpses beneath the veil of reality. But I also have the heart of a suspense writer. I like the grit and sinew of the real world, its pulse-pounding excitement and dangerous unpredictability.

While writing WHEN I WAKE, I drew on my lifelong interest in Mesoamerican history to invent the Storm Goddess, her mask, and the woman who carries her legacy. Threading that alongside the real-world details of Veronica's deafness and her relationship with Dugan Gallagher was just the kind of challenge that makes my artistic motor hum.

So much so that I've decided to pull threads of suspense, romance and magic forward into my next Warner book, EYE OF THE JAGUAR, which will be released next summer. Set in the Museum of Antiquities that Veronica founded, the story concerns a stolen Mayan dagger that might very well be cursed, museum curator Anna Lundgren who's determined to get it back, and a killer who can't take his eyes off of her. Homicide detective Gil Garcia, whom you may remember from my earlier novel BEFORE I SLEEP, has more than a few reasons of his own to keep his eye on Anna. EYE OF THE JAGUAR is turning out to be my most suspenseful and surprising novel yet. I hope you will watch for it.

I'm going back to my keyboard now.

Best wishes,

Rachel Lee

RACHEL LEE, winner of numerous awards for her best-selling romantic fiction, is the author of Silhouette's #1 miniseries, Conard County. She also writes lighthearted contemporary romances as Sue Civil-Brown. But suspense fiction that zings like a high-tension wire with excitement and passion has become her signature style—and has made her previous Warner book, *Before I Sleep*, one of the best romantic reads of the year! As *Romantic Times* says, Rachel Lee is "an author to treasure."